D1483820

WAR
&
WAR

LÁSZLÓ KRASZNAHORKAI

WAR & WAR

Translated from the Hungarian by GEORGE SZIRTES

A NEW DIRECTIONS BOOK

This edition of *War and War* was published with the assistance of a grant from
the Hungarian Book Foundation.

Memorial for György Korin, the hero of László Krasznahorkai's novel *War and
War*, on p. 253: Bronze plaque by Imre Bukta (1999) at *Hallen für neue Kunst*,
Schaffhausen (Switzerland). 40 x 50 cm. Photo: Raussmüller Collection.

Manufactured in the United States of America
First published as New Directions Paperbook 1031 in 2006
Published simultaneously in Canada by Penguin Books Canada Limited
New Directions Books are printed on acid-free paper.

Library of Congress Cataloging-in-Publication Data
Krasznahorkai, László.
  [Háború és háború. English]
  War and war / László Krasznahorkai ; translated from the Hungarian by
George Szirtes.
    p. cm.
  ISBN 0-8112-1609-8 (alk. paper)
  1. Archivist—Fiction. I. Szirtes, George, 1948– II. Title.
PH3281.K8866H3313 2006
894'.51134—dc22   2005035047

10 9 8 7 6 5 4 3

New Directions Books are pubished for James Laughlin
by New Directions Publishing Corporation,
80 Eighth Avenue, New York 10011

TABLE OF CONTENTS

WAR

&

WAR

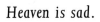

Heaven is sad.

I • LIKE A BURNING HOUSE

1.

I no longer care if I die, said Korin, then, after a long silence, pointed to the nearby flooded quarry: *Are those swans?*

2.

Seven children squatted in a semicircle surrounding him in the middle of the railway footbridge, almost pressing him against the barrier, just as they had done some half an hour earlier when they first attacked him in order to rob him, exactly so in fact, except that by now none of them thought it worthwhile either to attack or to rob him, since it was obvious that, on account of certain unpredictable factors, robbing or attacking him was possible but pointless because he really didn't seem to have anything worth taking, the only thing he did have appearing to be some mysterious burden, the existence of which, gradually, at a certain point in Korin's madly rambling monologue—which "to tell you the truth," as they said, "was boring as shit"—became apparent, most acutely apparent in fact, when he started talking about the loss of his head, at which point they did not stand up and leave him babbling like some half-wit, but remained where they were, in the positions they had originally intended to adopt, squatting immobile in a semicircle, because the evening had darkened around them, because the gloom descending silently on them in the industrial twilight numbed them, and because this frozen dumb condition had drawn their most intense attention, not to the figure of Korin which had swum beyond them, but to the one object remaining: the rails below.

3.

Nobody asked him to speak, only that he should hand over his money, but he didn't, saying he had none, and carried on speaking, hesitantly at first, then more fluently, and finally continuously and unstoppably, because the eyes of the seven children had plainly scared him, or, as he himself put it, his stomach had turned in fear, and, as he said, once his stomach was gripped by fear he absolutely had to speak, and further-more, since the fear had not passed—after all, how could he know whether they were carrying weapons or not—he grew ever more ab-sorbed in his speech, or rather he became ever more absorbed by the idea of telling them everything from beginning to end, of telling someone in any case, because, from the time that he had set out in se-cret, at the last possible moment, to embark on his "great journey" as he called it, he had not exchanged a word, not a single word, with anyone, considering it too dangerous, though there were few enough people he could engage in conversation in any case, since he hadn't so far met anybody sufficiently harmless, nobody, at least, of whom he was not wary, because in fact there really was nobody harmless enough, which meant he had to be wary of everyone, because, as he had said at the beginning, whoever it was he set eyes on it was the same thing he saw, a figure, that is, who, directly or indirectly, was in contact with those who pursued him, someone related intimately or distantly, but most certainly related, to those who, according to him, kept tabs on his every move, and it was only the speed of his move-ments, as he later explained, that kept him "at least half a day" ahead of them, though these gains were specific to places and occasions: so he had not said a word to anyone, and only did so now because fear drove him, because it was only under the natural pressure of fear that he ven-tured into these most important areas of his life, venturing deeper and deeper still, offering them ever more profound glimpses of it in order to defeat them, to make them face him so that he might purge his as-sailants of the tendency to assail, so he should convince all seven of them that someone had not only given himself up to them, but, with his giving, had somehow outflanked them.

4.

The air was full of the sharp, nauseous smell of tar that cut through everything, nor did the strong wind help because the wind, that had chilled them through to the bone, merely intensified and whipped the smell up without being able to substitute anything else for it in return, the whole neighborhood for several kilometers being thick with it, but here more than anywhere else, for it emanated directly from the Rákos railway yard, from that still visible point where the rails concentrated and began to fan out, ensuring that air and tar would be indistinguishable, making it very hard to tell what else, apart from soot and smoke, that smell—composed of the hundreds and thousands of trains that rumbled through, the filthy sleepers, the rubble and the metallic stench of the rails—comprised, and it wouldn't be just these but other, more obscure, almost indiscernible ingredients, ingredients without name, that would certainly have included the weight of human futility ferried here by hundreds and thousands of carriages, the scary and sickening view from the bridge of the power of a million wills bent to a single purpose and, just as certainly, the dreary spirit of desolation and industrial stagnation that had hovered about the place and settled on it decades ago, in all of which Korin was now endeavoring to locate himself, having originally determined simply to cross over to the far side as quickly, silently and inconspicuously as possible in order to escape into what he supposed to be the city center, instead of which he was having, under present circumstances, to pull himself together at a cold and draughty point of the world, and to hang on to whatever incidental detail he could make out, from his eyelevel at any rate, whether this was barrier, curb, asphalt or metal, or appeared the most significant, if only so that this footbridge, some hundred meters from the railway yard, might become a passage between the non-existing to the existing section of the world, forming therefore an important early adjunct, as he later put it, to his mad life as a fugitive, a bridge that, had he not been detained, he would have rushed obliviously across.

5.

It had begun suddenly, without preamble, without presentiment, preparation or rehearsal, at one specific moment on his forty-fourth birthday, that he was struck, agonizingly and immediately, by the consciousness of it, as suddenly and unexpectedly, he told them, as he was by the appearance of the seven of them here, in the middle of the footbridge, on that day when he was sitting by a river at a spot where he would occasionally sit in any case, this time because he didn't feel like going home to an empty apartment on his birthday, and it really was extremely sudden, the way it struck him that, good heavens, he understood nothing, nothing at all about anything, for Christ's sake, nothing at all about the world, which was a most terrifying realization, he said, especially in the way it came to him in all its banality, vulgarity, at a sickeningly ridiculous level, but this was the point, he said, the way that he, at the age of forty-four, had become aware of how utterly stupid he seemed to himself, how empty, how utterly blockheaded he had been in his understanding of the world these last forty-four years, for, as he realized by the river, he had not only misunderstood it, but had not understood anything about anything, the worst part being that for forty-four years he thought he had understood it, while in reality he had failed to do so; and this in fact was the worst thing of all that night of his birthday when he sat alone by the river, the worst because the fact that he now realized that he had not understood it did not mean that he *did* understand it now, because being aware of his lack of knowledge was not in itself some new form of knowledge for which an older one could be traded in, but one that presented itself as a terrifying puzzle the moment he thought about the world, as he most furiously did that evening, all but torturing himself in the effort to understand it and failing, because the puzzle seemed ever more complex and he had begun to feel that this world-puzzle that he was so desperate to understand, that he was torturing himself trying to understand was really the puzzle of himself and the world at once, that they were in effect one and the same thing, which was the conclusion he had so far reached, and he had not yet given up on it, when, after a couple of days, he noticed that there was something the matter with his head.

6.

By this time he had lived alone for years, he explained to the seven children, he too squatting and leaning against the barrier in the sharp November wind on the footbridge, alone because his marriage had been wrecked by the Hermes business (he gestured with his hand as if to say he would explain about it later), after which he had "badly burned his fingers with a deeply passionate love affair" and decided: never, never again, would he even so much as get close to a woman, which did not mean, of course, that he led an entirely solitary life, because, as Korin elaborated, gazing at the children, there was the occasional woman on the occasional difficult night, but essentially he was alone, though there remained the various people he came into contact with in the course of his work at the records office, as well as the neighbors with whom he had to maintain neighborly relations, the commuters he bumped into while commuting, the shoppers he met while shopping, the barflies he'd see in the bar and so forth, so that, after all, now he looked back at it, he was in regular contact with quite a lot of people, even if only on the most tenuous of terms, occupying the furthermost corner of the community, at least until they too started to melt away, which probably dated from the time that he was feeling increasingly compelled to regale those he met at the records office, on the staircase at home, in the street, at the store and in the bar, with the regrettable news that he believed he was about to lose his head, because, once they understood that the loss was neither figurative nor symbolic but a genuine deprivation in the full physical sense of the word, that, to put it plainly, his head, alas, would actually be severed from his neck, they eventually fled from him as they might flee from a burning house, fleeing in their droves, and very soon every one of them had gone and he stood alone, very much like a burning house in fact: at first it being just the matter of a few people behaving in a more distant fashion, then his colleagues at the records office ignoring him, not even returning his greeting, refusing to sit at the same table and finally crossing the street when they saw him, then people actually avoiding him in the street, and can you imagine, Korin asked the seven children, how painful this was? how it hurt me most, more than anything, he added, especially with what was happening to the vertebrae in his neck, and this was just when he most needed their support, he said, and while it was plain to see that he would have been pleased to explore this matter in the most intricate detail, it was equally obvious that it would have been wasted on the seven children because they would not have been able to respond in any way, being bored of the subject, particularly at the point when "the geezer started going on about losing his head" which meant "shit" to them, as later they would tell their friends, and looked at one another while the oldest nodded in agreement with his younger companions as if to say, "forget it, it's not worth it," after which they simply continued squatting, watching the confluence of rails as the occasional freight car rattled by below them, though one did ask how much longer they were going to stay there as it was all the same to him, and the blond kid next to the senior one consulted his watch and replied merely that he'd tell them when it was time, and until then he should shut the fuck up.

7.

Had Korin known that they had already arrived at a decision, and specifically at this particular decision; had he in fact noted the meaningful gesture, that nothing would happen, but, since he hadn't noted it, he wasn't to know and, as a result, his perception of reality was incorrect; for to him it seemed that his current predicament—squatting on the ground with these children in the cold wind—was increasingly fraught with anxiety precisely because nothing was happening, and because it wasn't made clear to him what they wanted, if indeed they wanted anything at all, and since there was no explanation forthcoming as to why they were refusing to let him go or just leave him there, having succeeded in convincing them that the whole thing was pointless because he really had no money, he still felt that there should have been an explanation, and indeed had found one, albeit the wrong one as far as the seven children were concerned, he being aware of exactly how much money was sewn into the lining on the right side of his coat, so their immobility, their numbness, their failure to do anything, in fact the utter lack of any animation whatsoever on their part, took on an ever greater, ever more terrifying significance, though if he had looked at it another way he might have found it progressively more reassuring and less significant; which meant that he spent the first half of each moment preparing to spring to his feet and make a dash for it and the second half remaining precisely where he was, apparently content to stay there and to keep talking, as if he had only just begun his story; in other words, he was equally disposed to escape or remain, though every time he had to make a decision he chose, in fact, to remain, chiefly because he was scared of course, having constantly to assure them how happy he was to have found such sympathetic listeners and how good it all felt, because he had so much, it was extraordinary quite how much, to tell them, really and truly, because when you took time to think about it, "extraordinary" was absolutely the right word to describe the complex details of his story which, he said, he should tell so it would be clear to them, so they should know how it was that Wednesday, at what precise time he could not remember but it was probably some thirty or forty hours ago, when the fateful day arrived and he realized that he really did have to embark on his "great journey," at which point he understood that everything, from Hermes down to his solitary condition, was driving him in one direction, that he must already have started on the journey because it was all prepared and everything else had collapsed, which is to say that everything ahead of him had been prepared and everything behind him had collapsed, as tended to be the way with all such "great journeys," said Korin.

8.

The only streetlights burning were those at the top of the stairs and the light they gave out fell in dingy cones that shuddered in the intermittent gusts of wind assailing them because the other neon lights positioned in the thirty or so meters between them had all been broken, leaving them squatting in darkness, yet as aware of each other, of their precise positions, as of the enormous mass of dark sky above the smashed neon, the sky which might have glimpsed the reflection of its own enormous dark mass as it trembled with stars in the vista of railway yards spreading below it, had there been some relationship between the trembling stars and the twinkling dull red lights of semaphores sprinkled among the rails, but there wasn't, there was no common denominator, no interdependence between them, the only order and relationship existing within the discrete worlds of above and below, and indeed of anywhere, for the field of stars and the forest of signals stared as blankly at each other as does each and every form of being, blind in darkness and blind in radiance, as blind on earth as it is in heaven, if only so that a long moribund symmetry among this vastness might appear in the lost glance of some higher being, at the center of which, naturally, there would be a miniscule blind spot: as with Korin . . . the footbridge . . . the seven kids.

9.

A total dickhead, they told a local acquaintance the next day, a total dickhead in a league of his own, a twat they really should have got rid of because you never knew when he'd inform on you, 'cause he'd had a good look at everybody's face, they added to each other, and could have made a mental note of their clothes, their shoes and everything else they were wearing that late afternoon, so, yeah, that's right, they admitted the next day, they should have got rid of him, only it didn't occur to any of them at the time to do so, everyone being so relaxed and all, so laid back, like a bunch of dopes on the footbridge while ordinary people carried on leading ordinary lives beneath them as they gazed at the darkening neighborhood above the converging rails and waited for the signals for the six forty-eight in the distance so that they might rush down to the embankment, taking up their positions behind the bushes in preparation for the usual ritual, but, as they remarked, none of them had imagined that the ritual might have ended in some other fashion, with a different outcome, that it might not be completed entirely successfully, triumphantly, right on target, in other words with a death, in which case of course even a pathetic idiot like him would be an obvious danger because he might inform on them, they said, might get into a funk and, quite unexpectedly, inform on them to the cops, and the reason it worked out differently, as it did in fact, leaving them to think the thoughts they had just thought, was that they hadn't been concentrating, and can't have been, otherwise they'd have realized that this was precisely the kind of man who presented no danger because, later, he couldn't even remember what, if anything, had happened at about six forty-eight, as he had fallen ever deeper under the spell of his own fear, the fear that drove his narrative onward, a narrative that, there was no denying, apart from a certain rhythm, lacked all sense of shape or indeed anything that might have drawn attention to his own person, except perhaps its copiousness, which resulted in him trying to tell them everything at once, in the way he himself experienced what had happened to him, in a kind of simultaneity that he first noticed added up to a coherent whole that certain Wednesday morning some thirty or forty hours before, two hundred and twenty kilometers from here in a ticket booth, at the point when he arrived at the front of the queue and was about to ask the time of the next train for Budapest and the cost of the ticket, when, standing at the counter, he suddenly felt that *he should not ask that question here*, at the same moment recognizing in the reflection in the glass over one of the posters above the counter, two employees of the District Psychiatric Unit, disguised as a pair of ordinary numbskulls, really, two of them, and behind him, at the entrance, a so-called nurse whose aggressive presence made his skin prickle and break into a sweat.

10.

The men from the District Psychiatric Unit, said Korin, never explained to him what he had wanted to know, which was the reason he had attended the unit to start with, and that was the matter of how the whole system that held the skull in place, from the first cervical vertebra through to the ligaments (the Rectus capitis), actually functioned, but they never explained it, because they couldn't, chiefly because they themselves had not an inkling, their minds being shrouded in a wholly impenetrable darkness that resulted in them first staring at him in astonishment, as if to indicate that the question itself, the mere asking of it, was so ludicrous that it provided direct and incontrovertible proof of his, Korin's, madness, then giving each other significant glances and little nods whose portent was (was it not?) perfectly clear, that they had dismissed the subject, as a consequence of which he made no further enquiries regarding the matter but, even while steadfastly bearing the enormous weight of the problem, literally, on his shoulders, tried to solve the problem himself by asking what that certain first cervical vertebra and the Rectus capitis actually were, how (sighed Korin) they performed their crucial functions and how it was that his skull was simply propped on the topmost vertebra of his spinal column, though when he thought about it at the time, or so he told them now, the idea of his skull being fixed to his spine by cerebro-spinal ligaments, which were the only things holding the lot together, was enough to send shivers down him when he thought of it, and still did send shivers down him, since even a brief examination of his own skull demonstrated the patent truth that this arrangement was so sensitive, so brittle, so vulnerable, in fact one of the most frail and delicate physical structures imaginable, that he concluded it must have been here, at this particular juncture, that his problems had begun and would end, for if the doctors were incapable of coming to any worthwhile conclusion after looking at his x-rays, and things had turned out as they had done so far, then, having steeped himself to some degree at least in the study of medicine, and having conducted an endless self-examination based on this study, he had no hesitation in declaring that the pain he was in had its root cause here, in that arrangement of tissue and bone, where vertebra met ligament, and that all attention should be focused on this point, on the ligaments, on which precise point he was not yet certain though he was certain enough about the sensation that spread through his neck and back, week by week, month by month, constantly increasing in intensity, knowing that the process had started and was proceeding irre- sistibly, and that this whole affair, if one considered it objectively, he said, was bound to lead to the terminal decay of the union of skull and spine, culminating in a condition, *not to beat around the bush*, for why should one, said Korin pointing to his neck, whereby this frail piece of skin finally gave out when he would inevitably lose his head.

11.

One, two, three, four, five, six, seven, eight, nine sets of rails could be distinguished from the vantage point of the footbridge, and the seven of them could do little but count them over and over again, concentrating their attention on the confluence of rails in the per- ceptibly deepening darkness accentuated by the red lights of the signals while waiting for the six forty-eight to appear at last in the distance, for the tension that had suddenly appeared on everyone's hitherto relaxed countenance was occasioned by nothing more at this stage than the impending arrival of the six forty-eight, the mark they had set out to mug having failed, after their first couple of attempts, to provide sufficient entertainment in the short period of their waiting, so that within fifteen minutes of having cornered him, even if they had wanted to, they would have remained inca- pable of listening to a single word more of the seamless and end- less monologue that, even now, cornered as he was, flowed unstop- pably from him, because he kept on and on regardless, as they explained the next day, and it would have been unbearable had they not ignored him, because, they added, if they had continued to pay

attention to him they would have had to do him in if only to preserve their own sanity, and they had, unfortunately, ignored him
for the sake of their sanity, and this resulted in them missing the
chance of eliminating him, for they really should have eliminated
him good and proper, or so they kept repeating to themselves, particularly since the seven of them would normally have been perfectly aware what failing to eliminate a witness might cost them, a
witness like him, who would never completely vanish in the
crowd, not to mention the fact that they had begun to get a reputation in certain important places as "cut-throats," a reputation they
had to protect, and killing him would not have been difficult, nor
indeed a new proposition to them, and this way they would have
been taking no chances.

12.

What had happened to him—Korin shook his head as if he still
could not believe it—was, at the beginning, almost inconceivable,
nigh unbearable, because even at first glance, following an initial
survey of the complex nature of what was involved, one straight
look told him that from now on he'd have to abandon his "sick
hierarchical view of the world," explode "the illusion of an orderly
pyramid of facts" and liberate himself from the extraordinarily powerful and secure belief in what was now revealed as merely a kind of
childish mirage, which is to say the indivisible unity and contiguity
of phenomena, and beyond that, the unity's secure permanence and
stability; and, within this permanence and stability, the overall co-
herence of its mechanism, that strictly-governed interdependence
of functioning parts which gave the whole system its sense of direction, development, pace and progress, in other words whatever suggested that the thing it embodied was attractive and self-sufficient,
or, to put it another way, he now had to say No, an immediate and
once-and-for-all No, to that entire mode of life; but some hundred
yards on he was forced to reconsider certain aspects of what he had
originally termed his rejection of the hierarchical mode of thinking
because it seemed to him that he had lost nothing by rejecting a particular order of things that he had elevated into a pyramid structure,
a structure that self-evidently needed correcting or rejecting in per-
petuity as misleading or inappropriate, no, strange to say, he had lost

nothing by the rejection, for what had actually happened that certain night of his birthday, could not be accounted loss as such but rather gain, or at least as a first point gained, an advance in the direction of some all-but-inconceivable, all-but-unbearable end—and in the gradual process of walking the hundred paces from the river to the point where the struggle had begun, and having been granted a glimpse of the terrible complexity ahead, he saw that while the world appeared not to exist, the totality of that-which-had-been-thought-about-it did in fact exist, and, furthermore, that it was only this, in its countless thousands of varieties, that did exist as such, that what existed was his identity as the sum of the countless thousand imaginings of the human spirit that were engaged in writing the world, in writing his identity, he said, in terms of pure word, the doing word, the Verb that brooded over the waters, or, to put it another way, he added, what became clear was that most opinions were a waste of time, that it was a waste thinking that life was a matter of appropriate conditions and appropriate answers, because the task was not to choose but to accept, there being no obligation to choose between what was appropriate and what was inappropriate, only to accept that we are not obliged to do anything except to comprehend that the appropriateness of the one great universal process of thinking is not predicated on it being correct, for there was nothing to compare it with, nothing but its own beauty, and it was its beauty that gave us confidence in its truth—and this, said Korin, was what struck him as he walked those hundred furiously-thinking paces on the evening of his birthday: that is to say he understood the infinite significance of faith and was given a new insight into what the ancients had long known, that it was faith in its existence that had both created and maintained the world; the corollary of which was that it was the loss of his own faith that was now erasing it, the result of which realization being, he said, that he experienced a sudden, utterly numbing, quite awful feeling of abundance, because from that time on he knew that whatever had once existed, existed still and that, quite unexpectedly, he had stumbled on an ontological place of such gravity that he could see—oh but how, he sighed, how to begin—that Zeus, for instance, to take an arbitrary example, was still "there," now, in the present, just as all the other old gods of Olympus were "there," as was Yahweh and The Lord God of Hosts, and there alongside them, the ghosts of every nook and cranny, and that this meant they had nothing and yet everything to fear, for nothing ever disappeared without trace, for the absent had a structure as real as the structure of whatever existed, and so, in other words, you could bump into Allah, into the Prince of the Rebel Angels, and into all the dead stars of the universe, which would of course include the barren unpopulated earth with its godless laws of being as well as the terrifying reality of hell and pandemonium which was the domain of the demons, and that was reality, said Korin: thousands upon thousands of worlds, each one different, majestic or fearsome; thousands upon thousands in their ranks, he continued, his voice rising, in a single absent relationship, that was how it all appeared to him then, he explained, and it was then, when he had got so far, continually reliving the infinite capacity of the process of becoming, that the trouble with his head first started, the predictable course of which process he had already outlined, and possibly it was the sheer abundance, the peculiar inexhaustibility of history and the gods that he found hard to bear, for ultimately he didn't know, nor to this very day was it clear to him, precisely how the pain that started suddenly and simultaneously in his neck and his back, began: the forgetting, subject by subject, random, ungovernable and extraordinarily rapid, first of facts such as where he had put the key that he had only just now been holding in his hand, or what page he had got to in the book he had been reading the previous night, and, later, what had happened on Wednesday, three days ago, in the time between morning and evening, and after that, whatever was important, urgent, dull or insignificant, and finally, even his mother's name, he said, the scent of apricots, whatever made familiar faces familiar, whether he had in fact completed tasks he had set for himself to complete—in a word, he said, there was literally nothing that stayed in his head, the whole world had vanished, step by step, the disappearance itself having neither rhyme nor reason in its progress, as if what there was left was somehow sufficient, or as if there were always something of greater importance that a higher, incomprehensible force had decided he should forget.

13.

I must somehow have drunk of the waters of Lethe, Korin explained, and while disconsolately wagging his head as if to convey to them that the un-

derstanding of the manner and consequence of events would probably always lie beyond him, he brought out a box of Marlboros: *Anyone got a light?*

14.

They were roughly the same age, the youngest being eleven, the
oldest perhaps thirteen or fourteen, but every one of them had at
least one slipcased razor blade nestling by his side, nor was it just a
matter of nestling there, for each of them, from the youngest to the
oldest, was capable of handling it expertly, whether it was of the
simple "singleton" kind or the triple sort they referred to as "the
set," and not one of them lacked the ability to yank the thing forth
in the blink of an eye and slip it between two fingers into the tense
palm without the merest flickering of outward emotion while gazing steadily at the victim so that whichever of them happened to be
in the right position could, quick as a flash, find the artery on the
neck, this being the skill they had most perfectly mastered, a skill
which rendered them, when all seven of them were together, so
exceptionally dangerous that they had begun to earn a genuinely
well-deserved reputation, only through constant practice, of
course, the practice that enabled them to achieve their current level
of performance and involved a carefully planned course of training
that they carried through at constantly changing venues, repeating
the same moves a hundred times, over and over again, until they
could execute the moves with inimitable, blinding speed and such
perfect coordination that in the course of an attack, they knew instinctively, without saying a word to each other, not only who
would advance and who would stand, but how those standing
would form up, nor was there any room for boasting, you couldn't
even think of it, so faultless was their teamwork, and in any case,
the sight of gushing blood was enough to stop their mouths and
render them dumb, disciplined and solemn, perhaps even too
solemn, for the solemnity was something of a burden to them,
leaving them with a desire for some course of action that would
lead rather more playfully, more fortuitously, that is to say entailing
a greater risk of failure, to the fact of death, since this was what
they all sought, this was the way things had developed, this was
what interested them, in fact it was the reason they had gathered

here in the first place, the reason they had already spent a good many afternoons, so many weeks of afternoons and early evenings, passing the time right here.

15.

There was absolutely nothing ambiguous about the way he moved, said Korin next day in the MALÉV office, the whole thing being so completely normal, so ordinary, the reaching for his cigarettes so perfectly innocent and harmless that it was merely a kind of instinct, the result of an on-the-spur-of-the-moment notion that he might lessen the tension and thereby ease his own situation by a friendly gesture such as the offering of cigarettes, for really, no exaggeration, it was just that and nothing more, and while he expected almost anything to happen as a result, what he did not expect was to find another hand holding his wrist by the time his had reached the Marlboros in his pocket, a hand that did not grip the way a pair of handcuffs would, but one that rendered him immobile and sent a flood of warmth lapping across his wrist, or so he explained the next day, still in a state of shock, while at the same time, he continued, he felt his muscles weaken, only those muscles that were grasping the pack of Marlboros, and all this happened without a word being exchanged and, what was more—apart from the child nearest to him, who had responded so nimbly and with such breathtaking skill to the gesture he had misinterpreted—the group did not move an inch, but merely glanced at the falling Marlboro pack, until one of them eventually lifted it up, opened it and drew out a ciga-rette, passed it on to the next, and so forth to the end while he, Korin, in his terror, behaved as though nothing had happened, nothing significant at least, or, if anything had happened it was only by an accident so minor and so unworthy of mention as to be laughable, an accident that left him gripping his wounded wrist with his blameless hand, not quite understanding what had hap-pened, and even when he did eventually realize, he merely pressed his thumb against the tiny nick, for that was all it was, he told them, a miniscule cut, and when the expected rush of panic, with its atten-dant throbbing, trembling, and loud noises in the head began to die away, an icy calm had lapped about him in much the same way as the blood had lapped about his wrist, in other words, as he declared the next day, he was utterly convinced that they were going to kill him.

16.

The work in the records office, he continued in a quavering voice, having waited for the last of the children to light his cigarette, did not involve, as did that of so many others, at least as far as he personally was concerned, a process of humiliation, blackmail, of wearing people down; no, not in his case, he stressed: on the contrary, he was bound to say, that after "the sad turn of events in his social life," it was precisely his work that remained most important to him, that was his sole consolation both in the obligatory and voluntary after-hours areas of his specialization; it was the one thing, in the fundamental and, as far as he was concerned, fateful, process of the last few months of coming to terms with a reality which involved acknowledging the not-so-much bitter as amusing evidence that showed history and truth had nothing to do with each other, that demonstrated to him that everything he, in his capacity as a local historian, had done to explore, establish, maintain and nurture as history, had in fact given him an extraordinary freedom and raised him to a state of grace; because once he was capable of considering how any particular history served as a peculiar—if one regarded its origins, accidental, and if one considered its outcomes, cynically concocted and artificially articulated—a peculiar blend of some remaining elements of the truth, of human understanding and the imaginative re-creation of the past, of what could and could not be known, of confusion, of lies, of exaggerations, of both fidelity to— and misuse of—given data, of both proper and improper interpretations of evidence, of inklings, suggestions and of the marshaling of a sufficiently imposing body of opinion, then the work in the records office, the labor of, what was referred to as, the classifying and ordering of archive material, and indeed all such enterprises, represented nothing less than freedom itself, for it did not matter in the least what task he was currently engaged on, whether the classification was within general, median or specific categories, whether it was filed under this or that heading; whatever he did, whichever section of that almost two-thousand-meters' length of archival corridor he dealt with, he was simply keeping history going, if he might put it

that way, while knowing, at the same time, that he was entirely missing the truth, though the fact that he knew, even while he was working, that he was missing it, rendered him calm and equable, gave
him a certain sense of invulnerability, the kind that comes to a
man who recognizes that what he is doing is as pointless as it is
meaningless, and furthermore that, precisely because it lacks point
and meaning, it is accompanied by an entirely mysterious yet quite
inimitable sweetness—yes, that was the way it was, he said, he really
did find freedom through work, and there was just one problem,
which was that this freedom wasn't quite enough, for, having tasted
it these last few months and having realized how rare and precious it
was, it suddenly seemed insufficient, and he had started to sigh and
pine for a greater, an absolute freedom, and thought only of how
and where he might find it, until the whole issue became a burning
obsession that disturbed him in his work in the records office, because he had to know where to seek it, where absolute freedom
might reside.

17.

All this, of course, indeed his whole history, originated in the distant
past, said Korin, as far back as the time he first announced the fact
that though an utterly mad world had made a madman of him, pure
and simple, it didn't mean that that is entirely what he was, for while
it would have been stupid to deny that sooner or later, naturally
enough, that was how he'd "finish up," or rather, sooner or later,
reach a state resembling madness, it was obvious that whatever
might in fact happen, madness was not a particularly unfortunate
condition that one should fear as being oppressive or threatening, a
condition one should be frightened of, no, not in the least, or at least
he personally was not scared of it, not for a moment, for it was simply a matter of fact, as he later explained to the seven children, that
one day the straw actually did "break the camel's back," for now that
he recalled it, the story did not begin beside that certain river but
much earlier, well before the riverside events, when he was suddenly
seized by a hitherto unknown and unfathomably deep bitterness that
resonated through his entire being, a bitterness so sudden that one
particular day it simply struck him how bitter, how deathly bitter he
was about that which he used to refer to as "the state of things," and

that this was not the result of some mood that quickly appeared then disappeared but of an insight that illuminated him like a bolt of lightning, something, he said, that branded him forever and would remain burning, a lightning-insight that said there was nothing, but nothing worthwhile left in the world, not that he wanted to exaggerate, but that was how it was, there really was nothing worthwhile in his circumstances, nor would there be anything lovely or good ever again, and though this sounded childish, and indeed he recognized that the essential aspect of that which he had distilled from his entire history, was, as he was content to acknowledge, childish, he began to peddle this insight regularly in bars, hoping to find someone that, in his "general state of despair," he might regard as one of those "angels of mercy," seeking such a one constantly, determined to tell him everything or to put a pistol to his own head, as he did, he said, without success, thank heaven; so, in other words, though the whole thing was perfectly idiotic, no doubt, that was how it started, with this sense of bitterness that created a whole "new Korin," from which point on he began to ponder over matters such as how things fitted together, and if their condition were such and such, what the implications might be for him personally, and once having understood that there were absolutely no personal implications, and furthermore, having grasped that he had reached his absolute limit, he then decided that he would resign himself to it, to say OK, fine, that's how things are, but then, if that was the case, what should he do, give up? disappear? or what? and it was precisely this question, or rather the fact that he approached this question in such a "so-what's-the-point-of-it-all" manner, that led directly to the fateful day, meaning that certain Wednesday morning when he concluded that there was nothing for it but to take immediate action, this being the direct conclusion he had reached, albeit by a dauntingly difficult route, and the seven of them here were witnesses, he said, still squatting in the middle of the footbridge, to the daunting difficulty of it, right from the time by the river when he first understood the complexity of the world, then by developing an ever deepening comprehension which in someone like him, a local historian of some godforsaken place, involved getting to grips with the inordinate wealth and complexity of possible thought about a world that didn't exist, as well as with the strength to be derived from the creative power of blind faith, and all this while forgetfulness and the constant terror of losing his head crept up on him, so that the taste of freedom he had enjoyed in the records office might carry him through to the end of his quest, after which there would be nowhere left to go and he would have to decide, and indeed declare, that he himself would no longer allow matters to proceed as they might have wanted to proceed, but mount the stage "as an actor," not as others around him tended to do, but quite differently, by, for instance, after one enormous effort of thinking, simply leaving, yes, leaving, abandoning the place allotted to him in life, leaving it forever, not simply in order to be in an indeterminate elsewhere, but, or so the idea came to him, to locate *the very center of the world*, the place where matters were actually decided, where things happened, a place such as Rome, had been, ancient Rome, where decisions had been made and events set in motion, to find that place and *then* quit everything; in other words he decided to pack up his things and seek such a "Rome"; for why, he asked himself, why spend his time in an archive some two hundred kilometers southwest of Budapest when he could be sitting at the center of the world, since one way or the other, it would be his last stop on earth? and the idea having come to him it began to crystallize in his constantly aching head and he had even begun to study foreign languages, when, one late afternoon, having stayed behind in the records office, vaguely checking the shelves, as he put it, utterly by chance, he arrived at a shelf he had never before explored, took down from it a box that had never been taken down, not at least since the Second World War, that was for sure, and from this box labeled "Family Papers of no Particular Significance" took out a fascicule headed IV. 3 / 1941–42, opened it and, in doing so, his life changed forever, for there he discovered something that decided once and for all what he should do if he still wanted to "carry his plan through" and to make "his last good-byes"; something that finally determined him to put all those years of thinking, proposing and doubting behind him, to let those years go, to let them rot in the past, and not to let them determine his future but to act right now, for the fascicule headed IV. 3 / 1941–42 had left him in no doubt what should be done, what to do in order to recover the dignity and meaning whose loss he had been mourning, what important thing there remained for him to do, and above all, where he should seek that which he so much lacked: that peculiar, furiously desired, greatest, very last freedom that earthly life was capable of offering.

The only things that interested them, they said the next day while hanging about in front of the Bingo Bar, were the slingshots, the kind used by anglers for laying out bait, not the mind-numbingly idiotic claptrap the geezer spewed continuously, without any prospect of an end, for he was incapable of stopping, so that eventually, after an hour or so of it, it became clear that it was his own repulsive gabble that had turned him into a head-case, though as far as they were concerned, they said, it didn't add up to anything, so it was completely pointless for him to talk himself into a frazzle, since the geezer meant as much to them as the wind on the footbridge, wind, that, like him, just kept blowing because it was impossible to shut either of them up, not that they gave it a thought, why would they? since he wasn't worth it, let him talk wind, the only things that mattered being the three slingshots, how they worked and how they would employ them when the six forty-eight arrived, and that was what they'd all been thinking about just before this creep arrived, of the three professional model ground-baiting slingshots they had got as a bargain, for nine thousand Forints, at the Attila József flea market, the three professional *German* ground-baiting slingshots they had tucked under their bomber jackets, and they wondered how these would perform, for people said their projectile power was vastly greater than that of the Hungarian sort, and, of course, far superior to that of hand-held missiles, some people even claiming that this German gear was not only more powerful but almost ensured that your aim was one hundred percent effective, and that it was, according to its reputation, no argument about it, the best on the market, chiefly because of the track-device, attached to the handle below the fork, that steadied your hand in case it accidentally trembled, thereby reducing the uncertainty factor to a minimum by holding the arm firm all the way to the elbow, or so it was said, they declared, or so they say, but not in their wildest dreams would they have imagined what really happened after that, since this piece of goods was brilliant, its capacity absolutely phenomenal, they said, or so said the four of them who were not among the first to use it, absolutely phenomenal, they said.

19.

Another long freight train rumbled by below them and the footbridge shook gently along its whole length until the train was
gone—leaving two blinking red lights in its wake—when the noise
of the very last car began to fade along with the rattling of wheels,
and, in the newly settled silence, after the two red lights disappearing in the distance, just above the rails, no more than a meter high,
a flock of bats appeared and followed the train toward the Rákos-
rendezö, utterly silent, without the least sound, like some medieval
battery of ghosts, in close order, at even pace, indeed at a mysteriously even pace, swooping strictly between the parallel lines of the
rails, suggesting somehow that they were being drawn toward Budapest or riding in the slipstream of the train as it went, the train
that was showing them the way, carrying them, drawing them,
sucking them on so that they could travel perfectly, effortlessly,
with steady, spread wings, reaching Budapest, at a precise height of
one meter above the crossties.

20.

Funnily enough he didn't smoke, said Korin, and he only happened
to possess this pack of Marlboros because somewhere on his journey
he had to get some change for the coffee machine and the man in
the tobacconists he wandered into, would only oblige if he bought a
pack of cigarettes, so, what could he do but buy one, but he didn't
throw it away because he thought it might come in useful some
time, and would you believe it, he added, he was so pleased that it
had actually come in useful, even if he himself had no use for it, or
rather, only on one occasion, said Korin raising his index finger, for
he had to be honest about it, there was one single moment, and only
one, when he would happily have lit a cigarette, which was the time
when he returned from the IBUSZ bus company's ticket office without having accomplished his mission, all because of the two male
nurses from the Psychiatric Unit; for he was aware of their eyes following him as he walked away, then as they looked at each other, not
in any significant way, or at least not yet, not yet in a way that might
show they were resolved to act, though soon enough they did start
off after him, a fact of which he was absolutely certain without hav-

ing to look back over his shoulder, for every cell in his body knew they were close behind him, after which, said Korin, he went home, straight home without a thought, and started packing, and though the apartment was already sold, and many of his possessions already cheaply disposed of, a disposal that involved the wholesale liquidation of a terrifying pile of accumulated notes, scraps, diaries, exercise books, photocopies and letters, not to mention photographs, and, apart from his passport, all his official documents including his birth certificate, his TB inoculation card, his personal ID, etc., the lot tossed on the fire, and yet, having survived the entire process and come through feeling that no earthly possession remained to burden him, the moment he stepped into his room he experienced a sense of utter despair, because now that he was ready to leave immediately, the very copiousness of his preparations for leaving had appeared to be an obstacle: he was incapable of resolving himself to simply go, even though the feeling of long preparation, he said, was misleading because there had not really been "copious preparations" as such, since one generous hour was all that had been needed for him to free himself of his material possessions and make ready to go, and please imagine, he continued, raising his voice, imagine that one bare hour was enough after all those months of forethought to set out, there and then, on his long journey, to open the door and leave the apartment to which he would never return, a single hour for his plans to be carried out and become reality, to leave everything forever, but then, just when he was as ready for departure as he could ever be, there he was, stuck, standing plumb in the middle of the cleared apartment, looking around, and without any sense of regret or emotion, casting his eyes over the vacancy when he suddenly understood that one hour was enough for any of us to dispose of everything, to stand plumb in the middle of our forsaken apartment and step out into the melancholy womb of the world, said Korin, and well, at that point, he would happily have flicked a lighter and smoked a decent cigarette, which was strange, but all of a sudden he desired the taste of cigarettes and wanted to draw heavily on one, to take a good deep breath, blow out the smoke, nice and slowly, and though this was the only occasion on which he felt like this, and had never desired a cigarette before nor since, not once, never in his life would he understand what it was all about.

For an archivist, said Korin, and especially for a head-archivist-in-waiting such as him, there were a great many fields to master, but he can tell them one thing, that no archivist, not even a head-archivist-in-waiting, such as, in fact, he was in all but name, was in possession of essential information regarding the practicalities of travel on the buffers car or caboose of freight trains, and that was why, when in deciding that the nature of his permanently fugitive status was such that he couldn't trust to buses, passenger trains, or even to the exigencies of hitchhiking, for a person committed to "any route that was fixed and might be inspected at any point" was vulnerable to discovery, identification, and easy arrest, he had set out on this veritably terrifying Calvary, and just imagine what it was like, said Korin, for someone who, as they already knew, had been used to restricting his movements to the four fixed points of his personal compass, to wit his apartment, the pub, the archive and, let us say, the nearest shop, and had never—he wasn't exaggerating—really never, not even for an hour, ventured beyond them, and now suddenly found himself off limits, in the deserted, wholly unfamiliar back end of some railway yard, stumbling over tracks, balancing on crossties, keeping an eye on signals and points, ready to dive into a ditch or behind a bush at the first sight of a train or a rail-yard employee, for that's how it was, rails, crossties, signals, points, being constantly prepared to throw himself on the ground, and, right from the start, to leap on or off a moving car, while being in a permanent state of anxiety that extended over the whole two hundred and twenty kilometers of the journey, anxiety in case he was spotted by a night watchman, a stationmaster or someone checking the brakes or axles, a terrible experience on the whole, he said, even having got so far, knowing how much was behind him; bad even to think of having undertaken such a journey, for he couldn't say what was the most exhausting, most embittering part of it, the cold that ate into your bones in the caboose or the fact that he had no idea where he could or dared to sleep, for the space was so narrow that he had no room to stretch his legs and consequently had constantly to be standing up and lying down, then standing up again, a process which naturally drained him, not to mention the other privations, for example having nothing but biscuits, chocolates or coffee at railway cafés for sustenance after two days of which he was permanently nauseous, and so you see, he told the seven children, the whole thing, believe me, was shit-awful, not only the cold and lack of sleep, not just the stiff leg or the nausea, no, for even when they had eased off somewhat and everything was generally fine there remained the perpetual anxiety every time the train departed for whatever perfectly appropriate destination was announced on the boards of the engine, that by the time they passed through it, leaving the town or village behind, be that place Békéscsaba. Mezőberény, Gyoma or Szajol, he immediately lost confidence and that uncertainty grew in him mile by mile so that pretty soon he was on the point of leaping off and boarding a train in the opposite direction, though he hadn't ever actually done that, for, he said, he would invariably decide that there was more choice at a major stop, and then would immediately regret his decision not to leap when there was still time but to stay on, at which point he would feel utterly lost and have to remain on full alert in case the journey took him into still more dangerous territory where anyone might come along—railway workers, night watchmen, engine-drivers, or whoever—for that would really be the end of everything, and then he would have to leap from the car into any cover that might be on offer, whether that was a ditch, a building or some shrubbery and that was precisely how he came to be here, said Korin, how he arrived, frozen through, desperate for food, for something salty preferably, or actually not too salty, but in any case, if they didn't mind, he would happily move on now and get into the city center for he urgently needed to find some shelter for the night until the MALÉV airline ticket-office opened the next morning.

22.

It was remarkable that the chosen stone, which was about the size of a child's fist, had succeeded at the first attempt in shattering one of the windows, so that they could not only hear it over the clatter-ing of the train but see it too, as one of the many speeding panes of glass broke in a fraction of a second into a thousand tiny splinters and shards, for the train had arrived, as they explained the next day, a few minutes late, they said, but they attacked it as soon as it ap-peared, rushing down the embankment to the prearranged cover, and as soon as the train hove into sight they leapt into action, fir-ing, three of them with slingshots, three with regular ones, one with only his bare hands, but all coordinated in attack formation, firing, peppering the six forty-eight, so that a window in the first carriage was immediately blown to pieces, not that they were satis-fied with that alone but launched a second wave of attacks and had only to watch out for the possible shriek of the emergency brakes, though that was something they had to devote intense attention to in order to make an on-the-spot assessment as to whether the brakes had been applied or not, and no, they hadn't, because there was not a squeal that might signal its possible application, for there was probably overwhelming panic up there by the window where people had been sitting and the whole thing, difficult as it was to figure, they said as they gave a detailed account of the affair in front of the Bingo Bar, was the work of less than a minute, no more per-haps than twenty seconds, or maybe even less, they added, since it's really tough to be precise about it, though one thing was certain, which was that they were, all of them, on full alert, as they had to be, listening out for the possible application of the emergency brakes, but since there was no evidence of that in that certain twenty seconds or so, they tried a second volley, and they could hear its effect, that it struck the carriages on the side with terrific force, with a loud ta-ta-ta-ta-ta-ta, to show that one of the last vol-leys had once more reached its target, that another window had been smashed, for they could hear it as the train roared by at ter-rific speed, making a terrific racket as the glass shattered, though later, when they sized it all up, that is to say once they had with-drawn to a safe distance and, in their own fashion, with ever greater elation, considered the matter in detail, the general feeling was that the second direct hit must have been on the mail car, whereas the first, and their voices broke with excitement at this, was a perfect bull's-eye, a word they kept repeating, going round and round in circles like a finger tickling a sensitive spot, repeating the words, passing them on, one to the other, so that by the end they were all choking, gagging, gurgling, helplessly rolling on the ground with lunatic laughter, a laughter that, once it had possessed them, would not let go now, and had gripped them in the past, so they kept exclaiming, bull's-eye! all the while clapping each other on the shoulder and hitting each other, repeating: bull's-eye! fuck it all! what about that then! what do you say to that, you prick! you prick! you prick! wrestling and pounding each other, crying, bull's-eye! until they were exhausted, at a safe distance from the scene of the crime, from the surmise that they had actually killed someone, without Korin suspecting any of this of course, for he wasn't even sure what happened to the seven children once they had suddenly leapt up and disappeared from the bridge, disappeared like camphor, as if they had never been there at all, all seven of them, all seven storming off into eternity, at which point he too took off, not glancing back, simply running in the opposite direction, anywhere to be away from the place, with but one thought pounding through his head, to be away, away, as far as possible from here, his chest shaking with the single urge, his one imperative in his great haste not to miss the route into town, for that was the point after all, to reach central Budapest and find some place where he could shelter for the night, warm himself, and perhaps get a bite to eat, but, failing that, to find some accommodation, some free accommodation, for he couldn't spare the money not knowing how much the ticket next day would cost him, as he explained at the MALÉV office, for all he wanted was some place where he would be left in peace, that was all he desired when, quite unexpectedly, he found his way free again, the children suddenly having disappeared, without explanation, without a word, while he, with his stiff leg, no longer clutching the wound that had stopped bleeding, seized the unhoped-for chance of escape, running and running until he could run no more, getting ever closer to the denser lights up ahead, slowing to a walk in his exhaustion, utterly drained by the terror he had just endured, so that he no longer cared what people said to him, and frankly he no longer gave a damn whether he ran into his pursuers or not, but stared directly in the eyes of those going the opposite way, confronting them in mid-gaze, seeking the one man that he, in his hungry, spent condition, might find it worth his while to address.

23.

That's the kind of person I am, said Korin, and spread his arms wide, having arrived at a crowded place and spotted a young couple, yet immediately conscious of the impossibility of telling them who he

was, and of the general lack of interest likely to be evinced by anyone else in the matter, simply adding: *You wouldn't happen to know a place
where . . . where I might spend the night?*

24.

The music, the venue, the crowds, or rather, that mass of young
faces; the dim light, the volume of noise, the wreaths of rolling
smoke; the young couple he had addressed and the way they
helped him when he, like them, was being frisked at the cash-desk,
the way they led him in and explained where things were while
constantly reassuring him that, of course, they could solve his
problem, the best solution being to enter and remain in the
Almássy, where there was likely to be a real hard-core gig, with
Balaton as the main band featuring Mihály Víg, and he needn't
worry because it would be the kind of gig that would go on till
dawn; and then it struck him, the extraordinarily dense crowd of
people, the stench and, by the end, all those dazed, empty, sad eyes
everywhere, in other words what with everything happening so
suddenly and all at once, said Korin the next day at the MALÉV office, after those long days of solitude followed by the hour of terror
when he was attacked on the railway bridge, he suddenly felt utterly exhausted and had barely spent a minute in there before his
head ached and he felt dizzy, unable to adjust to anything, his eyes
being accustomed to neither the dim light nor the smoke, his ears,
after all the mad panic he had been through, unable to cope with
the peculiar, quite unbearable racket, and, heaven knows, at first he
was incapable even of movement—as he recounted next day—
among this "crush of desperate pleasure seekers," being hemmed
in, rooted to the spot, then gradually swept one way then the other
by close groups of perspiring dancers, eventually fighting his way
through to the wall where he managed to insert himself between
two silent huddles who happened to be hanging about there; and
there, and only there at last could he try to come to terms with the
noise level by adopting some kind of defensive posture against it
and against all the misfortunes that had so unexpectedly befallen
him, to begin to collect himself and assemble his thoughts, for,
having reached this point of security, however infernally crowded
and chaotic it was, his capacity for thinking had simply been shot

to pieces, shot utterly to pieces, and the more he tried to concentrate the more his thoughts fell apart, so he would have far preferred to abandon the idea of thinking altogether and lie down in a corner, but that was out of the question, though that, on the whole, was his last coherent thought in a long time, the last decision he was capable of making while he continued standing there, gazing first at the band while one thought after another disintegrated before rising to the surface, then at the mass of people, then at the band again, attempting, without success, to catch something of the words of the rapid succession of songs, hearing only the odd phrase, such as "it's all over" and "everything's finished," responding chiefly to the ice-cold melancholy of the music that immediately communicated itself to him despite the sheer volume of noise, and he gazed at the three performers, at the green-haired drummer who stood at the back thrashing his drums while solemnly staring straight ahead, at the blond bass-guitarist beside him lazily rocking his body to the rhythm of the music and the singer, a man of roughly the same age as Korin himself, with his microphone at the front whose severe expression suggested terminal exhaustion and the desire to talk of nothing but terminal exhaustion, who occasionally directed his severe expression at the seething mass below him, as if he would happily have climbed off the stage and disappeared forever but remained there and continued singing, and, to tell the truth, Korin explained, there was something in this ruthless melancholy that incapacitated him, drugged him, defeated him, that tightened his throat, so that frankly, those first two or three hours of the hard-core gig at the Central club in Almássy Square simply offered him no refuge at all.

25.

Teflon heart, they hummed along in chorus with the singer, but pretty soon the THC appeared and there was no problem, only a few jolly little tours of the place as usual, so that, as they said to a close friend on the telephone the next day, they lost sight of him, having come in with them and disappeared in the heaving throng, though he was a truly weird guy the way he came up to them in the square and told them he was such and such a kind of guy, asked them if they knew anywhere to stay; just imagine, they told the friend, that, literally, that was all he said, that he was such and such a kind of guy, without going into any detail as to just what kind of a guy he was, that was the line he took, no shit, eh? and the clothes he wore! that enormous, long dark-gray overcoat smelling of mothballs, his great lanky body and his comparatively tiny, round, bald head with these two big ears sticking out, so he looked fucking incredible, they repeated time and again, like some old bat on its hind legs, meaning Korin of course, for who would have failed to recognize himself from such a description, and even though he did not forget them, the young boy and the girl who had brought him in, he did not think there was even the glimmer of a chance of seeing them ever again, not, at least, in this crowd, for after two or three hours, having finally warmed himself through and begun to get used to the atmosphere of the place, he ventured away from the wall to seek some sort of bar, to find a drink, above all, not of course, he added to himself, anything alcoholic, for he had utterly forsworn alcohol a few months ago, and so he launched out into the seething mass to buy himself a Coke, a small one at first, then a larger one, then another large one, not the bottled kind but cans from the machine, which were just as satisfying and, after the third, his stomach being full, his hunger had quite vanished, and the evening having worn on into the small hours, he made it his top priority to explore the possibilities of the environment of the Central in Almássy Square, and soon located some of the possible nooks and crannies where he might see out the rest of the night, somewhere security wouldn't find him even should the hard-core gig finish before dawn; and so he traipsed up and down, climbed stairs, tried a few door handles without anyone paying him the slightest attention for, by this time everyone, every boy and every girl, without exception, was wholly, but truly wholly, lost to the world, and he was confronted by an ever growing sea of glassy eyes, stumbling into ever more bodies on his way, some of them choosing to flop against him like sacks, impossible to stand them upright again, so that by the end there was an extraordinary scene wherein, eventually, the whole of Almássy Square was laid out on the floor or stretched over the stairs or collapsed on the stone floor of the toilets, like the remnants of some peculiar battlefield where defeat is an idea that slowly creeps over the combatants, as if radiating from within them, the singer continuing to sing until, finally, he stopped, not, as it struck Korin, at the end of a song, but somewhere in the middle, abrupt as death, removing his guitar and silently, with, if possible, a look more solemn and severe than before, leaving the stage somewhere at the back in the wings; and since Korin knew by now precisely where he would go to "spend the night" should it ever begin to wind down, as it did now, the singer having ended the evening in his own strange manner, Korin quickly left the hall, took a door to the left, climbed a few stairs to a room behind the stage where they stored scenery, full of junk, folding screens, miscellaneous items of furniture and sheets of plywood that afforded a good hiding place, and he was in the corridor on his way to precisely that point of refuge when suddenly the singer appeared opposite him, his face ravaged, and cast one sharp glance at him, at Korin that is, said Korin, and the thought occurred to him, he added next day, that this figure storming past him with long strides, his long hair flowing, was probably Mihály Víg, and was briefly flustered but quickly realized that the singer was not in the least interested in what a stranger was doing there, so Korin too walked on and slipped into the scenery storeroom, behind a wardrobe and a screen, found a warm piece of curtain material, lay down on it and wrapped the remainder around himself, made himself at home in other words, and the moment he put his head down he not so much fell asleep as fainted from exhaustion.

26.

It was an inexpressibly beautiful, unbelievably tranquil scene he found himself in as he sensed in every cell of his body, sensed it, he explained the next day, rather then saw it, because his eyes were closed, his two arms spread and relaxed, his legs slightly open, comfortable, the lush lawn beneath him softer than any down, light breezes playing about him like delicate hands, and the gentle waves of sunlight as intimate and close as breathing . . . together with the luxuriant vegetation that enfolded him, the animals drowsing in the distant shade, the azure canvas of sky above him, the earth an aromatic mass below, and this thing and that, he said, infinite, endlessly flowing in an as-yet-incomplete harmony yet permanent, immobile, echoing his own permanence and immobility, lying there, stretching, fixed as if by nails in his horizontal, immersed, practically submerged position, as if peace were this dish of dizzying sweetness and he the table, as if such peace and such sweetness really existed, as if there were such a place and such tranquility, as if such a thing existed, said Korin, as if it were possible.

27.

He couldn't really claim, he told the stewardess at the MALÉV office the next day, to be one of those to whom courage comes readily and without an effort of the will, someone capable of addressing strangers or using the fact that they were both waiting for something as an excuse, but having her, the stewardess, beside him like this, a stewardess who was so lovely with her smile and those two little dimples, he had found himself, having sat down a few minutes ago, tempted to dart brief glances in her direction, but recognizing that this was a shifty way of behaving, he had abstained and would prefer to come clean now and admit that he did in fact want to look at her, hoping that this disclosure might not prove too offensive or sly and that the young lady would not be angry, regarding it neither as a pass nor as a clumsy attempt to draw her into conversation, for nothing was further from his mind, but the stewardess being not only lovely but beautiful in a way that he couldn't forbear to remark on, he hoped she might not regard it as a proposition, oh no, apologies in advance, certainly not a proposition because he was beyond propositioning anyone, he said, it was merely the beauty, the sheer extraordinary beauty he discerned in the young stewardess lady that so overwhelmed him, as she would understand, wouldn't she? said Korin, for it wasn't a case of him, Korin, wishing to be intrusive, but rather of her beauty inadvertently intruding on him, and while he was at it, he added, elaborating on his theme, let him at least in all humility properly introduce himself, György Korin, though he wouldn't really want to delve into his occupation, for anything he might say on that subject would pertain only to his past, though he would have plenty to say, particularly today and particularly to her, about himself some time later and only then, though the prospect of doing so was pretty dim, and the most he could do for now was to let her know why he had eventually plucked up courage to speak to her, which was to tell her what a strange, in fact utterly extraordinary dream he had had last night, though he rarely dreamt, or rather hardly ever re-

membered his dreams, last night being a unique exception, for he
not only dreamt but remembered precisely every last detail of the
dream, and she should imagine a place of inexpressible beauty, of
unbelievable tranquility that he could sense in every cell of his
body, for though his eyes were closed he could feel his two arms
spread out, relaxed, his legs slightly open, comfortable, and she
should imagine, he said, a lush lawn, softer than any down, the
light breezes playing about him like delicate hands, and, lastly,
imagine the gentle waves of sunlight intimate and close as breathing, the density of the luxuriant vegetation that enfolded him, and
the animals drowsing in the distant shade, with the azure canvas of
the sky above and the aromatic mass of soil below, and so on, this
thing and that thing, infinite, endlessly flowing in an as-yet-incomplete harmony yet permanent, immobile, echoing his own permanence and immobility, lying there, stretching, fixed as if by nails in
his horizontal, immersed, practically submerged position, as if
peace were a dish of dizzying sweetness and he the table, as if such
peace and such sweetness really existed, as if there were such a
place and such tranquility, as if such a thing existed, if you know
what I mean, said Korin, as if it were possible, do you see, young
lady? the whole experience being so, you know, convincing,
though if there was anyone who might be skeptical of such a
dream, it would be the dreamer himself, Korin, though there was
nothing in his life that had not been unlikely, right from the start,
just think of him, György Korin, living in a small provincial town
some two hundred and twenty kilometers southeast of here,
though how to begin, it is so damned difficult, really practically
impossible to describe how it all began, but, if he didn't bore her,
for he had to wait here in any case, he would try to describe one or
two minor incidents in his life if only that she might have some
idea who he was, who it was talking to her and addressing her, in
fact who was it she was having to put up with for having suddenly
been addressed like this, without formalities or introductions.

28.

She had, she felt obliged to respond, been runner-up in a beauty
contest, and though nothing could have been further from her mind
than involving herself in a conversation with the man who had set-

tled himself beside her, this being of all possible options open to her the last she would choose, as she had more than once tried to convey to him, she nevertheless drifted into communication somehow and found herself answering when she should have kept quiet and even responding, if only with a word or two, when she should have turned her head away, so that she was genuinely unaware that she had become involved with a complete stranger in exactly the conversation she had wished to avoid, explaining to him how dog-tired she was, because to take this moment as an example, she had no idea how long she would have to wait, and how utterly unaccustomed she was to waiting like this so that she might meet and have the responsibility of escorting a passenger in a wheelchair, an old Swiss lady, and to do something she had never done before, that is to transport her to the airport and assist her onto the night-flight to Rome; and so, in telling him this, she had entered into an informal conversation with this man despite her best intentions, and whether it happened this way or the other, who cares, she didn't particularly mind in the end, she told the others once they were on board, it was only the beginning that was so weird, for she thought she was dealing with a lunatic or something, the kind who talks to himself, but he wasn't that, he was different, perfectly harmless, with rather nice big ears, and she had always had a weakness for big ears because they made the face look sweet, and in any case she could have stood up and left him any time she wanted, but was happy enough for him to tell her practically his entire life story, because it was simply irresistible, she just had to listen, and cross her heart, she did listen, though, to tell the truth, it was hard to know whether he was telling the truth, for could it really be that someone of such advanced age as forty-something, who knows how old exactly, could sell up and go to New York, not because he wanted to make a new life for himself but because he wanted to end his life there, for nowhere else would do, as the man kept saying, but "the very center of the world," which New York might be for all she knew, anyway he was pretty convincing, she continued in the cabin, it was impossible to think otherwise, though it is natural to be a little skeptical in view of everything one hears nowadays, none of it true, and though this man, of course, did not seem to be the sort of person whose word you'd doubt, far from it, in fact after a while she herself had seriously told him such things as she hadn't told anyone else, for they did have to wait an awfully long time, and she had, in this way, so to speak, opened up to him for he himself was so earnest that she grew quite upset, and somehow she kept feeling that she might be the very last person ever to listen to him, it was really that sad, and he was so fulsome in praise of her beauty that he had asked why she did not enter a beauty contest since she would be sure, absolutely certain, to win it, in response to which she did at last confess that once, in a moment of weakness, she did in fact enter one but had come away so terribly disillusioned with what she saw that she felt quite embittered by the experience of entering in the first place, and it was so nice when his answer to this was that she should not have been named runner-up, because that was clearly ridiculous and wholly unfair, but should have been awarded first prize.

29.

I need a ticket for the next flight, said Korin at the desk, and when he leaned across it to explain the matter to the clerk who was staring into her computer, making it clear to her that this was no ordinary journey, nor he an ordinary traveler, meaning he was not a tourist, not on a family visit, nor was he a businessman, all she said, after a lot of hemming and hawing and shaking of heads, was that she would be grateful if he would stop leaning across her desk, and that his one very faint hope of success lay in a so-called "lahsminih" flight, though he would have to wait for that too in order to discover whether it was in fact worth waiting, and so, if in the meantime, he would be so good as to return to his seat . . . but Korin begged her pardon, asking what that meant, and she had to enunciate it clearly, syllable by syllable, "lahs-min-ih" while he kept turning it over and over in his mind, aloud, until his English lessons of the last few months kicked in and he realized that what she meant to say was probably "last minute," yes, that was it, now he understood, he said, though he was far from understanding anything until, on his puzzled return to the bench, the stewardess explained it to him, though it transpired that he would also need a "so-called visa," and naturally he didn't have one, at which point the stewardess's beautiful face darkened for a minute, and everyone looked at him repeating, *Visa?* does he, Korin, mean to say he has no visa? but does he know what this means? does he understand that it can take up to a week to obtain a visa? and how can he present himself at the desk with an on-the-spot request for a ticket? indeed, too bad, the stewardess nodded in melancholy fashion, then, seeing how Korin had sunk back beside her in desperation, advised him that he shouldn't despair and that she would have a go, and, so saying, she stepped across to the nearest telephone and began phoning, ringing first one place then another, though because of all the noise Korin couldn't understand a word she was saying, and after half an hour or so someone appeared announcing that it would be all right, sir, regard the problem as solved, and Korin solemnly declared that the stewardess was not only enchantingly lovely, but that she could work magic in other ways too, until the man returned to inform Korin that the visa would cost him fifteen thousand, fifteen thousand! Korin repeated aloud, the color draining from his face as he stood up, but the man merely repeated fifteen thousand, saying Korin could, if he wished, try going to the consulate himself, and stand in the long queue on his own, perhaps returning after three or four days, he might have the time to spare, but if he didn't this was the price, there was not much chance of anything else turning up, in consequence of which Korin excused himself and popped into the toilet, took three five-thousand bills from the lining of his coat, came out and handed the money over to the man who told him that everything would be all right, he could relax, for he would fill the necessary parts of the form out for Korin, then take it in and go through all the proper procedures which meant he could stop fretting, it was all in the safest possible hands, he would have his darn visa by that afternoon and could therefore, he winked before disappearing with the appropriate information, take it easy for the next ten years, sleep soundly for ten years; and so Korin told the desk clerk that he would after all have need of a ticket for the next flight, then sat down again beside the stewardess and confessed that he had no idea what would happen to him if the old lady in the wheelchair happened to arrive, for, to tell the truth, he had never flown before, had no idea what to do, was in constant need of advice and his prospects, which had brightened so dramatically, would immediately cloud over again if she was required to attend on the old lady with the wheelchair and so leave him.

30.

All eyes in the office were directed at them, from the woman sitting behind the reception counter, through the agents at their desks in the background to the scattered individual browsers of brochures desirous of travel; not a pair of eyes but was fixed on them, on the whole incident, or rather what it signified, for there was no ready explanation for it: for the extraordinary beauty of the stewardess, since how could someone so beautiful be a stewardess or, indeed, a stewardess so beautiful; for the unwashed, smelly figure of Korin in his rumpled greatcoat, for how could someone traveling to America present such an appearance, or conversely, how could someone presenting such an appearance aspire to visit America; and above all for the fact that two such people could be in easy commerce with each other, on the best of terms, lost in a conversation so deep that its ultimate subject was beyond conjecture for it was being conducted in such passionate terms that it conveyed nothing beyond the passion itself, not even hinting at whether they were meeting for the first time or renewing an old acquaintance, both possibilities, as far as the office was concerned, remaining open: in other words the sight of such beauty borne with such regal modesty in combination with a figure of such beggarly degeneracy represented a serious disturbance in the even tenor of official life, indeed, as far as this sphere of existence was concerned, it signified a slowly developing scandal, since the stewardess was certainly no kind of queen, nor Korin a beggar, and therefore all anyone could do was to watch and wait, wait for this curious still life to disintegrate, to be snuffed out, liquidated, since there could be no doubt that scene on the bench was in fact a kind of still life, Korin with his degenerate beggarly appearance, his defenseless otherworldliness, and the stewardess with her enchanting body, that body's simmering sensuality; a still life therefore with peculiar rules of its own meriting the peculiarly intense interest of its environment, as the stewardess herself explained later on the plane, an interest that she herself finally noticed, and when she saw how everyone was looking at them, it confused her, she said, and there was even something frightening about it, about everyone's eyes, the way they were looking at them, how should she put it? as if it were one single face staring and in a truly frightening fashion, frightening and comical, as she told them all about it on the way to Rome.

31.

My predecessors were, on the whole, relaxed, said Korin after a period of silence, then, pulling a sour face, he scratched the top of his head and carefully accenting every word, added—but I was always fraught.

32.

The nipples delicately pressed through the warm texture of the snow-white starched blouse while the deep décolletage boldly accentuated the graceful curvature and fragility of the neck, the gentle valleys of the shoulders and the light swaying to and fro of the sweetly compact masses of her breasts, though it was hard to tell whether it was these that drew all eyes inexorably to her, that refused to let the eyes escape, or if it was the short dark-blue skirt that clung to her hips and bound her long thighs tightly together while indicating the lines of her belly, or indeed if it was the lush and sparkling black hair that tumbled over her shoulders and the clear high brow, the beautifully sculpted jaw, the thick soft lips, the pretty slope of the nose, or those shining eyes in the depths of which two unquenchable spots of light glowed and would glow there forever, that arrested them; in other words men and women caught in that moment in the office were quite unable to decide what it was that had such a spellbinding effect, so spellbinding that they could do nothing but stare at the several parts constituting this fever-inducing beauty, and what was more—bearing in mind the contrast between such a bountiful display of loveliness on the one hand and their own commonplace existence—they stared at her quite openly, the men with crude, long-suppressed hunger and naked desire, the women with a fine attention to the accumulation of detail, from top to bottom and back again, dizzy with the sensation but, driven by a malignant jealousy at the heart of their fierce inspection, surveying her with ever less sympathy, ever greater contempt, remarking, once the thing was over, or rather once this scandalous pair had disappeared separately through the exit of the MALÉV office, the women first, that it wasn't a matter of prejudice, for they too were women, and one woman always regards another in that light, so there could be no question of prejudice, but it was a little much the way this little strumpet of a stewardess, as one or two of them quickly interjected, pretended she was an innocent little angel, a meek, ready-to-please little princess, while, so the women in the office snorted once it was possible to get together behind the desk and address the subject properly, that tight blouse, the ultra-short skirt clinging to her ass giving an occasional glimpse of the long thighs and the white panties between the thighs, and the very fact that every part of this body, literally everything, was clearly on display, and was practically screaming for attention . . . well, they had seen quite enough of such apparent artlessness before and knew all too well how to work the little dodges that brought out the best but hid that which should be invisible, nor would they say anything but, really! the shameless deception of it, a blatant whore parading herself like some refined, regal presence, that! they all agreed, no one would be taken in by nowadays, and later on, before they went home, stopping for a brief chat in the park or a bar, the male employees who had witnessed the scene, a customer or two, or managers further up the chain, contributed to the ongoing discussion by adding that such women were on to a winner every time, that she had a fantastic body, and these huge tits that really thrust themselves at you, and what's more, they added, she had a sweetly swaying round ass, and tits like that, and an ass like that, not forgetting, they added, a snow-white set of teeth and a charming smile, and given those shapely hips and a bit of graceful movement, and, to top it all, a glance, a perfectly timed glance that told you, you whose throat was quite parched by the sight of her, that you would be wrong, seriously wrong, if you thought that you would be at the receiving end of all this, because the glance also told you that the woman confronting you was a virgin, and what is more precisely the kind of virgin who has no idea what she has been created for, in other words, taking it all into account, the men declared as they sat in the park or in the bar, if you took her on, they jabbed their fingers at their listeners, that would be the end of you, and they set out once more to describe the woman they had seen at the MALÉV office from her nipples down to her slender ankles, set out but could never finish what they started, since this woman, they kept repeating, was quite beyond words, because what did they achieve by telling you about the skirt glued to the hips and those long thighs, no more than the hair tumbling over her shoulders, those soft lips, the brow, the chin, the nose, really now, what did it add up to? they asked, for it was impossible, simply impossible to capture her in words, because what one ought to capture in beauty is that which is treacherous and irresistible, or, let's be perfectly honest: she was the vision of a truly magnificent, majestic female animal in a dismally synthetic world of sickness.

33.

If anyone really and truly wished him success in his venture, it was she, declared the stewardess to the other crew members on board, though she was sure, she added, that once she had left him he would quickly have come unstuck and got pretty well nowhere, and most likely his name would have been dropped from the stand-by list after the Swiss lady in the wheelchair had turned up—almost three and a half hours late—which was when she had taken her leave of him, pushing the woman through the door of the office, yes, they'd have dropped his name off the list, the stewardess repeated with growing certainty, no doubt about it, absolutely none, not that she knew precisely who it was that would do the dropping, the people who are normally responsible for such decisions, she expected, policemen, psychiatric workers, security personnel, the usual suspects, because the way he looked it was a miracle that he had got within hailing distance of the MALÉV office, and no one who had had the briefest contact with him could believe he would get any further, so why should she believe it, however she might wish it were otherwise, for to get across town, out to the Ferihegy airport and past the ticket inspectors, the customs people, the security guys, then to go on to America, no, no, no, the stewardess shook her head, it was unimaginable that he could manage all that, and even now, some two hours later, when she thought back over it, it all seemed like a dream to her, not that she had had a dream as strange as that in a long time, she confessed, nor had she any idea what it all added up to, this memory she now had stored away, for she was still too close to it, she couldn't really see anything, had no idea who he *actually* was, or anything about him except that she had immediately started making excuses for him and defending him without being able to make any categorical statements about him, in other words to defend him from some as-yet-unknown accusation, for example that of lunacy, for though he did at first sight appear to be a lunatic, he was, as she had already said, no fool, but, how should she express it, there was something about him, about this man, that was so solemn, so unusual, so—she felt justified in using the word—so startling in its absolute solemnity, that she couldn't but be struck by his sheer desperation, him being absolutely set on something, even though he couldn't articulate what it was, and no, she wasn't joking, she's not leading them on, not just saying all this, and after a good sleep she would get over the experience, and once she was through it all, she said, pointing at herself, through all this "may I talk to you" business, all this "intensity," really, it would be she herself who would be thought crazy for getting involved in the first place, right? ah no, not at all, she would quite understand it if her colleagues thought she was crazy, so she would shut up now, leave off the story of this great soul-shaking encounter, and she was sorry to have bored them, and had a good giggle herself among the general merriment, adding only that it was sad the way we meet people by chance, spend time talking to them, acknowledge the fact that they have had some effect on us, then we lose them and never ever see them again, something genuinely sad, whatever anyone says, she repeated, laughing, really very sad.

34.

It was Hermes, said Korin, Hermes lay at the heart of everything, that was his starting point, that was the foundation of his deepest intellectual experiences, and though he had never spoken of this to anyone before he simply had to tell the young lady stewardess that it was to Hermes he had been ultimately led, having time after time attempted to discover that hermetically-sealed beginning, had time after time attempted to understand it, to solve it, to get to the bottom of it, and not least of all, to recount it to those people that fate had so far brought him into contact with, to tell them how it was that he realized that he was not intended to be an ordinary archivist, not that he didn't want to be an archivist, for indeed he was most sincerely an archivist, but not an ordinary one, and what he sought to discover, what he constantly sought the answer to, was the reason why he wasn't ordinary; and so he kept going over and over things that had happened, extending his explorations ever further back in time, and there was always something there, something new about his past that made him think, this is it, I've got it, or rather he searched and searched for the source, the *origo* of this revolution in his life which eventually, some thirty or forty hours ago, had led him here, and to ever newer potential sources and *origos*, ever newer starting points and beginnings, until he reached the conclusion, he was pleased to say, the actual conclusion he had been seeking and the name of that conclusion was Hermes; for truly, he said, Hermes, for him, was that absolute *origo*, it was that encounter with the hermetic, the day, the hour he first encountered Hermes, when—if he might so put it—he became acquainted with the world of the hermetic and was afforded a glimpse into it, into that which Hermes presented as a world, the world of which Hermes was the ruler, Hermes, this Greek god, the twelfth of twelve, with his mystery, his lack of fixity, his copiously multifaceted existence, his secret forms, the dark side of his being shrouded in a deeply suggestive silence, who had had such a mesmerizing effect on his imagination, or, more precisely, had completely captured his imaginative faculties and made him restless, had drawn him into a sphere from which there was no escape, for it was like being under a spell or a curse or an incantation, since this is what Hermes was to him, not a god who led but one who misled, swept him off course, destabilized him, called him, drew him aside, seduced him from below, whispered to him from the wings; but why him, him in particular, why this archivist working some two hundred and twenty kilometers from Budapest, he could not tell, nor should he seek after reasons, he felt, but simply accept that that was the way it was; it was the way he had learned of Hermes, possibly through the Homeric Hymns, or maybe from the psychoanalyst Kerényi, possibly from the marvelous Graves, who the hell knew or cared how, said Korin, this being, if he might so put it that way, the induction phase which was quickly followed by the next phase, the phase of deeper exploration in which the towering, unrivalled work of Walter F. Otto, that is to say his *Die Götter Griechenlands*, was the sole guide, and in that book, exclusively one specific chapter in the Hungarian edition, which he read and reread until it came to pieces in his hands, which was the point at which restlessness and anxiety entered his life, when things were no longer as they were, the day after which everything looked different, had changed, when the world showed him its most terrifying face, bringing on a

sense of dissociation, offering the most terrifying aspect of absolute freedom, since knowledge of Hermes, said Korin, entails the
loss of one's sense of being at home in this world, of the sense of
belonging, of dependence, of certainty, and this means that suddenly there is an uncertainty factor in the totality of things, because, just as suddenly, it becomes clear that this uncertainty is the
only, the sole factor, for Hermes signifies the provisional and relative nature of the laws of being, and Hermes brings and Hermes
takes such laws away, or rather allows them liberty, for that is the
whole point of Hermes, said Korin to the stewardess, for whoever
is granted a glimpse of him can never again yield himself to any
ambition or form of knowledge, because ambition and knowledge
are merely ragged cloaks, if he might use such a poetic turn of
phrase, that one may adapt or cast off at a whim according to the
teachings of Hermes, the god of the roads of night, of night itself, a
night whose domain the presence of Hermes extends into day,
since as soon as he appears anywhere he immediately changes
human life, appearing to let days be, appearing to acknowledge the
powers of his Olympian companions, and allowing everything to
appear as though life continued to proceed according to the plans
and schemes of his own, while whispering to his devotees that life
was not quite like this, leading them into the night, showing them
the inconceivably complex and chaotic nature of all paths, making
them confront the unexpected, the accidental, the out-of-the-blue,
the dangerous, the deeply confused and primitive states of possession, death and sexuality, expelling them, in other words, from
Zeus's world of light and thrusting them into hermetic darkness, as
he had thrust Korin ever since Korin had understood that a glimpse
of him had induced a restlessness in his heart, a restlessness that
could never cease once Hermes had revealed himself to him, a
revelation that quite ruined him, for if there was one thing he did
not wish to suggest it was that this discovery, this glimpse of Hermes, indicated that he felt any love for Hermes, said Korin, no, he
had no love for Hermes whatsoever but was simply frightened of
him; and this is how things were, this is what happened and no
more than this, that he had been scared by Hermes as would any
man have been, any man who had realized at the moment of his
ruin that he had been ruined, that is to say had come into the possession of such knowledge as he did not at all wish to possess, as

was precisely the case with him, with Korin, for what did he desire that others did not? he had no desire to be different, to stand out from the crowd, he had no such ambitions, preferring relationships and security, homeliness and a clear and simple life, in other words absolutely ordinary things, though he lost these in the blinking of an eye the moment Hermes entered his life, and made of him, as he is happy to admit, a servant, an underling, since from that moment the underling began rapidly to distance himself from his wife, his neighbors and his colleagues, because it seemed hopeless even to try to explain, elaborate, or confess to the fact that it was a Greek god that lay at the root of the unmistakable changes in his behavior, not that he had any chance of getting others to sympathize with him, Korin told the stewardess, for just imagine him turning one day to his wife, or to his colleagues at the archive and saying to them, I am aware that you will have noticed a peculiar change in my behavior, well, it's all on account of a Greek god; just imagine the effect, said Korin, the way his wife would react to such a confession, or his colleagues to this explanation, in other words things could not have turned out otherwise than they did, a quick divorce, the rapid progress from peculiar looks at the office to being ignored, in fact some went so far as to avoid him altogether and refused to acknowledge him in the street, which was, said Korin, deeply hurtful, coming as it did from his own colleagues, people he met every day of his life, being utterly ignored in the street by them, thanks to Hermes, and everything flowed from that right down to the present moment, not that he was complaining, merely establishing the facts, for what cause had he for complaint, though there was a time when he was no more than a simple, perfectly orthodox archivist who had every hope of progressing to the post of chief archivist, but now instead of that, would you believe it, said Korin, here he was in Budapest, in Budapest, if he might be allowed to jump forward in time, at the Budapest offices of MALÉV where he trusted and genuinely believed that he would receive a visa and a ticket enabling him, Korin, not only to get to the world-famous city of New York, but in doing so to achieve, and here he dropped his voice, the chief aim of his hermetic state of uncertainty, not to mention the fact, he added, that should he desire compensation, which he did not; or should he wish to exchange his state for some other, which he did not; an exchange of states might serve as a form of compensation, and though this kind of exchange was against the rules it was not in fact impossible, for it was not impossible that he might, any day now, get to see the deity, Hermes, personally, at some moment, for such moments did exist, moments when things were really calm, moments when he glanced toward a shady corner, afternoons when he had fallen asleep and woke to a flash of light in the room, or perhaps when it was getting dark and he was rushing somewhere the god might be there beside him, keeping pace with him, visible as the moon, waving his caduceus at something that was not him, in the distance before disappearing.

35.

The visa arrived but they were still sitting in the same way in the same place on the bench set out to accommodate those who were waiting, since the old woman had not yet turned up, and on being shown the visa the people at the desk had nothing to add concerning his chances of getting a ticket, telling him off instead, asking him what his problem was, what was he getting so uppity and impatient about, constantly jumping up and down like that instead of sitting down calmly and waiting to be called in his turn at the right time, because there were people out there who had been waiting for weeks, to which Korin naturally replied with an acquiescent nod, assuring the staff that he would stop being a nuisance to them, that from now on, having got the point, he would, he promised, no longer impose on them, and so saying, sat back down on the bench beside the stewardess and said nothing for the next few minutes, simply waited, clearly anxious in case his behavior had set the staff against him, which, he explained to the stewardess, would harm no one but him, then, suddenly, as if he had forgotten everything he had said earlier, he turned to her again and continued from where he had just now left off, informing her that nothing would please him more than spending the entire week here, in continual conversation with her, though he himself did not quite understand what the hell it was that inspired him to launch out on his monologue, a monologue, furthermore, that was exclusively about himself, for he had never done anything like this in his life, not once, Korin told the stewardess, gazing into her eyes, for it would have been inconceivable before, in fact if anything characterized him as he had been it was a reluctance to talk about himself, he'd not say a word to anyone on the subject, and if now he felt impelled, it was possibly because he was frightened that he might be attacked, fearing that they were on his trail, which was by no means a certainty, more a simple likelihood, in other words it must be this or some other related cause that made him launch out on this torrent of words, feeling that he had to tell all, the bit about the riverbank, about the psychotherapy, the hierarchy, the amnesia, about freedom and about the center of the world so that he, who had never previously been aware of having the least talent for it, might at last initiate someone else into the secret story of the last years, the last months, the last day, telling them what happened at the archive, in the caboose, on the railway bridge and on Almássy Square; telling, in other words, everything, or, to be more accurate, the essential parts, though telling only the truly essential parts was becoming steadily harder, and not only because the whole consisted of individual details, details of which there was a maddening surfeit, but also because—a most humdrum problem— it made his head ache, or to be more precise made the headache he already had exceed its usual intensity so that it was becoming quite unbearable, or rather, he corrected himself, not even so much his head as his neck, his shoulders and the base of his skull, just there, he pointed out to the stewardess, and when you took all these pains into consideration, the whole effect, when it put its mind to it, could become unbearable, and there was nothing he could do about these attacks for nothing would help, not massage, not turning his head this way and that, not moving his shoulders about, nothing, the only cure was sleep, sleep alone could shift it, the complete and utter mental relaxation, the loss of all self-consciousness, though that was precisely the problem, that he never could relax his self-consciousness, never free himself of the tension in his head, he had to hold it just as he was now doing, though, naturally, it led to the cramping of the muscles and strained the ligaments, so that eventually the constitution of his whole upper body was in open revolt, at which point he had no option, if the young lady would be so kind as to forgive him, but to lie down here on the bench, only for a minute of course, but lie down he must if only to relieve the strain on his muscles and ligaments, from the *trapezius* and the *splenius*, from the *sub-occipital* and the *sternocleidomastodeus*, for somehow the pressure had to be lifted or else the thing he had long feared would come to pass, that is to say his head would drop off, because that would surely happen, the whole caboodle would just collapse, and then there would be no New York, no nothing, said Korin, it would all be over before you could say Jack Robinson.

36.

The stewardess stood up to make room for Korin, who gradually, carefully, arranged himself full-length along the bench but no sooner had he closed his eyes than he had to snap them open again because the door to the street was suddenly thrown open and a whole crowd of people thrust themselves through it, or to put it more precisely, erupted into the office with such brutal force it seemed they wanted to smash everything in their way, impatient of the slightest objection, shouting harsh instructions left and right, fore and aft, to the effect that the person they were delivering, who was now shoved forward in a brilliantly glistening ebony-black wheelchair, and who was now advancing through the ranks of would-be ticket purchasers and employees, had a quite particular reason for bursting in like this and had an absolute right to run people down while no one had any cause or justification to question this privilege; in other words, albeit half a day late, and to Korin's deepest disappointment but to the stewardess's great relief, the old woman from Switzerland had finally arrived in her very own skin-and-bone, dried-out body, her face fallen in and scored over with a thousand wrinkles, her gray eyes tiny and lightless, her lips cracked, her ears decked out in an outsize set of gold earrings that dangled right down to her shoulders, her whole presence immediately, silently, declaring that it was with precisely this body, this face, these eyes, these lips and just these enormous earrings that she intended to determine what was going or not going to happen in the next few minutes; nor did she in fact say anything at all, and as to her entourage, it was clear that there was no communication of orders to them either, it being more a case of now a little this way, now a little faster, now a touch slower, while they kept their eyes firmly glued to her, hanging on to her the way the golden earrings did to her ears, until, with one gesture as minimal as the act of breathing she made it clear what she wanted, which way she wanted to go, which route they should take to which desk, a decision that neither the employees nor those waiting for tickets had any power to resist, for those behind the desks stopped working and the queues broke up, simultaneously bringing to an end the situation in which Korin, still cursed with his headache, and the stewardess found themselves, since Korin had, at the very least, after the first moment of terror, to sit up in order to convince himself that the deputation had not come for him, and the stewardess had to snap into action and announce that it was she whom MALÉV had, after the necessary formalities, together with the Helping Hands service, sent to conduct the elderly lady to her chosen, specially selected flight, where she would be her supporter and aide, to be in the strict sense of the word, her *guide* on the road to the Ferihegy airport.

37.

The meat-filled pancake *à la Hortobágy* was fine, the old lady's translator conveyed to the nervous official, but the air—and here every member of the entourage allowed himself a smile—did not meet with Frau Hanzl's approval, no, *eure Luft*, as the old lady repeated in her loud, cracked rather masculine voice, shaking her head in a disillusioned manner, *ist einfach unqualifizierbar, versteht ihr?, unqualifizierbar!* after which, having indicated that she wished the computer monitor to be turned in her direction, she jabbed her finger at one of the lines, from which point everything happened improbably fast: no more than a minute or two had elapsed before her entourage was in full possession of a ticket and the stewardess had been informed what her duties were to be regarding "the acutely sensitive Mrs. Hanzl who was in the habit of making all her own arrangements for travel," and the shiny ebony-black wheelchair containing the acutely sensitive Mrs. Hanzl, was already turning and thundering across the hall toward the exit so that Korin, who was looking this way and that in panic, had barely time enough to dash over to the stewardess and condense into a single sentence everything she absolutely had to know, since, he stared at her in desperation, there was so much he had not had time to say, the most important things in fact, having neglected to inform her of the very reason he had to get to New York and what he had to do there, indicating his coat sleeve and the manuscript of which he had not said a word so far though it was by far the most important aspect of the whole thing and the stewardess would understand nothing if she did not know that, for that manuscript—he grabbed her hand and tried to delay the gathering momentum of the procession—was the most extraordinary piece of writing that anyone had ever produced, but he could talk to the stewardess all he liked for she was no longer listening, having only time enough to smile and beg his forgiveness for having to get on now, in response to which Korin himself could do no more than run ahead, to prop the door open before the onrushing wheelchair, and raise his voice above the din of the agitated procession of escorts to remark what a wonderful, unforgettable day it had been, and that the young stewardess lady should allow him to file away the two tiny dimples of her smile in his memory forever, to which she replied smiling, with precisely those two tiny dimples, that he was most welcome to file them away, whereupon she waved and disappeared behind the closing door, leaving Korin alone in the suddenly ear-splitting silence with only the eternal memory of those two little dimples to console him.

38.

For 119,000 Forints he could have a week in Iceland, one bored official told him, rattling the figures off; for 99,900 a week on the Nile, for 98,000 a week in Tenerife, for 75,900 five days in London, 69,000 for a week in Cyprus or Mallorca, 49,900 for a week on the Turkish Riviera, 39,900 for a week in Rhodes, 34,900 for the same in Corfu, 24,900 for Dubrovnik or Athens-Thessaloniki, 24,000 for a week at the Cloisters in Meteora, Jesolo was 22,900, Salou in Spain 19,900, or he could have eight days in Kraljevica for 18,200 Forints, and if none of those appealed to him, he told the customer standing at the desk, for he appeared to be dithering, then, the agent turned his head away and made a moue with his mouth, he was perfectly free to go elsewhere, and so saying he pressed a button on his computer, tipped his chair back and stared at the ceiling with an expression that clearly declared that he, for his part, had given out as much information as he felt bound to and was not going to give out one bit more.

39.

What ticket for what flight? Korin enquired at the desk later when they called him up to tell him the news, and started massaging his forehead the way people do when they want to summon up their lost concentration, cutting the operative short by asking: *Tomorrow? What do you mean tomorrow?*

40.

There were four of them altogether, three female adults aged between fifty and sixty, and a girl who looked about eighteen but was certainly no more than twelve years old, each of them arriving with a steel bucket full of cleaning apparatus and carrying a half-sized industrial mop in her left hand: four buckets, four mops and four sets of gray cleaners' lab-coats, ensuring their clear identification and function and explaining why they were now ready and waiting for something, squinting upward at everyone else, fixed in this inferior position keeping their eyes peeled for a sign from their supervisor who stood in the doorway of a glass cubicle, and when the sign eventually came they were set to go about their business, carefully at first, with a number of uncertain preparatory gestures, then, as the last of the officials and employees disappeared through the door, and the shutters at the front clattered down, switching to full speed with the mops and buckets, the four of them in their uniforms, two in front, two remaining on the street side, wringing out the cloths wound around the mops then dipping them into water again, the mops dripping, two on one side, two on the other, the cleaners taking long extended strides, solemnly, without a word, so that the only sound audible was of the four improvised mops sliding quickly across the fake-marble slabs of the floor, and then, as they reached the center and passed each other, one or two slight smacking sounds, then that sliding noise across the floor again, to the end of the room, then a dipping and wringing and back again, as wordless as before, until the girl reached into the pocket of her coat to turn on a small transistor, turning up the volume, so from that moment they moved in a dense, echoing, monotonous aspic of sound, like machines, with mops in their hands, their empty whey-colored eyes fixed on their damp mops.

II • THAT INTOXICATING FEELING

I.

On 15 November 1997, in the staff conference room of Terminal 2, Ferihegy Airport, having gone over all the standard procedures with the crew and acquainted them with the expected weather conditions, the passenger numbers, as well as the nature and status of the cargo, the captain summed up by telling them that he expected a smooth, trouble-free journey, and so Flight MA 090—a Boeing 767 equipped with two CF6-80C2 engines offering a maximum operating distance of 12,700 kilometers, fuel capacity of 91,368 liters, wingspan of 47.57 meters and capable of carrying a load of 175.5 tons, including 127 tourist-class and 12 luxury-class passengers—taxied down the runway and, having reached the average takeoff speed of 280 km/hour, rose above the ground at 11:56 precisely, attaining its full cruising height of 9,800 meters near the city of Graz by 12:24, at which point, the north-north-westerly headwind not exceeding the usual thresholds, it aligned itself along the Stuttgart-Brussels-Belfast axis that would lead it out over the Atlantic Ocean, where it adapted itself to the given coordinates, so that within 4 hours 20 minutes it arrived at the South Greenland checkpoint, and being four minutes short of an hour from its destination, began its descent, at first by 800 meters, then, having received its instructions from the Newfoundland center, dropping gradually and smoothly from a height of 4,200 meters, by now under the command of New York and district Air Control, according to the given timetable, arriving on the terra firma of the New World at Gate L36 of John F. Kennedy Airport at precisely 15:25 hours local time.

2.

Oh yes, yes, Korin nodded enthusiastically at the black immigration officer, then, the question being repeated time and again with ever greater irritation, when it had become quite pointless referring to his documents, and it was useless nodding and saying yes and yes over and over again, he spread his arms, shook his head and said in Hungarian: *Nekem te hiába beszélsz, én nem értek ebből egy árva szót sem,* in other words, *It's no use you talking to me, I don't understand a single word you're saying,* adding, usefully, in English, *No understand.*

3.

The room into which they led him down a long narrow corridor reminded him of nothing so much as the kind of closed boxcar in which they used to carry corn, the walls being lined with gray steel, not a window anywhere and the doors capable of being opened only from outside, which was why it was like suddenly being dumped in an empty boxcar, Korin explained later, because there were two things, he said, that suggested such a boxcar: an unmistakable smell and the way the floor was gently vibrating, which, once they closed the door on him and left him alone, really did make him feel as though he had found himself in a stinking freight car, an American one, but a freight car all the same, for as soon as he stepped in, he explained, he could smell the corn and feel the floor vibrating under him, the corn smell quite unmistakable since he had plenty of opportunity to experience it on his way to Budapest, and the vibration, likewise, he was convinced, was not a trick of the senses brought on by the flickering of the neon light, for there was nothing incidental or uncertain about it, it was a decided tingling he felt in the soles of his feet, and what's more, when he accidentally touched the wall he could feel that it too was vibrating, and you may imagine, he added, how a man feels under such circumstances, as he indeed did feel, since he understood precisely nothing of what was going on or what they wanted of him, what it was they were asking of him, and what on earth this whole thing was about, and so he took out the notebook in which he had jotted the most important words while still on the aircraft, because he didn't like the idea of using the phrase book, the one in his pocket, feeling it wouldn't help him when he got into conversation with someone, being too formal, too inconvenient, too slow with all those pages you had to flick through, looking words up, and in any case he found with this particular phrase book that he tended to flick past the place he wanted, or that those specific pages of the selected letter were somehow stuck together so whole sections flicked by in one go, and when he deliberately tried to slow the movement of the pages for fear of going past them, his anxiety and solicitude made him so nervous that he flicked past the page anyway, which meant that he had to start all over again, fiddling impatiently, holding the phrase book in a different kind of grip, searching through page by individual page, the entire process, in other words, resulting in a dramatic slowing down, that being the reason he took to the notebook, writing out the likely most important words, finding a system that would facilitate their recovery, speeding up the leafing-through process, and had indeed discovered such a system and had prepared everything on the long journey, though of course had to take it out again, and most pressingly now, if he wanted to get out of these dire straits; he had to take it out to find an English sentence that would help him make up something, to find an excuse, so it shouldn't spoil that intoxicating feeling, the delight he felt surging in him, for here he was, he had succeeded, succeeded in the face of what he might have described as impossible odds, and for this reason, if for no other, he had to find a comprehensible phrase which would make it clear to the authorities why he was there and what he wanted, moreover a phrase that referred exclusively to the future, for he had decided, and was determined, to speak of nothing but the future, as he had told himself, and later explained, having resolved to keep quiet about anything that might have dampened his spirits and soured this intoxicating feeling, though he would never, under any circumstances, lie to himself about the fact that there was indeed something sad about it, something that hurt him when he got off the plane and attempted to look back in the direction of Hungary, hurt because Hungary was invisible from here, for apart from the sense of arriving in a place where no pursuer could reach him and the fact that he, this tiny dot in the universe, an insignificant archivist from the depths of a dusty office two hundred and twenty kilometers from Budapest, was actually standing here, in A-me-ri-ca! and that he could now look forward to putting his Great Plan into immediate operation—because all these things were genuine occasions for the delight he felt as he descended the steps of the aircraft along with all the other passengers—and yet, while the others were rushing onto the bus he gazed back across the concrete runway in the booming wind and sighed that never again would he cut his ties with such an overwhelmingly glad sense of arrival, never again would there be a past, never again Hungary, in fact he said it out loud when the stewardess ushered him onto the bus with the rest and he looked back for a last time to where Hungary should have been, the Hungary that was now lost forever.

4.

There's nothing wrong with the guy, the airport security official entrusted with the interrogation of Central European immigrants reported to his superior, it's just that he arrived without any baggage, not even a scrap of hand-luggage, just a coat, in the lining of which he himself had very probably, as indeed he confirms through the interpreter, sewn a strange document and an envelope containing some money, and since he had nothing else, no backpack, not even a plastic bag, no nothing, it constituted a problem—go on, Andrew, his superior nodded—because it's possible that he might have had baggage that had disappeared, but, if so, where was it, that's why they decided to interrogate him, and the guys did interrogate him, absolutely, thoroughly, according to the rule book, with a Hungarian interpreter present, but they found nothing suspicious, the guy was, for all intents and purposes, clean, and it looked as though he was telling the truth about the baggage, that he really had traveled without any, so, as far as he was concerned, the security man said, he could be allowed through, and yes, he had cash, quite a lot of it in fact, but Eastern Europeans weren't expected to carry credit cards, and his visa and passport were in order, besides which he was able to show them a business card with the name of a hotel in New York City, where he intended on staying, a fact they would check within twenty-four hours, at which point the matter would be closed because in his personal opinion—go on, Andrew, his superior encouraged him—that would be enough, the guy was just some innocent, perfectly ordinary, crackpot scientist who can sew what he likes where he likes, and if he wanted to stitch his asshole together—the security guard flashed his blindingly white teeth—that was up to him, they should leave him alone, in other words his recommendation would be to wish him a nice day and let him through—OK, that's one problem less then, his boss assented—as a result of which, within half an hour, Korin was free again, though clearly not entirely conscious of the process that had led him thus far, his mind having been otherwise preoccupied, especially toward the end of the interview when he noticed how the interpreter had begun to pay close attention to what he was saying, a line of argument he was keen to pursue to its conclusion, the burden of which was that, perhaps, later, if he succeeded in doing what he set out to do, even the United States of America would have cause to be proud of him, because this country was precisely the place where his Great Plan became a reality, but no, the interpreter stopped him in his tracks, slowly running his hands through his snow-white hair which was parted in the middle and sticking to his scalp, to say, however nice a guy he was, Korin should understand that there wasn't time to go into that now, to which Korin replied that, naturally, he completely understood, and he would not detain him any longer, and would only add, one, that it was a matter for him of something perfectly wonderful concerning his place in the scheme of things, in other words the reason he had flown here constituted less of a danger, if he might so express it, than did the flight of a butterfly above the city, that is to say, he explained, from the city's point of view; and two, he said, he would like to be permitted to offer a word of thanks, if no more, to the kind interpreter on whose assistance he had been forced to rely in the moment of his predicament, and that he would hold him up no longer, and that all he wanted was to thank him, to thank him once more, or, as they say here, Korin consulted his notebook, *thanks, many thanks, mister.*

5.

I gave him my card, the interpreter recalled with irritation, later, in bed, furiously turning his back on his alarmed lover, only to be rid of him, because there was no other way, but the skunk kept blabbering on, blab-blab, and fine, I said, fine pal, we don't have the time right now, here's my number, give me a call sometime, OK? that's all, no more, I mean what is that? so he gave him the card as a piece of courtesy, just a lousy business card, the kind you leave anywhere, in a sad kind of way, sowing your seed like some piece of fertilizer shit, though he wouldn't do that anymore, said the interpreter shaking his head as if terminally embittered by the experience, because he'd had it, nothing worked out for him, there was no hope, he'd never come to anything in this place; after four whole years in America, nothing but shit, shit, shit, shit, shit, shit, shit, he cried beating his pillow: the Immigration Office job was shit, and yet he had to be grateful for them taking him on like that on a part-time contract basis, yes, grateful for that shit, and he was but what the hell did it all add up to, since one moment was all it took and they sacked him, without a word, with such greased-lightning speed that it wasn't until he was outside that he took it in, that it was all on account of a stinking business card, but that's how it was, that's what it's like with scum, that's what it's like interpreting in such a shit institution, interpreting for shitheads and dumb asses, you really deserve what's coming to you for that, it takes just a split second and they've kicked you out on your ass, because these shitheads, and these shithead Hungarians really are shitheads, dumb asses, and the passport officers were the dumbest of the lot, them and the customs staff, the security guards and the rest, the whole filthy lot of them, asses, terminal idiots, the interpreter repeated, his head bobbing up and down with hysteria, shit-heads, shitheads, shitheads, everyone, and thank you, Mr. Sárváry, they said, but, as you know, this is a serious breach of protocol here, initiating or accepting the offer of personal contact like that, it's regulations, etc. etc., which is shit, the interpreter exclaimed, on the point of tears in his fury, that's what this fucking animal says to me, pronouncing it Sárváry all the time, though he knows perfectly well it is pronounced Shárváry, the bastard, the fucking animal, and what can you do with fucking asses like that, there's no end to it, ever, and so saying the interpreter buried his head in the pillow again, because he just can't take the filthy routine any more, he is a poet, a poet, he suddenly screamed at his lover, a poet and a video artist, not an interpreter, is that clear? and he could wipe his ass with the lot of them, people like that, like that filthy nigger, his ass, that's how little they're worth compared to him, because, do you think, he bent over his lover's face, do you think for a moment that they have the foggiest idea who or what he is, because if you really believe it, go up close to one of them and have a good look and you'll see that they are all asses, asses or shitheads, he choked and turned away again, throwing himself on the bed-covers, then, turned back to face his lover and continued once more: and he had helped him, helped the idiot, that shithead idiot, because he himself was the biggest shithead of them all, on this whole filthy continent, because why should he help anyone, who had asked him to help, who would pay him a fucking dime more for helping, just because he tried to help that helpless shithead, precisely this particular fucking halfwit, who was probably still standing there, holding his lousy business card instead of sticking it up his ass and fucking off up some shit's creek, yes, he was willing to bet that the guy was still standing there, as if rooted to the ground, with his simpleton's face, like some cow, because he had no fucking idea what even "baggage" meant, though he had explained it to him, but he still just stood there; and it was as if he were standing in front of him now, he could see it so clearly, standing there like a guy who had shit himself once and for all without anyone nearby to wipe his ass for him, like all those of his kind, now please don't be angry darling, the interpreter lowered his voice, addressed his lover, asking her not to be angry on account of him losing his self-control like that, but it wasn't just his self-control he had lost but his job too, and why lose it, darling, all on account of some shit-head, like all the rest, all of them, really, every last single one of them.

6.
Just head for the Exit signs, Korin said to himself aloud, it's Exit you want, there where it says Exit, head for there and don't be diverted, because he was likely to get lost, and there it was, yes, Exit, here, this way, straight on, and he took care not to disturb anyone, though who the hell cared whether he spoke to himself or not, after all there were thousands of people here who were doing exactly the same, hurrying confusedly this way or that, keeping their eyes on boards and signs indicating directions, turning now left, stopping, waiting, turning back, then heading right, stopping, then

back again, eventually going straight on, onward and onward to ever more and ever new confusion; just like Korin, in fact, who had to keep his eye on the word Exit and nothing else, everything being postulated on the position of the Exit sign which must not be lost sight of, a task that required all his concentration, for nothing must disturb that concentration, because a moment's inattention in this crazy traffic and all would be lost, gone forever, and he would never find the right way again, nor should he allow any uncertainty in his procedure, he told himself, but to keep going, all the way down corridors and steps, not bothering his head with doors, corridors and steps on either side of him, not even glancing at them, and even if he did catch sight of them, to make as if he were blind as he passed those side doors opening out either side, and refuse to be distracted by facts like the word Exit appearing on one or other of them, albeit in different lettering, to move past them and ignore them, for he felt he was in a crazy warren, not any old warren, he later added, but one in which even the pace was crazy, everyone moving at a furious pace, so he always had to make spur-of-the-moment decisions, such decisions being the hardest of all for he had to choose one of two possible routes in a split second, and every so often, as he proceeded down the corridors and stairs, such snap decisions had to be made, and each time he made one he would happily have gone on but for some sign that planted a seed of doubt in him so he had to stop again, disconcerted by a confusing sign in a disorientating place, and had to decide again in the blinking of an eye, which of the damn corridors was the main one, this one or that one; in other words what was confusing was not so much the question of the most direct route, it was having to decide so quickly, under conditions of such tension, constantly to be seeking and moving and making headway without ever stopping, and, what is more, moving in the certain knowledge that the whole idea of stopping was impossible for stopping as a possibility was absolutely out of the question, a fact etched on each and every occasion for the Door Out of There was perpetually about to be closed and one had to hurry, to positively dash, each according to his capacity, but in any case without stopping, moving, seeking, making headway toward the Exit, which—and this was the second problem—was an utterly mysterious concept since it was impossible to know what was understood by the idea of an exit, which for him meant primarily a way of getting out of the building into open space, to a bus or taxi that would take him into town, providing the taxi was not too expensive, though he would have to wait and see about that, but whether his idea of the whole exit thing as a passage through to an open space was correct or not was impossible to say so he was forced to move forward with ever greater uncertainty, as he later explained, making uncertain progress along corridors and stairs, not knowing whether they were the right corridors and stairs, and feeling pretty frightened by then, he admitted, until, at a certain point, he suddenly felt his feet slipping from under him, when it occurred to him that he had probably been taking the wrong route for quite some time, and that was when he got really scared and in his state of fright he could no longer even think straight, in fact did not think at all, but did what his instincts were urging him to do, which was to trust to the crowd, to accept its judgment and go with the flow, adapting himself to its pace, drifting with it, like a dried leaf in autumn, if he might be allowed such an antique turn of phrase, like a leaf in a fierce gale, hardly seeing anything anymore because of the speed and fury, everything about him being too agitated, too heavy, too flickering, so the only thing clear to him in all this, in the pit of his stomach, was how utterly different it was from what he had been expecting, which meant that he was more scared than ever, he told them, for fear was what he felt, fear in the land of the free, terror even while celebrating a remarkable triumph, because everything hit him all at once, and he had to understand it, to grasp it, to see it clearly, and then had to try to find his way out of it, while all the time corridors and steps came at him, one after another without end, and he was driven along with the rest in a maelstrom of conversation, weeping, shouting, screaming and some kind of wild laughter, and, every so often, through waves of drumming, growling and the general din, noting the word Exit, yes, there, that way, straight ahead of him.

7.

Before the widening entrance to the arrivals hall, in the four corners of an area of roughly four by four meters, four black-uniformed and helmeted guards, clearly trained for special duties, equipped with handguns, tear gas, rubber truncheons and God knows what else, stood motionless, each capable of looking in thirty-six directions at once; four guards with stony expressions on their faces, their legs spread, in an area roped off with a piece of red tape that was just long enough to get round the four by four square meters and keep the crowd at bay, which was all the evidence of the clearly unique security system that first greeted the constant flow of people: no visible cameras, no sign of detachments behind the walls ready to leap out at a word of command, no peculiar collection of vehicles at the entrance to the airport, nor a squad of chief inspectors based somewhere in the building, keeping watch over all eighty-six thousand and four hundred seconds of the day, and this must have been unique, a truly unique security concept, to involve only four visible guards and four lengths of red tape for what these had to defend from which was constantly flowing their way, a whole horde of people comprising people from town, people passing through, aliens, assortments of professors, amateurs, collectors, addicts, thieves, women, men, children, the aged, all, all coming and going, for everyone wanted to see it, everyone tried to push to the front in order to get a really good view of it, of those four lengths of tape, and what the guards were guarding, which was a massive pillar covered in black velvet and lit from above by white spotlights, protected by bulletproof glass, for everyone wanted to see the *diamonds*, as they were referred to for the sake of simplicity, those diamonds that added up to the world's most valuable diamond collection according to the advertisements, and there they really were, twenty-one miracles, twenty-one incarnations of pure carbon, twenty-one brilliant and matchless stones with the light imprisoned in them forever, their presence arranged by the Gemological Institute but drawing on the kind offices of various other corporations and well-disposed individuals, not forgetting, since it is diamonds on a global scale we are talking about, the publicly acknowledged guiding hand of De Beers Consolidated Mines in the background, twenty-one *rarities*, as the catalogues had it—which, in this case, was no exaggeration, for they were assembled according to the four classic categories of diamond quality, that is to say, Color, Clearness, Cut and Carat, qualities that, apart from the FL and IF classed groups, would not be applicable to any lower class of diamond—a list in which they attempted to give a comprehensive account of the terrifying world of facet, dispersion, brilliance and polish in twenty-one stars, as the text had it, of an entire universe, the very intention of so doing, or so they wrote, being unusual, since it wasn't just one or two matchless beauties with which they intended to enchant the public but the idea of matchless beauty itself, beauty in twenty-one distinct forms that were not only extraordinary but utterly different from each other, and here they were, practically every sort you could imagine within the River, Top Wesselton, and Wesselton color range, the twenty-one perfect gems as measured by the Tolkowsky, Scandinavian and Eppler scale, including those cut in Mazarin, Peruzzi, Markiz and emerald fashion, in Oval form, Pear-shaped, Navette and Seminavette, from fifty-five carats through to one hundred and forty-two carats, and, of course, the two sensations, the sixty-one carat amber-colored TIGER'S-EYE in an ORLOV silver clasp, all offering a truly extraordinary, mind-blowing radiance under the bulletproof glass, and all this in the most unexpected place, at the most vulnerable point of the busiest airport in the United States of America, precisely where such a billion-dollar splendor was plainly least secure, though it was under the care of four hefty security guards standing with legs spread and four lengths of red official tape.

8.

Korin entered the last of the corridors, saw the arrivals hall in the distance, and as soon as he had seen it, or so he recalled in the course of a conversation later, he knew at once that he had taken the right route, the right route throughout, and that's it, as he said to himself, thank God, he had left the warren behind and could walk a little faster now, feeling a degree more liberated and less anxious with each step, steadily regaining his good spirits, that intoxicating feeling, setting about the last few hundred meters in this state of mind, until, about a third of the way down, as he was approaching the hall with its light, noise and promise of security, he suddenly spotted a figure among the oncoming crowd, a short, rather scrawny young man of about twenty or twenty-two years of age, more a boy really, in checkered trousers, with a strangely dancing sort of walk, who seemed to have taken particular notice of him, who having got within ten paces of Korin suddenly looked at him full in the face and smiled, his face brightening at the sight, showing the kind of surprise and delight one feels when one unexpectedly comes across an acquaintance one hadn't seen for a long time, his arms spread wide in greeting, accelerating toward him, in response to which Korin too, as he said, began to smile uncertainly, with an enquiring expression, while, in his case, slowing down, waiting for the point of meeting, but when the moment arrived and they came up level with each other, something quite unbelievable happened as far as Korin was concerned, something because of which, his view of the world immediately darkened, something that made him double up and squat down on the ground, because the blow affected him precisely in the solar plexus, yes, that was exactly what happened, said Korin, the boy, probably out of sheer devilment, on the spur of the moment, had chosen some arbitrary victim from among the new arrivals, had raised his eyebrows and approached him in an apparently friendly manner, then smacked him in the solar plexus, without saying anything, without a word, without conviviality, without any sign of recognition, without any of the warmth you might expect when meeting an old acquaintance, and simply fetched him a blow, but a big one, as the Trinidadian boy told the bartender in his local bar, just like that, biff, he demonstrated with a violent movement, properly fucking the guy over in the pit of his belly, with such power, said the Trinidadian boy to the bartender, that the guy clutched his stomach, doubled up, and without a sound, not a peep, but he was flat out on the floor, as if lightning had struck him, said the Trinidadian flashing his decaying teeth, like he was a piece of shit dropped from a cow's ass, you understand, he asked the bartender, just one biff and the guy didn't say so much as moo, but collapsed, just like that, and by the time the guy looked up, he himself had disappeared into the crowd, like the earth had instantly swallowed him, vanished, as though he had never been, while Korin just stared, dumbstruck, slowly being scraped off the ground, blinking this way and that, utterly astonished, seeking explanation in the eyes of the two or three people that had hoisted him up by the arms, but they gave no explanation, nor did anyone else as he went on his way, and it clearly did not seem to have meant anything to anyone, since they were wholly unaware of his presence, or where he had been, or that he had appeared one-third of the way down the corridor leading to the arrivals hall of JFK airport.

9.

It was still hurting when he reached the diamonds, and when he stepped into the hall with a painful expression etched into his face he entirely failed to notice either the diamonds or the seething crowds as he approached them, nor did the presence of the diamonds have anything to do with the hand with which he covered his stomach, for the pain was such that he was quite incapable of removing it from that spot, the pain affecting his stomach, his ribs, his kidneys and his liver, but still more his sense of injustice at the wickedness and sheer unexpectedness of the assault on his person, and that was a pain that infected every cell of his being, which was why the one idea in his mind was to get out of there as quickly as possible, looking neither left nor right, just moving in a straight line, onward and onward, not even noticing when the significance of the hand on his stomach changed from being a physical comfort and protection to an emblem of general, unconditional uncertainty in the face of dangers facing him, dangers that singled him out, but in any case, as he explained a few days later in a Chinese restaurant, that's how it happened, his hand just assumed this position, and when he eventually succeeded in fighting his way through the packed chaos of the hall, and arrived, if not in the fresh air, at least under some concrete arcade, he was still using his left hand to ward off anyone in his vicinity, trying to communicate to everyone near to him the fact that he was extremely frightened and that in this state of fear he was prepared for any eventuality, that no one should approach him, and in the meantime he walked up and down, seeking a bus stop before he realized that while the place abounded in bus stops there was in fact not a single bus in sight, and so, fearing that he might be condemned to stay there forever, he crossed over to the taxi stand and joined a long queue at the head of which was a commissionaire of some sort, a big man dressed like a doorman at some hotel, and this was a very wise thing to have done, as he said later, throwing his lot in with the queue opposite the concrete arcade, because this meant he was no longer lurching this way and that in an ever more advanced state of helplessness, for having got so far he had arrived at a point in the vast institution of the airport where he no longer had to explain who he was and what he wanted, since everything could be decided in his own good time, and so he waited his turn in the queue, slowly shuffling forward to the big commissionaire, the natural end point of his despairing, yet fortunate decision, because it was all likely to be smooth going from here once he showed him the slip of paper he had received from the stewardess in Budapest, with the name of a cheap, often tried and trusted hotel on it, after examining which the commissionaire nodded and told him the cost would be twenty-five dollars, and without any further ado sat him in a huge yellow cab, and there they were moving past street cleaners, having already rushed down the lanes of the highway that led to Manhattan, Korin still holding his stomach, his hand clenched into a fist, unwilling to move it from there, prepared to defend himself and beat off the next attack just in case the space between himself and the driver should suddenly be barred off and someone throw a bomb in through the cab window at the next red light, or in case the driver himself should lean back, the driver who at first glance he took to be Pakistani, Afghan, Iranian, Bengali or Bangladeshi, and grabbing a great blunderbuss cry, Your Money— Korin nervously consulted the phrase book—Or Your Life!

10.

The traffic made him dizzy, said Korin in the Chinese restaurant, and he was in constant fear of assault at every road and traffic sign that flashed before him and remained in his mind as if engraved there—Southern State Parkway, Grand Central Expressway, Jackie Robinson Parkway, Atlantic Avenue, and Long Island, Jamaica Bay, Queens, Bronx and Brooklyn—because as they journeyed further and further into the heart of town, he said, it was not the unimaginable, hysterically pounding, mortally dangerous totality of the whole as exemplified by the Brooklyn Bridge, say, or by the sky-scrapers downtown that he had read about and the effect of which he had anticipated from the information given in his heavily thumbed travel guides, but odd small details, the apparently insignificant parts of the whole, that struck him, the first subway grille next to a sidewalk from which the steam was perpetually pouring, the first, swaying, wide-bodied old Cadillac they passed by the gas station and the first enormous shiny steel fire truck, and something beyond that, that silenced something in him, or, something that, if he might put it that way, burned its way into his mind without burning it quite through, for what happened, he continued, was that as the taxi swept on without a sound, as if they were slicing through butter, while he was still holding his left hand in the defensive position, looking out of the window, now left and now right, he suddenly felt, and felt most intensely, that he should be seeing something that he wasn't seeing, that he should be comprehending something he was not comprehending, that there was, from time to time, right in front of his eyes, something he should be seeing, something blindingly obvious, but that he did not know what it was, knowing only that without seeing it he had no hope of understanding the place he had arrived at, and that as long as he failed to understand it he could only keep repeating a phrase he had been repeating to himself all afternoon and evening, something to the effect of *Dear God, this really is the center of the world* and that he, there could no longer be any doubt about it, had arrived there, at the center of the world; but he got no further with this thought and they turned from Canal Street onto the Bowery and soon enough braked to a halt outside the Suites Hotel, that being their destination, said Korin, and that's how it had been ever since, he added, meaning that he still hadn't a clue what it was he should be seeing in that vast city, though he knew full well that whatever it was, was right there before him, that he was actually passing through it, moving through it, as indeed he had been when he paid $25 to the silent driver and got out in front of the hotel, when the taxi started back again, and he was left gazing, simply gazing at its two receding red lights until it turned at the crossroads and set off in the direction of the Bowery, toward the heart of Chinatown.

11.

Twice he turned the key in the lock and twice he checked the security chain, then stepped to the window and watched the empty street for a while, trying to guess what was going on down there, and it was only after he had done that, he explained several days later, that he was capable of sitting down on the bed and thinking things through, his whole body still trembling, and he couldn't even begin to think of not trembling, because as soon as he tried he started remembering, and there was no way but to sit there and tremble, unable to calm down and think things through, for it was achievement enough, after all, to simply sit down and tremble, which is what he did for minutes on end, and, he wasn't ashamed to admit it, in the long minutes that followed the trembling he cried for a full half hour, for he was, he admitted, no stranger to crying, and now that the trembling had begun to diminish the crying took over, a kind of cramp-inducing, choking form of sobbing, the kind that makes the shoulders shake, that comes on with excruciating suddenness and stops excruciatingly slowly, though that was not the real problem, not the trembling and weeping, no: the problem was that he was obliged to face so many issues of such gravity, of such variety and of such impenetrable complexity that when it was over, that is to say after the concomitant hiccupping had also stopped, it was as if he had stepped into a vacuum, into outer space, feeling utterly numb, weightless, his head—how should he describe it?—clanging, and he needed to swallow but couldn't, so he lay down on the bed, not moving a muscle, and started feeling those familiar shooting pains in the nape of his neck, pains so intense that at first he thought his head was about to be ripped off, and his eyes started to burn and a tremendous tiredness overcame him, although it was not impossible, he added, that all these symptoms had been there for a long time, the pain, the burning and the tiredness, and that it was only that some switch had been turned on in his head to turn the lot on, but, well, never mind, said Korin, after all that you may imagine what it felt like to be in such outer space, in this state of pain, burning and fatigue, and then begin, at last, to get his head together and deal with everything that had happened and attempt to cope with it systematically, he said, all this while sitting in a cramped-up position on the bed, going first through each and every symptom, saying, this is what hurts, this is what burns, and this, meaning everything, is what exhausts me, then attending to the events, one after another, from the very beginning if possible, he said, from the surprisingly easy way in which he managed to smuggle money through Hungarian customs without any official intervention, this being the act that made everything possible because, having sold his apartment, his car, and the rest of his so-called effects, in other words when he had converted everything to cash, he had had to think about converting that cash, little by little, into dollars on the black market, but knowing that the chances of getting official permission to take the accumulated sum across the border were negligible, he had sewed the money, along with the manuscript, into the lining of his coat, and simply walked through Hungarian customs, out of the country, without so much as a dog sniffing at him, thus relieving himself of the most terrible anxiety, and it was this success, in every sense, that facilitated the untroubled flight across the Atlantic, and there hadn't been a major hurdle since, not, at least, that he could remember, apart from the less than major issue of a pus-filled zit at the side of his nose and the problem of constantly having to look for his passport, for the slip of paper with the hotel's name on it, for the phrase book and the notebook, to check constantly that he hadn't lost them, to see if they were still where he thought he had put them, in other words, but there had been no problem with the flight, his very first experience of flying, no fear, no pleasure, only an enormous relief, that was until he landed and that was where such problems as he had began, starting with the Immigration Office, the boy, the bus stop, the taxi, but chiefly the problems in his own mind, he said, pointing to his head, where it was as if everything had clouded over, where he had an overwhelming feeling of being suspended in transit, a fact he understood once he had arrived on the first floor of the hotel, just as he understood that he had to change, to change immediately, and that that change must be a wholesale trans-for-mation, a transformation that should begin with his left hand which he must finally relax and to relax generally, so that he might look ahead, because, in the end—and at this point he stood up and returned to the window—everything, essentially, was going well, it was only a case of finding what people referred to as peace of mind, and of getting used to the idea that here he was and here he would stay; and having once thought this he turned back to face the room, leant against the window, took in what lay before him—a simple table, a chair, a bed, a sink—and established the fact that this was where he would be living and that this was where the Great Plan would to be put into effect, and having made a firm decision in this respect he felt strong enough to pull himself together, not to collapse and not to start crying again, because he very easily could have collapsed and started crying again, he confessed, there on the first floor of the Suites Hotel, New York.

12.

If I multiply my daily forty dollars by ten, that gives me four hundred dollars for ten days, and that's nonsense, Korin said to the angel at dawn, once his jet-lagged sleepless night had eventually yielded him some sleep, but he waited for an answer in vain, there was no answer, the angel just stood there stiffly and continued staring, staring at something behind his back, and Korin turned over and told him, *I've looked there already. There's nothing there.*

13.

For a whole day he did not move out of the hotel, not even out of the room, for what was the point, he shook his head, one day wasn't the end of things, and he was so exhausted, he explained, that he could hardly crawl, so why should he rush into action, and in any case, what did it matter whether it was today, tomorrow, the day after, or whatever, he said a few days later, and that's how it all began, he said, in all that time doing nothing but checking the security chain, and on one occasion, when after failing to get a response to their knocking the cleaners had tried to get in using their own key, sending them away saying No, No, No, but apart from such alarms, he slept like the dead, like one beaten to death in fact, slept through most of the day while keeping an eye on the street at night, or at least those parts of the street he could actually see, watching dazed and for hours on end, letting his eyes graze over everything, identifying the stores—the one selling wood panels, the paint warehouse—and because it was night and there was little movement nothing changed, the street seemed eternal, and the tiniest details lodged in his mind, including the order of the cars parked by the sidewalk, the stray dogs sniffing round garbage bags, the odd local figure returning home, or the powdery light emanating from streetlamps rattling in gusts of wind, everything, all etched on his memory, nothing, but nothing, escaping his attention, including his awareness of his own self as he sat in the first-story window, sitting and staring, telling himself to remain calm, that he would rest during the day gathering both physical and mental strength, for it was no small thing this experience he had been through, it was enough, and if he itemized everything that had happened to him—being pursued at home, the scene on the railway bridge, the forgetting of his visa, the waiting and the panic at the Immigration Office, plus the assault at the airport and the taxi ride with that oppressive feeling of being blindly swept along by events—and added up all these individual experiences, the experiences of a man alone, without defenses or support, was it any wonder he didn't want to venture outside? he asked himself and, no, it was no wonder he didn't, he muttered time and again, and so he continued sitting, looking out, waiting by the window, numbed, rooted to the spot, thinking that if this was how things had shaped up on the first day following his arrival, they had shaped up even worse on the second after another fainting fit, or what seemed like a fainting fit, though who knows which day it was anyway, perhaps it was the third night, but whenever it was he had said exactly the same thing then as he had the previous night, swearing that he would not go that day, not yet, on no account that day, perhaps the next, or the the day after that, for certain, and he got used to walking round and round the room, from window to door, up and down, in that narrow space and it would be hard, he told them, to say how many thousands of times, how many tens of thousands of times, he had made the same round trip by the third night, but if he wanted to describe the total sum of his activity the first day all he could say was *I just stared*, to which, on the second day, he might add *I walked up and down*, for that was the sum total of it, pacing up and down, satisfying his hunger occasionally with a biscuit left over from the supper he had been served on the flight, continuing to go round and round between window and door until he all but dropped with fatigue and collapsed across the bed without having decided, even now that the third day was in prospect, what he should do.

14.

Rivington Street was where he was and down to the right and to the east was Chrystie Street, with a long windy park at the end, but if he went down and turned left it led to the Bowery, he noted after days of sleeping and nights of watching, uncertain how long he had been there, but on the day, whichever day it was, when he finally ventured out through the doors of the Suites Hotel, because, whatever day it was, he simply couldn't stay in any longer, he couldn't keep saying to himself *not today but tomorrow, or the day after,* but had to emerge and brave the streets if for no other reason than that he had eaten all the biscuits and his stomach ached from hunger, in other words because he had to eat something, and then, having done so, find a new place, *immediately,* Korin emphasized in the firmest of terms, *immediately* since paying forty dollars a day made it impossible for him to stay there more than a few days, and he had already stayed those few days as a consequence of which the amount he had permitted himself was exhausted, and while this liberality, he told himself, might have been excused in the light of his early shock, he could not imagine it being prolonged, for four times ten made four hundred dollars for ten days, and three times four hundred, that made one thousand two hundred dollars a month, which is a lot even to think about, said Korin, so definitely no, I don't have an infinite amount of money, and so he went out but in order to be sure of knowing his way back he twice walked the distance between Chrystie Street and the Bowery, then stepping out into the desultory Bowery traffic and marking out the first useful-looking shop on the far side, nor was he wrong in marking it out, or rather there was nothing wrong with the marking-out, only with his nerve, for he lost his nerve as soon as he was about to enter the shop because it struck him that he had no idea what to say, that he didn't even know the words for "I am hungry," that he couldn't say a single word of English because he had left the phrase book upstairs in the hotel, or so he discovered when he felt in his pocket, and this left him helpless, without the merest notion of what to say however he racked his brains, and so he walked up and down a while considering what to do, then made a snap decision, dashed into the shop, and in his despair picked up the first edible item he recognized among the boxes, which happened to be two big bunches of bananas, then, wearing the same desperate expression as that with which he had barged in, he paid the frightened shopkeeper and was out again in a flash, rushing off, cramming one banana after another into his mouth at which point he noticed something about two blocks up on the other side, a big red-brick building with an enormous sign on the front, and though he couldn't in all honesty say that the sight of it solved everything, or so he explained later, it did at least make him realize that he should pull himself together, so he stopped there on the sidewalk, the bananas still in his hands, talking to himself, wondering whether this behavior was really worthy of him, for was he not a hopeless nincompoop, an utter fool, to be behaving like this, with such utter lack of dignity, he muttered, muttering "calm down," standing in the Bowery, holding his head while clutching a bunch of bananas in his hands; was he not in danger of losing the last vestiges of his dignity, when the whole point was that everything would be all right, everything would be just fine, he repeated, if he succeeded in retaining it.

15.

The Sunshine Hotel lay approximately as far up as the point where Prince Street opens on to the Bowery, and where, a little further on, you come to Stanton Street, and there stands the great red-brick building with its huge sign bearing the single word SAVE, picked out in letters of burning scarlet, which is what struck Korin's eye at that considerable distance, and was the sight that calmed him down, for having dashed out of the shop gobbling a banana, it seemed some benevolent hand had addressed the sign directly to him, he added, though by the time he got to it and read it properly he might easily have been disappointed, since the word written there was not SAVE but SALE, and the store below was simply some kind of car-showroom/auto-rental business—and disappointed he might indeed have been if he had not noticed something less likely to disappoint him, a smaller sign on the left of the building reading The Sunshine Hotel 25 dollars, that was all, no other information such as where The Sunshine Hotel was actually to be found; but the figure quoted and, as with SAVE, the attractiveness of the word, Sunshine, which he found easy enough to translate, exerted a further calming influence and roused his curiosity, since what was it he had decided to look for a little while ago if not some such thing, an immediate change of accommodation, and at a sum of twenty-five dollars, Korin calculated, well, twenty-five, that's thirty times twenty, which makes six hundred, together with thirty times five, that adds up to seven hundred and fifty dollars a month, which was not bad at all, and certainly much better than paying one thousand two hundred for Rivington Street, and thinking this he immediately began looking for the entrance but the only building next to the big red-brick one was a filthy, decaying, six-story house without any signs or notices at all, only a brown door in the wall, where it was worth enquiring, he decided, for, surely, he could pronounce the words Sunshine Hotel, could he not, and he would, would he not, make some kind of sense of the answer, so he opened the door and found himself descending a steep set of stairs which led nowhere but to an iron-barred door, at which point, he explained, he might well have turned back with a bad feeling about the whole place, had he not heard the sound of human speech beyond the door, hearing which he decided to rattle the bars, and did so, and saw too late that there was in fact a bell available, and actually heard someone cursing the rattling of the bars, at least it sounded like cursing, said Korin, and indeed there, on the far side of the bars, was an enormous, rough-looking, shaven-headed man who took a good close look at Korin, then, without saying anything, returned whence he came, but already Korin heard a buzzing noise and there was no more time to think but he had to step through the opening barred door into a narrow hallway with more iron bars guarding a window and a small office behind it, and a small vent through which he had to speak when someone pointed at him, all he could do being to repeat the words "Sunshine Hotel" to which came the answer, "Yeah, Sunshine Hotel" indicating the other set of iron bars, at which Korin had hardly taken a glance than he started back, for he only saw the people there for the fraction of a second and did not dare catch their eyes again, they looked so terrifying, but the personage beyond the glass and metal grille somewhat suspiciously asked him, "Sunshine Hotel?" to which Korin had no idea what to answer, for should he say, Yes, that was what he was looking for, and add, yes but no thanks, and as he later recalled, he couldn't remember what the hell he said then, not having the faintest idea what to answer to the question, but what was sure was that a few seconds later he was outside in the street again, putting as much distance between him and the place as he could, as quickly as he could, all the while thinking that he should immediately ask someone for help, a voice inside him urging him on, keeping step with his own pace, telling him to hurry back to Suites Hotel in Rivington Street, seeing only those shady figures and their grinning faces, until he reached the hotel doors, hearing nothing but that buzzing and the cold sharp snap of the lock over and over again, while being pursued all the way from The Sunshine Hotel to Suites Hotel by some terrible indefinable rank smell that had first assailed his nose in there, as if to ensure that there should be, at least, one thing that morning that, if he might so express it, he asked his fellow diners at the table of the Chinese restaurant, he would never forget regarding the moment he first entered the fearsome precincts of New York.

16.

There was nothing else the interpreter could do, he being the way he was, which is to say someone who took certain things then gave them back, for that was what had happened, he had taken away something then given it back, which was not, of course, to say that this made everything all right, but at least he'd be receiving six hundred a month for a while, and this was still more than before, the utterly drenched interpreter told the wholly uncomprehending Mexican taxi driver, it was better than nothing, although if there was something he had not foreseen, he said, pointing to Korin who was sleeping in the backseat with his mouth wide open, it was him, indeed there were many things he could anticipate, added the interpreter vigorously shaking his head, but he would never have dreamt that this man would have the gall to ring him up, especially seeing that it was precisely because of him that he had been fired, dropped like a piece of shit, but this guy did not fuck around, no, he went and called him up thinking that because he had given him his damned card it meant that he could just call him up, which he did, begging him to see him and help him, because, the halfwit lummox was completely lost in New York, the interpreter went on, lost, you hear? he asked the Mexican driver, lost, would you believe it, he exclaimed and slapped his knee, as if that mattered to anyone in a town where everyone is utterly lost, and he would have slammed the phone down on him and let the stupid asshole go hang himself, when the guy blurts out that he has a bit of money and he needs accommodation and someone to help him out these first few days, the shithead, that kind of thing, in fact precisely that kind of thing, and something about standing by him, adding the detail that he could pay up to six hundred dollars a month but no more, he apologized on the phone, because he had to spread his money carefully, he said, because, Korin didn't really know how to put it, Mr. Sárváry, but he was a little exhausted by the journey, and tried to explain how he was not an ordinary passenger, that he wasn't simply visiting New York but had a mission to accomplish there, and that time was really pressing now and he had need of help, someone to assist him, which, of course, didn't mean doing a lot, in fact practically nothing, only being a particular someone to whom he could turn in difficulties, that was all really, and if it was at all possible, Korin had asked him, could he come for him now, in person, because he still had no idea what was what, or, to put it another way, he had no idea even where to put himself, that he knew neither the how nor why of anything, though when asked where he actually was, he did at least know the name of the hotel, so what else could he do, for six hundred rotten dollars he dashed straight down to Little Italy, because it was there, by the Bowery, that the guy was hanging out, all for six hundred dollars, the interpreter exclaimed and gazed at the taxi driver in hope of comprehension or sympathy, that was why he got straight onto the subway, yes, he jumped to it for six hundred lousy dollars, not that that was how he had imagined it, no, he hadn't the faintest inkling, that this was the way he would be spending his time when he arrived in America, that this was how he would end up, that all he could call his own would be an apartment on West 159th paid three years in advance, and that, of all impossible things, it would be this guy who'd get him out of trouble, though that was precisely what had happened, for the guy having asked him the question it came to him in a flash that he had a back room for which six hundred was laughable but every little bit helped, so he told him on the phone he'd be there in an hour and Korin had echoed him, crying out in delight, "An hour!" going on to assure him that he, Mr. Sárváry, had saved his life, then went down into the lobby and paid his bill, which was one hundred and sixty dollars, as he rather bitterly informed him some time later, going out into the street and sitting on the corner of a wooden fence by the wood-paneling store opposite the hotel, and blessed the moment when, after his disturbing encounter at The Sunshine Hotel, he finally realized that he had reached the limit, there was no point in hanging around, and if he wanted to avoid complete and utter failure he had to have immediate assistance, and there was in fact only one person on whom he could call, just one, whose number was somewhere on a business card in one of his pockets, and having found it and read the ornate typography with some care, it turned out to be Mr. Joseph Sárváry, at 212-611-1937.

17.

It might be the first time this has happened in the USA but I haven't come to start a new life, Korin protested right at the beginning, and not being able to decide whether his companion, who, having consumed his beer, had slumped heavily across the table, had heard him at all or was fast asleep, he put down his glass, leaned over and put his hand on the man's shoulder, carefully looking around him and adding rather more quietly: *I would rather like to finish the old one.*

18.

He paid for everything: the hot meal at the Chinese, the vast amounts of beer they consumed, the cigarettes that followed, and even for the taxi that took them to the Upper West Side, absolutely everything, and, what's more, with a joyful equanimity that was the sign of an inexpressible lightening of spirit, for, as he kept saying, he had seen no light at the end of the tunnel, the ground beneath his feet had begun remorselessly to shift, until the interpreter reappeared, and he could only thank him, and thank him again, for minutes on end, which made the whole thing even more intolerable, said the interpreter in the kitchen, for after that the words started pouring from his mouth and he told him everything in the smallest detail from A through to Z, from the point of leaving the airport, in such fine detail he practically described every step, the way he put one foot in front of the other, and the mind-blowing tedium! that was no exaggeration, he said, it really did take hours, because he started with the guy who allegedly knocked him flat before he had even reached the arrivals hall, then how he failed

74

to find a bus that would have taken him downtown, but how he had found a taxi instead and who the driver was, and how his hand was on his groin all the way into Manhattan, and then some strange business about something he should have seen through the window on the journey but didn't, and so they proceeded, no joking, yard by yard, missing nothing on the way, into Manhattan, and then what it was like at the hotel, seriously, going through each item of furniture and every little thing he did through the days he spent there, how he didn't dare leave the room though he eventually did so in order to buy some bananas, and that's no joke either, laughed the interpreter leaning on the kitchen table, though it sounds like a joke, but believe me, it wasn't, that's the kind of guy this guy really was, and he managed to find his way into some kind of prison too, telling me about iron bars, and how he escaped from there, in other words he is utterly screwed up, his head's screwed up, you can see it in his eyes, he's some kind of word nut, an absolute blabbermouth, and, what's more, he has a constant theme, to which he keeps returning, that he has come here to die, and because of this, he says, though it's an innocent enough matter, he has started to feel a bit uncomfortable with it, because though this spiel about dying is probably part shit, it is, in the end, not altogether to be ignored, because even though the guy looks innocent you have to take such things seriously, so that even she, he said pointing to his lover across the table, has to keep her eyes on him all the time, which is not to say there is any cause for anxiety for if there were he wouldn't have allowed the guy in, no, there isn't, for this guy was simply—and he would, said the interpreter, swear on it if he had to—talking out of his ass and you couldn't take anything he said seriously, though one could never be too careful, there's always that chance in a thousand, and what happens then, what if the guy happens to do it here at his place, the interpreter sucked his teeth, that wouldn't be nice, but what the fuck else was he to do, for just this morning everything had looked hopeless, he couldn't get a hundred together for the evening, and now, if you please, it's not even three o'clock yet and here are six sweet hundred-dollar bills, a full Chinese meal, plus fifteen beers, a pack of Marlboros, not at all bad going given his black mood that morning, seeing that it had all dropped into his lap, just like that, this guy with his six hundred, this little moneybags, grinned the interpreter, that's six hundred dollars a month, which is nothing to sneeze at, not a sum you can just say No to, because, after all, what's the situation, the guy crashes here, said the interpreter, giving a wide yawn and leaning back in his chair, and it'll be all right, he'll survive, and this guy, Korin, is not going to get under his feet, since his needs seemed to be minimal, meaning a table to work at, a chair, a bed to sleep on, a sink, and a few common household items, that was all he wanted, no more, and he knows he has been provided with all these things, and he can't thank him enough for them, or stop telling him how he has relieved him of a great burden, and you can have enough of this shit, he said, he had no wish to hear it all again, so he had left Korin in the back room, which is where he had stayed, alone, running his eyes over and over the place, this back room, his room, he had said aloud, but not too loud, not so that Mr. Sárváry and his partner should hear him, for, really, he didn't want to be a nuisance to anyone, nor would he, he decided, be a nuisance, then sat down on the bed, got up again, went over to the window, then sat back down on the bed once more, before getting up again, and so it went on for several minutes, since the feeling of joy continued welling up in him, overwhelming him, so time and again he had to sit down or stand up and eventually achieved complete happiness by pulling the table ever so gently over to the window, turning it so the light should fall fully on it, drew up the chair, then sat on the bed and stared at the table, at the arrangement of it, stared and stared, gauging whether the light was falling on it in the best possible way, then turning the chair a little so that it was at a different angle to the table, so it should fit better, staring at that now, and it was plain that the happiness was almost too much for him, for he now had somewhere to live, a place with a table and a chair, because he was happy that Mr. Sárváry existed in the first place, and that he should have this apartment on the top floor of 547 West 159th Street, right next to the stairs to the attic, and without the resident's name on the door.

19.

In his childhood, Korin began in the kitchen the next morning while the interpreter's lover was busily working at the gas burner with her back to him, he had always found himself taking the

loser's side, though that was not quite right, he shook his head, for
to put it more precisely, it was the story of his entire childhood he
was talking about: being with losers, spending all his time with
losers, not being able to deal with anyone else, only with unfortu-
nates, the failures, the mistreated and the exploited, they being the
only ones he sought out, the only group to whom he felt drawn,
the only people he felt he understood, and so he strove to follow
them in everything, even in his school textbooks as Korin recalled
now, sitting on the edge of the chair by the door, recalling how
even in literature classes it was only the tragic poets that moved
him, or, to put this more precisely, the tragic ends of the poets
themselves, the way they were neglected, abandoned, humiliated,
their life-blood ebbing away along with their secret personal
knowledge of life and death, or that, at least, was the way he visual-
ized them while reading the textbooks, having, as he did, an in-
born antipathy to life's winners so that he could never be part of
any celebration or feel the intoxication of triumph, for it just
wasn't in him to identify with such things only with defeat, and
that identification was immediate, instinctive, and ran to anyone at
all who had been condemned to suffer loss; and so that's that, said
Korin, as he rose uncertainly from the chair, addressing the immobile back of the woman, though this condition, the pain he felt at
such times, had about it a peculiar sweetness that he experienced as
a warm sensation running right through him, irradiating his entire
being, whereas when he met with victory or with victors, it would
always be a cold feeling, an icy-cold feeling of repulsion that seized
him, that spread through his entire being, not hatred as such, nor
quite contempt, but more a kind of incomprehension, meaning
that he could not understand victory or victors, the joy experienced by the triumphant not being joy to him, nor was the occasional defeat suffered by a natural victor truly a defeat, because it
was only those who had been unjustly cast out by society, heart-
lessly rejected—how should he put it?—people condemned to
solitude and ill fortune, it was to them only that his heart went out
and, given such a childhood, it was no wonder that he himself had
constantly been swept to the side of events, grown reserved, timid
and weak, nor should it be surprising that as an adult, having been
easily swept aside, having grown reserved, timid and weak, he had
become the personification of defeat, a great hulking defeat on two

legs, although, said Korin taking a step toward the door, it wasn't simply that he recognized himself in others similarly fated, that wasn't the only reason things had turned out as they did, despite such a self-centered and infinitely repulsive beginning: no, his personal lot could not entirely be regarded as particularly harsh, for after all he did actually have a father, a mother, a family and a childhood, and his deep attraction to those who had been ruined and defeated, the full depth of it, had been determined not by himself, far from it, but by some power beyond him, some firm knowledge according to which the psychological condition he had experienced in childhood, which sprang out of empathy, generosity and unconditional trust, was absolutely and unreservedly right, although, he sighed, trying to get the woman to pay minimal attention as he stood in the doorway, this might be a somewhat tortuous and superfluous attempt at explanation, since, there might be nothing more at the bottom of all this than the fact, to put it crudely, that there are sad children and happy children, said Korin, that he was a sad little child, one of those who throughout his life is slowly, steadily consumed by sadness, that was his personal feeling, and perhaps, who knows, that is all there is to know, and in any case, he said as he quietly turned the handle of the door, he did not want to burden the young lady with his problems, it was time he got on with things back in his room, and this whole account of sadness and defeat just sort of came out, and he didn't quite understand why it should have done so, what had got hold of him, which was ridiculous, he knew, but he hoped he hadn't intruded on her time, and that she could happily carry on cooking and so, he added by way of farewell to the woman still standing with her back to him by the burner, he was off now, and so . . . goodbye.

20.

If we ignored the toilet that was next to the steps leading up to the attic in the stairwell, the apartment consisted of three adjoining rooms plus a kitchen, a shower and a small store-cupboard of some sort, that is to say three plus one plus one plus one, in other words six spaces, but Korin only poked his nose round the other doors when the occupiers went out in the evening and when he would finally had the opportunity of examining his surroundings, to see where he had wound up a little more closely, but he hesitated here, he hesitated there, at every threshold and was content merely to cast a desultory glance inside, because, no, he wasn't interested in the dreary furniture, the torn wallpaper with its patches of damp, the empty wardrobe and the four or five collapsed shelves hanging off the walls, nor was he curious about the ancient suitcase employed as a nightstand, or the rusty, headless shower, the bare light-bulbs and the security lock on the front door with its four-figure combination, because, rather than drawing conclusions from such evidence, he preferred to concentrate on his only real concern which was the question of how he should screw up courage and talk to the owners on their return, addressing them to some such effect as, please, Mr. Sárváry, if you would be so kind as to spare a little time for me tomorrow, and it was clear from all that followed that this was the only reason he stumped round the apartment for hours, this being the only thing he wanted, and the only thing he was preparing himself for, practicing for, so when they came home at about one in the morning he should be able to appear and present his latest, and, as he now promised, his really last request, pleading, Mr. Sárváry . . ., which he practiced aloud, and finally succeeded in actually saying at about one in the morning, appearing in front of them as soon as they entered and starting, Please, Mr. Sárváry, asking him if he would be so kind as to escort him to a store the next day, a store where he could purchase the items necessary for his work, since his English wasn't, as they knew, quite good enough yet, and while he could somehow piece together a sentence in his head he'd never be able to understand the answer, for all he needed was a computer, a simple computer to help him with his work, he stuttered while fixing him with his haunted eyes, and this would entail, he imagined, an insignificant invest-ment in time to Mr. Sárváry, but to him, said Korin, grabbing hold of his arm while the woman averted her head and went off into one of the rooms without a word, it would be of enormous bene-fit, since he didn't only have this ongoing problem with English but knew nothing at all about computers either, though he had seen them at the records office, of course, back home, he ex-plained, but how they worked he was sorry to say he had no idea, and was equally clueless as to what kind of computer he should buy, being certain only of what he wanted to do with it, which was what it depended on, retorted the interpreter who was obviously ready for bed, but Korin felt it natural to check that it depended on what he wanted to do, to which the interpreter could only reply: yes, on what you want to do, what, I, enquired Korin, on what I want to do? and spread his arms wide, well, if the interpreter had a moment he would quickly explain, at which point the interpreter pulled a long-suffering face, nodded toward the kitchen, and went through with Korin close behind him, taking the seat opposite him at the table, the interpreter waiting while Korin cleared his throat once, said nothing, then cleared his throat again and once again said nothing but kept clearing his throat for an entire minute or so, like someone who had got into a muddle and didn't know how to get out of it again, because Korin simply didn't know where to start, nothing came, no first sentence, and though he would dearly have loved to begin something kept stopping him, the something that got him into the muddle that he did not know how to get out of, while the interpreter kept sitting there, sleepy and nervous, wondering why, for God's sake, he could not get started, all the while stroking his snow-white hair, running his finger down his center parting, checking whether this line that ran from his crown to his forehead was properly straight or not.

21.

He stood in the middle of the records office, or rather he had advanced into the more powerfully lit area having emerged from among the shelves, with no one around, everyone having gone home since it was after four, or possibly even half past four, advancing into the light clutching a family file, or to be more accurate, the sub-file or *fascicle* containing the historical documents of the Wlassich family, stopped under the big lamp, unpacked the sheaf of papers, separated them out, riffled through them, examined the material revealed with the intention of getting the files into some order if that were necessary, for after all they had lain undisturbed for many decades, but going through the various leaves from journals, letters, accounts and copies of wills, somewhere between the miscellanea and other official documents, he discovered a *pallium* or binder, under the reference number IV.3/10/1941-42 that, *as he immediately noted*, did not seem to fit, that is to say to fit the official description "family documents" because it wasn't a journal entry or a letter, not the estimate of a financial estate, not a copy of a will, nor any kind of certificate, but something he immediately recognized, as soon as he picked it up, as altogether different, and though he knew this as soon as he set eyes on it he did nothing at first, just looked at it as a whole, casually leafing through, to and fro, observing the year of entry, picking out names of individuals or institutions, and riffling through again to get some handle on the kind of document it was so that he might be able to conduct further work on it and so recommend an appropriate course of action, this entailing a search for some number or name or anything that might help him place it in the right category, though this proved fruitless since the one hundred and fifty to one hundred and eighty pages, or so he calculated, carried no accompanying note, no name, no date, no clue in the form of a postscript as to who had written it or where, in fact not a thing, nothing, as Korin observed with furrowed brow as he sat at the big table in the records office, so what on earth is it, he wondered as he set to examining the quality and nature of the paper, the competence and idiosyncracies of the typing and the style of the layout, but what he found did not match anything that related to other material either in the fascicule or the various palliums, in fact it was clearly unrelated, distinct from anything else, and this being the case he realized it required a different approach, so he actually decided to read the text, taking the whole thing and starting at the beginning, sitting himself down first, then, slowly, carefully, making sure the chair did not slip from under him, sat and read while the clock above the entrance showed first five, then six, then seven, and while he did not once look up, proceeding to eight, nine, ten, eleven o'clock already, and still he sat in exactly the same place in exactly the same way, until he did glance up and saw that it was seven minutes past eleven, even remarking loudly on the fact, saying, what the heck, eleven-o-seven already, then quickly packing the things away, tying up the string once more, leaving that which had remained unidentified or could not be identified in another file bound up with string, putting it under his arm, then going round, still holding the package, turning off the lights and locking the glazed entrance door behind him with the idea that he would continue his reading at home, starting all over again from the beginning.

22.

Back home, so Korin broke the momentous silence that had descended on him, back home he used to work in an archive where
the day generally ended at about half past four or a little earlier,
and one day on one of the back shelves he found a file that contained a mass of papers that hadn't been disturbed in decades, so,
having found it, he brought it out to get a better idea of its contents, took it to examine under the big lamp over the main table,
opened it up, spread it out, nosed around in it, leafed through it,
and investigated the various *palliums*, intending, he told the sleepily
blinking interpreter, to put them into order should they require ordering, when suddenly, while examining various journals, letters,
accounts and copies of wills referring to the Wlassich family, along
with other miscellaneous documents the file contained, as he was
looking through these he came upon a *pallium* registered in the system as number IV. 3 / 10 / 1941-42, a number he still remembered
because it didn't fit, which is to say it didn't fit the family-
documents category that the Roman numeral IV indicated in the
archive, and the reason it didn't fit was because what he discovered
there was not a diary, not an estimate of the financial estate, not a
letter, not even the copy of a will, nor was it a certificate of any
kind, or indeed a document as such, but something quite different,
a difference that Korin actually spotted straight away, as soon as he
started turning the pages, examining it all, turning the papers to
and fro in order so that having discovered some clue as to its nature
he might be able to furnish it with the appropriate note of advice
or suggest a correction, which was a way, he explained to the interpreter, of preparing the file for further work, and that was why, he
said, he was seeking a number, name or anything at all to help him
assign it some known category, but however he looked he didn't
find one among the one hundred and fifty or, at a rough estimate
one hundred and sixty-odd typed but unnumbered pages that,
apart from the text itself, contained no title, date or indeed any information as to who had written it or where, nothing at all in fact,
and there he was staring at the stuff, Korin continued, completely
puzzled, embarking on a closer examination of the quality and
weight of the paper and the quality and typeface of the script, but
he found nothing there that accorded with other "*palliums*" in the
fasciscule, "*palliums*" which did however accord with each other and

therefore made a coherent package: apart, obviously, from this single manuscript, as Korin emphasized to the interpreter who had started to nod off in his exhaustion, which had nothing to do with the rest and made no coherent sense whatsoever, so he decided to look at it again from the beginning, he said, meaning he sat down to read through it from the start to finish, sitting and reading, as he recalled, for hours on end while the clock in the office moved on, unable to stop reading until he reached the end, at which point he turned off the lights, closed up the office, went home and started reading it once more because there was something about the way the whole thing had fallen into his hands, so to speak, that made him want to reread it straightaway, indeed immediately, as Korin stressed in a significant manner, because it took no more than the first three sentences to convince him that he was in the presence of an extraordinary document, something so out of the ordinary, Korin informed Mr. Sárváry, that he would go so far as to say that it, that is to say the work that had come into his possession, was a work of astonishing, foundation-shaking, cosmic genius, and, thinking so, he continued to read and reread the sentences till dawn and beyond, and no sooner had the sun risen but it was dark again, about six in the evening, and he knew, absolutely knew, that he had to *do something* about the vast thoughts forming in his head, thoughts that involved making major decisions about life and death, about not returning the manuscript to the archive but ensuring its immortality in some appropriate place, for he understood as much even at such an early point in the proceedings, for he had to make this knowledge the basis of the rest of his life, and Mr. Sárváry should understand that this should be understood in its strictest sense, because by dawn he had really decided that, given the fact that he wanted to die in any case, and that he had stumbled on the truth, there was nothing to do but, in the strictest sense, to stake his life on immortality, and from that day on, he declared, he began to study the various repositories, if he might so put it, of eternal truth so that he might discover what historical methods had been employed for the preservation of sacred messages, of visions, if you like, concerning one's first steps on the road to eternal truth, in quest of which methods he considered the possibility of books, scrolls, films, microfiches, encryptions, engravings and so forth, but, finished up not knowing what to do since books, scrolls, films, microfiches and the rest were all destructible, and were in fact often destroyed, and he wondered what remained, what could not be destroyed, and a couple of months later, or he might just as well say a couple of months ago, he was in a restaurant when he overheard two young people at the next table, two young men, to be precise, he smiled, arguing about whether, for the first time in history, the so-called Internet offered a practical possibility of immortality, for there were so many computers in the world by then that computers were for all purposes indestructible, and, hearing this and turning it over in his mind, the personal conclusion that Korin himself came to, the conclusion that changed his life, was that that which was indestructible must perforce be immortal; and thinking this he forgot his food whatever it was, needless to say he couldn't now recall what it was he was eating, though it might have been smoked ham, left it on the table and went straight home to calm down, going down to the library the next day to read the mass of material in the form of books, papers and discs available on the subject, all of which were replete with technical terms hitherto unfamiliar to him, but seemed to be the work of excellent and less-than-excellent authorities, reading which he grew ever more convinced about what he should do, which was to establish the text on that peculiar sounding thing, the Internet, which must be a purely intellectual matrix and therefore immortal, being maintained solely by computers in a virtual realm, to lodge or inscribe the wonderful composition he had discovered in the archive there, on the Web, for in so doing he would fix it in its eternal reality, and if he managed to accomplish this he would not have died in vain, he told himself, for even if his life was wasted, his death would not be, and that was how he encouraged himself in those early days, by telling himself that his death had meaning, even though, said Korin dropping his voice, his life had none.

23.

It's perfectly all right, you can walk beside me, the interpreter encouraged Korin who was continually hanging back next day as they proceeded down the street, through the subway and finally up the escalators on 47th Street; come along now, catch up, stop hanging back, here, walk beside me, it's all right, but it was no use calling and gesturing, for Korin, involuntarily perhaps, kept falling ten or twenty paces behind, so in the end the interpreter gave up and thought to hell with him, as he recounted later, if he wants to trail behind then, very well, let him, after all it means damn anything to him where he chooses to walk, the essential point being, as he decided and made perfectly plain to Korin, that this was the last time they ventured out together, for frankly he had no time to spare, he was so busy, and he would help it this time, but that in the future Korin would have to stand on his own two feet, all by himself, right? he snapped, because it very much looked as if this was going in one ear and out of the other as far as Korin was concerned, lurking behind him like some retard, when he should at least listen, the interpreter barked furiously and pointlessly, for Korin was all ears and it was only that he had a hundred, no a hundred thousand other matters to attend to at the moment, this being the first time since his terrifying journey from the airport to The Sunshine Hotel that, thank God, he could look around in anything like normal fashion, the first time that he felt at all capable of comprehending events around him, even while being afraid, as he confessed next morning in the kitchen, afraid then and still afraid, without knowing what precisely it was that he should or should not be afraid of, what he should or should not look out for, and therefore, naturally, in a state of high alert at every step, right from the first, as he followed the interpreter, careful that he should not fall too far behind but at the same time careful not to hurry too much, careful to drop in his subway token at the machine precisely as required, fearing that the expression on his face, which might not be sufficiently indifferent, should call too much attention to him, in other words taking care to behave in an appropriate manner without knowing what an appropriate manner might be, which was why he was following Mr. Sárváry, in this exhausted condition, to a shop with the sign Photo above it on 47th Street, so tired that he was barely capable of dragging himself along as they stepped in and had immediately to mount some stairs, which meant dragging himself up the stairs too, so that by this time he hardly knew where he was or what was happening as Mr. Sarváry, he told the woman, had a word with a Hasidic Jew behind a counter who replied something to the effect that they would have to wait, though there were very few other people in the shop, in fact only a single customer before them, but even so they waited at least twenty minutes before the Hasidic Jew came out from behind the counter, led them to a mass of computers and started to explain something of which he, Korin, as he said, naturally understood not a word, and only caught on when Mr. Sárváry informed him that they had found the best possible model for his purposes and asked him if he would like to create a *home page*, when, seeing his clueless expression, he gestured in a hopeless comical manner, said Korin, and, thank heaven, decided the matter for himself, so that all that remained was for him to fork out the sum of twelve hundred and eighty-nine dollars, which he did, in return for which he received a small light package to carry home, and so they started back though Korin did not so much as dare to ask a question on the way, because he was keenly aware of the value of twelve hundred and eighty-nine dollars on the one hand and of the small light package on the other, and so they proceeded silently through the subway, changing trains once or twice, and so forth, making their way toward 159th Street in silence, without a word, and though a word is not much, it was probably the case that Mr. Sárváry was also exhausted by the traveling, for they continued thus in absolute silence, he and the interpreter, the latter sometimes casting a forbidding look at him whenever he felt that Korin was on the point of saying something, for he was determined not to endure another idiotic monologue, preferring silence, at least until they got home, when, the interpreter told him, he would explain how the thing worked and what he had to do, as indeed he did, explaining everything, turning the computer on and showing him which key to press and when to press it, though he was not prepared to do more than that, he said, demonstrating for the last time what each key was for and how he could get the necessary diacritics, then asked him not for the agreed two hundred as he had intended the previous night when he offered to help with the purchase, but for four hundred, straight out, as a loan, seeing the guy seemed to be made of money, not just the cash in his overcoat, he laughed to his partner, sitting with her at the table, saying, just imagine the overcoat, the money being all sewn into the lining like that and him having to poke his hand in and get it out of there so he could pay the store, imagine that, have you ever heard anything like it, as if it were some kind of purse, he roared with laughter, and the guy just peeled off the four hundred greenbacks, like that, which makes a round thousand, sweetheart, then he left him, continued the interpreter, but before leaving he told him, perfectly straight, Mr. Korin, pal, you won't survive long round here like that, because if you don't take that money out of your coat lining there are people out there who can smell the stuff, and it's beginning to stink to high heaven, so the next time you stick your nose out of the door, someone or other will kill you for the sheer smell of it.

24.

A conventional computer, the interpreter explained, normally consists of a monitor in a case, a keyboard, a mouse, a modem and various items of software one has to learn to use, and yours, he told Korin who was nodding without understanding anything, comprises all these items, and beside these has the extra facility, he pointed to the unwrapped laptop, not only of being plugged immediately into the Internet, which goes without saying, but of providing you with a template for a ready-made home page, which is all you need, for having put down a deposit of two hundred and thirty dollars, you have already paid for a provider several months ahead, so there is nothing else left for you to do except—but wait, let's go from the top again, he sighed seeing Korin's terrified expression—first you press this, he put his finger on a button at the back of the computer, to switch the set on, and when you do that these little colored icons appear, do you see? he asked pointing at each one of them, do you see all these? and began to go over it all again using only the simplest words and in the least technical detail, because the guy's level of understanding, he told his partner, was negligible to the nth degree, and that's not taking the speed of his reactions into account, so, never mind, he said, let's start at the beginning, from the point at which you see what you do see on the monitor, at which point you should do this and that, and he would have gone on to explain why this or that action was necessary and what various things meant, but quickly realizing that this was utterly useless, he taught him only that which was mechanically required and made him practice it, since, when you came down to it, he told her, the only way was to make him go through the basic actions, everything but everything, time and time again, so as soon as he demonstrated something he asked him to repeat it and in this way, said the interpreter, after some three hours, the guy eventually learned the secrets of creating a home page, so though he hadn't the faintest idea what he was doing he was capable of opening Word in Office 97 and typing in some piece of text, and, when he had finished for the day, of formatting what he had done as hypertext, saving it, then dialing up his server, typing his codename, his password, his provider, his own name, *etcetera etcetera*, just about everything he needed to know in order to send the information to his home page, using his personal password, so that he himself could check that his text had got onto the server and that the material could be searched on the basis of a few key words using the search engine, and this, all this, said the interpreter, still somewhat incredulously, had to be accomplished with the most primitive of methods seeing that the guy's brains were like cheese, full of holes, in one ear and out of the other, and whenever he was told something new his brow completely creased up with the effort, like the whole guy was one enormous straining mass but you can see the stuff that had just entered his head leaking out again, right out so there was nothing left, so you may imagine, as Korin himself said in the kitchen the next day, you may imagine what he went through trying to learn it all, for not only did he admit that his mind was not what it had been, but confessed outright that, as a mind, it was useless, ruined, kaput, finished, no good for anything anymore, and it was only thanks to Mr. Sárváry's remarkable, enchanting gift of pedagogy, not to mention, Korin added with a forced smile, his endless patience, that he finally got something right, and, why deny it, there was no one more surprised than he that he should have at his command this miraculous, incredible triumph of technology that weighed no more than a few ounces, and it worked, against all the odds it actually worked, he told her, highly animated, just imagine, young lady, there it was sitting in his room, the machine, on the table, right in the middle of it, adjusted precisely to its central position, and all he had to do was to sit down in front of it and everything was under way, everything functioning as it should, he suddenly laughed out loud, simply because, and for no other reason, than that he had pushed this or that button, and it was all as Mr. Sárváry said it would be, so with a couple more days of practice, he quietly told the woman, who was before the gas burner as usual, with her back to him, saying nothing, he could start work, just a couple more days, he repeated, then after a couple of days of concentrated practice he could get the job properly started, wholeheartedly commit himself to it, put his back into it, make a real go of it, in other words a day or so and he'd be sitting there, writing something for posterity, for eternity, he, György Korin, on the top floor of number 547 West 159th Street, New York, for the price of one thousand two hundred and eighty-nine dollars all told, of which two hundred and thirty was deposit.

25.

He searched for most secure place possible in the room then, taking the interpreter's advice, took the remaining money out of his coat lining, attached it to a string and stuffed it nice and deep between the bedsprings, folded the mattress back over it and smoothed out the bedclothes, checking from a variety of viewpoints, some standing, some squatting, to ensure that there should be nothing there to catch a stranger's eye; and this being taken care of, he was ready to get on with other things, for he had decided that between five in the afternoon and three in the morning, when, the interpreter had warned him, the single telephone line would be unavailable for working on the computer, he would start exploring the town in order that he might have some idea of where things were in relation to where he was, and in what particular corner of the city he now found himself, or, to put it another way, to discover what he had achieved in picking the center of the world, New York, as the most appropriate setting for the execution of his plan to comprehend the eternal truth and die, which was why, he told the woman in the kitchen, he now had to orient himself in it by walking everywhere until he got to know the place, which he did on the day after he had bought the computer and started to learn to use it, shortly after five o'clock when he descended the stairs, left the house and started walking down the street, just a couple of hundred yards and back at first, then repeating the exercise several times, glancing over his shoulder to ensure that he would know the buildings again by sight and later, after a good hour had passed, venturing down as far as the subway on the corner of 159th and Washington Avenue, where he took a long time studying the subway map without daring to buy a token, board a train or explore any further that day, though he had gathered courage enough by the next to purchase a token and board the first available train, riding down as far as Times Square because the name had a familiar ring to it, then walking along Broadway until he was perfectly exhausted by the effort; and this is what he did, day after day, always returning either on the bus the interpreter had recommended or on the subway, the result being that after a week of these ever more intrepid ventures, he had begun to learn to live in the city and no longer felt a mortal fear of traveling or of making a purchase at the Vietnamese store on the corner, and, more importantly, was no longer fearful of each and every individual who happened to stand next to him on the bus or pass him in the street: and all this he learned and it made a genuine difference, though one thing hadn't changed, not even after a week, and that was his high anxiety level, the anxiety, that is, of knowing that despite all he had so painstakingly learned he still understood nothing of it, and that, because of this, the intensity of his feelings had not abated, and that he was still in thrall to the state of mind he first experienced on that unforgettable first taxi ride, the feeling that, among all these enormous buildings, he should be seeing something, but that however he peered and strained his eyes, he was failing to see it, and he continued to feel this every moment of his various journeys from Times Square to the East Village, from Chelsea to the Lower East Side, in Central Park, downtown, Chinatown and Greenwich Village, and the feeling was gnawing away at him, so that whatever he looked at reminded him with a ferocious intensity of something else, but what that was he had no idea, not a solitary inkling, he told the woman who continued to stand silently with her back to him at the stove, cooking something in a gray saucepan, so that Korin had courage enough to talk to her but not to address her directly nor tactfully to compel her to turn around for once and say something herself, which meant he was restricted to talking to her, genuinely talking to her, on those regular occasions they met in the kitchen at noon, telling her anything that came to his mind, hoping in this way to discover a way of engaging her in conversation or understanding why she never spoke, for he felt instinctively drawn to her, more, at any rate, than to anyone else in the building, and it was plain from his daily noontime exertions that he was seeking to establish some favor with her, talking to her all the time, every noon, telling her about everything from his experiences with the computer to his feelings about skyscrapers, staring at her bent back by the stove, at the greasy hair hanging in bunches over her thin shoulders, at the straps dangling at the sides of the blue apron covering her bony hips, and watching how she used a dishtowel to lift the hot pan from the fire then vanish from the kitchen into her room without a word, her eyes averted, as if she were permanently frightened of something.

26.

He had become quite a different person in America, Korin told her after a week, no longer the person he had been, by which he didn't mean that something essential in him had been destroyed or mended, but that little details, which for him were not so little after all, his forgetfulness, for example, had utterly vanished after two days, that is if you can talk about forgetfulness vanishing like that, though in his case, said Korin, it really was a matter of vanishing, since he had noticed a couple of days ago that he really had stopped forgetting, that he actually remembered things that happened to him, they stayed in his head, and he no longer had to rummage through a mass of material to find whatever he had lost, though it was true, he said, that he had precious little material to rummage through, nevertheless he could now be sure of finding what he had lost, in fact he no longer had even to look, which hadn't been the case before when he used to forget anything that happened by the next day, for now he had a perfect recollection of what had happened, where he had been and what he had seen, specific faces, particular stores, some buildings, they all came immediately to mind, and to what could he attribute this, said Korin, if not to America, where, the very air was probably different, and not only the air, but the water too for all he knew, but whatever it was, something was radically different, for he too was different, nor was his neck or shoulder giving him the trouble they had before at home, which must mean that the permanent state of anxiety to which he was prey must have diminished, so he could forget the anxiety about losing his head, and that was truly a relief for it left

the way open for him to pursue his necessary goal, and he wondered whether he had told the young lady, Korin enquired in the
kitchen, that the entire notion of America had, ultimately, come
about as a result of his decision to put an end to his life, and while
he was absolutely certain that he should do so he didn't actually
know what means to adopt to this purpose, for all he knew when
he first formulated the idea was that he should quietly disappear
from this world, collect his thoughts and vanish, nor did he think
any different now really, since he wasn't here to seek fame by de-
vising some peculiarly ingenious way of disposing of himself, advertising himself as the unselfish self-sacrificing sort, the kind we
see so many of nowadays, he was by no means one of them, no,
that was the last thing on his mind, because what he was interested
in was something altogether different, something—and here he recalled the terrible grace of fate that set these thoughts off in his
head, and wondered how should he put it, then decided, he said,
to put it like this—that from the moment when it was his luck to
make the discovery of the manuscript he was no longer just a man
determined to die, as until then he had had every right to believe, a
fated figure, as the phrase has it, the sort of person who already has
death in his heart, but someone who continues working, let us say,
in his garden, watering, planting, digging, then suddenly discovers
an object in the ground that catches his eye, a discoverer, you see,
that's how the young lady too should imagine it, said Korin, for
that is what happened to him, for, from that time on, whatever
happened it was all the same to the man working in his garden because the object that glimmered there before him had settled matters, and that's just what had happened to him in a manner of
speaking of course, in a manner of speaking, for he had discovered
something in the records office where he had been working, a
manuscript for which he could find no source, no provenance, no
author, and what was strangest of all, Korin raised a warning finger, without a clear purpose, something that would never have a
purpose, and therefore not the kind of manuscript he'd rush to
show the director of the institution, though that is what he should
have done, but one that made him do something an archivist
should never do: he took it away, and by doing so he knew, knew in
his bones, that from that moment on he had ceased being a true
archivist, because by taking it he had become a common thief, the

document being the one genuinely important item he had ever handled in all his years as an archivist, the one undeniable treasure that meant so much to him he felt he couldn't rightly keep it to himself, as one kind of thief would, but, like a different kind of thief, had to let the whole world know of its existence, not the world of the present, he had decided, since that was wholly unfit to receive it, nor the world of the future since that would certainly be unfit, not even the world of the past which had long lost its dignity, but eternity: it was eternity that should receive the gift of this mysterious artifact, and that meant, as he realized, that he had to find a form appropriate to eternity, and it was following the conversation in the restaurant that the idea suddenly came to him, that he should lodge the manuscript among the millions of pieces of information stored by computers which, following the general loss of human memory, would become a momentary isle of eternity, and now it didn't matter, he wanted most firmly to emphasize this, it really didn't matter how long computers preserved it, the essential thing was, Korin explained to the woman in the kitchen, that the thing should be done just once, and that all the extraordinary mass of computers that had once been interconnected, or so he suspected, a suspicion confirmed by much subsequent thought on the matter, would, all together, have given birth to, produced between themselves, a space in the imagination that was related not only or exclusively to eternal truth, and that this was the right place in which to deposit the material he had found, since he believed, or that was the opinion he had arrived at, that once he connected one eternal object with the world of eternity it didn't matter what happened next, it was all the same where he ended his life, whether it was in darkness, in the mire, Korin dropped his voice, on a footpath, by a canal or in a cold and empty room, it made no difference to him, nor did it matter how he chose to end it, with a gun or by some other means, the important thing was to begin and complete the task he had set himself, here at the center of the world, to pass on that which, if it didn't sound too portentous to put it like this, had been bestowed on him, to plant this heartbreaking account, of which he could say nothing valuable at this stage since it would be on display on the Internet in any case, other than that, crudely speaking, it concerned an earth on which there were no more angels, that it was set in the theoretical heart of the world of ideas, and that once he had accomplished his mission, once he had finished, it didn't matter where he ended up, whether that was in mire or in darkness.

27.

He sat on the bed with his coat in his lap holding a small pair of scissors he had borrowed from his hosts in order to unpick the delicate stitches he had used to secure the top of the secret pocket he had sewn into the lining, so that he might finally extract the manuscript, and was ceremonially about to set about his task, when suddenly, barely audibly, the door opened and the interpreter's partner stood at the threshold with an open glossy magazine in her hand, not entering but looking across the room, somehow beyond Korin, and hovered there for a moment, more timid and tongue-tied than ever, not looking in the least likely to break her perpetual silence but rather on the point of disappearing once more and beating a hasty apologetic retreat, when finally, perhaps because both she and Korin were equally disconcerted by her unexpected appearance, she pointed to a photograph in the open magazine and asked, very quietly, in English: "Did you see the diamonds?" and when Korin, in his surprise, was unable to emit the merest squeak by way of an answer but continued to sit as if rooted to the spot with the coat in his lap, the very scissors frozen in his hand, she slowly lowered the magazine, turned around, and as noiselessly as she had entered, left the room, closing the door behind her.

28.

The eternal belongs to eternity, said Korin loudly to himself, then, since he had taken a long time entering a single page, he perched on the windowsill holding the second, gazing out at the lights on the fire escapes of the building opposite, scanning the flat desert of the rooftops and the furiously racing clouds in the strong November wind, and added, *Tomorrow morning, it must be done by tomorrow.*

III • ALL CRETE

1.

According to the manuscript's superbly honed and supple sentences, the kind of craft the ship most resembled was an Egyptian seagoing vessel, though it was impossible to tell what tides had borne it hither, for while the powerful winds currently blowing might have carried it from Gaza, Byblos, Lucca or indeed from the land of Thotmes, it might just as likely have been swept across from Akrotiri, Pylos, Alasiya, and if the storm had raged particularly fiercely, even from the distant isles of Lipari, and in any case, one thing was certain as Korin typed the letters, which was that the Cretans who had gathered on the shore had not only never seen one like it but had not even heard of such a craft, and that was chiefly because, firstly, they pointed out to each other, the stern was not raised; secondly, that instead of a full complement of twenty-five/twenty-five oarsmen, there were thirty/thirty, originally at least, fully equipped; and thirdly, putting all that aside, they remarked as they studied it from the shelter of an enormous cliff, the size and shape of the sail was now in shreds and its extent could be estimated, though the straining ornamental figurehead on the prow and the unusual positioning of the double row of arching tangles of rope all looked unfamiliar, unfamiliar and terrifying, even in the throes of destruction as huge waves drove the craft from Lebena into the bay at Kommos then cast it against a rock, turning the vessel on its side as if to exhibit the broken body to the frightened locals, saving it from further damage and raising it above the foaming waters, introducing it, as it were to human eyes in order to demonstrate how the combination of water and storm could, should it wish to, deal with such a vast mechanism; how thousands of unstoppable waves could toy with this previously un-known, peculiarly constructed ocean-going trader on which every-thing had died or at least seemed to have died, and had, indeed, to be dead, the Cretans muttered to each other, for surely no one could survive such turmoil in this lethal gale, not even a god, they added from the shelter of the cliff, for, as they said on shore as they shook their heads, no one could remain in one piece under such catastrophic, demonic circumstances, not even a god newly born, for none such could be born.

2.

They are here for eternity, Korin explained to the woman in the kitchen, while she stood at the stove in her usual position with her back to him, stirring something in a pan, and not giving the slightest sign of having understood or given any heed to what she was hearing, and he didn't go back to his room for the dictionary as he often had done, but abandoning hope of explaining the notion of *eternity* and *here-ness*, tried to move the conversation on instead by pointing to the pan in confusion, asking: *Something delicious . . . as usual?*

3.

It wasn't until the next day that the storm had abated to the extent that a small boat from Kommos dared venture out on the waters and row over to the rock, and so it was only then, Korin wrote, once the wind had dropped, early next afternoon, that they discov-ered that what had seemed from a distance to be a wreck beyond salvaging, was most certainly a wreck, but at a closer view, not en-tirely beyond salvaging, and the improvised rescue party was as-tonished to discover three, and maybe even four survivors in one of the main cabins that had not been flooded: three, they signaled by hand to those on the shore, and a possible fourth lashed to this or that post, the four unconscious but certainly alive, or at least three of them were alive and the heart of the fourth was also possibly beating, so they cut these four free of the posts and brought them out, they being the only four for the rest had been engulfed in the flood and drowned, some sixty, eighty or even hundred of them, they said later, who knows how many dreaming their last by the time they found them, but no longer in any position to feel pain, as they put it; while these three, the rescuers said, or maybe even four, had miraculously survived, and so they quickly brought them out of the cabin and transferred them to the boat immediately, one after the other, and set off back again leaving the rest, the entire ship, just as it was, since they knew exactly what would happen, what would come to pass, as, in two days, it did, when a powerful wave broke the by now utterly shattered wreck into two, whereupon it slid off the rock and, suddenly, almost unbelievably quickly, within a few minutes, sank beneath the surface, so that a quarter of an hour later the last of the waves was sweeping smoothly over the place it had been and across the shore where stood the entire village of the small fishing community of Kommos, every man, woman, child and dotard, mute and still, since within a quarter of an hour nothing, but nothing, remained of that huge, strange and terrifying vessel, not even the very last wave, only the three living survivors and a fourth who might survive the catastrophe, four, all in all, out of the sixty, the eighty, the hundred, only four.

4.

In the days of painful recuperation that followed they pronounced their names differently each time so the locals tended to stick to the names they claimed to have heard on the first day, in other words they referred to one as Kasser, one as Falke, one as Bengazza and the fourth as Toót, feeling that this was probably the most correct version, assuming that everyone took it for granted that the four names—names that sounded peculiar to their ears—were merely approximations, and not within hailing distance of the possible originals, though to tell the truth this was the least of their problems, for contrary to their earlier experience of those cast on their shores, those whose names, origins, homelands and fate would bit by bit, and in fact fairly quickly, become plain, with these people everything—names, origins, homelands and fate— became progressively more mysterious, that is to say their foreignness and peculiarity did not diminish but grew in astonishing fashion with the passing of days, so that by the time they were well enough to leave their beds and ventured with extreme caution out into the open air, that moment being described in that wonderful *chapter*, said Korin, pronouncing the word *chapter* in English, in particular detail, there stood these perfectly mysterious four men of whom less than nothing was known because they consistently avoided questions put to them in Babylonian, the *language*—Korin used the English word again—they shared, albeit both sides spoke it only brokenly, by answering to something different, so that even Mastemann, a recent foreign castaway from Gurnia, to the east of the island, a man not much given to doubts but willing to state his opinions forcefully, appeared to be in doubt, yes, even he, Mastemann, fell silent as he watched them from behind the wagon as they strolled silently through the tiny village, as they ambled behind the fig trees and eventually settled down to dawdle in an olive grove and watch the sun decline on the western horizon.

5.

The whole document, Korin said to the woman, seemed to be speaking of the Garden of Eden, every sentence of the manuscript that described the village and the shore, he said, dwelling on the unsurpassable beauty of the place, as though it were not some message it was conveying but more as if it were wanting to conduct itself back into paradise, for it not only mentioned this beauty, elaborated on it and proclaimed it, but lingered on it, in other words it established, in its own strange way, the fact that this peculiar beauty, Korin stressed the word "*beauty*" in English, was not simply an aspect of the landscape but all it contained, that calm, and, yes, delight, the calm and delight it radiated, suggesting that whatever was good was indisputably eternal, and in this way, Korin continued, embellishing the picture for her, it established the fact that, having been created good, everything continued very good, all of it, the brilliant red sunlight, the dazzling white of the cliffs, the subtle green of the valleys and the grace of the people inhabiting it, commuting as they did between the cliffs and the valleys, or, to put it another way, said Korin, everything—the red and white and green, the grace of the mule-drawn wagons as they trundled along, the octopus nets drying in the wind, the amulets around people's necks, the ornamental hairpins, the workshops offering pots and pans, the fishing boats and the mountain shrines, in a word the earth itself, as well as the sea and the sky (the sky, he said in English)—but really everything was calm and delightful, and, what was more, real, real in the full sense of the word, or that at least was how Korin described the state of affairs, when, having finished the morning's work, he attempted to sketch the place out for her, though his efforts as usual were doomed since it was clearly pointless describing anything to her in whatever painterly detail, now or at any time, for she not only stood there as indifferent as ever, but, as he saw when she happened to turn a little, she had been thoroughly beaten up, in other words it was not just a matter of having no idea in what language to speak to her, that is if she was listening at all to the monologue Korin had been trying to deliver in Hungarian since about eleven that morning to about half-past twelve, going on to one, that afternoon—a monologue supplemented with the odd English word he had gleaned from the dictionary—but that the blown veins were clearly visible on her face, her eyes were swollen and there were abrasions on her brow, possibly because she had ventured out at night and had been attacked by someone on the way home, it was impossible to tell, though it was deeply disturbing to Korin, who, for that very reason, pretended not to have noticed anything and went on speaking, picking up his monologue in the evening until the interpreter finally appeared in the kitchen when, summoning his courage, he rushed over to him and asked him what had happened, and who was it who had dared assault the young lady: assaulted her! the interpreter expostulated, beside himself, to his lover, her! he bellowed at the figure crouched, wide-eyed with terror at the end of the bed, while he paced furiously up and down the room, for God's sake, who does he think he is? what business was it of this dumb asshole what they did or didn't do with their lives, for God's sake, who does he think he is, does he think he can sniff around us like some damned dog and try to hold us to account about our lives! well, excuse me, but that's not okay! he growled at his lover, yes, he sent him on his way all right, the sly pitiful asshole, let him rot up someone else's ass, he told him all right, until there was hardly any breath left in him, left him gasping, saying he only meant to this or only meant to that, to which he, the interpreter, replied simply that if he wanted to avoid a busted nose like hers, he will shut the fuck up right now with questions, at which point, naturally, Korin slid off like some damn snake, into his own room and closed the door behind him so quietly it would not have disturbed a fly, the interpreter insisted, for that door made no noise, no sir, no noise whatsoever.

6.

Night fell and the stars came out, but the four of them would not return to Kommos, for after carefully and repeatedly checking the security of the place they remained where the sunset found them, to the north of the village and a little above it in the olive grove where they leaned against an ancient tree trunk and sat for a long time, silent, in the deepening darkness, until Bengazza spoke in that low murmur of his and told them it might be as well to say something to the villagers, he had no idea what, but didn't they think it would be proper to invent something assuring about what they were doing here, to which, for a long time, he received no answer, for it seemed no one wanted to break the silence, and when it was broken it was on a different subject, a remark of Kasser's to be precise, to the effect that there was nothing lovelier than this sunset over the hill and the sea, to which Falke replied that nothing could be finer than these extraordinary colors in the deepening darkness, this wonderful spectacle of the interplay between transition and permanence, for all interplay between transition and permanence has a remarkable theatricality, being like an enormous performance involving a beautiful fresco of something that does not exist and yet suggests evanescence, mortality, that sense of dying away, perfectly encapsulating the idea of extinction; not forgetting the ceremonial entrance of color, added Kasser, the breathtaking glory of scarlet, lilac, yellow, brown, blue and white, the demonic aspect of the painted sky, all this, all this; and so much else, suggested Falke, since they had not yet mentioned the thousand significant tremors of the soul such a sunset occasions in the viewer, the deep trance-like state certain to be produced in the viewer by contemplation of the phenomenon, in other words, said Kasser, the sense of hope suffusing the moment of parting, the setting forth, the spellbinding image of the first step into darkness; yes, but also the sure promise of calm, rest and the approach of dreams, all this, all at once and so much more, added Falke; and how much more, echoed Kasser, though by that time the grove was cooling, and since the linen loincloths they had been lent by way of raiment were inadequate against the chill they started back toward the village, making their way down the narrow path between the tiny stone cottages to occupy the one that had stood empty at the time of their arrival and which they had been offered by their brave rescuers and the squid fishers of Kommos as a temporary shelter for as long as they needed it, they were told; and so they entered and lay down on the beds, on what, inside the shelter, felt like a pleasant evening at Kommos, their entering and lying down being followed, as usual, by a short uninterrupted sleep, by which time it was dawn already, the new day arriving rose-hemmed, the very first light of course finding them up and about, outside the hut, beside a fig tree on the dew-drenched grass, all four of them squatting and staring at the early veils of sunlight, watching the sun rise across the bay in the east, for they all agreed that the earth had nothing lovelier to offer than sunrise; dawn, in other words, said Kasser, that miraculous ascent, the breathtaking spectacle of the rebirth of light, the distinguishing of objects and outlines, the wild celebration of the return of clarity and vision; in fact the celebration of the return of everything, of the very idea of wholeness, said Falke, of order, of the rule of law, and of the security they both offer; of birth, and the primal ritual of the dawn of things in general, and nothing surely can be more beautiful, said Kasser; and they hadn't yet spoken of what happens to a man who has seen all this, the silent observer of this entire miracle, said Falke, for even if all this meant the going down of the sun, dawn, with its own reason and clarity, would still signify a beginning and appear as the wellspring of some benevolent power; and of security too, added Kasser, for there was this sense of complete security about each and every morning; and so much more, put in Falke, though by that time it had grown bright as daylight and the morning had entered Kommos clad in its own splendor and magnificence, and was bidding it welcome, so one by one the castaways slowly stirred themselves, returning to the hut, for they all agreed with Toót when he quietly remarked that yes, indeed, it was all very well, and it was all true, but perhaps it was time to start on the food the people of Kommos had presented to them, the food—the dates, the figs and the grapes, time, in other words, to eat.

7.

Twelve days had passed since the ship ran aground in the storm, but the people of Kommos, wrote Korin, knew no more about the four survivors than they had that first day, from the single answer they had succeeded in eliciting from one of them, other than which they hadn't much clue how to set about the matter, for when they asked them to say something about their original destination or at least how they had got here, they were told that this was the very place they had set out for, since, as far back as they could remember, all four castaways, this was the shore they had always desired to wash up on, and they smiled as they answered the people of Kommos, then promptly began questioning them, with pretty specific questions at that, such as where the strategically most important defense works of the island were situated, about how many troops comprised the regular armed forces, what the locals generally felt about war, and what their opinion was of the martial prowess of the Cretans, this kind of thing and when the Kommosians answered that there were no defense works, no regular army just a fleet at Amnissos, and that weapons tended to be used only on ceremonial occasions by the young men, the castaways nodded and smiled knowingly as if these were precisely the answers they had been expecting, and having finished this conversation all four of them were in such good spirits that the fishermen were at a loss to understand why, and so they went on, observing them as, day by day, they grew steadily calmer and more at ease, as they tended to spend ever more time with the women at the mill and at the oil wells and with the men in their boats or their workshops, always offering to lend a hand, so that every blessed evening they could climb the hill above the olive groves and spend part of the night under the starry sky, though what they did there and what they talked about remained a complete mystery to the villagers, and even Mastemann could do nothing but continue listening, sitting all day by his cart in the square at Kommos, simply sitting and staring while the cats he kept in their various cages occasionally let loose a maddening squall of yowling because, as people explained to the four castaways on the boats and in the workshops, Mastemann, who was supposed to be this cat-dealer from Gurnia, tended to pretend that he was waiting for a customer to buy a cat off him, though the cats he had first brought with him were all gone, though really, said the Kommosians, he was waiting for something else, but what it was, he, naturally, refused to reveal, so Mastemann's appearance in Kommos, Korin pointed out, was generally regarded as a sinister phenomenon, and they looked on him now with apprehension even though he was only sitting there next to his cart, stroking a ginger cat on his lap, for since he had come things had gone badly in the village: there were no fish in the sea and there was no luck to be had in the olive grove either, which had begun to dry out, or so the women muttered among themselves, and even the wind there was acting strangely however they climbed to the highest shrine bearing sacrifices, however they prayed as they had been taught to Eileithyia, for nothing changed, Mastemann remained casting his shadow across Kommos, though they very much hoped that whatever Mastemann was waiting for might come to pass, because Mastemenn might leave then, and they might perhaps have their old lives back along with the luck, and even the birds in the sky might find some rest, for just imagine, as their frightened husbands said, even the birds, the gulls and the swallows, the lapwings and partridges were flying hither and thither, banking and swooping, screeching and flying into the houses as if they had lost their minds, seeking some corner as if they wanted to hide, so no one could understand what was happening to them, but everyone hoped the day would arrive when Mastemann left together with his ginger cat and those others in their cages, that he would get into that cart of his and vanish down the road he had come by, that led to Phaistos.

8.

He had read it through countless times, thought Korin as he sat in the kitchen next day—when, after a long period of silence behind the door, he judged that the interpreter must be out of the way— for really, he had been through it at least five, maybe as much as ten times, but the manuscript's mystery was by no means diminished, nor did its inexplicable meaning, its curious message, become any clearer, not for a second, in other words, he said, his position now was as it had been in the beginning, for that which he did not understand at the first reading was precisely what he failed to understand at the last, and yet it cast a spell on him, and would not allow him to escape the sphere of that moment of enchantment which constantly drew him in, even as he continued devouring the pages, and as he devoured them the conviction grew ever stronger, as it would in any man, that the mystery obscured by the unknowable and inexplicable was more important than anything else could possibly be and because this conviction was, by now, impossible to shake he felt no great need to try to explain his own actions to himself, to ask why he should have dedicated the last few weeks of his life to this extraordinary labor, since what after all did it consist of, he asked the woman rhetorically, but getting up at five o'clock in the morning (five o'clock, he said in English), a time he had naturally woken at for many years, drinking a cup of coffee, hoping not to disturb anyone with the minimal chinking and tinkling this involved, and by half past five or going on six to be sitting at the laptop, pressing the appropriate keys, everything going hunky-dory until about eleven when he would rest his back and neck, lying down for a while, and, as she knew, this would be the time that he gave an account of his morning's activity to the young lady, keeping her up to date with his progress, and once he had done so he would grab some canned food at the local Vietnamese downstairs, have it along with a roll and a glass of wine, then carry on working flat out till five when, according to their agreement, he would turn the computer off, pass the line to his kind host, the interpreter, put on his coat and go for a walk in town till about ten or eleven, not, he must confess, without a touch of fear, for he felt afraid but had got used to it because, in any case, he wasn't frightened enough to abandon this daily five o'clock excursion, because . . . and he couldn't remember if he had mentioned this or not, he had this feeling, how to put it, that he had been here before, or rather, no, he shook his head vigorously, that wasn't the best way of putting it: it was not that he had actually been here but rather that he seemed to have seen the town somewhere before, and he knew how ridiculous this must sound, since how could he have seen it from Köröspart, but what can he do, however ridiculous it sounded it was the truth, he said, that he had a *quite extraordinary feeling* when he was walking around Manhattan gazing at these enormous mind-boggling skyscrapers, no more than a feeling it is true but one he could not forget or dismiss, which was why, every day at five, he made the decision to explore it all, though exploring it all, in the literal sense, was of course out of the question, for he was dog tired by then, and at ten or eleven at night he would return and there was the computer so he could read all he had written that day, and it was only then, after he was finished, having checked that there was not one single mistake just before he went to bed, only then could he put it from his mind, as they say, and that was how days passed, or rather how his life here in New York passed, that is what he would write home if there were someone to write to, and that is what he is saying now, that the fact is he would never have thought the last weeks could have been so beautiful, he said, stressing the words *the last weeks* in English, after all he had gone through, but that he did not think about at all now, which was precisely why he was telling the young lady all this, since it might happen to the young lady too, that there might be a bad time in her life, *a bad period*, said Korin, but then would come a change, *a turning point*, when, from one day to the next, life would be different and everything would work for the good, for whatever might occasionally happen to a person, Korin said to the woman consolingly, this change, *this turning point* could happen to anyone from one day to the next, that was the way things were, for you can't live your whole life, he said gazing at the woman's thin bent back, under the same terror, that *shudder*, then, noting with alarm how the woman's shoulder gradually started to tremble with an ever more violent sobbing, he added that one must believe in the transformation, *hope* and *turning point* and *shudder*, and he now would beg the young lady to try to believe in this kind of turning point, because things would turn out for the best, he said, dropping his voice; for the best, of that you can be sure.

9.

What they were discussing in the grove that evening while watching the vast mass of the sea swaying far below, was the fact that there was a hard-to-define but potent relationship between man and landscape, between observer and the thing observed, a kind of marvelous correspondence by the light of which man could understand everything, and furthermore, said Falke, this was the only time in all human existence when you could genuinely, without the least doubt, comprehend everything, all other attempts at universal comprehension being no more than a fond fancy, an idea, a dream, whereas what we have here, said Falke, is all real and genuine, no fleeting illusion or mirage, not a conveniently fabricated, devised, dreamed-of substitute, but an actual glimpse into the very processes of life, that being what a man engaged with the landscape was offered a brief glimpse of, of life in its winter quietude, of life in the explosive energies of spring, a sense of the greater whole perceived through its details; nature is itself in fact, said Kasser, the first and last of undoubted certainties, the beginning and end of experience and at the same time of rapture too, because if anywhere, it was here and only here, before the unity that is nature, that one could begin, that one could be shaken by something whose essence is beyond our comprehension, but which we know has something to say to us; the only way to begin and be shaken, said Kasser, is in the unique position of being able to observe the radiant beauty of the whole, even if this very observation involved no more than rapt wonder at this very same beauty, for it was indeed beautiful, said Kasser indicating the wide horizon of the sea swaying below them, and beautiful too the unbroken infinity of the waves, the evening light glimmering on the foam, though the hills behind them were beautiful too, and beyond them the valleys, the rivers and the woods, beautiful and rich beyond all measure, said Kasser, for when man properly considers what he means when he talks about nature he finds himself at an utter loss, for nature was rich beyond every measure, and that's only taking into account the millions of entities that comprise it, leaving out the billions of processes and sub-processes at work in it; though one should ultimately point, added Falke, to the single divine manifestation, the omnipresent immanence, as we refer to the unknown end of that process, an immanence that while remaining beyond proof, nevertheless, in all probability, permeates those untold billions of processes and entities; and so they conversed on the hill in the olive grove that evening when, after a long silence, Toót mentioned that there was something they should discuss regarding the disturbing behavior of the birds, and from that point on, said Korin to the woman a couple of days later, the question of what that behavior meant, what should be done about it and how they themselves should respond to it, cropped up ever more frequently, until the day arrived when they had to admit that these so-called disturbing signs were evident not just in the birds—*the birds*, he said in English—but in the goats, cows and *monkeys* too, and that they had to keep an eye on this frightening change in the behavior of animals, on the goats, for example, who could no longer be kept on the mountainside because they'd fall to their deaths, or the cows who for no discernable reason lost control and started running, or the monkeys who swept screaming through the village, but apart from the screaming and the scampering, did nothing else out of the usual; and once this was pointed out of course there remained little of the joy and harmony that had characterized their early days, and while they continued to work beside the men and women, and though they visited the *oil mills* and took part in the torchlit *octopus fishing*, when they visited the olive grove after that, they made no secret of the fact that the joy had gone forever, a fact no one could deny, the time being ripe for them to admit it, as Bengazza did in the end, however painful it seemed, for it meant they had to leave this place and he claimed to see the harbingers of some terrible cosmic cataclysm, a *heavenly war*, he said, in the transformation of these animals, a war more terrible than anyone could imagine, as if there really existed something that could not be identified with nature, something, he said that would not allow this beautiful corner of this beautiful island to remain, that was impatient with these Pelasgians who had founded a peaceable domain and would not give themselves over to destruction, *ruin*, as they regarded it a scandal, said Bengazza, as something wholly intolerable.

10.

Mastemann remained silent and reserved any opinion he might have had on anything to himself, breaking his silence, wrote Korin, only when he felt like approaching the women who hurried to and fro across the main square, calling them in order to commend the infinite range of choice he offered, a choice lacking nothing, he smiled as he pointed to his cages full of cats, from the Libyan

White and the Marsh Cat, the Nubian Kadiz, the Arab Quttha and the Egyptian Mau, as well as the Bubastine Bastet, the Omani Kaffer and even the Burmese Brown, everything the heart could desire as he put it, offering not only what there was in store right now, but also what would be stocked in the future, in a word literally everything they could imagine, he went on, albeit in vain as far as his listeners were concerned, for he did not succeed in holding the attention of any of the busy women, in fact he tended to frighten them as much as his cats did, so the women hurried on, their hearts in their mouths, a little faster if anything, practically running, leaving the tall gangling figure of Mastemann in his long black silk cloak alone in the center of the square, in splendid isolation, to return to his usual place beside the cart as if his wasted words were of no concern to him, to pick up a cat and continue stroking it; and so he would go on all day in the shadow of the cart as if nothing and no one in the whole wide world were of the slightest interest, appearing to be a man incapable of being shaken out of his dour calm by any event whatsoever, even when, as actually happened, Falke stopped by the cages and tried to engage him in conversation, when Mastemann simply kept silent, fixing his light blue gaze on Falke's eyes, staring and staring while Falke asked him, "Have you been there?" pointing toward Phaistos, "for people tell me they have a most wonderful palace, a remarkable work of art, marvelous architects; or indeed beyond it to Knossos, though I expect you have," Falke sounded him out, "and you must have seen the frescoes there and perhaps even the Queen too?" he asked, but there was not the slightest flicker in the eyes of the other who continued watching him, "and then there are those famous vases, jugs and cups and jewels and statues, Mr. Mastemann," Falke enthused, "there above the sanctuary, what a sight, Mr. Mastemann, and this entire one thousand five hundred years, as the Egyptians tell us, is after all, and we should acknowledge it as such, an unrepeatable, unique miracle?" but his enthusiasm had no effect at all on Mastemann's dour expression, in fact, said Korin, nothing Falke could say made any difference whatsoever so what could he do, meaning Falke, but bow his head in confusion and leave Mastemann in the middle of the square, leave him to sit in the shadow of the cart alone again, stroking the ginger cat in his lap, seeing that he knew not Phaistos, nor Knossos, not the Regal Goddess with her serpents at the very top beyond the sanctuary.

11.

He would find it difficult, said Korin to the woman next day as she was sweeping round the oven, her eyes averted after having finished the cooking, really difficult, he said, to give precise descriptions of Kasser, Falke, Bengazza and Toót, because even now, after everything, after hours and hours of study, following day after day of the most intense absorption in their company, he still could not say exactly what they looked like, who was the tallest for example, who was short, which of them was fat or thin, and to be honest, if he absolutely had to say something he would have attempted to get around it by saying that they were all four of them of middling stature and of average appearance, though he could see their faces and expressions from the moment he started reading as clearly as anything, as clearly as if they were standing before him, Kasser delicate and thoughtful, Falke gentle and bitter, Bengazza tired and secretive, Toót harsh and distant, faces and expressions you see once and never forget, said Korin, and the delicate, bitter, tired, harshness of the four of them so impressed itself on him that he could still see them as clearly as he did that first day, moreover, he was forced to admit before he went any further, that it was enough for him to think of them to feel a tug of the heart, since the reader knew as soon as he came across them that the situation of these four characters, not to put too fine a point on it, was, beyond doubt, vulnerable, that is to say that behind those delicate, bitter, tired and harsh features it was all *vulnerability*, defenselessness, he said, yes, that's the kind of rubbish he came out with, imagine it, the interpreter recounted to his partner late next night in bed, he didn't know, he said, from day to day what delightful tidbit to regale him with and chiefly not, why or in what language, but today, when he was careless enough to walk into the kitchen the man was there and collared him in the doorway, giving him this unbelievably idiotic story, offering it to him like it was lady luck or something, something about these four guys in the manuscript and their vulnerability, I ask you, excuse me sweetheart, but who the fuck cares whether they were vulnerable or not, only God in his infinite mercy cared what the hell they did in that manuscript, or what he was doing in that back room, the only thing that mattered being that he paid the rent on the dot and not stick his idiotic nose into other people's affairs, because, and here he kept addressing his partner as "sweetheart," it was their business, and their business alone what they did or did not do, or, to repeat, whatever difficulties they may occasionally encounter, do in fact encounter, was a matter entirely for themselves alone, and he very much hoped that nothing relating to them was adverted to in these kitchen conversations while he, the interpreter was away, that his sweetheart never attempted to give anything away regarding their private life, never even mentioned it in fact, because, to be honest, he didn't even see what the point was of these great pow-wows in the kitchen, moreover in Hungarian, a language of which his sweetheart was almost totally ignorant, but all right, she can let the fool blather on, he couldn't forbid that, but the subject of them, or his new job, was out of bounds to her, just remember that, and, propping his head on his hand as he lay in bed, he hoped his sweetheart had made proper note of this, his free hand creeping toward the woman, then, he changed its mind, and moved his hand to the parting of his snow-white hair, tracing the line from the bridge of his nose upward, mechanically checking that no strand of hair had accidentally strayed across from one side to the other to disturb the clean line of the parting in the middle.

12.

My feeling is that nothing follows it, said Korin quite unexpectedly after a long silence, then, without explaining what it was he was referring to or why the phrase just came to him, he looked out of the window at the desolate rain and added, Only a great darkness, a great closing down of the light, and after that how even the great darkness is switched off.

13.

It was pouring outside, a blast of icy wind blowing off the sea, people no longer walking but rather fleeing down the streets, seeking some warm place, and it might also be regarded as a form of flight when Korin or the woman ran down to the Vietnamese, stopping just long enough to buy whatever they usually bought, Korin his accustomed can of something to heat up, along with wine, bread and some sweet confection, the woman a package of chili beans, lentils, corn, potatoes, onions, rice, or oil when any of these things had run out and a cut of meat or a bit of poultry on top of that, after which they immediately hurried back into the apartment that neither would leave till the next such excursion, the woman settling to her cooking, doing a little cleaning or washing in between, Korin sticking to his strict routine, having bolted his dinner to return to the table in order to work till five, when he saved the file, turned off the set and remained in his room, doing nothing, just lying on the bed for hours without moving as if he were dead, staring at the bare walls, listening to the rain beating on the window, then drawing up a blanket and allowing his dreams to flood over him.

14.

Then one day he burst into the kitchen to announce the fateful day had arrived though the nature and manner of its coming was impossible to predict, he said, even immediately before the event; for of course there would be considerable *anxiety* in Kommos, a constant stream of visitors bringing every kind of *sacrifice* to the shrine but questioning the priestesses too, their watching with concern the fate of the animals, looking for signs in the plant world, examining earth, sky, sea, sun, wind and light, the length of shadows, the wailing of infants, the flavor of meals, the breathing patterns of the aged, everything just so as to get some inkling of what was to happen, to discover which day might prove to be the fateful one, the *decisive day*, though no one anticipated it when it came and only once it had actually arrived did they realize it was here, the circle of attendants recognizing it in an instant and rapidly carrying news of it far and wide, for truly it was enough to catch a glimpse of it in the main square, said Korin, enough to take stock of it, frozen as they were in terror as it appeared in the approach to the square, teetered forward then collapsed in the middle and remained there, perfectly still; enough for them to acknowledge that this was it, the final sign, that there was nothing more to come and that it was the end of all terrified anticipation and agonizing worry: for the time of fear and flight had arrived, since if a lion, *a lion*, for this is what happened, descended into a place of human habitation only to die in the main square then nothing remained but fear and flight, and asking the gods time and again what it meant, this lion in the main square, what it was doing there clearly in agony, limping and gazing into the eyes of tinkers and oil-workers as they rushed to and fro, gazing, it seemed, into the eyes of each and every person individually and then collapsing, rolling over onto its side on the cobbles, what could all this mean, they asked; and this was the last sign, the very last and clearest sign that told them disaster had struck, for it certainly had struck precisely as they thought it would, precisely as they understood disaster to strike, all of them, *everybody*, so Kommos fell quiet and children and birds began to squawk in the silence while men and women started packing, getting their things together, storing their belongings away and considering what to do—and carts were already standing by their dwellings, shepherds and cowherds already driving their flocks, and all the ceremonials were concluded, all the farewells said, the prayers said at the shrine before the last hesitation at the topmost bend in the road to look back, to shed a tear, to feel the bitterness and panic of that last look, said Korin, all this happened and within a few days everyone had gone and Kommos was deserted, everyone having gathered in the mountains in the hope of security and better defense, of explanation and escape, and that's how it happened that within a few days everyone was on the road to Phaistos.

15.

Mastemann vanished, a local fisherman explained to Toót up in the mountains, quite simply vanished from one moment to the next, and the strangest thing of all was that nothing remained of him, not his cloak or his cart, not even a cat hair, though many people were willing to swear that up to the moment before the lion died he was still there but as soon as it died he had vanished, and Toót must understand, said the fisherman, that not one person recalled seeing the cart trundle away anywhere, no one had the faintest clue where the cart was or what happened to the cats, or even heard the cats make any kind of noise, the only thing they were certain of being that by that first evening in all the panic as people set to packing up their houses and drawing up their boats on the strand, the spot Mastemann had occupied was perfectly empty, as empty as if this had been the moment he had been waiting for, as if the dead lion were the sign for him to depart, and in the light of this it was no surprise if people felt that being rid of Mastemann was just as unsettling as his presence had been, and stranger still, said the fisherman, no one felt that they had truly got rid of him, it was merely that he had gone absent, and that's how it would always be from now on, some people said, for wherever Mastemann's shadow falls it remains forever, the fisherman concluded, while Toót waited for his companions to pass on all he had heard to them but they were not to be bothered with it at the moment, so he waited to speak until they had finished their conversation, waited so long in fact that he forgot it all, or rather, noted Korin, that he lost the desire to communicate it, because he preferred to listen to Kasser speaking about time and to the squealing of the cart next to theirs as it worked its slow way up the steep path, then turning his attention to the breathing of the oxen drawing the cart, to the buzzing of the wild bees above and the evening light catching the tack and gear close to the ground, and lastly the song of a solitary unknown bird from somewhere in the dark among the dense trees.

16.

It was a slow procession, the path steep and narrow, parts of it only just accommodating a single cart, and in many places narrowing at some water-drenched point, or *gulch*, that was altogether too narrow to pass through, so they had to support one side of the cart and hold it in the air while the two inner wheels rolled on, first unloading any heavy items, of course, so that the six to eight people following each vehicle could lift it at all, to get hold of it, raise it and convey it past the dangerous stretch, no wonder then that their progress through the mountains was slow, as slow as you may imagine, said Korin, nor should one forget that it was impossible to move at all in the heat of the day, the sun being so hot that they had to withdraw into the shade, lead the animals to shelter and throw damp skins and canvas over their heads so they should not suffer from brain fever; and so they continued, day after day, the weakest among them already dizzy with exhaustion, an exhaustion clearly visible in the animals too, until they finally reached the Messene plain and saw the mountain rise above it with the *palace* on the mountainside, and here they could comfort their tired children by muttering, see, there is Phaistos, we've arrived, encouraging each other too before settling in a shady wooden glade, *a grove*, said Korin, and spending the entire day staring at the gentle slope of the mountain ahead of them, admiring the palace walls as they glimmered in the sunlight, observing the mass of roofs above, all but Kasser growing silent and meditative, Kasser, from whom, now that they were lying in the shade of a cypress tree, words began to pour in an unstoppable stream, his utter exhaustion being the likeliest cause for this flood of speech, the probable *reason* why he talked and talked, saying that if a man systematically thought about everything he had to leave behind the list would be practically endless, for one might as well begin with one's birth, in his opinion, that birth being as much a miracle as the chance of him perishing in this beautiful place, for here, after all, was this wonderful building towering above them, one side of it overlooking the Messene plain, the other facing Mount Ida, with Zakro, Mallia and Kydonia in the far distance, and, of course, Knossos too, never mind the stone shrines, the temples of Potnia, the workshops where vases, rhytons, seals and stamps were made, the jewels, the murals, the songs and dances, the ceremonies, the games, races and sacrifices; for they had heard of all these in Egypt, Babylon, Phoenicia and Alasiya, for the true marvel and the real loss, if everything was indeed to be lost, said Kasser, would be Cretans themselves, *the man in Crete*, said Korin, that people who had vision enough to bring these wonders into being and who now, it seemed most likely, were about to be lost along with all their ideas, their infinite capacity, their temperament and love of life, their skill and courage: unprecedented miracle! unprecedented loss! Kasser exclaimed and his companions remained silent because they understood that Kasser deeply felt what he was saying, and so they watched the *torchlights*, said Korin, of Phaistos, as evening slowly descended in awed silence, and even Toót remarked that he had never seen a more beautiful sight, then cleared his throat, lay down on the ground, resting his head on his linked hands, and before falling asleep warned the others that they had had enough awe for one day, because tomorrow morning they would have to find the great harbor, ask whether there was an available ship and find out where it was going; that their task was precisely this and nothing more, that this should be their first concern in the morning, he said, his eyelids drooping before eventually closing.

17.

They saw the palace of Phaistos in the distance, said Korin, and marveled at the famous steps quite close to them on the western side, but took their leave of the Kommosians who, bearing their news and fears, hurried inside, and having obtained directions to the harbor, set out down the steep twisting path, and it was still the morning, soon after sunrise, just as the four of them were making their way to the sea, Korin told the woman, that it happened, that suddenly the sky above them darkened, that there was darkness in the morning, a dense, heavy, impenetrable darkness that covered them all in an instant, and they stared at the sky terrified, stumbling on through the incomprehensible dark, hurrying ever faster, finally in a desperate dash as fast as their legs could carry them, and it was pointless gazing at the sky in blind, hopeless fashion, because the darkness was total and terminal, there was no way out of it, no escaping it, because it was eternal night that had enveloped them, Bengazza cried out in terror, his whole body trembling, *perpetual night*, Korin whispered to the woman by way of explanation, at which the woman, who was still standing by the oven, possibly because of the unexpected whispering turned around in fright before attending to her pots and pans, giving them a stir, then sighed, stepped over to the ventilation window, opened it and looked out, wiping her hand across her brow, then closed the window again and sat down in her chair by the oven with her back to Korin and waited patiently until the food in the pan was ready.

18.

Down in *the harbor* it was impossible to move for the crowd: there were local Luvians, Lybians, Cycladesians and Argolisians, but also people from Egypt, Cythera, Melos, Cos, and, a number from Thera who were a considerable throng by themselves, in other words, a very mixed gathering, said Korin, all in the same state of panic and confusion, and maybe it was precisely the way they were rushing to and fro, shouting, falling to their knees then running on that calmed Toót and his companions sufficiently for them to gain an advantage over those who had lost their heads, so instead of dashing into the sea as so many of those who had streamed to the harbor had done and were still doing, they withdrew from the general hysteria into an obscure corner, and remained there a good while, and for a long time could think of nothing but how best to prepare for death; but eventually, when they saw that the catastrophe had not yet overtaken them, they began to calculate the chances of escaping, of *running away*, and, according to Bengazza, there was some such chance, the odds today being no longer than they had been yesterday, for there was the sea in front of them, said Bengazza, and all they had to do was to discover whether there was a boat that could accommodate all four of them, and they should at least try, he said, pointing to the torchlit harbor, *the bay*, and so, by merely speaking about the possibility of escape, he succeeded in encouraging the others, all but Kasser, who fell silent as though Bengazza's words had had no effect on him, but hanged his head not saying a word, and when the others agreed that they should make the effort, that they should after all try and set off for the shore, he continued sitting in that corner, hanging his head, not moving, showing no desire to leave, so that in the end they had to pick him up bodily, for, as he explained a good deal later once they were safely on board a ship bound for Alasiya, he felt that the terrible darkness above them and the ash that began soon enough to fall on their heads signified the imminent coming of the last judgment, and that they should not hope or try to escape, nor weigh the chances of doing so, and he personally abandoned hope once he saw the flakes of ash drifting in the air, for he felt, and afterwards knew, knew authoritatively, that the whole world—and he was thinking particularly of Knossos—was in flames, was certain that the earth was on fire, as were the worlds above and below it, that this really was the end, the end of this world and of worlds to come too, and, knowing this, he could not speak, could not explain, and therefore allowed himself to be carried by the others to the shore, allowed himself to be cast this way and that by the maddened crowd, let himself be thrown on board a ship, though he was not aware of what was happening to him or around him, then sat at the front of the ship, *at the prow*, said Korin, and, Korin added, this was how the chapter ended for him, with Kasser sitting at the prow, gazing into vacancy, the prow rising and falling along with him as the whole craft rises and falls in the waves, and this is how I still see him, said Korin, swaying and dipping at the prow of the ship, Crete enveloped in utter darkness behind them, and somewhere in the uncertain distance, Alasiya, their refuge, ahead of them.

19.

One thing the young lady should know, said Korin as he entered the kitchen the next day to take his place at the table, was that when he first arrived at this point of the narrative back in the far-distant records office, the point when they disappear on a boat to Alasiya, he was somewhat puzzled, for while he found *the story*, or whatever it was, utterly enthralling, as he had already said, he understood nothing of it, and believe me, young lady, this is no exaggeration, for as the young lady herself might have discovered, a person might think he has understood what he has read the first time, but doubt everything the second time round, even to the extent of doubting whether he had had the feeling of understanding in the first place, and he, he being the person in question, had found himself in such doubts the second time round, questioning the authenticity of his first reading, for Toót's speech was fine in itself and he had noted the fact of the four of them being pulled from the water, had seen them enjoying a few delightful weeks getting to know an earthly paradise, then watched them facing the last judgment, and this was all very interesting, for people do write this kind of thing, but having considered the totality, he did still want to ask what it was about—*so what* were Korin's English words—and admittedly this was a crude way of putting the question, perhaps even a little *coarse*, but this was precisely the form in which the question had arisen at the time, in as rough and ready form as that, in the feeling that this was all very wonderful, brilliant, wholly engrossing *etcetera*, but in the end, *so what*, what did it mean to anybody, what was it all about, why should anyone invent something like this, what was the writer secretly or overtly trying to do, was he retreating from the world by bringing these four characters out of the mist and thick fog, tossing them to and fro in a timeless universe, in an imagined world lost in the mists of legend?; what indeed was the point of it he asked himself, said Korin, and continued asking the question for a long time with much the same result, which was in fact no result at all, for he had no better answer to it now than he had back then in the records office where he first read it, raising his head from the manuscript for a moment to take breath and think, just as he had raised his head a few moments ago when he was busily transferring the document to his home page, and now this *All Crete* episode was there on his *home page*, Korin triumphantly announced, open to the world's inspection, or to be truly precise, open to the inspection of eternity, and the young lady would know what that meant, that is to say anyone could now read the Cretan episode, by which he meant, the young lady should understand, that anyone at any time in eternity could read it, for all they had to do was to click on the site in the AltaVista search engine, one click and they were there, and there it would remain, Korin enthused, his eyes fixed on the woman, thanks to Mr. Sárváry who had helped him set up the site, the whole first chapter was there for eternity, just a few clicks away, he raved, but if he thought this news would brighten the life of the woman sitting by the oven he was sorely mistaken because he hadn't even succeeded in getting her attention, and she continued sitting bent over in her chair, occasionally turning to the burner, removing a pot or turning the heat up under it, shaking or stirring with a wooden spoon whatever was bubbling inside it.

20.

The Minoan kingdom, said Korin—along with the Minotaur, Theseus, Ariadne, the Labyrinth, the one thousand, five hundred once and once-only years of peace, all that human beauty, energy and sensibility, with the double-axe, the Camera vase, the goddesses of opium, the sacred caves—the cradle of European civilization, or as they refer to it, the first flowering, in the fifteenth century BC, then Thera, he added bitterly, then the Mycenaean and Achaean hordes, the incomprehensible, agonizing and utter destruction, young lady, that is what we know, he said, then fell quiet and since the woman who was sweeping the floor had just reached him, he raised his feet to let her sweep under his chair, having done which she started toward the door to continue her work, but then stopped, turned and very quietly, as if to thank Korin for raising his feet, addressed him in a strange Hungarian accent, saying jó, meaning "right," then continued to the door, sweeping the corners of the room, and gave the threshold a brush before sweeping everything carefully into a heap and brushing it onto the pan then opened the ventilation window and emptied the lot into the strong wind so the sweepings drifted past the miserable roofs and ragged chimneys up into the sky, and when she closed the window they could still hear one empty can bouncing as it was blown away, the noise falling away, falling silent behind the window, silent among all those rooms and chimneys, under the sky.

21.

There'll be snow soon, said Korin in Hungarian, staring out of the window, then rubbed his eyes, cast a glance at the alarm clock ticking on the kitchen cupboard then, without a word of good-bye, left the kitchen closing the door after him.

IV • THE THING IN COLOGNE

1.

If they were worried about security, they could put their minds at ease, since security as far as he was concerned was completely assured, began the interpreter, strictly keeping to the orders he had received at the beginning that he should sit straight in the Lincoln, gaze calmly ahead and not turn round, then added that if there were to be any problem it could only be with his partner but that she was simpleminded, in other words a genuine mental case, and therefore could safely be ignored, for he had rescued her a year ago from some utterly hopeless predicament in the filth of a Puerto Rican swamp where she lived beyond hope, without family or possessions, without a thing in the world at home or indeed in the U.S. when she crossed illegally over the border, without a scrap of ID, nothing, till fate threw them together, and they should know that she owed her life to him, everything, in fact more than everything because she was in no doubt that if she misbehaved she could lose everything in the blink of an eye, as she would fully deserve to: in other words she was no great prize but that's how she was, and she'd do for him, because while it was true that she was simpleminded, she could cook, sweep and warm his bed, if they knew what he meant, as he was sure they did, and, well, there was someone else living in the apartment with them, but he didn't count because he was a nobody, a crazy Hungarian, who drifted in and out and was there for only a couple of weeks until he found himself proper accommodation, a guy who was staying in the back room, said the interpreter pointing to the house for they were just passing it, there, and he let it out to him as one Hungarian to another, because they took pity on him, a poor lunatic you wouldn't even notice because he lacked any distinguishing feature, and that really was all, the mad Hungarian, the Puerto Rican and himself, that's the way it was, and when he said it was completely secure it was the honest truth, for there were no friends, just them, nor was he part of a group of any sort, there were only a couple of guys at the video store he occasionally talked to, and the people he knew at the airport from the time he worked there, and that really was all, then having got so far he told them they could ask him anything, but no one stirred in the backseat and no questions were asked, they simply continued in funereal silence as they made another circuit of the interpreter's block, so when he was eventually able to get out and go up to the apartment he had a lot to think about when he met Korin on the stairs, the interpreter on his way up, Korin heading down, saying Good evening Mr. Sárváry, though it was clear that Mr. Sárváry was deeply preoccupied but, if he did not mind, he would like to tell him here on the stairs, since they hardly ever met otherwise, that he regretted the unfortunate incident, the misunderstanding, which as far as he was concerned was utterly innocent, for he felt no compulsion at all to pry or interfere in others' lives, that being completely alien to his character, and if there had been a misunderstanding it was entirely his fault, it truly was, Korin shouted after the interpreter; in vain however, since his last words were directed at the wall alone, the interpreter, who was already on the next floor, having dismissed him with a wave of his hand as if to say, for God's sake leave me alone, so that Korin, after a moment or two of confusion, continued on his way downstairs and at ten minutes past five precisely, stepped out into the street, because he was starting again, that is to say he could start anew, for the rainy, stormy, intolerable weather of the last few days had vanished to be replaced by a dry cold, and he could go out again and carry on walking around New York in search of the mysterious secret, as he had described it to the woman, taking the subway to Columbus Circle, then stretching his neck to gaze up at the skyscrapers as he trudged along Broadway, Fifth Avenue or Park Avenue to the towers of Union Square, turning down toward Greenwich Village, making his way on foot into SoHo, along Wooster, Greene and Mercer Streets, beyond Chinatown, toward the World Trade Center where he caught the subway returning to Columbus Circle and Washington Avenue, utterly exhausted by then, and as ever, not having solved the mystery, back to the apartment on 159th Street to read over what he had done that day, and if he found it satisfactory, to save it with the appropriate key, that is to say, as he remarked, doing everything properly, according to a system that was correct and reassuring, or rather, he said, as the story grew and lengthened and the days passed, but he felt no anxiety or terror on this account, rather the opposite in fact, for he was perfectly content knowing this was his last home on earth, that everything would remain in this fatal state of balance between eternity and the march of time, that it was all going according to plan, ever growing on the one hand, ever diminishing on the other.

2.

In the corner of the room, opposite the bed, the TV was switched on and turned to a permanent advertising channel where a cheerful handsome man and an attractive cheerful woman were offering diamonds and diamond-encrusted wristwatches to viewers who were invited to phone in and order the items at declared-to-be-sensational prices via a telephone number continuously scrolling in the right-hand bottom corner of the screen while the jewels and watches, as well as the precious stones set in them, regularly flashed and sparkled in a carefully directed beam of light, for which first the woman then the man jokily begged pardon, apologizing for the fact that no one had yet provided them with a camera that would eliminate the glare, and so the jewels would have to carry on flashing and glimmering, laughed the woman looking directly at the viewers, and yes, they'd just have to twinkle and blind people, the man laughed along with her, nor was their laughter in vain, in this room at least, for while the interpreter's partner went about her business without showing the slightest sign of amusement, he, having lain for days, fully dressed, on the unmade bed staring at the television, regularly gave a little smile despite having heard these jokes a thousand times before, and when the female host said this or that and when the man said something else, or when the sign TELESTORE, TELESTORE, TELESTORE started flashing, he regularly smiled, not being able to help it, watching the woman flounce into view followed by the man running on to the sound of mechanical applause and the first items of jewelry appearing between the waves of artfully folded red velvet that glowed as though it were on fire, while the mindless twittering about weight, value, dimension and price continued, to be followed by the woman's quip about the camera, and the man's on the same subject, the lighting and the flashing, then the whole thing ended in a blur of music and waving good-bye, at which point the whole thing would start all over again from the beginning, from entrance through applause, through red velvet and the two quips, again and again, each time from the beginning with all the unbearable indifference associated with repetition, the effect of the whole being to impress on the viewer's mind the notion that this entering, applauding, flashing the red velvet and quipping were part of an eternal cycle, while he continued watching it from the bed in the darkened room, watching as if he were under a spell which dictated that he should laugh every time they laughed.

3.

The cathedral was magnificent, said Korin to her one day in the kitchen, simply magnificent, *enthralling*, they were enthralled and really it was impossible to say what was more spellbinding, the description of the cathedral, that is to say them being enthralled by the cathedral or the fact that the manuscript after the Cretan episode—you'll remember, he reminded her, that they were on the boat to Alasiya, leaving the dark apocalypse, *the day of doom*, behind them—in other words once the manuscript had finished with Crete, it did not move on or continue, did not explain itself or develop, but provided a *resumption*, a new start, and this was, he was quite convinced, the original, indeed unique thing about it, that a . . . what should he call it, a story? should begin and then go on by starting again, for what we must understand is that the author, this anonymous member of the Wlassich family, decided to start this narrative of sorts and proceeded with his main characters up to a certain point, but then decided against continuing, and therefore started the whole thing all over again, as if this were the most natural thing to do, a matter of course, not, he should add, regretting and throwing away what he had written so far, but simply starting again, and that is exactly what happened, said Korin, since the four of them, after the voyage to Alasiya, appear in a completely different world, the strangest thing being, he added, that the reader feels neither frustrated nor annoyed when this happens, nor does he complain about the tired literary cliché of time travel, thinking that was all he needed, more damn time travel from one epoch to another, doesn't the ham-fisted author realize we have had enough of such long-defunct literary devices, no, that's not what the reader says, no, he accepts it immediately and finds nothing wrong with it, finds it somehow natural that these four characters should have emerged from the clouds of prehistory to sit at a table by the window of a beer-hall on a corner of the Domkloster, which is in fact where they were sitting, gazing at what, for them, was a magical building, watching it go up day by day, seeing it rise one stone after another, and nor was it by chance that they were sitting in that particular beer-hall on the corner day after day either, for it was precisely this table in this particular beer-hall that afforded the best view of the construction, as close as you like and from the southwest; and it was from here that they could see most clearly that the cathedral, once completed, would be the most magnificent cathedral anywhere, and the key term here, stressed Korin to the woman, since the manuscript heavily emphasized it, was southwest, it was from the *southwest* that it had to be seen, from the foot of the so-called south tower, from a fixed point relative to it, from almost precisely where they sat at their table in fact, at a large table made of solid oak, their regular table as they felt fully entitled to refer to it, especially since Hirschhardt, the proprietor of the inn, a crude, rough-spoken fellow, had formally allowed it to become their regular table and reserved it for them, given his blessing to their appropriation of it in a wholly unexpected and most courteous manner, saying, by all means, *meine liebe Herren*, let it be reserved for your exclusive use, repeating this over and over again, which signified not only favor but a proper commitment, *a fact*, because that was the table they always took on entering from the moment Hirschhardt opened his doors, the table there by the window that gave the best view, and it must have seemed that they had been watching Hirschhardt from close quarters ever since they had woken at dawn for the moment Hirschhardt opened up they immediately appeared, having returned from the long morning walk they took at precisely the same time, a walk of many hours in the cold wind, from Marienburg, down the bank of the Rhine, left at the Deutz Ferry and into the Neumarkt, then cutting between St. Martin's Church and the Rathaus, through the Alter Markt, finally reaching the Cathedral by way of the narrow alleys of the Martinsviertel, making a circuit of the building, having exchanged not a word all the while, for the wind by the Rhine was chilly indeed and by the time they crossed the threshold of Hirschhardt's beerhall at about nine they were pretty well frozen.

4.

They were making their way through Lower Bavaria and had stopped at a market when Falke heard that something was happening in Cologne, said Korin, a fact he discovered as a result of the interest he showed in a work by a certain Sulpiz Boisserée at the bookstall where he had stopped to leaf through certain items, and he had become interested enough in one to linger and read more of it when the man at the stall, the bookseller, having been assured that Falke had no intention of stealing it but was seriously thinking of buying, told him his choice was a sign of the most refined taste, because something really important was in preparation at Cologne and furthermore that he, the bookseller, was of the opinion that it was of a magnitude to shake the world; and the book that Falke was holding in his hands was the best work on the subject and he was pleased to recommend it in the most earnest terms, its author being the young scion of a long-established family of tradesmen, who had dedicated his life to art, and had made it his chief aim to make the world forget an international scandal, if he may put it that way, by producing something spectacular of international significance to cover it; for the honorable gentleman would no doubt know, he leant closer to Falke, what precisely happened in 1248 when Archbishop Konrad von Hochstaden laid the foundation of the cathedral, and would no doubt also be aware what was to be the fate of the divine plan according to which the foundation stone of the world's highest and most magnificent sacred structure was then laid, because what he was talking about, of course, was the story of Gerhard, the architect and the devil, said the bookseller, specifically the extraordinarily curious death of Gerhard, after which in 1279 there was no one left who was capable of completing the building of the cathedral; not Meister Arnold who labored at it till 1308, nor his son, Johannes who carried on to 1330, nor Michael von Savoyen after 1350, in fact there was no one at all who could make any significant progress with the work, the point being, the bookseller continued, that after 312 years the building came to a halt and had remained in an infinitely sad skeletal condition with only the Chor, or choir, the Sakristei or sacristy, and the first 58 meters of the south tower completed, and rumor had it, as it would of course, that the reason for all this was Gerhard's pact with the devil, which in turn was to do with the rather confused story of the building of some kind of drain, but whatever the truth of that, what was certain was that in 1279 the architect in a state of *non compos mentis* as they call it, threw himself from the scaffolding, since when a curse had lain on the whole project so that no one over the centuries could really complete the work, the cathedral on the Rhine famously remaining in the condition in which it had been left, with enormous debts in 1437 when they installed the bell, and all the time it was Gerhard, Gerhard, whom people talked about, for that was where, they all suspected and not without reason, the *cause* of the failure lay, the bookseller said, and then came 1814, and in 1814, that is to say 246 years after the complete abandoning of the work, this enthusiastic, virtuous and passionate man, this Sulpiz, somehow succeeded in finding the thirteenth-century drawings of the cathedral, the very *Ansichten, Risse und einzelne Theile des Doms van Köln* that Gerhard himself had used, and had become slavishly devoted to them, thereby subjecting himself to a curse much like that suffered by Gerhard, and here now was the very book, said the bookseller, pointing to the volume in Falke's hands, and the news that 621 years after the laying of the foundations, the work was under way again, so the honorable gentleman had done well to pick the book up, and to carry on perusing it, and could for a ridiculously reduced price take it home with him and study it further, for this was a work that would bring him great joy in the possession, a discovery like no other, said the bookseller, lowering his voice, indeed there was nothing like it in the world.

5.

It was the name of Voigtel, the *Dombaumeister*, that most often came up, that and *Dombauverein* and *Dombau-fonds*, not to mention terms like

Westfassade and *Nordfassade*, and *Südturm* and *Nordturm*, and most importantly how many thousand tallers and marks were spent yesterday and how many today, this was what the grumpy Hirschhardt spouted day after day, continuously and unstoppably, while admitting that the cathedral, should it ever be finished, would be one of the wonders of the world, and the world of art, as he put it, was sure to turn its immediate attention to it, *although*, as he immediately pointed out, that would never happen, since the building would never be completed, given *such a Dombauverein* and *such a Dombau-fonds* and the constant bickering between the *Kirche* and the *Staat* about who should pay for what, and he couldn't see any good coming from it, despite the fact that it was supposed to be one of the wonders of the world, and so on and so forth, though this was Hirschhardt's manner generally, to be running things down, to be moaning, full of acid remarks and skeptical about everything, cursing now the stonemasons, now the carpenters, now the transporters, now the quarries at Königswinter, Staudernheim, Obernkirchen, Rinteln and Hildesheim, the point always being to curse someone or something, or so it seemed, said Korin, though equally there was no one who knew better what was happening outside his window, so he knew, for example, that at any particular moment there were 368 stone-carvers, 15 stone-polishers, 14 carpenters, 37 stonemasons and 113 assistants engaged on site, was aware of what had gone on at the last negotiations between representatives of church and crown; was informed about disputes between carpenters and stone-carvers, stone-carvers and stonemasons and between stonemasons and carpenters; knew who was sick and when, about shortages of provisions, about fights and injuries, in other words about truly everything there was to be known, so while Kasser and his companions had to put up with Hirschhardt and his grumbling, they were, nevertheless, obliged to him and to no one else for the information in whose light they could interpret events outside, events that might have remained hidden from them, for Hirschhardt also knew about Voigtel's predecessor as *Dombaumeister*, Zwirner, a man of inexhaustible energy who nevertheless died young, and about long-dead characters like Virneburg and Gennep, Saarwerden and Moers, and not only them but obscure ones like Rosenthal, Schmitz and Wiersbitzky, as well as being able to tell them who Anton Camp was, who Carl Abelshauser and

Augustinys Weggang were, how the winches, pulleys and traction equipment worked, and how the carpenters' tools, the hoists and the steam engines were constructed; in other words you couldn't catch Hirschhardt out on anything, not that Kasser and his companions even tried of course, in fact they hardly ever asked questions at all, knowing well that they would only be submitting themselves to one of Hirschhardt's latest rants, merely nodding now and then as he spoke, for what they appreciated above everything else in the beer-hall was silence, that and a tankard of light ale from the tap, in other words the early and midmorning when there was hardly anyone but themselves in the bar and they could sit by the window, sipping at their beer, watching the work on the cathedral outside.

6.

In Boisserée's *Ansichten* there was already a drawing of the west front, dated 1300, most probably by Johannes, son of Meister Arnold, that was a work of outstanding beauty in itself and revealed something of the remarkable ambition behind the design of the building, but the deciding factor, first for Falke and then, following his summary, for the others, was the print they had seen displayed throughout the empire, a print hung in barbershops and on the walls of inns, that Richard Voigtel colored in after the etching by W. von Abbema for the *Verein-Gedenkblatt*, probably to draw attention to events in Cologne, in other words a print of 1867 originating from the Nurenberg workshop of Carl Meyer, that was all, and it was this that informed their decision where to go, because through their eyes, said the manuscript, the vast scheme depicted in the print immediately revealed the remarkable possibilities of this monumental shelter, a shelter, added Korin, that the four of them, as Kasser told a stranger who had been more successful than others in pursuing the question of who they were, that is to say merely a set of obsessed fugitives, though that was not how they described themselves that day, a week later, to Hirschhardt for example, but as *simply expert defense-works engineers,* in Kasser's words when it seemed he had to say something to Hirschhardt, and that was all there was to it, he said, that was the chief reason the four of them had come, not simply to research, not only to analyze, but primarily, in fact above all, to admire all that was happening here, and in saying so they were not saying anything they would have had to deny elsewhere, for they did genuinely admire it from the moment they got off the mail-coach, caught their first glimpse of it and could not help but admire it, admire it there and then, the sight immediately and wholly captivating them, immediately for there was nothing with which to compare with it, because imagining it from Boisserée's book, working it out from the drawing and the print, was entirely different from standing at the foot of the south tower and seeing it in real life, an experience that confirmed all they thought and imagined, though they had to be standing precisely where they were, at the precise distance, at a precise point and a precise angle to the south tower, Korin explained in the kitchen, so that there could be no mistake, but they did not mistake the distance, the point or the angle, and saw it and were convinced that it was not simply the building of a cathedral at stake, not just the completion of a Gothic ecclesiastical monument that had been abandoned centuries ago, but a *vast mass,* a mass so incredible as to surpass any building they might have imagined, one of which every detail would be finished—altar, crossing, nave, the two main aisles, the windows, the gates in all the walls—according to plan, though it was not what this or that aisle looked like, nor what this or that window or gate looked like that mattered but the fact that it would be an entirely unique, immensely high, incredible vast mass, relative to which there would be a point, as Gerhard had said to himself some six hundred years earlier, a specific point, as every *Dombaumeister* right down to Voigtel whispered, a point from which this beautiful piece of Amiens-work would appear to be *a single tower mass,* that is to say an angle from which the *essence* of the whole would be visible, and this was what the four of them had discovered by studying the legend of Gerhard, the drawing by Johannes, the Abbema-Voigtel print, and now, following their arrival, the reality itself, when, astonished, they sought out the ideal place where they might contemplate their own astonishment, a point that was not difficult to find, the beer-hall in other words from where they could watch each day's progress and so be ever more certain that what they were seeing was not something they had imagined after seeing an architect's plan but true, extraordinary, real.

7.

Sometimes I would really like to stop, to abandon the whole thing, said Korin on one occasion in the kitchen, then, after a long silence, staring at the floor for minutes on end, raised his head and hesitantly added, *Because something in me is breaking up and I'm getting tired.*

8.

The day began at five in the morning for him, the time he naturally woke, which he did in a moment, his eyes snapping open, and he sat straight up in bed, fully conscious of where he was and what he had to do, that is to wash at the sink, draw a shirt over the undershirt in which he slept, grab his sweater and his plain gray jacket, slip on his long johns, climb into his trousers fixing the suspenders, and, lastly, to pull on the socks warming on the radiator and the shoes parked under the bed, all within a minute or so, as if time were continually pressing, so that he could be at the door listening out for any other movement—not that there ever was any at this time—before slowly opening it so it shouldn't creak or, more importantly, that the handle should not click too loudly, for the handle was capable of making a terrible racket if he didn't handle it properly, then out, out on tiptoe, into the connecting hallway and thence into the kitchen and the stairwell to knock on the door of the toilet—not that there was any-one in there at that time—to take a piss and a shit, return, put the water on to boil in the kitchen, prepare the coffee grounds the ten-ants kept by the tin of tea over the gas oven, brew the coffee, add sugar and, as quietly as possible, sneak back into his room where things would proceed according to a permanent, changeless routine that was never broken, which entailed sitting straight down at the table, stirring and sipping at his coffee, turning on the laptop and beginning work in the permanently gray light of the window, not forgetting to check first that all he had saved the day before was safe now, then he'd lay the manuscript open before him at the current page on the left-hand side of the machine, and scanning through, slowly trace the text word by word, using two fingers to type up the new material, till eleven when his back would hurt so much he had to lie down awhile then stand up and perform a few vigorous waist movements and some even more strenuous turns of the neck, before returning to the desk and continuing from where he had left off, until it was time to run down to the Vietnamese for that day's lunch, after which he would go to the kitchen to join the woman and spend a good hour or so, sometimes as much as an hour and a half with his notebook and the dictionary in his lap, talking to her, keeping her informed of each new development, then return to his room to eat and work again solidly till about five, but sometimes only till half past four, because by now he felt obliged to stop at half past and lie down on the bed again, his back, his head and his neck being too painful, though he only needed half an hour of rest by this stage, then he'd be up again to listen out at the door, for he didn't want to run into his host unless it was absolutely necessary to do so, and having assured himself that they wouldn't meet, he went out, wearing his coat and hat of course, into the stairwell, down the stairs, and as quickly as he could, out of the house altogether so he shouldn't meet anyone at all, for greeting people, when the occasion arose, was still a problem for him since he didn't know whether Good evening, or Good day or a simple nod and Hi was the most appropriate, in other words it was best not to have to decide, and once he was outside in the street he'd take his usual route into New York, as he thought of it, having finished which he would return the same way, enter the house, climb the stairs, often stopping a long time by the door if he heard the rumble of the interpreter's voice, waiting there sometimes a few minutes but occasionally a whole half hour before slipping down the connecting hallway into his room, closing the door so gently it created hardly a draft before relaxing and letting the air out of his lungs, before daring to breathe again once it was safe to do so, then remove his coat, his jacket, his shirt, his trousers and the long johns, place them on the chair, hang his socks over the radiator, tuck his shoes under the bed and finally lie down, dog tired, but still concerned to breathe as quietly as he could and to turn his body under the blankets with great care so the springs shouldn't creak because he was afraid, constantly afraid of being heard, for the walls were paper-thin and he regularly heard the voice of the man shouting.

9.

Now he keeps talking about this guy Kirsárt or whatever his name is, said the interpreter to his partner, shaking his head incredulously, like the other night there he is in the kitchen again and he is beginning to feel that the man is literally stalking him, hiding in wait somewhere between the front door, the kitchen and the hallway, just looking for that moment when he might "accidentally" bump into him, and what a ridiculous state of affairs, trying to evade someone, having constantly to be on the alert in his own apartment, having to hesitate before entering the kitchen in case the guy should be there, it really was intolerable, for after all he is perfectly aware of what the man is up to, hanging around behind doors, listening, but there are times he just can't avoid these so-called "accidental" encounters, like the one last night when he pounced on him too, asking him if he could spare a moment while he babbled on about how his work was progressing and about this Misfart, or Firshart, or whatever his name was, unloading all this nonsense on him, nonsense of which you can't understand a single word of course, because it's all confused and he talks as if he, the interpreter, should have some clue as to who the hell this Dirsmars was: the guy was crazy, crazy in the strictest sense of the word, crazy and scary, there was no doubt about that anymore, scary and dangerous, you could see it in his eyes, in other words it was time to put a stop to all this because if he didn't, he felt things would come to a bad end, and in any case it was fair to say that Korin's days were numbered because Korin would be out on his ass now that he'd had this great offer, which was the chance of his life, believe me, said the interpreter to his partner, and if it worked out, and the way it looked was that it would need divine intervention to foul things up now, it would mean the end of poverty for them, they could get a new TV, new video machine and everything, whatever she wanted, a new gas stove, a new pantry, in other words an utterly new life down to the last saucepan, don't you worry, and Korin would be sent packing too, there'd be no more need to hide from him or to scurry about like rats in their own apartment in order to avoid him, nor would she have to spend hours listening to the affairs of Birshart, no, Hirschhardt, Korin corrected him in confusion for he didn't know how to conclude the conversation he had unfortunately become engaged in, for Hirschhardt was his name and Mr. Sárváry should picture him as someone who hated any kind of mystery, for mystery meant ignorance, which was why he loathed mystery, was ashamed of it and tried to dispel it whatever way he could, in the case of Kasser and his companions, by taking note of any incidental, casual and, for the most part, misunderstood remarks and, in his own fashion, drawing quite unfounded conclusions from them, constructing an entirely arbitrary view of affairs on the basis of extremely shaky foundations, presenting himself to his fellow citizens as someone wholly in the know when he sat down at various tables and told tales about them, quietly so they shouldn't hear, suggesting that they were of some strange monastic order, the four of them there by the window, never saying anything, mysteriously coming and going, nobody knowing the least thing about them, what with their foreign names, not even where they were from, and of course they were all peculiar creatures, but they should regard them as refugees from the triumph at Königgrätz, or rather the hell of Königgrätz as anyone would say had they witnessed the Prussian victory on that notorious July 3 three years ago, a victory bought at the price of forty-three thousand dead, and that was just the Austrian casualties, Hirschhardt told the local drinkers, forty-three thousand in a single day and that was just the enemy, and, well, I ask you, he said, anyone seeing forty-three thousand dead Austrians is never going to be the same again, and that lot, said Hirschhardt indicating the four of them, were part of the entourage of the famous general, members of the strategic corps, in other words no strangers to the smell of gunpowder, and must have come face to face with death in many engagements, Hirschhardt concluded, his voice lingering on the word "death," but the hell of Königgrätz had shocked even them, for that was hell, it really was, for the Austrians he meant of course, he quickly added, in other words they were heroes of Königgrätz, and that's how they should be regarded, nor should they wonder that they did not seem in exactly high spirits: and, having heard this, people naturally did regard them as such, saying to each other as they walked into the bar, oh yes, indeed, there are the heroes of Königgrätz, before looking round for a vacant table or for their friends, calling for beers while surreptitiously casting sidelong glances in the direction of the window, assuring themselves that there, indeed, sat the heroes of Königgrätz, as Hirschhardt had told them time and time again, participants in that heroic battle, that great victory, which was a triumph looked at from one point of view but absolute hell from another, what with forty-three thousand dead, which was part of the history of the four men over there who were involved in the glorious battle and had had to witness the death of forty-three thousand people, all on a single day.

10.

Kasser and his companions were perfectly aware, Korin explained to the woman, that the landlord of the inn was talking all kinds of nonsense but since they observed that the result of the landlord's fabrications was that the locals by and large left them in peace, they only occasionally tried to broach the subject with Hirschhardt to ask him why he went about saying they were heroes of Königgrätz when they had never in their lives visited Königgrätz nor had ever claimed to have been there, adding that taking flight before the battle of Königgrätz was not the same as fleeing from Königgrätz itself and so forth, that they were not members of Moltke's entourage, not even soldiers, and had only tried to escape an impending battle, not emerged from the heat of one, though, truth to tell, they only occasionally pointed this out because there was no point telling Hirschhardt anything for Hirschhardt was incapable of comprehending and simply nodded, his broad, completely bald skull covered in perspiration, his face set in a false smile as if he knew what the truth really was, so that eventually they gave up trying altogether and Kasser picked up a train of thought he had long been following, *the original thread*, the thing they had been talking about since they first arrived, that is the notion of preparing themselves for utter failure, for that was a genuine, unarguable possibility, since history was undoubtedly tending toward the ever more extensive force, *violence*, although no proper survey of affairs should omit the fact that a marvelous work was under construction here, a brilliant product of human endeavor, the chief element of which was the discovery of sanctity, *holiness*, the holiness of unknown space and time, of God and the divine, for there is no finer sight, Kasser declared, than a man who realizes that there is a God, and who recognizes in this God the spellbinding reality of holiness while knowing that reality to be the product of his own awakening and consciousness, for these were moments of enormous significance, he said, resulting in momentous works, for at the center of it all, at the very apex of each and every achievement stood the radiant single figure of God, *the one God*, and that it was always the man with the vision, the one who beheld him, that was capable of constructing an entire universe in his own soul, a universe like a cathedral aspiring to heaven, and the remarkable thing, the thing in Cologne, was that mortal creatures felt the need for a sacred domain, and this was the thing that completely overwhelmed him, said Kasser, that this desire persisted in the midst of an undeniable failure, a precipitous collapse into ultimate defeat, and yes, Falke took over, that was indeed extraordinary, but what was still more extraordinary was the personal quality of this God, since man, in discovering that there might be a God in heaven, that there might indeed be a heaven beyond this earth, had found not only a kind of lord, someone who sat in a throne and ruled over the world, but a personal God to whom he could speak, and what was the result of that? what happened? asked Falke rhetorically—*what happened*, Korin echoed him—what happened, Falke answered his own question, was that it extended man's sense of being at home in the world, and this was the truly startling, truly extraordinary thing, they said, this all-consuming idea that weak and feeble man was capable of creating a universe that far exceeded himself, since ultimately it was this that was great and entrancing here, this tower man raised to soar way beyond himself, and that man was capable of raising something so much greater than his own petty being, said Falke, the way he grasped the vastness he himself created, the way he defended himself by producing this brilliant, beautiful and unforgettable, yet moving, *poignant*, thing, because of course he was not capable of governing such grandeur, unable to handle something so enormous, and it would collapse and the edifice he had created would tumble about his ears so the whole thing would have to start all over again, and so it would go on *ad infinitum*, said Falke, the systematic preparation for failure changing nothing in the desire to create ever greater and greater monuments that collapsed, it being a natural product of an eternal desire to resolve an all-consuming, overwhelming tension between the creator of vast and tiny things.

11.

The conversation continued into the late evening and ended with praise of the discovery of love and goodness, which, as Toót put it, may be regarded as the two most significant European inventions, and this, said Korin, was roughly when Hirschhardt did his round of the tables and totaled up the bills of the various drinkers so that he might send them home, and, while he was at it, to say goodnight to Kasser and his companions too; and so it went night after night, like clockwork, and no one imagined that it would all change soon or that the accustomed order of things would be overturned, not even Kasser's friends on their way back along the Rhine who felt a little heavy on account of the beer and spent their time discussing whether the peculiarly frightening figure who had recently appeared in the vicinity of the cathedral and whom they had spotted through the window, a gangling, exceedingly thin man with pale blue eyes wearing a black silk cloak, had anything to do with the building, for all they knew about him was what the ever informative Hirschhardt told them when they enquired, which was that he was named Herr von Mastemann, and while that was all he or anyone else knew, there was no lack of gossip on the subject, a gossip that varied from day to day so that now he was supposed to represent the State, and now the Church; now he was said to be from a country on the far side of the Alps, now from some northeastern principality; and while one couldn't exclude the possibility that one or other of these rumors was true it was impossible to be certain, for there was nothing but rumor, hearsay, said Korin, to go on, rumors such as that he had been seen with the master of the works, or with the foreman of the carpenters and eventually with Master Voigtel too, or that he had a servant, a very young man with curly hair whose only task seemed to be to carry a portable folding chair, to appear with it each morning in front of the cathedral, and to put it down dead in the center facing the west front so that his master might sit in it when he arrived and remain there for hours, immobile, in silence; rumors that women, the women, Korin explained in English, particularly the servant girls at the inn were head over heels in love with him, that he had made them wild; that here in the celebrated city of St. Ursula, the city of beer, he did not drink beer at all but—scandalously—confined himself to wine; in other words, said Korin, there were endless petty rumors but nothing firm, no convincing overall picture, nothing of the essence, as a result of which of course the evil reputation of this von Mastemann increased hour by hour while the whole of Cologne looked on and feared; so that in the end there was no chance at all of discovering the facts, the truth, said Korin, rumor having grown ever wilder and spread ever more quickly, people saying that the air grew significantly cooler as you drew closer to him and that those pale blue eyes were not in fact blue at all, nor were they real, but were actually made of a peculiarly sparkling steel, which must mean that this von Mastemann character was quite blind, and taking all rumors into account the truth itself would have seemed pretty dull so that no one actually sought it any longer and even Toót, who was the least likely to pay attention to idle chatter, remarked that cold shivers ran down his spine as he watched von Mastemann sitting immobile for hours, his two metal eyes sparkling and staring at the cathedral.

12.

The bad thing was getting ever closer, its progress irresistible, Korin explained in the kitchen, and there were any number of signs of its approach, but it was one word that decided the issue in Cologne, after which there could be no doubt as to what was to follow, this word being *Festungsgürtel*, said Korin, or rather the event associated with it, an event whose importance outweighed everything else, at least for Kasser and his companions, for while the febrile mood they observed both in town and at the inn, and the ever more frequent sight of military detachments patrolling the streets were enough to set them thinking, they could still not be certain as to the true nature of events, and could only be so once they heard the military snap of the word one day when the inn was full of the tramp of soldiers' boots and Hirschhardt sat down at their table to inform them that the army unit stationed in town, or rather the *Festungsgouvernor*, to give him his proper title, that is to say Lieutenant-General von Frankenberg himself—despite the fury of the archbishop—had ordered the vacating of the *Festungsgürtel* to make space for a shooting gallery, the *Festungsgürtel*, Hirschhardt emphasized the word, which, as you gentlemen must know, serves as the spiritual center of the building works, where they keep the stones, in what we call the *Domsteinlagerplatz*, right next to the *Banhof am Thürmchen*, and the order had just been given so Herr Voigtel had immediately to stop all further railway deliveries, thereby severely endangering the whole project, and to begin hoarding the stone surreptitiously and in a great hurry, the very tone of the order making it clear that it would have to be obeyed immediately and that there would be no appeal against it, and indeed what could Herr Voigtel do but rescue that which was still possible to rescue and to remove whatever he could, burying the rest, for it was pointless referring to the overriding significance of the progress of the cathedral, the answer would have been that its overriding significance was merely an aspect of the glory of the German Empire, for the word was *Festungsgürtel*, and that's what mattered, repeated Hirschhardt nodding significantly, then, seeing that his guests had fallen utterly silent, tried to cheer them with a discussion of the glorious prospects of the coming *Krieg* but without much success, for Kasser's little band just sat there with vacant stares, in shock, before asking more questions in an attempt to understand more clearly what had happened, without much success for Hirschhardt could only repeat what he had already said before returning to his group of carousing soldiers, perfectly at peace with himself it seemed, relieved of his normal gloom, prepared even to take the liberty, as he had never done before, of downing a big tankard with them and joining in a roaring chorus celebrating the glorious forthcoming victory over the filthy French.

13.

They put the money down at the end of the bar counter and left quietly so that Hirschhardt, who was caught up in the general heartiness, failed to notice their departure and without anyone else remarking that they had paid and disappeared; from which fact, said Korin, the young lady might be able to deduce what was to follow, and indeed there was no need for him to tell her what followed for it was plain as the nose on her face what would, effectively, follow, although it was quite different hearing it in his words to reading it on the page, there being no comparison between the two experiences, and particularly in the case of the passage on this subject, an extraordinarily beautiful passage about the last evening with their walk home along the bank of the Rhine and how they then sat on the edge of their beds at their accommodation, waiting for the dawn without saying a word, at which time a conversation did begin, albeit with some difficulty, a conversation about the cathedral of course, about the point to the southwest of it from where, henceforth, they would no longer—*never more* said Korin— have the privilege of observing it as a solid, perfectly compact mass, with those splendid buttresses, the wondrous relief work on the walls and the vibrant ornamentation of the façade that concealed the weight and mass of the whole, and their talk kept straying to the deep metaphysical aspect of this unsurpassable masterpiece of the human imagination, to heaven and earth and the underworld, and the governance of such things, the way these invisible domains were created, and, needless perhaps to say, how, from the moment Hirschhardt's account had made it clear what the order to clear the *Festungsgürtel* had meant, they had immediately resolved to leave the place, this *Cologne*, to depart at first light, said Bengazza, and allow the military art of destruction, *the art of soldiers* as Korin put it studying his dictionary, to replace the unique spirit of the art of construction, and he knew, added Korin, that as another chapter in the lives of Kasser and his companions drew to a close, that nothing had been resolved or had grown any less mysterious, that there was still no clue as to what all this was leading to or what the manuscript was really about, what we should think as we read it or listened to its words, for as we do so we keep feeling that somehow we are looking in the wrong place for clues, in studying, for instance, its descriptions of the shadowy form of Kasser, for naturally one would like to understand what it all added up to, or at least Korin himself would, but the details did not help: he was left contemplating the whole thing, the sum of the images, and that was all he could see as he worked at the keyboard transcribing the manuscript, watching Kasser and his companions speed away from Cologne that morning, the dust of the mail-coach billowing behind them; and the image of the curly-headed young servant as he appears in front of the cathedral, folding chair in one hand, the other casually in his pocket, a light breeze raising the locks on the young man's head as he puts the chair down directly facing the west front then stands beside it, waiting, and nothing happening as he continues to stand there, both hands now tucked into his pockets, there is no one about in the square at dawn and the chair is still vacant.

V • TO VENICE

1.

It was about quarter past two at night and even from a distance you could tell that he was very drunk, since from the moment he came through the door and bellowed Maria's name he kept blundering against the wall, and the sound of repeated thumps, scufflings and curses made that fact ever more unambiguously clear as he drew closer while she did her best to snuggle under the eiderdown showing neither feet nor hands, not even her head, but hid and shuddered, hardly daring to breathe, flattening herself against the wall so that there should be the greatest possible room left in the bed and so that she should occupy the smallest possible space—but just how drunk he really was could not be properly gauged from inside the room, only once, after a long struggle, he managed to find the door handle and turn it so the bedroom door was flung open, when it became obvious that he was on the point of losing consciousness, and then he did indeed collapse on the threshold, collapsed as soon as the door opened, and there was perfect silence, neither the interpreter nor the woman moving a muscle, she beneath the covers using every muscle to suppress her breathing so that her heart beat loud with fear, an effort she could not maintain forever with the result that, precisely because of the strain involved in trying to keep absolutely quiet, she finally gave a little groan under the sheets then spent minutes in petrified stillness, but still nothing happened, and there was no sound except the radio of the neighbor downstairs where the deep bass of Cold Love, by Three Jesus boomed faintly on without the petulant whine of the singer or the howl of the synthesizer, the bass alone penetrating to the upper floor, continuous yet fuzzy, and eventually she, thinking it possible at last that the interpreter would remain where he was now till the morning, tentatively put her head above the cover to take stock of the situation and maybe help a little, at which point, astonishingly and with extraordinary vigor, the interpreter leapt from the threshold as if the whole thing had been some kind of joke, sprang to his feet and swaying a little, stood in the doorway and with a possibly intentional evil half-smile on his face stared at the woman on the bed, until, just as unexpectedly, his expression suddenly became deadly serious, his eyes grew harder and as sharp as two razors, terrifying her to the extent that she dared not even cover herself with the sheet but simply trembled and hugged the wall as the interpreter once again bellowed MARIA, strangely extending the "i" as if mocking her or in hatred of her, then stepped over to the bed and with a single movement tore first the covers then her nightdress off her so she did not even dare to scream as the nightdress ripped across her body but crouched there naked, not screaming, prepared to be wholly obedient as the interpreter, in a voice that was more a croaking whisper, ordered her to turn on her front and raise herself on her knees on the bed, muttering, get that ass higher you filthy whore, as he pulled his dick out, though since he was speaking in Hungarian, she was left to guess what it was he wanted, as guess it she did, raising her buttocks while the interpreter entered her with brutal power, and she squeezed her eyes tight with the pain, still not daring to cry out, because he was squeezing her neck with equal power at the same time, so that by all rights she should have been screaming but instead it was tears that began to course down her face and she bore it all until the interpreter released his hold on her neck because it was her shoulders he needed to grasp, it being plain, even to him, that if he failed to do so the woman would simply collapse under the weight of his ever more violent thrusting, so he grabbed her again and with increasing frustration yanked her onto his lap though he was incapable of coming to a climax and eventually, having grown exhausted, simply tossed her aside, tossed her across the bed, then lay back, spread his legs and pointed to his softening member, gestured her over again, indicating that she should take the thing into her mouth, as she did, but the interpreter still failed to come so he hit her across the face with great fury, calling her a filthy Puerto Rican whore, and the force of the blow left her on the floor, where she remained because she had no strength left to get back on and try something else, though by this time the interpreter had lost consciousness again and lay flat out, starting to snore through his open mouth, leaving her with a faint vestige of hope that she might sneak away somehow, which she did, as far as possible, covering herself with a rug, and tried not to look at the bed, not to even glance at him lying there utterly senseless so that she might not see that open mouth with its trail of spittle, taking in air, the spittle slowly dribbling down his chin.

2.

I am a video artist and poet, the interpreter told Korin over lunch next day at the kitchen table, and he would be most grateful if Korin remembered once and for all that it was art alone that interested him, art was his *raison d'être*, it was what his whole life had been about, and what he would soon be engaged in again after an unavoidable break of a couple of years, and what he would then produce would be a truly major piece of video art of universal, fundamental significance, a statement about time and space, about words and silence, and, naturally, above all, about sensibility, instincts and ultimate passions, about humankind's essential being, the relationship between men and women, nature and the cosmos, a work of indisputable authority, and he hoped that Korin would understand that what he had in mind was of so immense a scope that even an insignificant speck in the human consciousness such as Korin will have been proud to have been acquainted with its creator, and will be able to tell people how he sat in the man's kitchen and lived with him for some weeks, that he took me in, helped me, supported me, gave me a roof above my head, or so he hoped, that was what he so he fervently hoped Korin would say, because nothing could stop it now, the success of the venture was guaranteed and it was impossible that it should not be, for the project was all systems go, the whole thing was about to get under way and would be accomplished in a few days, since he would have a camera, an editing room and everything else, and what was more, the interpreter emphasized with particular care, it would be his own camera, his own editing room and everything else, and here he poured more beer into their glasses and clinked his against

Korin's a little wildlly, then drained his down to the dregs, simply poured it down his throat, his eyes red, his face puffy, his hand badly trembling so that when he went to light his cigarette it took several goes with the lighter before he found the end, and if Korin wanted evidence—he sprawled across the table—here it was, he said, then pulled a stern face and, rising from the chair, staggered into his room returning with a package and slapping it down in front of Korin, there, he leaned into his face, there is a clue from which you might be able to deduce the contents, he encouraged Korin, pointing to a dossier bound with a rubber band, there, open it and take a look, so, as slowly and delicately as if he were handling a fragile decorated Easter egg, terrified that one abrupt movement of his might destroy the thing, Korin removed the rubber band and obediently began to read the first page when the interpreter impatiently slapped his fist on the sheet and told him to go on, relax, read it through, he might at last begin to understand who it was that was sitting opposite him, who this man József Sárváry really was, and all about time and space, he said, then slumped back down in his chair, propping his head on both elbows, the cigarette still burning in one hand, its smoke slowly winding its way into the air, while Korin, feeling deeply intimidated, thought he'd better say something and muttered, yes, he understood very well, and was most impressed, since he himself was regularly engaged on a work of art himself, much like Mr. Sárváry in fact, for the manuscript that preoccupied him was a work of art of the highest caliber, so he was very much in a position to understand the problems of the creative imagination, only from a great distance of course, since he himself had no practical experience of it except as an admirer whose task it was to devote himself to its service, his whole life in fact, for life was worth nothing otherwise, in fact it wasn't worth a stinking dime, the interpreter muttered as if to raise the stakes, turning his head away, still supporting it on his elbow, a statement with which Korin enthusiastically agreed, saying that for him too art was the only meaningful part of life, take for example the beginning of the third chapter which was utterly breathtaking, for Mr. Sárváry should just imagine, he had got to the stage of typing—and he begged to be excused for still referring to it as typing—the third chapter, the one about Bassano, in which it described Bassano and how the four of them continued toward Venice, the loveliest thing there, imagine, being the way it described them waiting for a passing stagecoach to pick them up while they walked slowly along the streets of Bassano, and how they were full of endless conversation debating what they considered to be the most marvelous creations of mankind, or perhaps when they talked about a realm of exalted feelings that might lead to the discovery of exalted worlds, or perhaps, still better, Kasser's monologue on love and Falke's response to that, and all the superstructure and supporting structures of their arguments, for that was roughly the manner in which their talk proceeded, meaning that Kasser developed the superstructure and Falke provided the support, but that Toót would chip in at times and Bengazza too, and oh Mr. Sárváry, the most wonderful thing about it all was that there remained a vital element of the story that was not even mentioned for some time, an element whose likely importance, once touched upon, became immediately apparent, and that was that one of them was injured, a fact about which the manuscript had said nothing so far, and only mentioned once, eventually, when it described them in the courtyard of the mansion at Bassano, at dawn, on the day when Mastemann, who had just arrived from Trento, was changing horses, and the innkeeper, bowing and scraping, led the horses in and told Mastemann that there were four apparently monastic travelers on their way to Venice and that one of them was injured but he didn't know where or to whom he should report the matter, since there was something not quite right about the whole company, he whispered, for no one knew where they came from or what they wanted, beyond the fact that Venice was their destination, and that their behavior was very strange, the innkeeper continued in whispers, for they spent the whole blessed day just sitting about or going for walks, and he was pretty certain they weren't real monks, partly because they spent most of their time talking about women, and partly because they talked in such an incomprehensible and godless manner that no mortal could understand a word of it, that is unless they themselves were of such heretical bent, and come to that, their very garments were probably a form of disguise, in other words he didn't like the cut of their jib, said the innkeeper, then, at a gesture from Mastemann, backed away from the carriage and an hour later was totally confused when in departing, the gentleman, apparently a nobleman from

Trento, said he would like to relieve the tedium of the journey by taking the four so-called monks with him if they wanted a lift, and what with the fresh horses having been harnessed, the broken strapping replaced, the trunks adjusted and secured on top of the carriage, the innkeeper rushed off as ordered, bearing this good news for the quartet without properly understanding—without understanding at all—why he was doing so, though much relieved by the thought that the four of them would be off his hands at last, so that by the time the carriage eventually rolled through the gates and set off in the direction of Padua he was no longer troubled by the effort of understanding but crossed himself and watched the carriage disappear down the road and stood for a long time in front of the house until the dust of the carriage vanished with them.

3.

Pietro Alvise Mastemann, said the man giving a curt bow while remaining in his seat, then leaned back, his face expressionless as he offered them places in a manner that made it immediately obvious that the undoubtedly grand gesture of the invitation owed nothing to friendliness, readiness to help, desire for company, or curiosity of any kind, but was, at best, the momentary whim of a haughty disposition; and since this was the case the actual seating arrangements presented a problem for they weren't sure where to sit, Mastemann having spread himself across one of the seats and the other being nowhere near wide enough to accommodate all four of them however they tried, for however three of them huddled together, the fourth, Falke to be precise, would not fit on, until eventually, after a series of attempts at finding some cramped position and with an endless shower of apologies, he finally lowered himself onto Mastemann's seat, insofar as he was able to do that, meaning that he shifted the various blankets, books and baskets of food slightly to his right and having done so squeezed himself against the walls of the carriage while Mastemann did not move a muscle to help but casually crossed his legs, leaned back at leisure and gazed at something through the window, all of which led them to conclude that he was impatient for them to settle down at last so that he might give the driver the go-ahead—in other words this was the state of affairs in those first few minutes nor did it change much afterwards, so Mastemann gave the signal to the driver and the coach set off, but the carriage itself remained silent though the four of them felt that now was the time, if any, for introducing themselves, though the devil only knew how to go about that for Mastemann was clearly uninterested in conversation and the embarrassment of not having gone through that formality weighed ever more oppressively on them, for surely that should have been the proper thing to do, they thought, clearing their throats, to tell him who they were, where they had come from and where they were going, that's what should have happened, but how to do this now, they wondered, glancing at each other, and for a long time saying nothing at all, and when they did finally break the silence it was to talk very quietly among themselves so as not to disturb Mastemann, remarking that Bassano was beautiful since they were able to see the picturesque massif of Mount Grappa, the Franciscan church with its ancient tower below, to walk the streets listening to the Brenta as it babbled by them and remark on how nice everyone was, how friendly and open, in other words, thank heaven for Bassano, they said, and thank heaven particularly that they had succeeded in moving on too, though the thanks in this case were due not so much to heaven, they glanced across at Mastemann, more to, in fact entirely to their benefactor, the gentleman who had offered them a ride and who, though they tried to catch his eye, continued to stare at the dust rising from the road to Padua, as a result of which they realized, and none too early, that Mastemann not only did not wish to speak, but preferred them not to speak either, that he wanted nothing at all from them—though they were mistaken in this—and was content with their sheer presence, pleased that they were there and that that was what he wished to convey with his silence, their presence being quite sufficient, and having reasoned so far they naturally concluded that it mattered little to Mastemann what it was they talked about, if indeed they did talk, and that made the whole journey more pleasant for them because having realized that they could continue the conversation they had been having in Bassano from precisely the point at which they left off, and were free therefore, Korin added, to develop the subject of love, the way love created the world, as Kasser put it, they continued to develop it while the carriage swept on and Bassano disappeared from sight altogether.

4.

Korin sat in his room and it was obvious that he didn't know what to do, what to believe or what he should conclude on the basis of all he had heard in the apartment since that morning, obvious because he kept leaping out of his chair, walking up and down nervously then sitting down again, before leaping up and repeating the procedure for an hour or so, not that there was any need for an explanation as such for he had been scared ever since the interpreter threw his door open, at about a quarter past nine and ushered him into the kitchen which looked as though a war had taken place in it, telling him that they owed it to their friendship to down, there and then, a quantity of ale that was good for you, and followed this with a monologue that seemed to consist chiefly of veiled threats as well as a lot of other unrelated things to the effect that something had come to an end yesterday and that this ending firmly closed a chapter, at which point Korin took over the conversation because he really did not want to know what it was that had brought the chapter to a close, and could see that the interpreter's mood might any minute swing to outright hostility and so he began talking in as uninterrupted a stream as he could manage, that is to say until the interpreter slumped across the table and fell asleep, after which he scampered back into his room but could find no rest there at all, and that's where the process of squatting on the bed then stalking the room began, or rather the struggle not to listen out for the interpreter or be too concerned as to whether he was still out there or had returned to his room, a concern that continued to preoccupy him until eventually he heard the sound of clattering dishes and bellowing, and decided it was enough, that it was time to work, work, he said, time to sit down at the computer and pick up the thread where he had left it, and so he continued working, managing to immerse himself in the work, and, he said the next day, he immersed himself in it so successfully that by the time he had finished for the day and laid down on the bed with his hands over his ears, the only thing he could see was Kasser and Falke and Bengazza and Toót, and when, despite the periodic clattering and bellowing, he finally fell asleep it was Kasser and his companions alone who occupied his head, and it was thanks to them that when he ventured out into the kitchen at the usual time the next morning he found a magical transformation, for it was as if nothing had happened there, for that which had been broken had been swept away and that which had been spilled wiped up, and, what was more, there was food in the pans again, the clock was still ticking on the cupboard, and the interpreter's partner was in her accustomed place, standing immobile with her back to him, all of which meant that the interpreter must be out as usual at this time of day, so, overcoming his astonishment, he took his place at the table in the normal way and immediately launched into his account, continuing where he had left off, saying he had spent the whole evening with Kasser, that Kasser's was the only face he saw that evening, or rather the faces of Kasser and Falke and Bengazza and Toót, and that was how he fell asleep, with nothing in his mind, but them, and what was more, he was pleased to tell the young lady, they were not only in his head but in his heart too, because this morning when he woke and thought things through he had come to the conclusion that for him they were the only people that existed, that he lived with them, filled his days with them, that he might even say that they were his only contact with the world, no one else, only them, he said, that these were the people who, if for no other reason than that theirs were the histories he had most recently read, were closest to his heart, whom he could see in clear detail, he added, even at this very moment how the carriage was conveying them to Venice, and how should he describe it to the young lady, he visibly pondered, perhaps by simply going through each detail as it arose, he said, and he would attempt to do so now starting with Kasser's face, those bushy eyebrows, the brilliant dark eyes, the sharp chin and the high brow; going on to Falke's narrow, almond-colored eyes, his great hooked nose, the locks of his hair that fell in waves down to his shoulders; then there was Bengazza of course, said Korin, with those beautiful blue-green eyes of his, the delicate, slightly effeminate nose and the deep furrows of his brow, and finally Toót with his small round eyes, snub nose and those strong lines running crosswise round his nose and chin that looked as though they had been carved with a knife—that was what he saw day after day, every minute of the day, as clearly as if he could reach out and touch them, and having got so far he should perhaps confess that waking this morning, or rather reawakening, he should say, the sight of them made him suddenly fearful, for after heaven knows how many readings he had gradually formed some kind of apprehension as to what it was they were escaping from, in other words where this strange manuscript was leading them, why it was doing so, why they seemed to have neither past nor future, and what it was that caused them perpetually to be surrounded by a kind of mist, and he simply watched them, he said to the woman in the kitchen, simply watched the four of them with their remarkably sympathetic faces, and for the first time, with a shock of fear, he seemed to know, to suspect, what the apprehension was.

5.

If there were just one sentence remaining at the end, as far as I am concerned, dear lady, it could only be that nothing, absolutely nothing made sense, Korin remarked next morning after his usual period of silence, then stared out of the window at the firewalls, the roofs, and the dark threatening clouds in the sky, eventually adding a single sentence: *But there are a lot of sentences left yet and it has begun to snow.*

6.

Snow, Korin explained in Hungarian, snow, he pointed to the swirling flakes outside, but he had left the dictionary in his room so had to go and fetch it in order to find the word in English, and having done so, repeating the words, *snow, snow,* he finally succeeded in attracting the woman's attention to the degree that she turned her head, and having adjusted the gas under the pans, and washing and putting away the wooden spoon, she came over to him, bent down and took a look out of the window herself then sat down at the table opposite him and they gazed at the roofs together, facing each other for the first time across the table as, little by little, snow covered the roofs, she on one side he on the other for the first time, though pretty soon Korin was no longer gazing at the snow but at the woman whose face at this distance simply startled him so much he was unable to turn his head away and not just on account of a fresh swelling that practically closed her left eye but because the whole face was close enough now for him to see the mass of earlier bruises and signs of beating, bruises that had healed but had left a permanent mark on her brow, her chin and cheekbone, bruises that horrified him and made him feel awkward for staring

at her, though he could not help but stare at her, and when this became clearly unavoidable and likely to remain the state of affairs,
the sight of her face drawing him back time and again, he tried to
break the spell by getting up, going over to the sink and filling
himself a glass of water, having drunk which he felt able to return
to the table and not stare at the face with its dreadful injuries but
concentrate on the story of the carriage, concentrating his gaze not
on the woman but on the ever thicker snow, telling himself that
while it was winter here it was spring back there, *Spring in Veneto*, the
loveliest part of the season in fact, the sun shining but not too hot,
the wind blowing but not at gale force, the sky a calm clear blue,
the woods covered in dense green on the surrounding hills, in
other words perfect weather for the journey, so that Mastemann's
silence no longer weighed on them, for they had accepted that this
was how he wanted to proceed and no longer felt inclined to wonder why, content to sit quietly while the carriage swayed gently
along the well-worn road, until Kasser picked up the subject of
pure love, that wholly pure love, *the clear love*, said Korin, and what
was more, he added, spoke only about that, not about the lesser
kinds of love, the wholly pure love of which he spoke being *resistance*, the deepest and perhaps only noble form of revolt, because
only love of this kind allowed a person to become perfectly, uncon-
ditionally, and in all respects free, and therefore, naturally, dangerous in the eyes of this world, for this was the way things were,
Falke added, and if we looked at love from this point of view, seeing the man of love as the sole dangerous thing in the world, the
man of love being one who shrinks in disgust from lies and becomes incapable of lying, and is conscious to an unprecedented extent of the scandalous distance between the pure love of his own
constitution and the irredeemably impure order of the world's
constitution, since in his eyes it isn't even a matter of love being
perfect freedom, *the perfect freedom*, but that love, this particular love,
made any lack of freedom completely unbearable, which is what
Kasser too had said though he had put it slightly differently, but in
any case, Kasser resumed, what this meant was that the freedom
produced by love was the highest condition available in the given
order of things, and given that, how strange it was that such love
seemed to be characteristic of lonely people who were condemned
to live in perpetual isolation, that love was one of the aspects of

loneliness most difficult to resolve, and therefore all those millions on millions of individual loves and individual rebellions could never add up to a single love or rebellion, and that because all those millions upon millions of individual experiences testified to the unbearable fact of the world's ideological opposition to this love and rebellion, the world could never transcend its own first great act of rebellion, because such was the nature of things, it was what was bound to follow any major act of rebellion in a world that really existed and was actually set in ideological opposition, that is to say it did not happen and did not follow, and now would never come to be, said Kasser, dropping his voice at the end, then it was silence and for a long time no one spoke, and there was only the voice of the driver in the seat above as he exhorted the horses up the hill, then just the rattle of the wheels as the carriage rolled and sped along the Brenta valley a long way from Bassano.

7.

Jó, said the interpreter's lover in Hungarian, pointing through the window and gave a fleeting smile at the falling snow outside by way of farewell before she winced with pain and touching her bruised eye, rose, went over to the burners and quickly stirred the food in the two pans—and with this the whole snow event ended as far as she was concerned, for from that moment not only did she not move from the burner but did not even glance at the window to see how the weather was doing, whether the snow was still falling or had stopped, nothing, not a movement, not even a glance to show that what had so plainly filled her with joy just now had anything to do with her, so Korin was forced to abandon the hope he had glimpsed in her face, the hope that had found solace in the peacefulness of falling snow, or, more precisely, the hope that this solace might find visible expression, in other words he himself snapped back into the old routine and continued as he would have done, though not quite from the same place in the story, for the carriage had reached Cittadella already, and after a short rest moved on toward Padua, Mastemann apparently overcome by sleep and Falke and Kasser too dropping off, so that only Bengazza and Toót were still in conversation, saying that of all possible modes of defense water was clearly the best and that's why nothing could be safer than building an entire town on water rather than anywhere else, or so Toót proclaimed, and went on to say that, as far as he was concerned, he desired nothing better than a place where the defense arrangements, *defense viewpoint*, said Korin in English, were so thorough, the whole conversation having begun with the question of what was the most secure place, a problem that arose first in Aquileia, then surfaced again at the time of the Longobard assault, was considered in a more sophisticated way under the rule of Antenoreo, and, appeared to have been solved after Malamocco and Chioggia, Caorle, Jesolo and Heracliana when, as a result of the Frankish advance into the Lido in 810, the Doge moved to the island of Rialto, a perfectly correct decision at the time, that led to the development of the urbs *Venetorum*, and the invention, on the Rialto, of the notion of impregnability; and it was this decision that brought the peace and trade that established the present conditions of the state, the arrival at the decision coinciding with the arrival of a true decision-maker; which was all very well, but *what* precisely did he have in mind, they heard the apparently sleeping Mastemann's voice asking from the seat opposite, an intervention so unexpected and surprising that even Kasser and Falke woke immediately, while the startled Toót turned courteously to answer that they had always believed that the best, most effective form of defense for a settlement must obviously be water, and that is why it was such a wonderfully unique solution to build a whole city on water, for, muttered Toót, there could be nothing better as far as he was concerned than such a place, a place where the considerations of defense lay as close to the heart of the enterprise as Venice, for, as Signor Mastemann will surely know, that was the way Venice actually came into being, with people asking themselves what was the most secure environment, for the question had first arisen at the time of the Hunnish incursions into Aquileia, and had been presented during the attacks of the Longobards, and had led to ever more sophisticated solutions under the rule of Antenoreo, Signor Mastemann, said Toót, until, after Malamocco and Chioggia, Caorle, Jesolo and Heracliana they finally came up with the real answer, that is to say following the invasion of the Lido by Pepin in 810, as a result of which the Doge moved his residence to the island of Rialto, this being the perfect answer and therefore absolutely correct, and it was only in consequence of this absolutely

correct solution that the *urbs Venetorum* came into being; and this discovery of the principle of impregnability on Rialto, that is to say
the decision predicated on peace and the development of trade, is
what had led to the state of affairs Venice enjoyed today, the arrival
at the correct decision having coincided with the arrival of the
maker of that correct decision—at which point Mastemann inter-
vened again, to ask yes, but *who* was it they were thinking of, and
he frowned impatiently, to which Bengazza replied, explaining that
it was he who not only embodied the soul of the republic, but
could articulate it too, making it clear in his will that the splendor
of Venice could only be preserved under conditions of peace, with
the conservation of the peace, said Korin, and in no other way, that man
being Doge Mocenigo, Toót nodded, it being part of the will of
Tommaso Mocenigo, and that that was what they were talking
about, that famous will, that magnificent document rejecting alliance with Florence which was, in effect, the rejection of war and
the first clear articulation of the concept of Venetian peace, and
therefore of peace generally; that they were discussing those words
of Mocenigo's whose fame had quickly spread throughout the local
principalities so that it was all perfectly public and no surprise to
anyone what had happened a fortnight before in the Palazzo
Ducale, and when they set out on their journey, it had been in utter
ignorance, not knowing where to go, so as soon as they heard
about the last pronouncements of Mocenigo at the end of March
concerning the will and about the first results of voting at the
Serenissima, they immediately set out, for after all where else
should fugitives from the nightmare of war find shelter, they ar-
gued, but in Mocenigo's Venice, a magnificent city that after so
many vicissitudes now appeared to be seeking to realize the most
complete peace yet known.

8.
They were passing through a chestnut grove that filled the air with
a fresh and delicate fragrance so for a while, said Korin, there was
silence in the carriage, and when they started up their *conversation*
again it turned to the subjects of beauty and intelligence, that is to
say the beauty and intelligence of Venice of course, for Kasser, noting that Mastemann remained distant and silent but was undoubt-

edly paying attention, attempted to show that never before in the history of civilization had beauty and intelligence been so aptly conjoined as in Venice, and that this led him to conclude that the matchless beauty that was Venice must have been founded on purity and luminosity, on the light of intelligence, and that this combination was to be found only in Venice, for in all other significant cities beauty was inevitably a product of confusion and accident, of blind chance and overweening intellect engaged in senseless juxtaposition, while in Venice beauty was the very bride of intelligence, and this intelligence was the city's cornerstone, founded as it was, in the strictest sense, on clarity and luminosity, the choices it had made having been luminously clear resulting in the greatest of earthly challenges finding their perfectly appropriate solutions; for, said Kasser, turning to the rest of the company while being fully aware of Mastemann's wakeful presence, they had only to consider how the whole thing began with those interminable assaults, the constant danger, or *continuous danger* as Korin put it, which had forced the Venetians of those days to move into the lagoon, and how that, incredibly, had been entirely the right decision, the first in a series of ever more correct decisions which made the city— every part of which had been constructed out of necessity and intelligence—said Falke, a construction more extraordinary, more dreamlike, more *magical* than anything mankind had hitherto produced, one that because of these incredible yet luminous decisions had proved itself to be indestructible, unvanquishable and utterly resistant to annihilation by human hands—and not only that but that this supremely beautiful city, Falke raised his head slightly, this unforgettable empire, he said, of marble and mildew, of magnificence and mold, of purple and gold with its dusk like lead, this sum of perfections built on intelligence, was at the same time wholly impotent and functionless, *absurd and useless,* an intangible, static luxury, a work of inimitable, wholly captivating and unrivalled imagination, an act of unworldly daring, a world of pure impenetrable code, pure gravity and sensibility, pure coquettishness and evanescence, the symbol of a dangerous game, and at the same time an overflowing storehouse of the memory of death, memory ranging from mild clouds of melancholy through to howling terror—but at this point, said Korin, he was incapable of continuing, simply unable to conjure up or follow the spirit and letter of

the manuscript, so the only practical solution would be, exceptionally, to go and get it and read the entire chapter word for word, for
his own vocabulary was wholly insufficient to the task, the chaotic
mess of his diction and syntax being not only inadequate but likely
to destroy the effect of the whole, so he wouldn't even try, but
would simply ask the young lady to imagine what it must have
been like when Kasser and Falke, traveling in Mastemann's carriage,
talked of dawn about the Bacino S. Marco, or the brand-new eleva-
tion of the Ca' d'Oro, since, naturally enough, they talked of such
things, and the talk was at such a transcendently high level it made
it seem they were rushing ever faster through the fresh and fragrant
grove of budding chestnut trees, and only Mastemann was proof
against such transcendence, for Mastemann looked as if it was of
no account to him who asked what and who answered, he being
concerned only with the motion of the carriage down the highway,
with its swaying, and how that swaying soothed a tired traveler
such as himself, as he sat in his velvet seat.

9.

Korin spent the night almost entirely awake, and didn't even undress until about two or half past two, but paced up and down between the door and the table before undressing and lying down,
and was quite unable to sleep even then but kept tossing and turning, stretching his limbs, throwing off the covers because he was
too hot then pulling them back on again because he was cold, and
eventually was reduced to listening to the hum of the radiator and
examining the cracks on the ceiling till dawn, so when he entered
the kitchen the next morning it was plain he hadn't slept all night,
his eyes were bloodshot, his hair stuck out in all directions, his
shirt wasn't properly tucked into his pants and, contrary to cus-
tom, he did not sit down at the table but, hesitantly, went over to
the burner, stopping once or twice along on the way, and stood directly behind the woman, for he had long wanted to tell her this,
he said, covered in embarrassment, for a very long time now he
had wanted to discuss it but somehow there was never the opportunity, for while his own life was, naturally, an open book and he
himself had said everything that could possibly be said about it, so
it can be no secret from the young lady what he was doing in

America, what his task was, why and, should he succeed in accomplishing it, what the result of that would be, and all this he had revealed and repeated many times, there was one thing he had never mentioned and that was what they, and particularly the young lady, meant to him personally, in other words he just wanted to say that as far as he was concerned this apartment and its occupants, and particularly the young lady, represented his one contact with the living, that is to say that Mr. Sárváry and the young lady were the last two people in his life, and she was not to be cross with him for speaking in such an excitable and confused fashion, for it was only in such turgid manner that he succeeded in expressing himself at all, but what could he do, it was only like this that he could convey how important they were to him, and how important was anything that happened to them, and if the young lady were a little sad then he, Korin, could fully understand why that might be and he would find it painful and would deeply regret it if the people around him should appear sad and this was all he wanted to say, that's all, he quietly added then stopped speaking altogether and just stood behind her, but because she glanced back at him for a moment at the end and, in her own peculiar Hungarian accent said simply *értek*, I understand you, he immediately turned his head away as if feeling that the person he had been addressing could no longer bear his proximity, and stepped away to sit down at the table and tried to forget the decided confusion he had caused by returning to the usual subject of his conversation, that is to say the carriage and how as it was nearing the outskirts of Padua, all the talk was of names, a range of names and guesses as to who would be the new Doge, who would be elected, in other words, following the death of Tommaso Mocenigo, who would rule in his place, whether it would be Francesco Barbaro, Antonio Contarini, Marino Cavallo, or perhaps Pietro Loredan or Mocenigo's younger brother, Leonardo Mocenigo, which was not unimaginable according to Toót, though Bengazza added that any of these were possible, Falke nodding in agreement that it was all possible, with one exception, a certain Francesco Foscari, who would not be elected for he was in favor of the alliance with Milan and therefore, problematically, of war and Kasser, glancing at Mastemann, agreed it might be anyone but him, the immensely wealthy procurator of San Marco, the one man against whom Tommaso Mocenigo, in that memorable speech, had warned, indeed successfully warned, the republic, for the forty-strong election committee had immediately responded to the power of Mocenigo's argument and demonstrated their own wisdom, by giving this Foscari fellow just three votes in the first round, and he would no doubt receive two in the next and then would shrink to one, and while they could not be certain of this, Kasser explained to Mastemann, for they had received no fresh news since the first round of the elections, they felt sure that a successor would already have been chosen from among Barbaro, Contarini, Cavallo, Loredan or Leonardo Mocenigo, or at any rate that the successor's name would not be Francesco Foscari, and since two weeks had elapsed since the first round people in Padua would probably know the result already, said Kasser, but Mastemann continued to refrain from comment and it was evident by now that it was not because he was asleep for his eyes were open, if only narrowly, said Korin, so it was likely that he wasn't sleeping, and he maintained this attitude to the extent that no one felt bold enough to persist with the conversation, so they soon fell silent and it was in silence they crossed the border of Padua, such silence that none of them dared break it, it being completely dark outside in the valley for a good while now, one or two fawns scattering before the carriage as they reached the city gates where the guards raised their torches so they could see the occupants of the seats and explained to the driver where their intended accommodation was to be found before stepping back and snapping to attention, allowing them to continue on their way into Padua, and so there they were, Korin summed up for the woman, late in the evening in the courtyard of an inn, the landlord and his staff running out to receive them, with dogs yapping at their heels and the horses swaying with exhaustion, a little before midnight on the April 28, 1423.

10.

The gentlemen would, he felt sure, forgive him this late and somewhat lengthy statement, said Mastemann's driver at the crack of dawn next day when having woken the staff he sounded his horn to gather the passengers together at one of the tables at the inn, but if something could serve to make his master's journey unbearable, that is beside the terrible quality of the Venetian roads which made his master feel as though his kidneys were being shaken out of his body, as though his bones were being cracked, his head split wide open and his circulation so poor that he feared to lose both his legs, that is on top of the tribulations already mentioned, it was the impossibility of talking, socializing, indeed of merely existing, so it was unusual for his master to commit himself in this way, and he had undertaken the exercise only because he felt it his duty to do so, said the driver, on account of the news, the good news he should emphasize, of which he had been instructed to speak this dawn, for what had happened, he said, drawing a piece of paper from an inner pocket, was that having arrived last night, Signor Mastemann—and they might not be aware of this—did not ask for a bed to be prepared for him, but ordered a comfortable armchair complete with blankets to be set opposite an open window with a footstool, for it was well known that when he was utterly exhausted and could not bear even to think of bed, it was only like this that he could get any rest at all, and so it was that once the servants found such an armchair for him, Signor Mastemann was escorted to his room, undertook certain elementary ablutions, consumed a meal, and immediately occupied it, then after three hours or so of light sleep, that is to say about four o'clock or so, woke and called him in, him alone, his driver, who by his master's grace was literate and could write, and honored him by effectively raising him to the rank of secretary, dictating a whole page of notes that amounted to a message, a message whose written contents, the driver explained, he had this dawn to pass on in its entirety and what was more in a manner that was clear and capable of withstanding any enquiry, so that he should be prepared to answer any questions they might have, and this was precisely what he would now like to do, to carry out his orders to a T by attending to them in full, and therefore he requested them, if they found any expression, any word, any idea less than clear the first time round, that they should say so immediately and ask him for elucidation, and having said all this by way of preamble, the driver extended the piece of paper toward them in a general kind of way so that no one actually attempted to take it from him at first, and only once he had offered it more directly to Kasser, who did not take it from him, did Bengazza accept it, seek out its beginning and start to read the single side of text that had been inscribed in the driver's finest hand, then having done so he passed the sheet on to Falke who also read it, and so the message circulated among them until it was returned to Bengazza once more, at which point they fell very silent and could only gradually bring themselves to ask any questions at all, for there was no point in asking questions, nor was there any point in the driver answering them, however patiently and conscientiously, for any answer would have failed entirely to touch on the meaning of the letter, if letter—*letter*—it might be called, added Korin to the woman, since the whole thing really consisted of thirteen apparently unconnected statements, some longer, some shorter and that was all: things like DO NOT FEAR FOSCARI and when they enquired after its significance the driver merely told them that as concerned this part of the message Signor Mastemann had merely instructed him as to the correct stressing of the words, telling him that the word FEAR was the one to be most heavily stressed, as indeed he had just done, and that was all the explanation they received, further probing of the driver being useless, as was the case with another statement, THE SPIRIT OF HUMANITY IS THE SPIRIT OF WAR, for here the driver started a recitation in praise of war, about the glory of war, saying that men were ennobled by great deeds, that they longed for glory but that the true condition required for glory was not simply a capacity to undertake glorious deeds but the glorious deed itself, a deed that might be attempted, planned and carried out only under circumstances of great personal danger, and furthermore, the driver continued, clearly not in his own words, a person's life was in continuous and extended peril only under the conditions of war, and Kasser stared at the driver in astonishment, at an utter loss, then glanced across at his companions who were just as astonished and at an equal loss, before running his eyes over the third statement saying VICTORY IS TRUTH, asking the driver if he had something to add to this subject too, the driver then replying that the election committee, as far as Signor Mastemann was aware, had sat in the election chamber for ten days in the course of which they had come to the conclusion that Cavallo was too old and incapable, that Barbaro was too crippled and vain, that Contarini was dangerous as he had autocratic tendencies, and that Loredan was required to be at the head of a fleet, not at the Palazzo Ducale, in other words that there was only one candidate worth discussing, the one man able to help Venice maintain her honor, the one man capable of victory, the one man chosen by twenty-six clear votes after ten days of debate to be the Doge of Venice, and that man, naturally, was the great Foscari, in response to which Kasser could only repeat the name: Foscari? are you sure? and the driver nodded and pointed to the bottom of the sheet where it was stated, and twice underlined, that Francesco Foscari, the noble procurator of San Marco, had been elected by twenty-six clear votes.

11.

If he were to describe their reaction, Korin ventured, simply as *indescribable*, it would be only an overused, hackneyed form of speech that the young lady should not take literally, for the manuscript was particularly sensitive and precise on the subject of Kasser's disappointment, dealing with it in great detail, and not only with that but with the whole morning after the exchange with the driver, at the conclusion of which they understood, not without considerable difficulty, that one purpose of the dawn message was to let them know that Mastemann did not envisage continuing the journey with them—and this was the point, explained Korin, this sensitivity, this refined eye, this proliferation of precise detail, the way *the manuscript had suddenly become extremely precise*, as a result of which an even stranger situation confronted him, for now, because of the valedictory at the end of the third chapter, it wasn't events at the inn at Padua following the appearance of the peculiarly well-prepared driver with his peculiar mission that he wanted to tell her about, but the *description* and its extraordinary quality, in other words not about how, having understood the matter, Kasser and his companions themselves considered the idea of continuing their journey with Mastemann to be out of the question, since according to the thirteenth part of the message the road to Venice that they had so desired to take, either with Mastemann or with anyone else, meant nothing to them now, not about that but about all those apparently insignificant events and movements that had now become extremely important, or to put it as simply as he could, said Korin to the woman in an effort to clear the matter up, it was as if the manuscript had suddenly recoiled in shock, surveyed the scene and registered every person, object, condition, relationship and circumstance individually while utterly blurring the distinction between significance and insignificance, dissolving it, annihilating it: for while events of obvious significance continued to pile up, such as that Kasser and his companions continued to sit at the table facing the driver until he rose, bowed and left to start preparations for the departure of the carriage, to secure the luggage, to check the straps and examine the axles, following this, if such a thing was at all possible, the narration focused entirely on minute particulars of utter apparent insignificance such as the effect of the sunlight as it poured through the window, the objects it illuminated and the objects it left in shadow, the sound of the dogs and the quality of their barking, their appearance, their numbers and how they fell silent, on what the servants were doing in the rooms upstairs and throughout the whole house right down to the cellars, on what the wine left in the jug from the previous night tasted like, all this, the important and the unimportant, the *essential and the inessential*, catalogued indiscriminately together, next to each other, one above another, the lot building up into a single mass whose task it was to represent a condition, the essence of which was that there was literally nothing negligible in the facts that comprised it—and this, basically, was the only way that he could give her some idea, said Korin, of the fundamental change that overcame the manuscript, while all the time the reader, Korin raised his voice, carried on without noticing how he had come to accept and realize Kasser's disappointment and bitterness, though it was only by registering this disappointment and bitterness that he could foresee what still lay ahead, for of course, much still did lie ahead, he said, the chapter leading to Venice would not abandon its readers at this point, only once Mastemann himself appeared at the turn of the stairs wearing a long dark-blue velvet cloak, his face stiff and ashen, and marched down to the ground floor, dropped a few ducats in the palm of the bowing landlord, then, without casting a glance at the travelers' table, left the building, got into the carriage and galloped off along the bank of the Brenta while they remained at the table, and once the innkeeper came and placed a small white canvas package in front of them, explaining that the noble gentleman from Trento had commanded him to pass this on, after his departure, to the man they said was wounded, and once they opened the package and established the fact that what it contained was the finest powdered zinc for the healing of wounds, only once that had been recounted did the third chapter end, said Korin standing up, preparing to return to his room, with this mysterious gesture of Mastemann's, then with their own settling of bills with the landlord, and, he hesitated in the doorway, with their farewells to him as they stepped through the gate into the brilliant morning light.

12.

All is of equal gravity, everything equally urgent, said Korin to the woman at noon the next day, no longer concealing the fact that something had happened to him and that he was on the edge of despair, not sitting down in his accustomed chair but walking up and down in the kitchen, declaring that either it was all nonsense, all of it, that is to say everything he was thinking and doing here, or that he had reached a critical point and was on the threshold of some decisive perception, then he rushed back into his room and for several days did not appear at all, not in the morning, not at five, not even in the evening, so on the third day it was up to the interpreter's lover to open his door and with an anxious look on her face enquire, *It's all right?* or *Okay?* for nothing like this had happened before—not even to stick his head out of the door, for after all anything might have happened, but Korin answered with a simple, *Yes, it's all right*, rose from the bed where he was lying fully dressed, smiled at the woman, then, in an entirely new and relaxed manner, told her that he would spend one more day thinking, but tomorrow, about eleven or so, he would appear in the kitchen again and tell her everything that had happened, but that wouldn't be until tomorrow, having said which he practically pushed the woman out of the room, repeating, "about eleven," and "most certainly," then the lock clicked shut as he closed the door behind her.

13.

Well then, all is of equal gravity, everything equally urgent, Korin declared the next day at precisely eleven o'clock, taking a long time to pronounce the words and holding his silence for a good while, at the end of which silence, having said all he had to say, he simply repeated, significantly: *Equal, young lady, and of the utmost importance.*

VI • OUT OF WHICH HE LEADS THEM

1.

They took the wardrobe down first, the big one they used for clothes in the back room, and it wasn't clear for some time why they were doing so, who had sent them or at first what they wanted, but they went about it, gripping their caps in their hands, gabbling away in a completely incomprehensible pigeon English, showing the woman a piece of paper with the interpreter's signature on it then pushing their way into the apartment and getting to work at something that seemed to mean nothing in particular, tramping up and down through the rooms, hemming and hawing, taking the odd measurement, nudging to one side any object that happened to be in their way, in other words clearly taking stock, making lists, arranging the contents of the apartment—from the refrigerator to the dishcloth, the paper lampshade to the blankets used for curtains—into a sort of order, stringing the items together on some invisible thread then classifying them by some specific criterion, but betraying nothing about that criterion, assuming it was known to them, so that, by the end, with an ostentatious look at the clock and a your-obedient-servant look at the inhabitants, all four of them sat down on the kitchen floor and started eating their breakfasts, while both the frightened woman shrinking into the background, and Korin who had been roused from his work at the computer and was now staring this way and that wide-eyed, were too startled to say a word, both remaining in their original states, the first of frightened confusion, the second of idiotically gaping, the interpreter being nowhere to be found and therefore unable to offer an explanation; and nor was he available the next day, so even though they grasped the fact that he must have consented to the process they had not the foggiest idea why the four men, having finished their breakfast, mumbling away in their incomprehensible mother tongue and throwing the odd word at them, began removing all the movable objects in the apartment and loading them onto a truck waiting outside the house: the gas-fire, the kitchen table, the sewing machine, everything down to the last cracked salt cellar, in other words systematically removing every last item from the apartment; nor did they understand the next morning, after the men had ruthlessly taken away the beds they had left the night before, what they wanted when they rang the bell again and threw a huge roll of tape made of some synthetic material down in the corner, and, screwing their caps up in their hands, chorused a brief *morning*, then continued the previous day's nightmarish activity, but this time in reverse, removing from the truck parked in front of the block countless numbers of wooden and cardboard boxes, among them certain heavy large items they could only manage between two or even occasionally four of them, using straps, dragging them upstairs for hours on end so that by noon the containers had piled up head high and there was nowhere to lie or sit or even move much, and the interpreter's lover and Korin stood beside each other, squeezed into a corner of the kitchen, staring at the extraordinary upheaval until, at about four o'clock, the men departed and suddenly there was silence in the apartment, at which point, seeking an explanation, they began tentatively to open the boxes.

2.

They were proceeding along the West Side Elevated Highway, all four in apparently very good spirits, yesterday's *catrafuse*, the Romanian for loot, being of immeasurable importance to them, a really big deal, they repeated to each other, slapping each other on the back, regularly breaking into laughter in the driver's cab, the process of sneaking off with the *bozgors'* or that bozo's gear, and rather than delivering it all to the agreed garbage dump squirreling it away at their pad behind Greenpoint, having gone much smoother than they had imagined it would, since the fake certificate of dumping went unnoticed by everyone, for who the hell would have noticed, since the *catrafuse* was of the kind that would have been chucked away in any case, and as for Mister Manea, their benefactor as they referred to him, he was unlikely to be interested in such things, or so they told each other, and now they had everything they needed, beds, tables, a wardrobe, chairs, stove and a mass of other little items, enough to furnish a complete apartment, which was nothing to be sneezed at, including coffee cups and shoe brushes, the lot, and all for a single dime that Vasile had thrown out of the cab in superstition as they were leaving, and to throw all this away at the dump, such a wardrobe, such a bed, such a table and chair and stove and coffee cup and shoe brush was out of the question, they had decided, no, they would neatly take it home and no one would have the faintest idea where that was, the point being to spirit the stuff away, and indeed why not do so in Greenpoint for that matter, and fit out the entire apartment of a completely vacant block overlooking Newtown Creek with it, their own apartment, not to put too fine a point on it, the one that, following their arrival in the New World a bare two weeks ago, Mister Manea had offered them for seven hundred and fifty dollars a week, that is to say one hundred and eighty-eight each, on top of the employment, a deal they immediately accepted the day before yesterday when they took stock of the load they were to carry, decided there and then, and began to haul the stuff downstairs, stuff that was to be their own, the tenants of the apartment counting for nothing, not for a moment, *Mā bozgoroaicā curvā împutitā*, they said with a courteous smile at the woman, and *Dāte la o parte bosgor împutit*, they said to the man with a sideways glance, and it would have been great to laugh out loud, but they didn't, just carried on shifting the stuff and left the laughing till later in the evening, when fully loaded up they set off toward Greenpoint, and then again now, when having got over their day of excitement, wondering whether they would be apprehended but weren't, nobody asking or checking anything, enquiring where they were really taking the *catrafuse*, no one at all, they could happily drive down the West Side Elevated Highway, leaving behind the horrendous traffic of Twelfth Avenue, in other words after, and only after all this, could they allow themselves to laugh as they sat in the driver's cab and laughed, after which they left off laughing for a while and stared out of the window, their eyes bright and their mouths wide open with astonishment at the blaze of headlights, their hands in their laps, three pairs of hands with fingers that could not be straightened, thirty terminally crooked fingers from the endless fetching and carrying; three pairs in their laps and one pair, Vasile's, turning the steering wheel now left, now right, as they cut their way through the unknown, terrifying core of the city that was the frozen center of all their hopes.

3.

They've gone, said Korin to the woman on the evening of the first day of the upheaval, and looked terribly sad in the empty apartment, indeed more than sad: broken, defeated, exhausted, and, at the same time, highly tense, continually rubbing his neck, turning his head this way and that, going into his room then coming out again, and repeating this several times, clearly unable to stay in one place, in-out, in-out all the time, and whenever he reached the kitchen he looked through the gap left by the open door into the back room to see the woman sitting immobile on the bed, waiting, then he immediately looked away and moved on, until the evening when he finally plunged in and entered and sat down beside her but carefully so as to reassure her, not frighten her, nor did he talk about the subject he had first thought to talk about, about the discovery in the landing toilet, or about what they should do should they find themselves evicted, since, for his part, he took it for granted that this wasn't about eviction, so no, he didn't want to talk about such things, he explained to someone else later, but— and this would be genuinely reassuring—about the three long chapters he would now have to recount in one big go, though he would happily leave them aside or quickly pass over them and not mention them at all, but he couldn't do this because then it would not be plain, *clear*, he said, that thing he had promised earlier to explain, and he couldn't just skip over those three great chapters, *three chapters*, himself these last few days, nor could he simply say, OK, now everything is *absolutely clear*, the devil take it, and I won't write up another line of it, though he might have said it because everything did in fact become *absolutely clear*, but he still had to finish it and not just abandon it like that, for *an archivist* does not leave things half done simply because he happens suddenly to have solved the puzzle, *the rebus*, for what actually happened was that he did in fact suddenly solve the puzzle, only once he had read through the entire material, that was true, but solve it he did and this led him to a comprehensive revaluation of his plans, in other words changed everything, though before he gets on to that, he declared, before he reveals what this is all about, he would say but one word: Corstopitum, that's it, and just Gibraltar, and just Rome, for whatever happened he had to get back to where he had left off, for it was only the actual sequence of events as always, in every case, that made it possible to understand something, it being a matter solely and exclusively of *Continuous Understanding,* he said, seeking out the most appropriate phrase in his notebook, which is why he must refer back to Corstopitum and the terrible weather there, for it was truly terrible, this melancholy realm of eternal drizzle, terrible, an enormity, this constantly droning, bone-penetrating zero domain of icy wind, though more terrible still, he added, was the superhuman effort of the manuscript to provide descriptions of Corstopitum, followed by Gibraltar and Rome, for from this point on beyond the fourth chapter it was no longer a matter of the established practice of minutely cataloguing selected facts and circumstances, but of the ever deeper and ever more intensive exploration of selected facts and circumstances, which the young lady should try imagining, he told her, though what she was listening to with such nervous intensity was not him but to noises outside while he was leafing through a black and white notebook on his lap so that, for example, he noted the chapter began with four mentions of Segedunum, that is the say the mouth of the Tyne, and moved west to the fourth (!) manned passing place, then, from there on to the road that led to Corstopitum, four times in a row, four times the same thing (!), only filling it out every so often with an extra clause or so, but usually just with some adjective or adverb to drive the point home, as if somehow it were four distinct acts of breathing he wanted to describe, and with it of course everything concerning the journey through fog and rain that could be contained in four breaths, and thus repeating four times the experience of traveling the army communication route to the Heavenly Vallum, four times the story of how they changed horses at Condercum, of what first impression Kasser and his companions formed of the Vallum fortifications, of the forests and the military posts along the way, and of how they were stopped six miles before Vindolava where it was only the energetic intervention of the commander of the troop and the providing of a pass by the *Praefectus Fabrum* that persuaded the centurion in charge of the fort to allow them to continue toward Vindolava, though he could say the same of the Gibraltar episode where the repetition of the descriptions took a different form, such that it kept referring back to the extraordinarily precise picture it had drawn, and by continually keeping that picture in front of the reader it etched the image of the whole ineradicably on his mind, for example how, in the fifth section, it preserved the spectacle witnessed by Kasser and the others when, having reached Calpe by the mainland route they arrived at an enormous inn with the name of Albergueria and having settled into their rooms there they went downstairs to exchange some money and looked out of the window to catch a first glimpse of the spectral gathering of galleons, frigates and corvettes, *naviguelas*, *caravelles* and a variety of hulks below in the fog-bound bay: craft from Venice, Genoa, Castile, Brittany, Algeria, Florence, Vizcaya, Pisa, Lisbon and who knows how many others kinds of vessels in that absolute graveyard stillness, that immediately declared what happens when you get a spell of *calma chicha*, the sea becalmed, said Korin, among the dangerously narrow, fatal straits of Gibraltar, and this was what confronted the mind of the reader, such an image and other images like it, drawn in lines of ever greater depth, and confronted him too when, between the writing of the fourth and fifth chapters the beginnings of an understanding burst upon him and he realized that this was how he should express the matter, as regards what still remained to understand.

4.

Usually it took about ten minutes or so to warm himself with his own breath, to lock himself in, undo his buttons, sit down and then just breathe and keep breathing until he felt the room beginning to warm a little, taking up position at about five o'clock or quarter past five when he was sure not to be disturbed, for it was too early for the others and he could relax, and what was more, he added much later one evening, this was the only place he could relax, because he needed this half hour in the morning, this security and silence in the landing toilet, and he did in fact sit there about half an hour waiting for the urge, so he had time to gaze and stare, and did indeed take the opportunity for gazing and staring, this being a time before he could actually begin to think, the sort of time when a man sleepily gazes at things, when he truly soaks up everything that meets his gaze, the world before him, and, as they say, he said, even a crack in the wall or the door or the concrete floor becomes intimately familiar to him, so it was no wonder that one morning he noticed that near the top of the wall on his right, a wall that had been tiled from floor to ceiling, one of the tiles was not quite as it should be, that something about it was different from the day before or the day before that, though he didn't notice that straightaway for while he was sitting with his trousers around his ankles, propping his head on his hands, he was looking down or ahead, at the bolt on the door, not up, and it was only after he had finished and pulled up his trousers that he happened to glance up and saw the change, which, he decided, consisted of the grouting around the tile having been removed, and it was so obvious that the grouting had gone that he couldn't help seeing it immediately, so he put down the toilet seat and stood on it so he could reach the tile, tapped it and could hear that it was hollow behind, and by carefully pushing at one corner of it succeeded somehow in extracting the tile, behind which—there!—he could see a deeper space had been created and that the space had been filled with little plastic sachets, full, God forbid, of a white powder much like flour, not that he looked too closely or dared open one because he was a little frightened, his first reaction being that it was bad things in there, though to be perfectly honest, as he confessed later, he didn't know what precisely bad things was, but he knew somehow, by some means, and it was somehow obvious that it was bad, and he didn't even begin to guess who might have put it there, for it might have been anyone, and the most likely explanation was that was one of the lodgers in the apartment below, so he put the tile back, finished buttoning his trousers, flushed the toilet and quickly returned to his room.

5.

There is an intense relationship between proximate objects, a much weaker one between objects further away, and as for the really distant ones there is none at all, and that is the nature of God, said Korin after a long period of meditation, but suddenly didn't know whether he had said that aloud or only to himself and cleared his throat a few times, then instead of returning to his interrupted story said nothing for a while, hearing only the shuffling of the newspaper as the interpreter's lover leafed through its pages.

6.

It was Kasser who suffered most from the cold, he said eventually, breaking his silence, from the moment they disembarked from the enormous *decareme* on the shores of the Tyne, received their horses, were joined by a body of armed escort that had been ordered for them, and set out on the road along the inner edge of the Vallum, and he was so cold that when they arrived at the first military post, *garrison* said Korin, he had to be lifted off his horse because he was so stiff, he said, that he could no longer feel his limbs or get them to execute his will, and was carried into the fort, sat in front of the fire and two gypsies were summoned to rub his back, his arms and his legs until they set off again, this time toward Condercum, moving on from there too in the same way, through several stops until, on the afternoon of the third day, they reached Corstopitum, that being their destination as well as their starting point according to the *Praetorius Fabrum* since they were bound to report some time soon on the condition of the Wall, which was why they made a tour of The Immortal Work of the Most Heavenly Caesar, after a good few days of rest of course which were necessary chiefly to allow the *vapors* of the brigantine medicinal herbs to take effect and cure Kasser's aches and pains, a treatment he might have been glad of when they arrived at Calpe following the vicissitudes of the journey from Lisbon, which, once again, caused him the most suffering, and it was in fact the figure of Kasser, said Korin with a distant look, Kasser alone of the four of them, that underwent some subtle yet definite transformation, *mutation*, in the second half of the manuscript, his sensitivity or oversensitivity, his vulnerability to injuries of various kinds, becoming ever more marked, a fact he mentioned now only because the attention of the others to Kasser became ever more intense, sometimes it being Bengazza, sometimes Toót asking him if "everything was all right" as they traveled on in the coach under the protection of the Prince of Medina, while at other times, at the Albergueria for instance, it was Toót who secretly tried to find some army surgeon, and succeeded in finding one in the "hope of alleviating the strange distress continually afflicting Señor Casser," explained Korin, shaking his head, in other words, after the fourth chapter there was an imperceptibly increasing, concentration, a matter of delicate emphasis—or *nuance*, as Korin put it—on Kasser, and this constant concentration cast an anxious shadow even across the first hours of their arrival—for example when they found a space at a table on the crowded ground floor of the Albergueria, and everyone was keeping a wary eye on whether Kasser was eating the food put before him by the landlady, and later, after supper, when they were trying to guess whether he was listening at all to the conversation around him in which a mass of people, each in his own peculiar language, was analyzing the worrying and somewhat nightmarish state of affairs in the bay with its gently rocking but stranded vessels in the thick fog, the hopeless vacuum of the fatally becalmed sea, and, closer to the shores of Gibraltar, the melancholy shades of drifting schooners from Genoa and Venetian *galera da mercato*, the joints of whose masts gave an occasional muffled shriek as they shifted slightly in the deaf air.

7.

According to the *Mandatum* of the *Praetorius Fabrum* they were commanded to inspect the condition of the Glorious Work so as to be able to form an opinion of the value of all that had been done so far, to offer technical advice on the remarkably continuous development and maintenance of the wall, on the human and other resources required for this maintenance, and to form a management committee of *ingeniarii* with legally binding powers, able to make decisions regarding the organization of time and space, to be set up in Eburacum where the VI *Legio Victrix* was stationed, though in actual fact, Korin told the interpreter's lover on the bed, they were being summoned and dispatched simply so they might admire and adore this unique structure, and so that they should declare their astonishment and rapture at the sight, the idea being that the aforesaid astonishment and rapture should strengthen the position of its creators, reassuring, above all, Aulus Platorius Nepost, the current *legatus* of *Britannia Romana* in distant Londinium, that the masterpiece constructed here was genuinely the most advanced, most glorious, most immortal work that could have been created; and it was clear from the chosen style of the *Mandatum*, from the ceremonial quality of its language, that this was what was expected of them, nor would they have happily undertaken the terrible overland journey and the even more terrible sea-crossing had they not been assured that the purpose of this great plan of the Most High Lord, *the Project*, was precisely to inspire such astonishment and rapture, and, it must be said, they were not disappointed, for Hadrian's Wall, as the simple soldiers referred to it, really did astonish everyone, being greater and different from what they had expected on the basis of what they had heard of it in the form of news or gossip before their arrival, chiefly in its physical substance as it snaked over miles and miles of the bare spine of the Caledonian hills toward its western limit at Ituna aestuarium, *bewitching* the spectator, including the four of them who after recovering from the ardors of the journey, which in the case of Kasser meant covering himself with a selection of furs from pelt of bear, fox, deer and sheep, walked the line of the Vallum for several weeks, so, yes, they were observers, said Korin, not technical advisers, as described in the markedly official document relating to their mission, and observers too they remained as guests of the Albergueria inn nestling, hidden by the sea, at the foot of Gibraltar, in Calpe, where they were registered as emissaries, *vicariouses*, of the cartographic council of King John II, though in actual fact it was the bay itself they had come to watch from the upper-story windows, in which bay, according to Falke, they were obliged to pay their respects to the limits, *the border*, as Korin had it, *of the world*, and therefore also the limits of certainty, of verifiable propositions, of order and clarity, in other words *the border* between reality and uncertainty with all the compelling attraction of unverifiable propositions, full of the unquenchable desire for darkness, for impenetrable fogs, for incredible outlandish chances, confronting, in brief, that which lay behind the realm of whatever existed, at the point where the human world had drawn the line of demarcation, added Bengazza, joining the conversation on the second evening, beyond which there exists, as they say, nothing, where, as they say: *nothing can be*, he declared raising his voice, the raising of his voice betraying for the first time the true purpose of their arrival here, *the aim*, said Korin, that being to wait here for news of the Great Event, the term referring to something Kasser had mentioned back in Lisbon, and at this point, said Korin, the young lady should know that in this fifth chapter all Christendom, but particularly the kingdoms of John and Isabella, was in a fever of hitherto unknown excitement, as were Kasser, Bengazza, Falke and Toót who, as true disciples and servants of the much respected Prince of Medina-Sidonia, Don Enrique de Guzmán, as well as of the Mathematical Junta of the court of Lisbon, believed that the daring expedition, rejected by John but fervently supported by Isabella was of greater, indeed very much greater significance than anyone could imagine, far more than a simple adventure, for, Toót remarked on their way here, if Señor Colombo's idiotic venture should achieve its aims, Gibraltar, and with Gibraltar the world, and with the world the notion of anything with limits, and with the end of limits the end of everything known, everything, but everything would come to a stop, declared Toót, for the hidden last term of the conceptual realm, the intellectual distinction set between that which exists and that which does not would vanish, he said, and so the definable and therefore correct, if immeasurable, fixed ratio between the divine and the mortal orders would be lost in the dangerous euphoria of discovery, in the hubris of the search for impossible things, in the loss of respect for a state of being that realizes errors and can therefore reject error, or to put it another way, *the fever of fate* was succeeded by *the intoxication of sobriety*, said Kasser, yes, if you looked at it like that, the place, Gibraltar, was of enormous importance, and he gazed through the window, saying, Calpe and the Heights of Abila, and the Gates of Heracles, whispering that places offering views of Nothing would henceforth be confronted by Something, then he fell quiet on this second evening, as did everyone else as they sat and gazed silently, a shadow slowly crossing their faces, and thought of all those ships becalmed, trapped in the bay by the much feared *calma chicha*, the bay down there in the fog, and the faint shrieks occasionally emitted by the masts of the ships drifting off shore.

8.

These two chapters, said Korin, with their increasing focus on Kasser, with their unrestricted use of the devices of repetition and intensification, these fourth and fifth chapters, should have quickly alerted the reader to the probable intentions of the writer and hence to the meaning of the manuscript at large, but he, in his dense, stupid, unhealthy way had managed to grasp nothing, but nothing of it in the last few days, and the mysterious, cloudy origins of the text, its powerful poetic energy, and the way it turned its back in the most decided manner on normal literary conventions governing such works, had deafened and blinded him, in fact as good as blasted him out of existence, like having a cannon fired at you, he said and shook his head, though the answer was right there in front of him all the time and he should have seen it, did in fact see it, and, furthermore, admired it, but had failed to understand it, failed to understand what he was looking at and admiring, meaning that the manuscript was interested in one thing only, and that was *reality examined to the point of madness*, and the experience of all those intense mad details, the *engraving* by sheer manic repetition of the matter into the imagination, was, and he meant this literally, Korin explained, as if the writer had written the text not with pen and words but with his nails, scratching the text into the paper and into the mind, all the details, repetitions and intensifications making the process of reading more difficult, while the details it gave, the lists it repeated and the material it intensified was etched into the *brain* forever, so that the effect of all those passages—the same sentences endlessly repeated but always with some modification, now with some filling out, now a little thinner, now simplified, now darker and denser, the technique itself delicate, light as a feather—said Korin, reflectively, the combined effect did not produce impatience, irritation or boredom in the reader but somehow immersed him, Korin continued, glancing at the ceiling, practically drowned him in the world of the text; but, well, we can say more about that later, he interrupted himself, because now we should continue with how the journey from Onnum to Maia and back got properly under way and how anyone who was not in their immediate proximity at their various stopping places or, in the evenings, at their various improvised shelters, might have thought that the journey from Onnum to Maia would be no different from the one from Maia to Onnum, with three *decurio* before them, four horsemen immediately behind, and the thirty-two soldiers of the *turma* or detachment on heavily armored horses at the back of the procession, though it wasn't a straightforward progress, a matter of continually moving ahead, said Korin shaking his head, not a simple journey at all along the serpentine route of the enormous Vallum, nor was it the matter of a single unbroken conversation, of *talking* after dark as they rested at the warm outposts of Aesica, Magnis or Luguvalium, engaged in seamless never-ending reflection by the fire as they sat on their bearskin rugs, going over and over what they had seen that day, checking that the selection of stones was appropriate for carving, noting the unparalleled skill in accommodating to natural conditions, keeping an eye on the haulage, the marking, the laying of the foundations and the faultless planning of the construction itself and admiring the expertise and invention of the military engineers of the II *Legio Augusta*; the skill of the execution itself—*the art of implementation*, said Korin in English—being as nothing compared to the idea of the Vallum, that is to say the Vallum's spiritual content, since its physical existence, said Bengazza, was the embodiment of the idea of a border and articulated with spellbinding clarity the distinction between all that was Empire and all that was not, a statement, said Falke, of simply staggering force, to show the two distinct realities the Vallum Hadrianum was there to divide, since at the bottom of all human intentionality, Toót took over, on the most fundamental level—in *the primary level of human*, said Korin—lay the longing for security, an unquenchable thirst for pleasure, a crying need for property and power and the desire to establish freedoms beyond nature; and man, he added, had gone a long way to achieving all this, the loveliest aspect of it being the ability to construct fastidious answers to insoluble problems, to propose the monumental in the face of the miscellaneous, to offer security in the face of defenselessness, to provide shelter against aggression, to develop refinement in the face of crudity and to seek absolute freedom in the face of constraint, in other words things to produce things of high order as opposed to those of a lower order, though you might put it as effectively, said Bengazza, to credit him with the creation of peace instead of war—*instead of war the peace*, in Korin's words—for peace was the greatest, the highest, the supreme achievement of man, peace, the magnificent symbol of which, as of the divine Hadrianus and of the permanence of the entire *Pax*, was the Vallum that stretched for mile after mile beside them, which demonstrated how one great symbol, with all its deep inner significance, might become its own perfect antithesis, for that is what they were talking about there in Gibraltar, at the table in the Albergueria, in the course of those endless unfinished conversations, the most important of them concerning the unquenchable human desire for the taking of ever greater, ever newer risks, the desire for a supreme, unsurpassable and ever new kind of daring that extended the scope of personal courage and curiosity, as well as the human capacity for *understanding* as they called it in the feverish din of their morning and evening gatherings on the enormous ground floor of the Albergueria, in those long days of enforced inactivity in 1493, while waiting for the most decisive news in human history, the news whether Admiral Colombo had returned in triumph or vanished forever in the immeasurable dusk at the ends of the world.

9.

Go round again, they told the driver from the backseat, turn right at the corner, do a circle and when you get back to 159th Street again take your fucking foot of the gas and cruise very slowly past the houses, because it wasn't true that they couldn't find it, it simply couldn't be true how much these fucking houses resembled each other, for they'd find the motherfucker, they most certainly would, they said, sooner or later it would all click into place, and they'd go round and round all night if need be, because it was somewhere on the right-hand side, either that house, said one of them, or the one next to the Vietnamese, said the other, having gone round three times already, and how the fuck could it have happened that they had really paid so little attention, but really, the driver called back, surely two normal mothers could not have given birth to such a pair of fuckheads, it being the third time they had gone around, then that guy comes out and they lay into him without even looking back and now nobody knows where to look for him, and don't anyone tell him how to handle the gas 'cause he'd leave them here to drown in their own shit, let them do the driving and try to find him by themselves, and when it comes to that, they retorted in the back, they'll just keep going round in circles until that lousy rat shows his stinking face, so let's stop here, one suggested, but no, the other snapped back, just keep going, and *whatthefuck*, the driver slammed his hands down on the wheel, is that what they really want, to spend the whole fucking night going around in circles in this filthy, rotten, shithole of a side street? and so they continued at a snail's pace down 159th Street, moving so slowly that pedestrians passed them by, turning at the next corner and circling the block to return to 159th Street, a Lincoln with three people on board, which was all the Vietnamese grocer saw when, after a while, he went out to see what the devil was going on out there, the car having passed the shop several times, reappearing every few minutes, and repeating this procedure time after time, a light blue Lincoln Continental MK III, he told his wife later, with decorative chrome flashing, with leather upholstery and dazzling rear lights and, naturally, the slow, dignified, hypnotic swaying of the spoiler.

10.

The Albergueria was not exactly an inn, said Korin to the woman on the bed, the sheer extent of it would tell you as much, since people don't build them of such size, of such astonishing, quite incredible largeness, nor was the Albergueria exactly "built" as such, if by building one meant something planned, for it simply grew, year by year, grew larger, higher, wider, more complete—*expansion* was the word Korin used—with countless rooms upstairs, ever more staircases, ever more floors full of nooks and hallways, exits and connecting passages, a corridor here, a corridor there in entirely incomprehensible order, while along this or that corridor, you might suddenly come across some vague focus of attention, a kitchen or a laundry with the doors removed, from which *steam* was continually billowing, or, equally suddenly, on some floor or other, between two guest rooms, you'd see an open bathroom with enormous tubs, the tubs filled with the steaming bodies of men surrounded by the slight running figures of Berber boys with towels covering their private parts, and stairs leading everywhere from inside these rooms, stairs that passed office-like quarters on certain levels, with commercial signs on the door and impatient queues of Provençals, Sardinians, Castilians, Normans, Bretons, Picardians, Gascons, Catalans and countless unclassifiable others, as well as priests, sailors, clerks, dealers, money-changers and interpreters, not forgetting a miscellaneous bunch of whores from Granada and

Algiers on the stairs and down the corridors, *whores* everywhere, everything so enormous, so confusing and so complicated that no one was able to comprehend it all, because there wasn't one single owner here but infinite numbers of them, each of them keeping an eye only on what was theirs and not caring about the rest and therefore lacking the foggiest notion of the place as a whole, which was in fact true of everyone there, and one should say, said Korin massaging the nape of his neck, that if this was the case on the upper levels, it was even more so on the ground floor, *down below*, for there chaos and incomprehensibility, *the impenetrable situation*, said Korin, was the general rule, it being impossible to be certain of anything, of whether, for instance, this space with its marvelously frescoed ceiling supported by roughly fifty columns and below it the vast, all-encompassing gloom constituted a dining hall, a customs house, a surgery, a bar, a financial exchange, a vast confessional, a marine recruitment agency, a brothel, a barber's shop, or all of these together at the same time; the answer in fact being "everything at the same time," said Korin, for the ground floor, the *downstairs* as he called it, was a monstrous Babel of voices morning, noon, evening and night, full of monstrous numbers of people continually coming and going, and what was more, added Korin blinking, it was as if they all existed in a slightly non-historical space, so that there were enemies and fugitives, hunters and pursued, the defeated as well as those about to be defeated; for here you would find the suspicious agent of a bunch of Algerian pirates consorting with the secret emissary of the Inquisition at Aragon, undercover Moroccan dealers in gunpowder in conversation with traveling salesmen from Medina carrying little statuettes of Stella Maris, Capocorsicans en route to Tadjikistan, Misur and Algiers walking shoulder to shoulder with beautiful melancholy homeless Sephardics who just a year ago had been expelled by Isabella, as well as crushed Sicilian Jews exiled by the Sicilians themselves, all of them in a state between genuine hope and despair, revulsion and dream, calculation and waiting for miracles, here, in the empire recovered but two years ago from the migrating Catholic Kings, every one of them living in expectation—*another expectancy*, said Korin—waiting to see if three frail *caravelles* would return and if they did so, whether the world would change, a world, which like the Albergueria with its becalmed ships in the bay, itself seemed becalmed, had suspended its activities, yet permitting all this—the chaos and confusion of the ground floor and the floors above ran riot—while outside some missing power, the power of *peace*, somehow balanced the equation, the peace that Kasser, Bengazza, Falke and Toót were happily enjoying on the journey from Lisbon to Ceuta—that's the way it was, and that *in point of fact*, was the state of affairs behind the thick and secure walls of the villa at Corstopitum too, for within them, he said, they felt a kind of inner calm settling on them, a calm that felt like being reborn, as Falke put it, after several weeks of having walked the length of the Vallum and returned—for Corstopitum to them meant security, the guarantee of which was the extraordinary wall constructed some thirty miles away from where they were—for the sensation for example, said Korin, of entering the baths of the villa that had been made available to them by the will of the *cursus publicus*, the joy of casting a glance at the wonderful mosaic floor and mosaic-covered walls, of sinking into the water of the basin and allowing the flush of hot water to reach every part of one's frozen limbs, was the kind of feeling, the kind of morale-raising luxury for the protection of which you required at least a proper Vallum or its equivalent, so that the kind of security experienced at Corstopitum, that calm and peace, signified a genuine triumph, a triumph over that which lay beyond the Vallum, the forces of barbaric darkness, of bare necessity, of savage passions and the desire for conquest and possession, triumph over all this, *triumph*, Korin explained, over what Kasser and his companions had seen in the wild eyes of a Pict rebel hiding in the scrub somewhere behind the tower of the fort at Vercovicium, over the state of permanent danger, triumph over the eternal beast in man.

11.

There was a noise outside the front door and the interpreter's lover jerked her head to one side and waited in case the door opened, her whole body tense, her eyes full of fear; but there was no further activity at the door so she opened the magazine she was reading and examined it again, gazing at a picture of what happened to be a brooch, a brooch with a sparkling diamond at its center at which she stared and stared until she eventually turned the page.

He arrived in the uniform of a centurion of the Syrian archers and a simple legionary's helmet with a plumed crest, wearing a short leather tunic, chain mail, neck-scarf, a heavy cloak, with a long-handled *gladius* at his side and the ring on his thumb that he never forgot to wear, though he would refer to him rather as a master of ceremonies, or, as Korin had it, a *master of ritual*, who appeared among the staff of the villa in the week following their return from the wall, though no one knew who had sent him, the *Praetorius Fabrum* or the *cursus publicus*, though it might have been the high command of the auxiliary cohorts or some unknown officer of the II Legion from Eboracum, but at any rate he turned up one day, flanked by two servants bearing a large tray full of fruits, the last of the original Pons Aelius rations, the three of them entering the central hall of the villa where meals were usually taken, he stepping in to introduce himself as Lucius Sentius Castus, then bowing his head, and with full consciousness of the effect he was having, after a moment of silence, called the attention of Kasser and his companions to his presence and announced that though no one had asked him to do this, no one, he repeated, had asked, it would be a great honor for him, *very dignified*, in Korin's words, if with the completion of his mission not only the mission but his very being were to cease, that he was a simple bearer of news who had come with both news and an offer, and with the conveying of these he would prefer to bring his emissary role to an end, or, if they might allow him to put it that way, that with the delivery of the news and the offer he would willingly vanish like the *Corax*, having said which he fell silent—*silence*, said Korin—and for a moment it seemed he was searching their faces for traces of understanding, then launched into what Korin considered to be an especially incomprehensible speech consisting almost entirely of signs, hints and references, which must, said Korin, have been in some kind of code, which, according to the manuscript, was perfectly understood by Kasser and the others, but seemed decidedly difficult to him, and he could form no clear picture of its subject since it demanded the establishing and interpretation of connections between objects, names and events that seemed entirely unconnected, not only to his own admittedly defective mind, but to any mind, since expressions such as *Sol Invictus, resurrection, the bull, the Phrygian cap, bread, blood, water, Pater, altar* and rebirth suggested that it was an adept of some deep mystery such as the cult of Mithras that was speaking, but what it all meant, Korin shook his head, was impossible to guess, for the manuscript merely rendered Castus's speech but gave no clue or explanation, not even in the most general way, as to its meaning, but, as so often in this chapter it merely repeated everything, three times, to be precise, in a row, and having done so, the text simply shows us Kasser, Bengazza, Falke and Toót recumbent in that refectory decorated with huge laurel branches, their eyes sparkling with excitement as they listen to this Castus character who, true to his promise, vanishes like the Corax or raven, an army of astonished servants behind them and the scented dates, raisins, nuts and walnuts as well as the delicious cakes, products of the confectioners of the Corstopitum Castrum lying on the tray in front of them, all of which make a very deep impression on a person, as do the broken sentences of Castus, though none of this actually leads anywhere— it didn't lead nowhere, said Korin—except into obscurity, into the densest, foggiest obscurity, or it might possibly mean, Korin declared, that the kind of total obscurity into which it led was of the so-called Mithraic sort, since, at the end of the speech, when Kasser on behalf of his companions silently nodded to him, Castus seemed to be indicating that some not-quite-definable Pater was awaiting them on the day of Sol's resurrection in the Mithraeum at Brocolitium, and that it would be he—Castus pointed at himself— or some other person, a Corax, a Nymphaeus or a Miles, who would come for them and lead them into the cave, though who precisely was to do that remained unknown as yet, but there would be someone, and that this person would be the leader, the guide, and so saying he raised his arms, fixed his eyes on the ceiling then addressed them, saying: please oblige me by also desiring that we may summon him, as we do, the blushing Sol Invictus, after the becoming manner of Acimenius, or in the form of Osiris the Abrakoler, or as the most hallowed Mithras, and you should then seize hold of the bull's horns under the crags of the Persian Dog, the bull who will take a firm stand, so that henceforth he should follow you, having said which he lowered his arms, bowed his head and added, very quietly: outum soluit libens merito then departed—leave taking, said Korin—the end of the fourth chapter being entirely steeped in puzzles, secrets, enigmas and mysteries, much like the text that followed, an extraordinarily and equally significant part of which was also comprised of such puzzles, secrets, enigmas and mysteries, though all this served to characterize only one of the groups waiting at the Albergueria, there being one recurring image involving some Sephardic and Sicilian brothers in which—whatever the Sephard or Sicilian's occupation, whether he be beggar, printer, tailor or cobbler, whether he be interpreter or scribe in Greek, Turkish, Italian or Armenian, or a money-changer, or a drawer of teeth, or whatever—*never mind*, said Korin—what you plainly saw was that suddenly he stopped being what he was and was transported to *another world*, that suddenly the tailor's scissors or the cobbler's knife ceased moving, the spittoon he was carrying or the *maravedi* he had counted out stood still in the air, and not only for an instant but for a minute or more, and the person, we might say, was lost in meditation—that he would *brood*, said Korin—and had entirely ceased to be a tailor or cobbler or beggar or interpreter and became something completely different, his gaze contemplative, oblivious to the calls of others, and then, since he continued in this state for some time, the person confronting him also fell silent, no longer addressing remarks to him nor shaking him, simply watching the peculiarly transformed countenance before him as it gazed, entranced, into the air, watching this beautiful face and those beautiful eyes—*beautiful face and beautiful eyes*, said Korin—and the manuscript kept returning to this moment as if it too were lost in contemplation, meditative, entranced, suddenly letting the text go and allowing his inner eye to gaze on these faces and eyes, this manuscript, said Korin, of which it was possible to know this much at least, or at least he himself knew this from his first reading of it, and indeed it was the one and only thing he knew about it from the very beginning, that the whole thing was written by a madman, and that was why there was no title page, and why the author's name was missing.

13.

It was getting late but neither of them moved while Korin—his dictionary and notebook in his hand—continued the story complete with explanations without once stopping and the interpreter's lover continued holding the same magazine in her hand, occasionally raising her head from it, sometimes folding it for a moment, but never putting it entirely aside, even when she turned toward the door, or, tipping her head on one side, listened out for something in the air, always returning to it, to the pictures in the black and white pages, with its list of prices for necklaces, earrings, bracelets and rings as they sparkled, colorless, on the cheap paper.

14.

Lewdness, erotica, passion and desire, continued Korin after a short pause for thought in obvious embarrassment before the woman, and explained that he would be misleading the young lady if he pretended they did not exist, if he attempted to keep silent about them or deny that they were an important aspect of all he had been talking about so far, for there was this other vital factor in the final collapse, the collapse, that is to say, of the text whose narrative was drifting toward Rome, for the text was deeply drenched in desire, a fact he simply could not deny on account of what followed, for the Albergueria was packed with prostitutes, and the sentences of the text, when they touched on the various levels of life in the Albergueria were constantly coming up against these prostitutes, and when they did so, he had to tell her straight, the text described them as extraordinarily shameless, the way they hung around the stairs and on landings, lounging in the corridors, or in the lit or darkened nooks of each floor or communicating passageway, nor was the text satisfied with pointing out their commodious breasts and buttocks, their swaying hips and slender ankles, their wealth of hair and the roundness of their shoulders, all of which constituted a colorful, variegated market, but insisted on following them as they picked up sailors, notaries, tradesmen or money-changers, entertained punters from Andalusia, Pisa, Lisbon, and Greece as well as adolescents and lesbians, strolled alongside aged priests who were continually blinking and gazing in terror behind them, lasciviously licking their lips and shooting come-hither glances at a random selection of already aroused customers then vanished into some darkened nearby room, and yes, blushed Korin, the text does indeed draw apart those curtains that should under any circumstances remain closed, and, no, he did not want to go into further detail regarding the subject, simply to indicate that the fifth chapter was unremitting in its portrayal of what went on inside these rooms, describing an infinite range of sexual practices, recounting the vulgar exchanges between whores and their customers, depicting the crude or complex nature of each sexual act, the cold or passionate expressions of desire, desire as it awakens or dies away, and noting the scandalously flexible rates offered for such services, though when it talks of these things it does not suggest that the world in which they happen was corrupt, nor was there anything high-handed or judgmental in its account of them, the text being neither euphemistic nor scatological, but rendered them remarkably methodically or, if he might so put it, with remarkable sensitivity, said Korin spreading his hands, and since this methodical and sensitive manner carried extraordinary power, it sets the tone of the text from the middle of the chapter onward so that whatever new or as yet unmentioned characters are discovered in the Albergueria their positions are immediately established in terms of desire, the first such character being Mastemann, who at this point, and possibly unexpectedly, turns up once more, having had enough of the dangerous and wasteful stillness of the becalmed bay, and is shown leaving a Genoa-bound *coca* and arriving on shore in a rowing boat to take a room on an upper floor of the Albergueria, accompanied by a few servants, yes, Mastemann, Korin raised his voice a little, Mastemann who had reason enough to weigh his decision carefully since he had to take into account the hatred—the *hate*, said Korin—felt by the inhabitants of Spanish-controlled Gibraltar toward Genoans, a hatred that extended to him; just as before, in the earlier episode, when Kasser and his companions first heard from guests arriving at their accommodation, from the first cohort of the *primipilus* at Eboracum, from the *librarius* of the *castrum* at Corstopitum, and finally from the Preatorius Fabrum himself, who had arrived in the seventh week of their sojourn in Britannia, about the hatred felt for the mysterious leader of the Frumentarians, who, it was said, Caesar held in the highest affection, and who was regarded by some as a genius and by others as a monster of depravity, as a man of the highest credentials on the one hand, an underling on the other, but whichever the case, he was referred to by all those dining under the friendly laurel branches of the shared refectory as *Terribilissimus*—the *Most Fearsome*, said Korin—an epithet applied first of all to the Frumentarius, said Korin, those cells of the imperial secret police implanted in the *cursus publicus,* who kept an unblinking eye on absolutely everyone, and were in the confidence of the immortal Hadrian, ensuring that nothing should remain shrouded in the fogs of ignorance, whether in Londinium, in Alexandria, in Tarraco, in Germania or in Athens, wherever, in fact, immortal Rome happened to be at the time.

15.

Kasser was very ill by then—*very ill,* said Korin—and spent most of the day in bed, rising only to join the others for the evening meal, but nobody knew what sort of disease was eating him because the only symptom he exhibited was extreme chill: no fever, no coughing, no pain of any sort, but a cold that continually shook his whole body, his arms and legs, everything trembling all the time, however they stoked the fire up, the two slaves allotted to the task continually feeding the flames, until the place was so hot that perspiration ran off them in rivers, all in vain, for nothing helped Kasser, and he continued to freeze while the doctor from Corstopitum examined him, as did physicians from Eboracum, prescribing various herbal teas, feeding him the flesh of serpents, and in general trying everything they could think of without any of it making the slightest difference, and his three guests, the three agents of the Frumentarius with their all-comprehending web of informants, headed by Mastemann, made him visibly worse, and were, in fact, a decisive factor in his deteriorating condition, so that after the visit of the *Praefactus Fabrium* he no longer rose to take his evening meal but had it brought to him by the others, and even then they couldn't really *talk* to him because he was either trembling so violently under the blankets and pelts that he was incapable of even contemplating conversation, or they found him lost in such a deep well of silence they didn't feel it worthwhile trying to rouse him from it; in other words the evenings—*the nights,* said Korin—passed with few words or in general silence, as did the days, the early and midmornings, in silence or with just a few bare words, Bengazza, Falke and Toót spending the time in composing their reports on the Vallum, and going to the baths in the afternoon, so that they might return to the peace of the villa by dusk, and that was how time passed on the surface, said Korin, or genuinely seemed to, with Kasser inside, shivering in his bed, and the rest writing their reports or enjoying the waters of the baths, though in actual fact they were all cultivating the peculiar art of not mentioning Mastemann, not even pronouncing his name, although the very air was heavy with his presence, with his physical form and history, a history they could glean in detail from the accounts given by the three visitors and one that weighed on their thoughts, so that after another week it had become obvious to them that they were not only keeping silent about him but that they were *waiting* for him, counting on him to act, and were convinced that as the *Magistere* of the *cursus publicus* of Britannia he would seek them out, said Korin, the manuscript being obsessed with the necessity of reminding the reader how they kept watching the events outside the villa, how they trembled when the servants announced the arrival of a guest, but Mastemann did not come to seek them out—*he was not coming*, said Korin—for that was not to happen until the next chapter, when, on the evening of his arrival, he announced himself as the special representative of the *Dominante* of Genoa and, wafting a cloud of subtle perfume around him, requested a place at their table which being granted he gave a curt nod, sat down, briefly examined their faces, then, before they could reveal who they were, set out on an encomium of King John as if he already knew who it was he was dealing with, telling them that in his eyes and in the eyes of Genoa, the king of Portugal was the future, the spirit of the age, *Nuova Europa*, in other words the perfect ruler whose dictates were based not on emotion, interest, or the vagaries of his fate, but on the reason that governed emotions, interest and fate, then having said so, turned his attention to discussion of the Great Tidings, to Colombo whom he referred to now as Signor Colombo and now as "our Cristoforo," and to their utter astonishment, talked of the expedition as of something successfully completed, then ordered some heavy Malaga wine from the landlady for everyone and announced the beginning of a new world—*a new world coming*, said Korin—in which not only Admiral Colombo but the very spirit of Genoa would triumph, and what was more, he raised both his glass and his voice, the all pervasive, all conquering spirit of Genoa, the spirit that, judging by the looks that followed Mastemann's least gesture, Korin explained to the woman, aroused in the lodgers of the Albergueria nothing but intense and the most wholesale hatred.

16.

Should we die, the mechanics of life would go on without us, and that is what people feel most terribly disturbed by, Korin interrupted himself, bowed his head, thought for a while, then pulled an agonized expression and started slowly swiveling his head, *though it is only the very fact that it goes on that enables us properly to understand that there is no mechanism.*

17.

The whores' fit of madness, he continued, could only be explained by the appearance of Signor Mastemann, though no one was clear about the reasons for it at the time because they all missed the most important thing, that Mastemann's presence produced a kind of magnetic field, the power appearing to emanate from his entire being, and it can't have been anything else, for as soon as Mastemann arrived and settled in on an upper level, the Albergueria changed: the ground floor fell silent as never before, silent, until he came down that first evening of his stay and sat down at an impromptu choice of table—that of Kasser's companions as it happened—at which point everything changed, for though life went on nothing was as it had been, so that tailors, cobblers, interpreters and sailors, though they continued where they had left off, all kept an eye on Mastemann, waiting to see what he would do, though what could he have done?—Korin spread his hands—since he simply sat down opposite Kasser's companions, talked, filled his glass with wine, touched his glass to theirs, leaned back and in other words did nothing to suggest that this universal stillness— *this general rigor,* said Korin—might have its origins in him, though one had to admit that it was enough to look at him in order to feel the terror he inspired with his frighteningly pale and immobile blue eyes, his pockmarked skin, his huge nose, his sharp chin and long, delicate, graceful fingers, his cloak black as ebony, especially when its scarlet lining flashed from beneath it, when the words froze in everyone's mouth: *hate and fear,* hate and fear being what he inspired in the tailors, cobblers, interpreters and sailors on the ground floor; though all this was nothing as to the effect he had on the prostitutes, for they not merely trembled before him but were completely beside themselves whenever he appeared, wherever they came across him, the nearest and loveliest girls of Algiers and

Granada immediately running to him and surrounding him, as if drawn by an irresistible magnet, swarming round him as though he had bewitched them, touching his cloak and begging him, please, to come with them, he needn't pay, they whispered in his ear, it could be the entire night, every part of them was his, anything he wanted, they crooned and burst into bubbles of hysterical laughter, jumping up and down, running about, hugging his neck, pulling at him, patting him, dragging him this way and that, sighing and rolling their eyes as if Mastemann's mere presence was a source of ecstasy, and it was perfectly obvious that once Mastemann arrived they had taken leave of their senses, though this meant that the thriving trade that had depended on them very quickly and most spectacularly went bust, for a new age, an *epoch*, had begun in which whores no longer sought financial rewards for their services but sought payment in orgasm instead, though orgasm was not to be had since there wasn't anyone left who could satisfy them, and men advised each other to leave them alone for they would only drain you to the dregs and use you rather than you using them, and everyone knew which way the wind was blowing, that the cause of all this was Mastemann, so that, under the apparent calm, the fear and hatred—*hate under the quietude*, said Korin—grew hour by hour, in a manner very similar to that experienced in Corstopitum, for you could hardly describe it as anything else but fear and hatred, as Bengazza and his companions detected in the general attitude toward the unknown Mastemann, as they heard the depressing accounts of the *primipilus* and the *librarius*, and marked the bitter words of the *Praetorius Fabrum* recalling how adept Mastemann had been at exploiting the well-oiled machinery of the *cursus publicus* ever since it started building up its network of agents, and how people had already feared and hated him then, though they hadn't even seen him, holding him in contempt and shuddering at his name despite the fact that there was no chance of actually meeting him, and it was only Kasser who did not reveal his feelings, said Korin, Kasser who remained inscrutable, without a stated view for he was incapable of saying a word and expressed no opinion either in Corstopitum when the others came to visit him, nor at the table in the Albergueria, where he hardly ever appeared now to take part in conversations, and when he did come, he only sat silently, watching the bay through the window, gazing at the wreath-like sails visible through the fog patches, that ghostly gathering of galleons, frigates and corvettes, the *naviguela, caravelles* and hulks as they waited so that, finally, after eleven days, the wind should begin to rise again.

18.

Castus returned precisely seven days later to tell them that their rhapsodic report on the divine Vallum had been passed to the *Praetorius Fabrum* and that having been delivered their business in Britannia was in fact done, and having done so bowed his head and once again addressed them as an emissary of the *Pater*, telling them that he was doing them an honor by addressing his task to them, the task being that they should follow him to Brocolitia for the sacred feast of *Sol* and *Apollo*, on the day, he raised his right hand, of the great sacrifice and the great feast, where he would see them through the purification ceremony required of those who wished to partake in the glorious day of the killing of the Bull and the rebirth of Mithras, though only Bengazza, Falke and Toót were to make the journey for Kasser was incapable of undertaking it, especially in weather that was, if anything, worse than before, as Kasser told Falke, very quietly, when asked, saying no, it was too late, he was beyond making the attempt, and the others should go without him, asking them to report everything in great detail on their return, and so Bengazza and the others gathered together the cloaks and masks required for the ritual, put on heavy fur coats and, following their instruction to the letter, proceeded without an escort and therefore in the utmost secrecy—and, for the first time in their adventures, without Kasser—setting out on their journey most of which, with a quick gallop and three changes of horse, they managed to complete in one short night despite the icy wind blowing in their faces, which made any kind of gallop a superhuman task, as they told Kasser later, on their return, but they made it in time, that is to say they arrived before dawn in Brocolitia where Castus directed them to the secret entrance of a cave a little to the west of the encampment, though Kasser had the feeling they were hiding something from him and gazed at them with ever greater sadness, not asking, nor expecting them to reveal what it was, but plainly knowing that *something had happened to them on the road,* something that they were keeping quiet about, and all the while their eyes sparkled as they spoke of Mithras's rebirth, of the gushing of the bull's blood, the feast, the liturgy and the *Pater* himself, how inspiring he was and how wonderful, yet Kasser noticed some subtle shadow in their sparkling eyes that spoke of something else, nor was he mistaken in this—*no error*, said Korin—the manuscript was clear on this point, for something did actually happen along the way, at the second stop, between Cilurnum and Onnum, where they had changed horses and drank a little hot mead and where they were suddenly confronted by something they might have anticipated but could not prepare, for as they were about to leave the precincts of the mansion and set out on the road again, a group of horsemen of unknown appearance, but reminiscent, if anything, of Swedish auxiliaries, burst out of the darkness, wearing chain mail, fully armed with *scutum* and *gladius*, who simply rode them down, so they had to dive into the ditch along with all their horses to avoid being killed, the assailants being a cohort in tight formation headed by a tall man in the midst of them, a man without insignia, wearing a long cloak that flowed behind him, who cast the merest glance at them as they clung to the ditch, a glance, that's all, then galloped on with his cohort toward Onnum, but a glance that sufficed to tell Bengazza who it was, and thereby confirm the rumors, for the glance was harsh and stern, though that is not quite accurate enough, said Korin, for stern would not quite do, it was something more like a blend of *seriousness and dourness*, as he put it, the kind of look a murderer gives his victim to inform him that his last hour has come, or, more to the point, Korin tried to sum up, his voice taking on a bitter tinge, it was the Lord of Death they saw in him, *the Lord of Death*, said Korin in English, from the wayside ditch on the road from Cilurnum to Onnum, and the narrative of the Gibraltar chapter merely pauses to point out how in one place it was the terrible distance dividing them and in the other the terrible proximity that frightened Bengazza and his companions, since it is probably superfluous to add, Korin explained, that when Mastemann sat down at the table with them at the Albergueria and embarked on a perfectly normal conversation they were aware of how close they were to such a terrifying face, a face that was more than terrifying, a face that froze their blood.

19.

He preferred Malaga wine, that heavy sweet Malaga, those first few evenings following his disembarkation, evenings he spent largely with Kasser's companions, ordering one flask after another, filling glasses, drinking, then refilling, encouraging the others not to hold back but to go on, have a drink with him, all of them, then, surrounded by his band of lovelorn whores; he talked endlessly—*talk and talk*, said Korin—talked so that no one dared interrupt him because he was talking about Genoa and a power the like of which the world had never seen—Genoa, he said, as if merely to pronounce it was enough, and: Genoa again, after which he rolled off a list of names beginning with Ambrosio Boccanegra, Ugo Vento and Manuel Pessagno, but seeing that these meant nothing to his listeners, he leaned over to Bengazza and quietly asked him if perhaps the names of Bartolomeo, Daniel and Marco Lomellini had a familiar ring; but they didn't for Bengazza, who shook his head—*no, he said*, said Korin—so Mastemann turned to Toót and asked him whether that phrase of Baltazár Suárez in which he says "these are people who consider the whole world not to be beyond their grasp" meant anything to him; but Toót answered in confusion that, no, it meant nothing, in answer to which Mastemann prodded him with his finger, saying that the perfection of the words, "the whole world," told him not only that the world would indeed be theirs, and pretty soon, but that they stood at the threshold of a momentous event, the period of Genoa's greatness, a greatness that would pass in the course of nature, naturally, though *the spirit of* Genoa would remain, and that even after Genoa was dead and gone its engine would continue to drive the world, and if they wanted to know what this Genoan engine consisted of, he asked them and raised his glass so that it caught the light, it was the power generated when the *Nobili Vecchi*, that is the world of the simple trader would be surpassed by the *Nobili Novi*, the trader dealing exclusively in cash, in other words by the genius of Genoa, boomed Mastemann, in which the *asuento* and the *jura de resguardo*, the exchanges and credits, the banknotes and the interest, in a word the *borsa generale*, the building up of the system, would produce an entirely new world where money and all that stems from it would no longer be dependent on an external reality, but on intellect alone, where the only people needing to deal with reality would be the unshod poor, and the victors of Genoa would receive nothing more nor less than the *negoziazione dei cambi*, and, in summing up, said Mastemann, his voice ringing, there would be a new world order, an order in which power was transformed into spirit, and where the *banchieri di conto*, the *cambiatori* and the *heroldi*, in other words roughly two hundred people in Lyon, Besançon or Piacenza would occasionally gather to demonstrate the fact that the world was theirs, that the money was theirs, whether it be *lira, oncia, maravédi, ducats, reale* or *livre tournois*, that these two hundred people constituted the unlimited power behind these things, just two hundred people, Mastemann dropped his voice and swirled the wine about in his glass, then raised it to the company and drained it to the last drop.

20.

Two hundred? Kasser asked Mastemann on their last evening together, and with this the packing—*the wrapping*, said Korin—began, for there was a moment the previous night as they were going up the stairs and heading for their rooms when they looked at each other and without saying a word decided that this was the end, it was time to pack up, there was no point in waiting any longer, for should the News arrive, even if everything should turn out as Mastemann had predicted, they would not be affected by it—*the news was not for them*, as Korin put it—for though they believed Mastemann, and indeed it was impossible not to believe him, his words were as hammer blows to Kasser and over the course of several evenings they were increasingly convinced of the coming into being of this new world, a world born diseased; in other words they had already decided to leave and Kasser's question, that Mastemann in any case had chosen to ignore, was only the *mood music* to all this, said Korin, so that when Kasser repeated the question—two hundred?—Mastemann once again pretended not to hear him though the others did and you could tell from their faces that the time had come, that once a wind sprang up there would be no point in prolonging their stay, and it didn't matter from which of the hoped-for directions the News did arrive, whether from Palos or Santa Fé, or whether they first heard it from one of the people around Luis de Santangel, Juan Cabrera or Inigo Lopez de Mendoza, this new world would be more dreadful than the old—*awful than the old*, said Korin—and Mastemann kept repeating the same message, even on this, their last evening, about how the wine from La Rochelle, the slaves, the beaver-pelts and wax from Britannia, the Spanish salt, the lacquer, the saffron, the sugar from Ceuta, the tallow, the goatskin, the Neapolitan wool, the sponge from Djerba, the oil from Greece and the German timber, all these things would become merely theoretical items on paper, you understand? allusions and statements, and what mattered was what was written on the *scartafaccio* and in the ledgers of the great *risconto* markets, that is what they should pay heed to, for that was what reality would be, he said, and downed another glass of wine; then the next day a bunch of sailors from Languedoc arrived with stories that they had seen a few *magogs* coming down to the sea at Calpe, this being the first sign, soon to be followed by many others, such as the Andalusian pilgrims who turned up one day to report that an enormous albatross was flying low over the surface of the water, so that everyone should recognize that they were no longer becalmed, that the iron grip of the *calma chicha* was loosening, that the lull was over—*the lull is over*, said Korin—and within a few hours delighted servants entered the room where Kasser's companions were lodged, and told the gentlemen who had been locked in there for days, that a wind had sprung up, that sails had been seen to tremble and that ships were moving, slowly at first then with ever greater speed, as the *Cocca* and frigates, the *karaks* and the galleons set off, so suddenly the Albergueria was a hive of activity, seeing which Kasser and his companions also made a start, their backs to Gibraltar, Ceuta before them, Ceuta where, in accordance with their earlier plans and with the preparation of a new navigational map, they should pick up a new commission from Bishop Ortiz, and in other words they knew what was to happen next, as they did at Corstopitum when they took their farewells before they crossed the channel, knowing what would await them on the beach at Normandy—*what comes at the beach of Normandia*, said Korin—and it was only Kasser who didn't know whether he would reach the other side, the others having wrapped him in the warmest fleeces and led him to the dormitory of the *carruca* reserved for their special use by the *cursus publicus*, helping him up and settling him in, then getting on their horses and escorting him in the face of terrible winds, through thick fog that surrounded them at Condercum, past the wolves that attacked them at the bridgehead of the Pons Aelius, then boarding the extremely fragile-looking *navis longa* awaiting them in the Roman harbor to face the enormous waves of a tempestuous sea, moving into the daytime darkness and falling across the shore, the sun in hiding, said Korin, and no light at all, no light whatsoever.

21.

He gazed vacantly for a long time, not saying a word, then took a deep breath indicating that he would close the account for the day, and glanced over at the woman, but for her the story had been finished some time ago and she was leaning back against the wall behind the bed, her head having dropped forward, her hair across her face, fast asleep, and Korin hadn't noticed until now, at the end, that she had had enough of the story, and since there was no need to take elaborate leave he rose carefully from the bed and left the room on tiptoe, returning after a moment's thought, to look out for a piece of rumpled bedding, an eiderdown left behind for them by the movers, and covered the woman with it, then went to his room and, fully dressed, lay down on his own bed but couldn't sleep for a long time, and when he did fall asleep it was in an instant so he had no time to undress or draw the blanket over him, the result of which was that he woke the same way the next morning, fully clothed, his whole body shivering, in the dark, and stood at the window gazing at the vaguely glimmering roofs, rubbing his limbs to warm himself, then sat down on the bed again, turned on the laptop, entered the password, checked that everything was still there on his home page, that he hadn't made any mistakes, any miscellaneous errors, and found no error, so, after performing the few ritual strokes demanded by the format he looked to see the first few sentences of the manuscript on the screen, then turned the computer off, closed it and waited for the eviction to begin, the eviction he said, though it wasn't an eviction that got under way, he said later, but rather a moving in, if he might put it that way, for moving in was what it most resembled, since boxes and packages kept arriving as he stood in the corner of the kitchen by the door with the woman beside him, gawping at the furious activity of the four movers, the head of the household, the interpreter being nowhere in sight, utterly vanished, as if the ground had swallowed him, and so the movers carried on shifting their endless boxes and packages until they covered every inch of available space, at which point the four workmen got the woman to sign another piece of paper then cleared off while they remained standing by the table in the kitchen staring at the upheaval, understanding nothing, until the woman eventually took the nearest package, tentatively opened it, tore the wrapping paper and discovered a microwave oven; and so she continued through other packages, one after another, Korin joining in and unwrapping, using his hands or else a knife, whatever served the purpose, uncovering a refrigerator, he said, a table, a chandelier, a carpet, a set of cutlery, a bathtub, some saucepans, a hair-dryer, and so on until they were done, the interpreter's lover walking up and down among the vast gallery of items, treading over mounds of wrapping paper, wringing her hands and darting panicky glances at Korin who did not respond but carried on walking up and down himself, stopping every so often to lean down, examine a chair, a pair of curtains, or some bathroom taps, checking that they really were chairs, curtains and bathroom taps, then went over to the front door where the workmen had left that purple polyester fabric, opened it up, examined it, and read aloud the writing on it saying *start over again*, and said to himself, this is an enormous length of tape, perhaps it is some sort of game, or prize, since everything was tied round with it, but his remarks meant nothing to the woman who continued marching up and down in the chaos, and this went on until they were both worn out and the woman sat down on the bed and Korin settled beside her as he had done the day before, for it was exactly the same, just as mysterious and worrying as it had been the previous night, or at least, as Korin explained much later, as far as he could judge from the interpreter's lover's look of deep anxiety, which was why everything went exactly the same as the night before, the woman leaning back against the wall behind the bed, casting frequent glances at the open door through which she could see the entrance, leafing through the same magazine full of advertisements, while Korin, in an attempt to divert her attention, picked up the story where he had left off last night, for all was ready, he announced, for the last act, the finale, the ending, and this was the important moment when he could reveal what was hidden there, to tell her about the realization that changed everything, the realization that made him alter all his plans and was, for him, a moment of dizzying enlightenment.

22.

There is an order in the sentences: words, punctuation, periods, commas all in place, said Korin, and yet, and he began swiveling his head again, the events that follow in the last chapter may be simply characterized as a series of collapses—*collapse, collapse and collapse*—for the sentences seemed to have lost their reason, not just growing ever longer and longer but galloping desperately onward in a harum-scarum scramble—*crazy rush*, said Korin—not that he was one of the those ur-Magyar fast-speaking types, said he, pointing to himself, he was certainly not one of them, though no doubt he had his own problems with gabbling and babbling, trying to say everything at once in a single sentence, in one enormous last deep breath, that he knew all too well, but what the sixth chapter did was something altogether different, for here language simply rebels and refuses to serve, will not do what it was created to do, for once a sentence begins it doesn't want to stop, not because— let's put it this way—because it is about to fall off the edge of the world, not in other words as a result of incompetence, but because it is driven by some crazy form of rigor, as if its antithesis—the short sentence—led straight to hell, as indeed it had tended to do with him, but not with the manuscript, for that was a matter of discipline, Korin explained to the woman, meaning that this enormous sentence comes along and starts to egg itself seeking ever more precision, ever more sensitivity, and in so doing it sets out a complete catalogue of the capabilities of language, all that language can do and all it can't, and the words begin to fill the sentences, leaping over each other, piling up, but not as in some common road accident to be catapulted all over the place, but in a kind of jigsaw puzzle whose completion is of paramount importance, dense, concentrated, enclosed, a suffocating airless throng of pieces, that's how they are, that's right, Korin nodded, it was as if— *all the sentences*—each sentence was of vital importance, a matter of *life and death*, the whole developing and moving at a dizzy rate, and that which it relates, that which it constructs and supports and conjures is *so complicated* that, quite honestly, it becomes perfectly incomprehensible, Korin declared, and it's better that it should be so, and in saying this he had revealed the most important thing about it, for the sixth chapter, set in Rome, was inhuman in its complexity, and that was the point, he said, for once this inhuman complexity sets in the manuscript becomes genuinely unreadable—unreadable and, at the same time, unrivalled in its beauty, which was what he had felt from the very beginning when, as he had already told her, he first discovered the manuscript in that far-off archive in distant Hungary, in the time before the deluge, when he had read it right through for the very first time, and he continued feeling this however often he reread it, still experiencing, even today, how incomprehensible and beautiful it was—*inapprehensible and beautiful*, as he put it—though the first time he attempted to understand it all he could make out was that they were standing at one of the gates of the walled city of Aurelianus, at the Porta Appia to be precise, already outside the city, perhaps some one hundred meters from the wall, gathered around a small stone shrine and looking down the road, the Via Appia, as it approaches from the south, straight as a die, and they are just standing there, nothing happening, in autumn or early spring, you couldn't tell which, at the Porta Appia, the door of the Porta being lowered, and, for the moment, just two guards, their faces visible at the arrow-slits of the maneuver room, with the scrub of the plains full of trampled weed on either side of them, a well by the gate with a few *cisiarii*, or vehicles for hire, ranged about it, and that was all he could make out of the sixth chapter, apart from the fact, Korin made a point of pursing his lips, that everything, but everything, was terrifically complicated.

23.

They were waiting by the shrine to Mercury, about a hundred to a hundred and fifty yards from the Porta Appia, Bengazza sitting down, Falke standing and Toót with his right foot on a stone, his arms folded and propped on his knee—nothing else happening, the very image of expectancy—*expectancy in the heart of things*, said Korin, for when the text was examined in greater detail it seemed that time had ceased and history itself had come to an end, so whatever appeared in those huge inflated sentences, whatever new element entered them, none of it led anywhere or prepared the way for anything, it was neither preamble nor closure, neither cause nor effect, simply one glimpsed element of a picture moving at unprecedented speed, a detail, a cell, a chunk, a working part of an indescribably complex whole that stood immobile in those gigantic sentences, to put it another way, said Korin, if he was not mistaken—and he did not wish to mislead—the sixth chapter was ultimately nothing but an enormous inventory, there was no other way to describe it, and the contradictions in it had, from beginning to end, always unnerved him, for what was he to do with those mutually exclusive statements, that were both true yet impossible, and no, no, no he knew he wasn't getting anywhere with it yet that's how it was, he said with a slight smile, the three of them standing there without Kasser, at one end of the Via Appia, watching the road as it approached them from the south, and, as they stand there, the monstrous inventory begins, from Roma Quadrata to the Temple of Vesta, from the Via Sacra to Aqua Claudia, and in one way it really does work, but in another, said Korin, his eyes beginning to burn, it really doesn't, it really does not work at all.

24.

He got up, left the room, then returned a moment later with a big wad of paper, sat down beside the woman, picked up the manuscript and searched through it for a while, then, begging her pardon for just this once having to have the text in front of him, chose a few pages, glancing over them and continued from where he had left off last time, at Rome, and how the road to Rome was filled with slaves, the *libertus* and the *tenuirs*, with makers of staircases and makers of women's shoes, with smelters of copper, blowers of glass, with bakers and workers at brick ovens, with Pisan weavers of wool and potters from Arretium, with tanners, barbers, quackdoctors, water-bearers, knights, senators, and fast on their heels, *accenti, viators, praeca* and *librarii*, then *ludimagisteri, grammatici* and rhetors, flower-sellers, *capsarii* and pastry-cooks, followed by innkeepers, gladiators, pilgrims and, bringing up the rear, *delators*, with *libitinarii, vespillons* and *dissignatori* all coming their way, or rather they had come their way for they were no longer actually coming, said Bengazza looking up the deserted road, while Falke agreed, saying no, because there's no *Forum*, no *Palatinus*, no *Capitol*, no *Campus Martius*, nor is there a *Saepta*, an *Emporium* on the banks of the Tiber, no gorgeous *Horti Caesaris*, no *Comitum* and no *Cura*, nor is there an *Arx*, a *Tabularium*, a *Regia* and no shrine of *Cybele*; no more marvelous temples such as those of Saturnus or Augustus, or Jupiter or Diana, for grass covers the *Colosseum* and the *Pantheon* too; nor is there a Senate to bring in laws, nor is there a Caesar in place, and so on and so forth *ad infinitum*, Korin explained; they just went on saying these things, one picking up where the other left off, the words pouring from them, words about the immeasurable quantity of gifts the earth had bestowed on them, for it brought forth corn, continued Toót, and it gave us firewood and stump-wood by way of the *Vicus Materarius* and honey, fruits, flowers and precious stones by way of the *Via Sacra*, cattle for the *Forum Boarium*, and swine for the *Forum Suarium*, fishes for the *Piscatorium*, vegetables for the *Holitorium*, and oil, wine, papyrus and herbs to the foot of Aventinus and the banks of the Tiber, but there is no incentive for this infinite store of earthly goods to flow in our direction, Bengazza took over, for there is no more life, no more festival, and never again will there be chariot races, or *Saturnalia*, for *Ceres* and *Flora* are forgotten; and there is no *Ludi Romani* to organize, nor *Ludi Victoriae Sullanae* either, for the baths are in ruins, the thermals at *Caracalla* and *Diocletians* are wrecks, and the pipes to carry the water are dry, dry as the *Aqua Appia*, empty as the *Aqua Marcia*, and who cares, said Toót, where Catullus, or Cicero or Augustus once lived, and who cares where those vast, imposing, peerless palaces used to stand or what wine they used to drink there, the *Falernian*, the *Massilian*, the *Chiosi* and the *Aquileian*, it's all the same now, no longer interesting; they no longer exist, no longer flow, nor is there any reason for them to, and that's the mad way it goes on from page to page, said Korin, leafing through a little helplessly, and he, of course, he added, was quite incapable of conveying the tight discipline that drove the whole thing, since it wasn't just a case of one thing after another, because, he should explain, alongside the inventory there was a sense of a thousand other incidental details, for, say a man reading about what the *cisiarii* were doing with their coaches between the *Forum Boarium* and the *Caracalla Thermae*, or some guards closing the gate—the iron bars and the wooden panels—at the *Porta*, then, for example, a pile of ceramic figures in relief glittering between the *Aquae*, the *Saturnaliae* and the *Holitorium*, and the dust settling on the leaves of cypresses, pines, acanthus and mulberry bushes on either side of the Via Appia, and, yes, that's precisely it, sighed Korin, details all and yet all part of a single thing, some cipher engraved in the heart of each long list, so you see, young lady, it isn't just a simple sequence, a row of items on a list, say, of the crowds flowing into Rome, followed by, let us say, the dust on the cypresses and then an endless catalogue of the goods arriving at their depots, and then, for example the *cisiarii*, no, it's not that, but the fact that these are all part of a single monstrous, infernal, all-absorbing sentence that hits you, so you begin with one thing, but then a second thing comes along and then a third, and then the sentence returns to the first thing again, and so on, so the reader's hopes are continually raised, said Korin glancing at the interpreter's lover, so that he thinks he has got some kind of hold on the text, believe me when I say, as I said before, he said, that the whole thing is unreadable, insane!!! and Korin trusted that the young lady understood by now that the whole thing was extraordinarily beautiful, and in fact moved him to an extraordinary degree every time he read through it, moved him deeply, until, about three or so days ago he got to this sixth chapter, until he arrived here, just a few days ago as he was typing up, by which time he had believed that it was finished, that the whole thing was doomed to remain obscure, when, ah yes, then, said Korin, his eyes shining, having typed the first few sentences of the sixth chapter, the manuscript—and there was no other way to put it—opened up before him, for how else could it have been that three or so days earlier he simply found himself with an open door in front of him, and that, wholly unexpectedly, after so much reading, astonishment, effort and agony, he should understand it, and it was as if the room were suddenly filled with a blinding light, and he leapt off the bed into the light and started walking up and down in his excitement, and he kept leaping and walking and understood everything.

25.

He read the enormous, ever longer sentences and typed them into the computer though his mind wasn't on it but somewhere else altogether, he told the woman, so everything that remained of the last chapter of the manuscript practically typed itself and there was still a good deal left, for there remained all the stuff about the journey, the modes of transport, and about Marcus Cornelius Mastemann, who by way of farewell, had decided to call himself *curator viarum*—about the journey, in any case, about how the route needed to be constructed, and in the most painstaking explanations of what was a *statumen*, a *rudus*, the *nucleus* and *pavimentum*, the regulated dimensions of roads, the two obligatory ditches on either side of them and about the positioning of the *crepinides* and the *milliarii*, the rules regarding notices, then about the workings of the *centuria accessorum velatorum*, the famous brigade founded by Augustus for the maintenance of roads, and then the means of transport themselves, about the countless carriages and carts, the *carpentum*, the *carruca*, the *raeda*, the *essedum*, and all the rest including the *birota*, the *petorritum*, and the *carruso*: vehicles on two wheels, the uncovered *cisium* and so forth until only Mastemann remained, or, more accurately, a description of the essential powers and responsibilities of any *curator viarum*, but all this, of course, contained in the central image of Bengazza, Falke and Toót standing by the shrine to Mercury, watching the Via Appia in case anyone appeared on it after all, and so, said Korin, he just kept writing, typing the last sentences into the computer while something completely different was going on in his mind, buzzing away continuously, shuddering, clattering, ticking away as he tried to sum up what it was he had seen in that great blinding light, for where did it all begin, he asked himself, but there, at the point when having left the records office, he took the manuscript home and read and reread it, time again, repeatedly asking himself what was the point of it, that it was all well and good, but what was it, and that this was the first question and the last too, holding within it the seeds of all the other questions, such as, for example, seeing the manuscript employed language what was the manner or pitch of it, what form of address was involved, for it was perfectly clear that it was not addressed to anyone in particular; and if it was not a letter, why it did not respond to the pressure of expectation demanded as a bare minimum by other works of literature; and what was it in any case if not a work of literature, for it was clearly not that; and why the writer employed a mass of amateurish devices while having not a scintilla of fear that he might sound amateurish, and besides that, why, in any case—Korin's agitation was evident in his expression—does he describe four characters with such extraordinary clarity then insert them at certain historical moments, and why precisely one moment rather than another, why precisely these four and not some other people; and what is this fog, this miasma, out of which he leads them time after time; and what is the fog into which he then drives them; and why the constant repetition; and how does Kasser disappear at the end; and what is this perpetual, continuous secrecy about, and the ever more nagging impatience, increasing chapter on chapter, to discover who Mastemann is, and why each episode concerning him follows the same pattern, as does the narrative of the others too; and, most important of all, why does the writer go *completely* mad, whoever he is, whether he is a member of the Wlassich family or not, and how did his manuscript find its way into the Wlassich *fasciculus* if he was not, might it by some accident; in other words, said Korin still sitting on the bed and raising his voice, what, *in the final analysis,* does the manuscript hope to achieve, for there must be some reason for its coming into existence, some cause, Korin kept telling himself whenever he thought of it, some reason for its presence here; and then came the day, hard to say precisely when in retrospect, he couldn't tell precisely now, three days ago or something like that, when suddenly there was light, and in that instant everything became clear, hard as it was to explain why then and not before, though he did think it was right, then, whenever it was, some three or so days ago, if only because he had thought about it for *precisely the right length of time* over the past few months, and because his thinking had taken precisely so much time to mature to a point at which it could at last become clear, and he himself most clearly remembered how, when he was having this experience, this blinding light and understanding thing, his whole heart was filled with a kind of warmth as he was unashamed now to say, if he might so put it, and furthermore it might have been better to begin with this, since it was very likely that this was how it began, and that the clarity could be traced back to this source, this warmth flooding through his heart, not that he wanted to get sentimental about it but that was how it happened, meaning that somebody, a certain Wlassich or other, had decided to *invent* four remarkable, pure, angelic men, and equip these four admirable, floating, infinitely refined beings with the most marvelous thoughts, and if one scanned through the story we are presented with, it seemed he was seeking a point from which he might lead them out of it, said Korin, indeed, he said, his hand trembling and his eyes glowing as if he had suddenly developed a fever, yes, he said, it was a way out that this Wlassich or whatever his name is, was seeking for them, but he could not find one that was wholly airy and fantastical so he sent them forth into the wholly real realm of history, into the reality of eternal war, and tried to settle them at a point that held the promise of peace, a promise that was never fulfilled, though he conjures this reality with ever more infernal power, with ever more devilish fidelity, ever greater demonic sensitivity, and populates it with the products of his own imagination, in vain as it turns out, for their path leads but from war to war, and never from war to peace, and this Wlassich, or whoever it is, despairs ever more of his one-person, amateurish ritual, and eventually goes completely off his head, for there is no Way Out, young lady, said Korin and bowed his head, and this conclusion must be agonizing beyond telling for the person who invented and had fallen in love with these four men—Bengazza, Falke, Toót and the ultimately vanishing Kasser—for they live so vividly in his own heart that he can hardly find the words to tell how he walks, walks up and down in his room with them, how he carries them out into the kitchen then back into his room, because something is driving him, and it is terrible to be so driven like this, young lady, said Korin to the woman, his eyes full of despair, for they have, as you might say, no Way Out, for there is only war and war everywhere, even within himself, and finally, and what's more, now that it is finished and that the whole text is sitting there on his home page, he really doesn't know what awaits him, for originally he had thought, and had made all his plans on that basis, that at the end he could set calmly out on his last journey, but now he must embark with this terrible helplessness in his heart, and he feels this is not the way it should be, that he should think of something, something at all costs, for he can't carry them with him, but should put them down somewhere, but he can't, his head can't cope, he is too stupid, hollow, crazy, and it does nothing but ache, and is heavy and wants to drop off his neck, for there is nothing but pain and he can't think of a damn thing.

26.

The interpreter's lover looked at Korin and quietly asked him in English, *What's there on your hand*, but Korin was so surprised that she said anything at all, and in any case she spoke too fast for him to understand, that for a while he was incapable of answering, just kept nodding and staring at the ceiling as if he were busy thinking, then put the manuscript aside and took the dictionary instead to look up a word he hadn't understood then suddenly slammed it shut and cried out in relief that he had understood, that it was a matter of "what's" and "there" not "Whatser," or what the hell, of course not, no, he nodded, it was clear now: "what is there on your," well, "hand" and he held both his hands out and inspected them but couldn't see anything unusual on them, until it occurred to him what the woman wanted to say, and he sighed and pointed with his left hand to a scar on the right which had been there for ages, an *old thing*, he said in English, not interesting—*no interesting*— the result of an incident a very long time ago, at a time when he felt bitterly disappointed, and he was almost embarrassed to mention it now for the whole disappointment was so childish, but what happened was that he had shot through it—*perforate with a colt*, as he put it, peeking into the dictionary, but it was nothing, it didn't cause him any problems and he had got so used to it he hardly noticed it anymore, though he would carry the mark around for the rest of his life that much was sure, as the young lady most certainly noticed, but what was a much bigger problem was that he had to carry this head around on this weak and aching neck, a neck that was groaning—he pointed to it and started massaging it with his palm and swiveling his head from right to left— under too great a burden, or rather the same problem kept recurring, for after a short transitional period of easement the old agonizing weight returned just as before so that he has felt, particularly in the last few days, as though the whole thing was genuinely ready to drop off, and having said this he stopped massaging and swiveling his head, picked up the manuscript again, shuffling its concluding pages while adding that he couldn't in fact tell where it ended because the text had grown so dense and impenetrable, one couldn't even decide precisely when it was taking place, at what point of history to locate it, for though the earthquake of 402 is mentioned in one bitter monologue, and a few crazy sen-

tences take a melancholy turn in referring to the terrible victory of
the Visigoths, to Geiserich, to Theodoric, to Orestes, to Odoacer
and even, at the end, to Romulus Augustulus, mostly there were
just names, said Korin, spreading his hands, references, flashes, and
the only thing certain was that Rome was dying there at the Porta
Appia, over, over, declared Korin, but was unable to continue because suddenly there was a loud noise outside, the drumming of
feet, a rattling and banging, and some cursing as well—after which
there was not much time left to meditate as to who it was, or what
it was, for the drumming, rattling, banging and cursing soon revealed their source to be a man, bellowing on the staircase, crying
Good evening, darling, a man abruptly kicking the door open.

27.

No need to ask anything, just be happy, the interpreter hesitated
swaying on the step, and while the great weight of bags and
satchels he was carrying might have explained the swaying, for
there were some round his neck and others hung on both shoulders, there could be no doubt about the real reason for his condition, for he was clearly drunk, the red eyes, the slow looks and the
stumbling speech immediately betraying the fact, not to mention
that he was in unprecedented good spirits and wished everyone
else to know it, for when he surveyed the apartment and noticed
the two figures emerging from among all the clutter of boxes
and packages he started laughing so violently that he was quite
unable to stop for several minutes, his laugher self-perpetuating,
leading to more and more laughter until he fell back against the
wall, quite helpless, the drool trickling from his mouth, but still
could not stop himself, and even when, for one reason or another,
he got tired and began to calm down, shouting at Korin and the
woman—what's up? how long you want to keep staring?—can't
you see this mass of bags and satchels I'm carrying—so that they
ran to help relieve him of his load it was still all in vain, in vain to
venture a step forward, for by the time he came to a second step
and had run his eyes over the chaos of boxes and packages, the
laughter seized hold of him again and he carried on laughing,
while choking out the words, *start over again*, in English, pointing at
the mess and falling flat on his face, at which point the woman

went over to him, helped him up and, somehow supporting him, got him over to the inner room where he flopped down on the bed, right on Korin's manuscript, dictionary and notebook as well as on the woman's magazine, gave a grunt and immediately fell asleep, his mouth open, snoring, though his eyes weren't fully closed so the woman did not dare move from where she was for she couldn't be certain that this wasn't a practical joke he was playing on them, a fact they never found out, because he was awake again, that is if he had really slept, a few minutes later and was bellowing once more—*start over again*—though this might have been a joke since he kept looking at the woman with a mischievous look on his face, eventually telling her to come closer, he wouldn't bite her, don't be afraid, let her sit down beside him on the bed and stop all that quivering because he'd smack her one if she continued like that, couldn't she understand that the days of their poverty were over, and that from this time on she too should behave as though she had a few nickels to rub together, for nickels there were now, he declared, sitting up on the bed, though he couldn't tell, he winked at her, whether she had noticed the fact, but their lives were changed in the blinking of an eye since he'd got his act together, since he'd gone down to Hutchinson's and signed up for the "start over again" deal in which they change everything in a single day, replacing old things with new, and true enough he had exchanged all the old shit cluttering up the place and here it was, all filled up with the new, because, by God, did he need a change, and it needed a stroke of genius like the Hutchinson's offer at Hutchinson's store, an idea so brilliant in its simplicity that it simply said: rid yourself of this shit at a day's notice, of every little trace of it, and completely re-equip yourself in the space of a day, and as soon as that was done then you could really *start*, in order to do which you need nothing more than to pick a convenient moment for the change, and he did find such a moment and did change, and not a moment too soon, for everything here was going downhill all too fast and he had had enough of counting dimes, wondering if he had enough change to buy something from the Vietnamese downstairs; enough, he had decided: he had made the decision, took hold of himself and had yanked himself out of the mire, changed and seized the moment of opportunity, that was the shortest, most efficient way he could put it, he said, stumbling over his words, and now, he sprang from the bed and started toward the door, he would find Korin and they would, he raised his voice, celebrate, so hey, where is our little Hunkie hiding, he bellowed into Korin's room, as a result of which Korin quickly emerged and said, Good evening Mr. Sárváry, but he was already being dragged away, the interpreter joyfully demanding to know where the damned bag was, then, after a cursory search, finding it himself by the front door, pulling out a couple of bottles, he raised them high in the air and shouted in English once more: *start over again*, so the woman had to fetch three glasses, a none too easy task, for first they had to look through the mess to find the boxes with glasses in them, but when they eventually did so the interpreter opened a bottle and poured half into the glasses and half on the floor, then raised his own glass to the alarmed Korin who was desperately trying to smile, saying, *To our new lives!* concluding the toast by clinking glasses with the cowering woman and declaring *And let bygones be bygones!* after which he made a sweeping gesture, dropped his glass without noticing it, and simply gazed into the air to signal that he was about to make a ceremonial announcement, a signal that was followed by a long period of silence eventually broken by nothing more than a simple: *that's over, that's over*, then he dropped his arms, his eyes cleared for a second, he shook his head, shook it again, asked for a new glass, filled it, ordered the woman to come closer, put an arm round her shoulder and asked her if she liked champagne but did not wait for an answer, pulling from his pocket a small package that he placed in her hand, tightening his grip on her at the same time, then leaned closely into her face, looked in her eyes and, in a whisper, asked her whether she liked the good life.

28.

He had been traveling by taxi for days, just as he was now, on his way home, drunk and carrying masses of stuff, the backseat entirely filled with it as was the trunk that he had packed right up before getting in, the one thing he didn't know, he said to the driver, being how the hell he was going to get all this up to the top floor, for he couldn't see how it could be done since it was too much for one man, you see? and so saying he lifted one of the bags, saying, this is caviar, and not just any old caviar but Petrossian Beluga, and this is Stilton cheese, and this thing is some kind of preserve, and, he peeked in deeper, what's this, ah yes, bagel with salmon cream cheese, and see this? he asked, grabbing another package off the floor, this is champagne, Lafitte, the most expensive brand, and cultured strawberries from Florida, and this, he searched around among the pile of paper bags, is Gammel Dansk you know, and then there's chorizo and herring and a couple of bottles of Bourgogne wine, best in the world, world famous, so he hoped he understood, the interpreter told the taxi driver, that there would be a big party at home tonight, in fact the biggest party of his life, and did he know what they were celebrating, he asked leaning closer to the grille so the driver should hear him over the noise of the engine, because it wasn't a birthday or a name-day, not a christening, no, no, no and no, he'd never guess because there were few people in New York who could celebrate what he was celebrating, and that thing was courage, his own personal courage, the fact, he pointed to himself, that he took the correct steps at the correct time, that he didn't shit himself, he never wavered when the decision had to be made, asking himself whether he dared or not, but went and decided without a second thought, and dared do it, and not just at any moment but at precisely at the best, most appropriate moment, not one moment too soon, not a moment too late, but when the moment was dead right, and that is why this night would be the celebration of his courage, and at the same time the decisive prelude to the re-launching of a great artistic career, and this was why they'd all be drunk out of their minds tonight, he could faithfully promise that, and the two of them could drink to that right now for he had a drop of something on his person somewhere that would do, and so saying pulled a flat bottle of bourbon from his pocket that he slipped through the driver's grille and the driver took it, licked the bottle's lip then, nodding and laughing silently, returned it to the interpreter, who said, OK, OK, if you want more just say the word, they could finish the bottle, there were more where that came from, the whole cab was full of goodies, and the only thing he didn't know was how in God's name he was going to get it all upstairs, all this stuff, he shook his head grinning, no, he couldn't imagine it was all to be carried up to his apartment, but actually, he had suddenly had an idea, like how would it be if they did it together for an extra dollar or two, seeing the cab wouldn't run away, and the driver smiled and nodded, fine, and he did in fact help carry but only to the bottom of the stairs, that much he agreed to, but no further, not up the stairs themselves and he laughed silently again and kept nodding, but eventually said he had to be getting on so he received only one dollar and the interpreter cursed him vigorously for his pains while struggling up the stairs a good many times until finally it was all piled up at the top, and it felt so good then kicking the door open, he told the woman next morning, he in bed, she standing by the door, it was so good to stand there watching her and the little Hunkie stare at him among that vast pile of boxes, packages, satchels and bags without the faintest idea what it was about, that he forgot his fury and would happily have hugged them, but maybe that was what he actually did, didn't he? before unpacking a table and two chairs, and, he was pretty sure, sitting Korin down opposite him, putting a couple of champagne bottles before him, switching to Hungarian and explaining to him how he should lead his life, how he should not go on like an idiot, that he should stop wasting his time and so on, though his listener didn't seem to be listening to all this good advice but only wanted to know where the Hungarian quarter was, the area that he, the interpreter, had told him was the best source of paprika salami in New York, and that seemed to be the most important thing to him because he could swear this was what he kept asking about, that place he thought was above Zabar's deli round about 81st or 82nd Street, but he wanted to get the street just right, and so it went on for ages, but he hadn't the foggiest idea why now, or indeed yesterday evening, when he just wanted to tell him what to do should he ever come to a crossroads where he had to make a choice, and how, if he did come to one, he should be brave and trust to his instincts: courage, he said, it was the importance of courage he tried to impress upon him, giving a broad smile as he lay in bed and stuffed his head into his pillow, but the guy had gone on muttering something like, Mr. Sárváry, Mr. Sárváry, and so the time passed, him saying he had done what he had set out to do and a lot of stupid things like that in his usual fashion, and—he had just remembered—that he then paid what was owing on the rent and finally, or so he thought, dipped into his pocket, searched through the pocket of his trousers, brought out all the money he had left, saying it had to be in there, and had asked him, that is to say the interpreter, to pay the provider an advance that would ensure permanent maintenance of his site, and, he even had some glimmering that at the end they kissed each other—he snorted with laughter into his pillow remembering this—and had sworn themselves to eternal friendship, or so he thought, but beyond that he couldn't remember a thing, so leave him alone now, he had a splitting headache with a bucket of snot for brains, leave him be, he just wanted to sleep now, sleep a bit, and if he's not here he's not here, who cares, but the woman just stood in the doorway crying and kept repeating, he's gone, he's gone, he's left all his things behind, but he's gone, his room is empty.

29.

In the corner opposite the bed the TV was on, a brand-new, large-screen, remote-controlled, two-hundred-and-fifty channel SONY MODEL, with the sound turned down but the screen was alive, the images continually running on a loop, the charming smiling man and the woman, and as the diamond show moved toward its conclusion the set darkened then flickered into life again, back to the beginning once more, the screen fading then brightening so that the room too began to pulse and twitch with the neurotic light, while the interpreter lay fast asleep, his legs spread out, with the woman beside him, turned away from him toward the window, on her side and still wearing her blue terry cloth bathrobe, having kept it on because she was cold, the interpreter having dragged all the covers off her this first night, so that she remained wide awake, unable to sleep for the excitement, on her side, her knees drawn up to her stomach, her eyes open, hardly blinking, while using her right hand under the pillow to support her head and extending the other arm along her body, her fingers bent, clutching a small box, gripping it tightly and never letting go, gripping it in sheer joy, staring straight ahead in the neurotically pulsing blue light, looking straight ahead and hardly blinking.

VII • TAKING NOTHING WITH HIM

1.

He did not look back once he set off but walked along the icy pavement toward the Washington Avenue stop, never glancing back over his shoulder, not, he explained later, because he had resolved not to but because everything now was truly behind him and nothing in front of him, only the icy sidewalk, and nothing inside him either except of course the four figures he was dragging with him toward Washington Avenue, that is to say Kasser and his companions; and that was all he remembered of that first hour after leaving the house on 159th Street, except the early dawn when it was still dark, with hardly anyone on the street, and the effort of slowly absorbing all the events of the previous night as he proceeded down the first two hundred yards or so along the ice, the way his savior, Mr. Sárváry, eventually fell silent after the great celebration and the countless toasts to their eternal friendship, the moment when he was free to return to his room, close the door and flop down on his bed and decide that he would take nothing with him, and, having decided that, closed his eyes; but sleep did not come, and later when the door quietly opened and there stood Mr. Sárváry's young lady, Korin's faithful listener through all those long weeks, who padded over to the bed quietly so as not to wake him, for he pretended to be deeply asleep, not wanting to have to say goodbye, since what could he say about where he was going, there was nothing to say, but the young lady hovered by his bed for a very long time, no doubt watching him, trying to tell whether he was really asleep or not, then, because he gave no sign that he was not, she squatted down beside the bed and very gently stroked his hands, just once, so lightly she was hardly touching him, his right hand that is, said Korin, showing the hand to his companion, the hand with the scar, and that was all, having done which she left as silently as she had come, and there was nothing to do after that but wait with as much patience as he could for night to be over, though that, alas, was very difficult, and he clearly remembered constantly checking the clock—quarter past three, half past three, a quarter of five—then he rose, dressed, washed his face, went to the toilet to do what he had to do there, and then a thought had suddenly occurred to him and he stood up on the seat to sneak a look at the sachets, the story being, he explained, that he had earlier discovered a hiding place behind one of the tiles that was full of little sachets containing a fine white powder and had immediately guessed what it might be, and that now he wanted to take another peek at them though he had no idea why, perhaps it was only curiosity, so he took down the tile again and found—not the packets but a vast amount of money, so much that he quickly put the tile back, and scurried into the apartment so as not to be seen by anyone on the lower floors, specifically by the person who had been depositing things in the toilet, so, having sneaked back, he closed the front door quietly behind him, folded the bedclothes in his room, piled them tidily on the chair he had positioned by the bed, looked round for the last time, saw that everything was precisely where it had been, the laptop, the dictionary, the manuscript, the notebook as well as little things like his few shirts and some underwear which would not need washing again, then left taking nothing with him only his coat and five hundred dollars; in other words there were no great tearful farewells, said Korin shrugging, and why should there be, why should he upset the young lady when it was certain that it would hurt her to see him leaving because they had got so used to each other, so no, it wasn't a good idea, he said to himself; he'd go the way he came, then he stepped out into the street and really there was absolutely nothing in his head except Kasser and the other three, and the sad thing was he had nowhere to take them.

2.

He clicked on the file, titled it *War and War*, gave it a proper file name, saved it, checking first that the address was working, then pressed the last key, switched the machine off, closed it, and carefully put it down on the bed, and having done so was quickly out of the house, running down the sidewalk in a panic with no idea where he was going, but then stopped, turned and set off in the opposite direction, as fleet-footed as before and, being just as uncertain, stopping once more some two hundred yards down the road to massage his neck and swivel his head before looking first ahead and then behind him as if seeking someone he failed to find, for it was early and there was hardly anyone on the street, and those few he saw were far away, a couple of blocks off at least, around Washington Avenue, with only some homeless under a mound of garbage directly opposite him on the other side of the road and a very old blue Lincoln turning out of 159th Street getting into second or third gear and passing him on its way back—but where to go now, he wondered, at a complete loss, just standing there, and you could see that he knew the answer to the question but had forgotten it, so he fiddled with a paper handkerchief in a pocket of his coat, cleared his throat, and poked his toe at an empty pack of Orbitos lying on the hard snow, but since the paper had almost completely come to pieces, it was hard work shifting it: still, he persisted and eventually succeeded to the extent that the pack turned over, and while he was poking the thing, clearing his throat and fiddling with the paper handkerchief in his pocket, his eyes darting now this way, now that, it is possible that he remembered where he wanted to get to.

3.

Red 1 and Red 9 were equally fine for him since they both ran from Washington Avenue to Times Square where he would have to switch to the black line by means of which he could get to Grand Central and the green line that would take him to the Upper East Side, since he wanted to get there as soon as possible, Korin explained to his companion, having gleaned from his landlord the previous night that there was a Hungarian quarter in New York, for that was when he decided that he would buy the gun there, since, after all, not speaking English, he realized that he needed to be instructed in Hungarian, which was why his landlord's mention of it in his monologue came at such a handy moment, for he didn't feel he could ask him, having already bothered him so much, and as for others, well, he didn't have the English and was therefore constrained to turn to a Hungarian to whom he could clearly explain his requirements and discover where the business might be arranged, for the language problem left him with no alternative, he immediately realized, but to find a Hungarian speaker, but once he found a seat opposite a large black woman on the Red 9 and began to examine the subway map above the woman's head, he decided that he would make the journey between Times Square and Grand Central on foot, for it was not clear to him from the map what the black line connecting the two signified, and it was chance, the merest chance that decided things, not he himself, for he simply sat opposite the huge black woman and recognized that however long he studied the subway map he would not succeed in working out what the black line between the green and red routes actually meant, so it had to be on foot, he decided, and that's how it turned out though he had no inkling what curious farewell gift the inscrutable will of fate had reserved for him on this, his last day, not the faintest idea, he repeated enthusiastically, but he had got thus far, he explained, everything on this last day worked out; he made smooth progress toward his ultimate goals, for it was as if something had taken him by the hand and was leading him there by the most direct route once he got off at Times Square, emerged from the subway and starting walking eastward, directly toward the tower he might almost say, immediately noticing that everything around him seemed to speed up, the whole world accelerating in extraordinary fashion as soon as he reached the street and made his way among the skyscrapers, pressing through dense crowds and gazing at the buildings, craning his neck, until it struck him that there was no point in seeking to discover a meaning in these buildings because however hard he tried he would not, said Korin, though it was a meaning he had been constantly aware of from the moment he first glimpsed the famous skyline of Manhattan from the window of his cab, a meaning of peculiar significance that he sought day after day each night about five P.M. after he had finished work and set out to walk the streets, particularly Broadway—trying in vain to give his thoughts some shape, first by meditating on the fact that the whole thing reminded him keenly of something, then by sensing that he had been here before, that he had seen this world-famous panorama, those breathtaking skyscrapers of Manhattan somewhere, but no, it was no good, the walks were all in vain, it was useless trying, he could not solve the puzzle, and, as he told himself this very dawn walking down toward the tower and the bustle of Times Square, he would have to leave without having found out, without having discovered or stumbled across the answer, without the least notion that in just a few minutes he would understand, said Korin, that in a few bare minutes he'd realize and achieve what he had set out to do, and that this would happen only a few minutes after setting off among the skyscrapers toward Grand Central Station.

4.

We pass things without any idea of what it is we have passed, and he didn't know, said he, whether his companion knew the feeling, but that was exactly what happened to him, in the most literary sense, for he had no idea what it was as he passed it, and only a few steps later, once he had slowed down, did he vaguely suspect something, and then he had to stop, stop right there and stand stock still, at first without knowing quite what the sensation was related to, racking his brains to find out the cause, but then he turned to retrace his steps and as he spun round he found himself in front of a huge store, the one he had just passed, a store full of television sets, several racks high and some twenty meters long of nothing but TV sets, all turned on, all working, every one of them showing a different program; and all this, he felt, was trying to tell him something very important though it was far from easy discovering what it was or why these advertisements, film clips, blond curls and western boots, coral reefs, news channels, cartoon films, concert excerpts and aerial battles should have anything to say to him, and first he stood puzzling in front of the display, then tried walking up and down in front of it still mystified, until, suddenly, having taken a step closer and leaned over, in the second row from the bottom, roughly level with his eyes, he noticed an image, a medieval painting, which must have been, there was no doubt about it, the thing that had stopped him as he passed, though he still didn't know why, so he leaned closer still and saw it was a work by Breughel, the one showing the building of the Tower of Babel, an image that, being a history graduate, he knew very well, the camera focusing on the detail where King Nimrod, stern, serious and very fearsome looking, arrives at the site, with his moon-faced chief adviser beside him escorted by a few guards and there are some stone carvers working in the dust in front of them, the film being probably some kind of documentary, said Korin, that at least being his impression, though, naturally enough, he could not hear the commentary through the thick glass of the window, only the racket of the street in which he stood, the sirens, the squealing of brakes and the blast of horns; and then the camera began to pull slowly away from the foreground and Nimrod, and to take in more and more of the picture until Korin stood facing the landscape and the enormous tower with its seven infernal levels, unfinished, abandoned and damned, straining toward the sky at the end of the world, and, ah now he understood! Babel! he declared aloud, ah if only everything was so simple: Babel and New York! for had he understood this he would not have had to traipse about the city all those long weeks seeking a solution to the mystery—and he continued staring at the picture, stopping by the window display until he noticed that a big adolescent boy in a leather jacket kept staring somewhat challengingly at him, when he felt compelled to move on, and doing so, step by step, he felt a sort of calm settling over him and he carried on toward Grand Central Station while the stores by either side of him began to open up, chiefly the smaller greengrocers and delicatessens at first, but a little bookstore too, the owner being in the act of rolling out a bookcase on castors and the case full of cut-price books before which Korin stopped, having plenty of time for he had never in his life felt so free, and looked through the brightly colored volumes as he always did on his five o'clock strolls whenever he passed such a store, picking out one book with a familiar picture on the cover, the title of the book being Ely Jacques Kahn, and, in smaller letters below it, the words New York Architect, with the 1931 foreword by Otto John Teegen, and masses of black-and-white photographs of big New York buildings, precisely the ones he had seen in the course of his walks, images of the same gaggle of New York skyscrapers—the *scraper-scape*, he muttered to himself, and the word *scraper-scape* began to ring in his ear—and then he turned over a few pages, not systematically page by page, but in a vague arbitrary fashion, jumping from the end of the book to the early pages, then from the early pages to the later ones, when, suddenly, on page 88 he came upon a photograph labeled "View from East River, 120 Wall Street Building, New York City" at which point, he said that afternoon in the Mocca restaurant, it was like being struck by lightning, and he went back to the beginning and leafed through the whole book properly, from "Insurance Building, 42-44 West Thirty-Ninth Street Building" through "Number Two Park Avenue Building," "N.W. Corner Sixth Avenue at Thirty-Seventh Street Building," "International Telephone and Telegraph Building," "Federation Building" and "S.E. Corner Broadway and Forty-First Street Building" right through to the end, when he checked the name on the front of the book once more, Ely Jacques Kahn, and again, Ely Jacques Kahn, then raised his eyes from the book jacket and sought the nearest such building in the direction of the Lower East Side and Lower Manhattan, and could not believe his eyes, he said, simply didn't want to believe his eyes, for he immediately found it: there stood the building in the book, as well as others whose pictures he had just looked at, and though there was undoubtedly some relationship between them, there was *at the same time an even greater relationship between them and the Tower of Babel as painted by Breughel*, and then he tried to find other such buildings, rushing down to the next intersection to see better, or rather to get a better view of Lower Manhattan, and discovered them immediately, and was so shaken by his discovery that, without thinking, he stepped off the sidewalk into the crosswalk and was almost knocked down, cars hooting at him while he continued to stare at Lower Manhattan even as he leapt back, mesmerized by the view, it having struck him that *New York was full of Towers of Babel*, good heavens, imagine it, he said the same afternoon in a state of high excitement, here he had been walking right amongst them for weeks on end, knowing that he should see the connection, but had failed to see it, but now that he had seen it, he announced with great ceremony, now that he had got it, it was clear to him that this most important and most sensitive city, the greatest city in the world, the center of the world, had deliberately been filled by someone with Towers of Babel, all with seven stories, he noted, his eyes screwed up, examining the distant panorama, and all seven stories stepped like ziggurats, a theme with which he was very well acquainted, he explained to his companion, having attended university some twenty years ago as a student of history, later a local historian, for they were dense with references to the towers of Mesopotamia, and not just the Babel of Breughel, but also to material from Koldewey too, the German amateur archeologist's name being Robert Koldewey, as he recalled perfectly clearly even now, the man who excavated Babel and Esagila and discovered Etemenanki, partly uncovered it and even made a maquette of it, so it was no wonder that when he arrived at John Fitzgerald Kennedy Airport, got into the taxi and took a first look to see the famous panorama that something immediately rang a bell with him, it was just that he didn't know what it was, couldn't put a name to it, though it was there lurking in some corner of his aching brain, reluctant to appear, hiding away, he said, until today, and frankly he didn't understand the way it all suddenly came together on this, his last day, but it was as if it had been all laid out before him and always had been, because ever since dawn he had this feeling that someone was taking him by the hand and leading him on, and that this book about Ely Jacques Kahn was, so to speak, thrust into his hands; for why on earth would he pick up this book rather than any other, and why should he have stopped precisely before that particular bookstore, why walk down that very street, why walk at all—oh, it was quite certain, Korin nodded smiling in the Mocca restaurant, that they were there with him, leading him, holding his hand.

5.

A king among stone carvers: the idea shocked everyone in Babylon, for it meant that whatever laws had governed them so far were now invalid and that there was no longer any foundation on which order might be built, and, this being so, from now on it would be the unpredictable, the sensational and the senseless that ruled their lives, and yet he walked among the stone carvers as any man might do, treading the length of the Marduk road, through the Ishtar Gate, over to the hill opposite, acting against all the ruling conventions and thereby advertising the fact that power was no longer with the empire, for leaving the palace without the appropriate retinue and the presence of the court, with just four guards as escort and, of course, the fearsome moon-faced chief adviser at his side was more than Babylon could bear, and when the chief adviser cried, The King, and the armed escort carelessly echoed the words, the stone carvers on the hillside thought someone was playing a joke on them and did not even rise to their feet and stop working at first, but when they saw it *really* was the king they threw themselves on the ground facedown until the adviser, communicating the king's wishes, ordered them to rise and to continue what they were doing, for such were the king's commands, he said, the king's expression stern and frightening, but somehow disturbing too, the eyes faintly idiotic, the eyes of a man bearing the authority of Nimrod's robes and scepter, *but among workmen*, and that's how the priests of Marduk knew that the last judgment must be near though sacrifices continued undisturbed on the altars, but there was the king, engaged in direct conversation with the stone carvers on the hillside, and news of this apocalyptic event quickly spread and terrified even those who had given themselves over to fierce pleasures and the evils of forgetfulness behind the thick but now useless walls of the city; and the four of them threw themselves on the ground once more but none of them dared answer such questions as they did not understand, for their hearts were in their mouths, loudly drumming in fear that the mighty Nimrod was standing before them in an act of madness, that the king himself was asking them whether the stone was hard enough, and they went on nodding, saying, yes, yes, hard enough, but the king gave no sign of having heard their answer and stepped away to join the guards who were openly grinning, then stood on a ledge that offered a perfect view with a deep chasm at his feet, the vast tower of Etemenanki rearing up before him on the far side, and stood immobile, a dry scalding breeze above the river blowing directly into his face; so Nimrod watched the builders at work, laboring at the enormous monument, that impossible structure rising before him, almost ready now, a perfect silence at his back, the hammers and chisels frozen in the workmen's hands as he surveyed his creation, Nimrod's challenge to the world, a triumph, a work of genius, an edifice of godless majesty designed to confront time itself—that, at least, was how Nimrod imagined it, said Korin to his new friend, for what else could it be, as they sat down for a drink at the Mocca restaurant, what else could it be if we are to believe Breughel rather than Koldeway, and he did believe Breughel in preference to Koldeway, for that was what he had assumed from the beginning, that Breughel's painting was correct, since after all one had to, in fact absolutely had to assume something, for there had to be a reason for him being in New York, and there had to be some mysterious guiding hand to lead him here so that he might accomplish his own humble task and receive a clear explanation of all these references to Babel, and why should all this be as it was, smiled Korin, his head swaying, if not to enable us to comprehend that this is what God's absence leads to, to the production of a miraculous, brilliant and utterly captivating kind of human being who is incapable, and always will be incapable, of just one thing, that is of controlling that which he has created, his own feeling being, he declared, that it was true, that there really was nothing more miraculous than man, for think, to take a random example, of computers, of satellites, of microchips, motor cars, medicines, televisions, of unmanned stealth bombers, a list so long we could continue it forever, and this was probably the reason and explanation for his own presence in New York, so that he should be able to sort the essential from the banal, in other words to understand that *that which is too big for us is altogether too big*, and having understood this to convey this understanding to others, because, and he couldn't emphasize this strongly enough, he, Korin, had to point out the true state of affairs, and he did not merely imagine but felt most clearly that something had taken him by the hand and was leading him.

6.

Oh yes, they knew Gyuri Szabó, the proprietor of the Mocca remarked as she was chatting with her friend on the phone that night, having got home, showered, turned on the TV and pulled the phone over, and he had taken the opportunity of bringing over some lunatic, giving him a table to sit at, yes, they let Gyuri in, he is no problem, he just sits himself down at the table and shifts about in his chair a bit, he's been there a week now among the customers, a quiet well-behaved decent enough kind of guy, with, yes, some strange ideas, but he was welcome to sit there, the problem was the other one, the one with a face like a bat, they never had this screwball before, the woman exclaimed, and he did all the talking, producing such a torrent of nonsense, she cried, well, you have no idea, and they drank Unicum with beer, the Hungarian way, eleven shots each, from four in the afternoon to two in the morning, so you may imagine, she said, the bat-faced one talking and talking and Gyuri Szabó listening, though he was drunk too just like the other guy, nor was there any point in telling him to behave himself when he came out of the john, they just went on as before though she should have closed up hours ago, the cash long having been dealt with, and still they didn't want to go, so in the end she had to say something, to turn off the light, which was something she hated doing as it reminded her of being back in Hungary where they do this lights-off-all-out business all the time, but there was nothing else she could do, she had to turn the lights off a couple of times until, thank heaven, they finally noticed, got to their feet and went out, though it was Gyuri Szabó she was sorry for, him being the son of old Béla Szabó from his second marriage, she told her friend, the one who was in charge of a department at Lloyds, yes, old man Béla's boy, yes and we always thought he was the artistic type, in other words a real decent guy, all heart, but the other man she knew absolutely nothing about, and to be honest, she was genuinely frightened of him, because you never knew what that kind of person was thinking or what he'd do next, though, truth to tell, he can't have been thinking much in particular and in any case, he paid, thank God, and, true, he upset a couple of chairs on his way out, but at least he was leaving and hadn't done anything to upset anyone, but as he left he complained of feeling sick saying he had to throw up, and the other guy said, go ahead, throw up, so Korin went a little way down into the doorway by the entrance and vomited and vomited until he felt better, then feeling fine, he went straight over to the cart to help push it even though his friend told him not to bother as he was used to doing it himself and he'd do it by himself this time too, but Korin paid no attention to him since that was what the man had told him the first time that afternoon when he had stopped a block away, down 81st Street, and Korin had asked whether he could help, at which point his accent gave him away, and they both immediately realized that the other was Hungarian, this being pretty simple with Korin's *can I help you*, and not much more difficult with the other's *no thanks*, Korin having spent several hours summoning up the courage to talk to someone without succeeding in finding either the courage or indeed anybody who looked Hungarian until suddenly he noticed a strange figure and was astonished to see that this figure was in the process of leaning a full-size store dummy against a bus stop on 81st Street, arranging it so it looked as though the dummy were waiting for a bus, having done which he chained the dummy's hands and feet to the bus stop and turned its head to face the oncoming traffic, raising its left arm a little so it would seem that the dummy was hailing a bus, after which he returned to his cart, ready to pull it further up the street, which was the point at which Korin first approached him and asked him if he needed a push for if he did he would be glad to help.

7.

He was used to doing this alone and would like to continue alone, the man told him, but having said it allowed Korin to help even though it was clear he had no need of it, for the plastic hands and feet protruding from under the loose tarpaulin cover of the cart showed that the whole thing was full of store dummies and would therefore weigh very little; but Korin did not let that discourage him and began pushing the back of the cart while the man got hold of the pole at the front and pulled it, the whole lot rattling and giving a considerable jolt each time there was a bump in the icy snow beneath, so that dummies began to slide off right and left and Korin or the man had to thrust them back among the rest; and so they pushed and pulled and pushed and pulled and within a few minutes had gotten pretty well used to it, arriving in the busy traffic of Second Avenue where Korin finally dared to ask whether the other, by any chance, could tell him where the Hungarian quarter was because he was looking for it, to which he received the answer that they were in the Hungarian quarter right now; in which case, Korin continued, perhaps the other might help him with some business, the business, Korin cleared his throat, that is, of buying a gun; an inquiry greeted by the other with a solemn echo—ah, gun—his face suddenly serious, telling him a gun could be bought almost anywhere, and this seemed for a while to conclude the conversation, neither of them saying a word until the man applied the brakes, dropped the pole on the stones, turned round and asked Korin directly to tell him what it was he was actually after, in response to which Korin repeated, a gun, a gun of any kind, no matter if it be big, small or of middling size, just a gun, and that he had five hundred dollars to spend on it, that sum comprising all his money, and that he was prepared to spend it all on a gun, just a gun; not that he wanted to frighten the other man with all this, he hastily added, for he meant absolutely no harm and would be quite happy to tell the whole story but wasn't there somewhere they could sit down and eat and drink something while he told it, he asked, and looked around for some such place because he had, after all, been out on the street since dawn and was chilled through to the bone, so a little warmth would be most welcome, and some food and drink too, and yes he'd love to drink something; but the other man would not let the matter rest and examined him further and at some length on the subject of the gun, Korin responding with further invitations to go and eat, pressing the man to be his guest and telling him that all would be revealed once they were sitting down together, so the man hemmed and hawed and said there were plenty of restaurants nearby and within a few minutes they were sitting in the Mocca, its walls lined with mirrors and decorative crockery, its ceiling papered in relief using some synthetic material, with just three melancholy looking guests at the tables and the crow-faced proprietress wearing oval glasses, her hair cut froufrou fashion, who suggested they eat something as well as drink, and though she did this in the most friendly manner only Korin took her advice and drank a goulash soup with pinched noodles, the other man refusing anything, merely taking one of the sugar packets provided on the table, tearing the end off and pouring it down his throat, flicking at the packet with his index finger to get all the sugar out, repeating this a few times in the course of their conversation; all he wanted, he said, being something to drink, which indeed they both did, downing one Unicum with beer, followed by another Unicum with beer, and another and so on while Korin talked and the man listened.

8.

The dummy sat by itself at a table near the counter and looked so convincing one might have thought it was a real person sitting there though it was of the same plastic material as the other dummies in the cart and as life-sized as those outside, and yet, in the light of the diner, its pink skin seemed more transparent and its gaze more meditative than theirs as it sat with its legs tucked under the table with perfect propriety, a propriety it was forced to exercise in order that it should be able to sit at all, with one hand in its lap and the other on the table, its head turned away a fraction, tipping slightly, so as to make it seem the face was gazing into the distance somewhat lost in thought—and as soon as the man saw it he immediately went to sit beside it, so that by the time Korin had removed his coat he too had to sit with the dummy and clearly found it difficult not to query its presence at first, though once he got used to it being there he accepted it and no longer felt any need to ask any questions, just glanced at it every so often, and after the fifth or sixth round of drinks, once the Unicum had well and truly gone to his head, he accepted the dummy to the extent that he even started including it in his conversation, a conversation that consisted primarily of his monologue of course, whose intention was to enlighten the other by telling him about the headaches, about his own revelation concerning Babel and to continue with his account of the time in the records office, the weeks at Sárváry's, the journey to America passing on to the manuscript, eternity, the gun, then, eventually, Kasser, Bengazza, Falke and Toót, and the way out, how they couldn't find it and how he carried them about inside him but felt extremely worried now even though earlier he thought he'd be perfectly calm, because they somehow stayed with him, were clinging to him, and he felt he couldn't get rid of them just like that, but what could he do, where and how could he solve the problem, he sighed, then went to the toilet on returning from which he was confronted in the corridor by the proprietress with the froufrou hairdo who begged his pardon but asked him, a little awkwardly, not to ply his companion with drink, because they knew him very well in the restaurant, and he was neither used to it, nor able to cope with it, to which Korin answered that neither could he himself, though the woman, rather impatiently, cut him short, saying it would do his companion no good at all, and adjusted her froufrou hair as she did so, because he was a very sensitive, good-hearted boy and he has this obsession with store dummies, populating the whole district with them, and it wasn't just in her restaurant he planted one but wherever they would let him, and they let him because he is such a quiet, gentle, decent sort of man, and he had left three dummies in Grand Central Station, as well as others in the public library, one at McDonald's, another at the cinema at 11th Street, and one at a nearby newsstand in front of the magazine shelves, but people said he had more at home, one sitting in the armchair in his room watching the TV, one at the kitchen table and one at the window supposedly looking out, in other words, said the proprietress, she couldn't deny that he was somewhat cranky but he was not mad, and he was only doing all this on account of some woman because, they say, he very much loved her, and she was simply asking Korin to understand, and more than understand, to look after him if he could, because you couldn't fill him with drink, it was just asking for trouble, to which Korin readily agreed, saying yes, he understood now, and that he would certainly look after him most carefully as he too thought he was a really nice man, confessing that as soon as he set eyes on him he really liked him, so, yes, he would look after him, he promised, but then immediately broke his word for as soon as he sat back down with the man at the restaurant he immediately ordered another round, nor could he be dissuaded from more on top of that, so he was truly asking for trouble, and this eventually did lead to trouble, though not in the form the proprietress had anticipated, for it was Korin who felt ill, extremely ill in fact once they had finished and while vomiting helped, it only relieved him for a few minutes, then he was ill again, and worse, no longer pushing the cart but clinging onto it, constantly telling the other man, whom he now referred to as his friend, that death meant nothing to him, while clinging on, almost allowing himself to be drawn, his feet repeatedly slipping on the snow, which by this time, that is to say about four or half past four, had frozen solid.

9.

They were going somewhere in the snow and it didn't matter to Korin where it was, nor did it seem to matter much to the other man, who occasionally adjusted the tarpaulin covering the dummies, then bent forward and blindly dragged the cart behind him in the sharp wind blowing down the avenues oriented north to south so that every time they passed one of these, which they did frequently, they tried to escape from it as soon as they could, fleeing from it, saying nothing at all for a long time, until the man

suddenly said something over his shoulder, something he must
have been thinking for a while, but Korin didn't hear him so the
man had to drop the pole, go over to Korin so he could get his
message through to him, which was that it was all very nice what
he had told him about the manuscript in the Mocca restaurant,
very nice indeed, he nodded, but of course he had invented the lot,
admit it, for beautiful as the Cretan, the Venetian and Roman
episodes were, he should calmly own up to the fact that they existed only in his imagination, to which Korin naturally responded
with a firm no, that no, he had not made it up, the manuscript existed and what was more was there on his bed on 159th Street if he
wanted to see it, he said, quickly grabbing the back of the cart because he had let go of it for a moment, and yes, said the other man
very slowly, because if it was true—he raised his head—it must be
beautiful and it would really be very nice to see it, and surely there
was something one could do about that road, that way out, and
you know what? he asked, we should meet tomorrow night about
six o'clock at my place, and Korin should bring that manuscript
with him, that's if it existed, for if it did exist it would be very
beautiful and he would like to show a page or two to the woman
he loved, he said gazing at the dummies under the tarpaulin, then
produced a business card from his pocket, pointed to the address
on it, saying, here, and gave it to Korin who put it away, and the
place would be easy enough to find, so let us say six o'clock, he
added before falling flat on his face and remaining motionless on
the snow while Korin stared at him for a moment before letting go
of the cart and taking a step toward the man to help him, but he
lost his balance in trying to do so and fell beside him where he lay
until the man, who might have been brought to his senses, or if
not precisely to his senses at least to consciousness by the cold before Korin was, extended his arms, pulled Korin to his feet, and
they stood there, with feet planted apart, facing each other, both of
them swaying for a whole minute or more, until the man suddenly
said that Korin was a likable guy but somehow lacked a center, and
with that he took up his place at the front of the cart, raised the
pole and set off along the snow once more, only this time Korin
did not follow him, for he hadn't the strength to do so, not even by
clinging onto the cart, but gazed at the man with his dummies
getting ever further and further away, reeled over to the nearest

doorway, pushed at the outer door and lay down by the wall at the foot of the stairs.

10.

Four hundred and forty dollars, that was what most upset him when he found the money on him, for where does a dirty little nobody like this get four hundred and forty dollars from, while he, said the man in the yellow overalls pointing to himself, he clears the crap from the house, fixes the drains, takes out the garbage and sweeps the filthy ice in front of the house for a hundred and eighty a week working his guts out to earn a pittance, and this creature has four hundred and forty dollars right there in his coat pocket, just like that, as he guessed when he saw him at the bottom of the wet stairs, thinking there's another filthy stinking bum lying in his own vomit, just as he suspected when he saw him at the bottom of the stairs, the sight of him making his blood boil, so he would happily have put a bullet in him, but contended himself instead with giving him a kick and was just starting to drag him outside when he found the four hundred and forty dollars in his pocket, counted the bills into his own wallet, and gave him such a kick his foot was still aching because he must have struck a bone his foot was hurting so badly; four hundred and forty, imagine it, his voice trembled with fury, well, he was so angry he booted him right out of that door and off the sidewalk too onto the street like the piece of shit he was, he was that disgusting, and boy was he disgusted, said the man in the yellow overalls grabbing the arm of the person living upstairs, and he was quite right to treat him the way he did, he thought, that's the way to deal with them, let them freeze their asses off outside, he said, his face reddening, let him lie out there till a car runs over him, and he just lay there, unable even to open his eyes he was in so much pain, but eventually managed to do so, heard the terrible car horns, saw where he was and started dragging himself toward the sidewalk without quite realizing the gravity of his situation or understanding why his stomach, chest and face hurt so much, then lay for a while on the edge of the sidewalk until it seemed someone was asking him if he was all right and he didn't know what to answer so he said yes, all right, but even as he did so it flashed across his mind that he wouldn't want a policeman to find him there and he grew agitated, thinking he had to move on as quickly as he could, so clambered to his feet seeing that it was light and that two school-age children were looking at him sympathetically, asking him again if he was all right and whether they should call an ambulance, an ambulance, Korin echoed, oh, an ambulance and tried to tell them that they were on no account to call an ambulance because there was nothing really wrong with him, it was just that something had happened, he didn't know what, but that everything was all right now and that they should leave him alone now, he'd be all right, until he realized that he was speaking Hungarian and quickly tried to find a few English words but nothing came, so he stood up and started down the sidewalk, walking with enormous difficulty, making it to the corner of Lexington Avenue and 51st Street, then stumbled down into the subway and felt better among the swirling crowds where a battered figure like him would not be so conspicuous, because he was truly battered and shattered, he told his friend later, so utterly shattered he couldn't imagine how he could ever be reassembled, but he got onto a train though he had no idea where it was going, nor did he care as long as it was away from there, and once he thought he was far enough away he got off and wandered over to a map and found the name of the station, which was somewhere in Brooklyn, but what could he do, what was there to do, he wondered in desperation, as he said later, and then he remembered what they had agreed when they parted, strange as it was that he should have forgotten everything about the last few hours except the fact that he had promised to deliver the manuscript to his new friend by six o'clock that evening, so the task was to get the manuscript, he said to himself, and he eventually found himself on a 7 train going back toward 42nd Street, but was very frightened, he said, since he realized how beaten up he was, not to say how dirty and stinking, with vomit all over him, frightened also that someone would stop him before he got home, but it was the last thing on anyone's mind to stop him, everyone steering clear of him rather than confronting him, and so he reached West 42nd, transferred to a 9 train to get home, home as he kept muttering, home, the word itself like a prayer, dragging his body homeward, his body feeling as if it had been broken into a thousand distinct pieces, finally reaching the house and climbing the stairs still feeling so terrible that it never occurred to him that he had left the apartment for the last time the night before, though he should have given that a thought, he told the man later, because then he might have understood more clearly why he felt so much like a corpse.

11.

The two of them were in the kitchen among the boxes, the woman lying twisted and spread-eagled, her face completely beaten in, the interpreter hanging on the central heating duct but the blood all over his face showing he had been shot several times with a machine gun at close range—and he couldn't scream, couldn't move, as he stood in the open door, but slowly opened his mouth without any sound coming out of it, and then he wanted to go back the way he came, to get out of there but his limbs simply wouldn't move, and when he was eventually able to move his legs they took him forward, closer to them, ever closer, and he felt a terrible pain in his head, so he stopped and stood still once again rooted to the spot and remained there for ages, standing and staring, unable to take his eyes off them, his face filled with horror, suddenly aged, and he opened his mouth again still without success, still silent, and took one more step forward but stumbled over something, the telephone, and almost fell, but instead of falling squatted down beside it and slowly punched in a number and listened a long time to the busy signal before realizing that he had dialed himself, and then he began searching in his pocket, but whatever he was looking for in an ever greater panic he couldn't find, not for ages, and then it was there, the business card; uh, he grunted into the receiver, repeating the sound idiotically, uh, uh, uh, they're dead, the pair of them, dead, the young lady and Mr. Sárváry, the man at the other end telling him to speak up and stop whispering, to tell him clearly what the matter was, but I'm not whispering, Korin whispered, they've killed them, both of them are dead, the young lady's waist is twisted right out of shape, and Mr. Sárváry is hanging there; then get out of there as quick as you can, the man shouted into the phone; uh, and everything is smashed up, said Korin, then held the receiver away from his mouth, looked up with a terrified expression, then rushed out onto the stairs, pushed open the door of the toilet, leapt onto the seat, raised the tile and removed the money, gripping it in his hands, then rushed back into the apartment, picked up the phone and told the man that he knew, he knew at last what must have happened and started telling him about his landlord's new job, about all his shopping, about the money in his hands, about the packets of white powder and the place where they were hidden and how he had discovered them, babbling on in ever greater confusion, ever more terrified by what he himself was saying as the man at the other end asked him again to stop whispering because he couldn't hear him properly, but it was quite certain now, Korin continued, and he never once thought it would be Mr. Sárváry, not while he . . . , and he began crying, uncontrollably sobbing, so whatever he said the other man could not hear him for the sobs, sobs that shook him and went on shaking him so he couldn't even hold the receiver, but then he picked it up again and listened and there was the man at the other end saying hello, are you still there? and when Korin replied that he was, the man told him to get out, and seeing that he had the money, hold on to it and bring it with him, definitely bring it with him and not to touch anything now but to leave the place, leave it now and come to his apartment or anywhere else he wanted to meet, can you still hear me? are you still there? the question hanging in the silent petrified air a long time but not receiving an answer because Korin had put the receiver down, screwed the money up in his coat and had started backing away, continually backing and weeping once more, finally stumbling down the stairs and out into the street, walking a couple of hundred yards and then beginning to run, to run as fast as he could, rushing on with the business card in his hand, gripping it so hard that his hand was all the time shaking with the effort.

12.

They were sitting in the three bucket chairs, the store dummy facing the TV, the man beside her and Korin beside him, and all was silent but for the hum of the television with the sound turned off and a washing machine in the bathroom grumbling, bucking and sloshing, none of them saying anything, the man having sat Korin down on his arrival and taking his place beside him but not asking anything for a very long time, just staring in front of him and thinking very hard, then eventually getting up, taking a glass of water and sitting back down again to reassure Korin that they would think of something but that first they had to clean his clothes because he couldn't move a step dressed like that, and then he helped him strip the clothes off though it was obvious that Korin did not really know what was going on or why it was necessary which meant that it was only with the greatest difficulty the man succeeded in unbuttoning him, but eventually his garments lay in a heap at his feet, and the man gave him a bathrobe, then removed anything that remained in the clothes before taking them into the bathroom and putting the lot—coat, underwear and all—into the washing machine, starting it up, then returning to the armchair to sit there and think even harder; and so they sat there a whole hour until the washing machine in the bathroom, with one final gasp, came to the end of its cycle, and the man said he had better know, roughly at least, what had happened otherwise he couldn't help to which Korin only answered that he had noticed the hiding place in the toilet before, but had believed one of the occupants downstairs to be responsible for it, since anyone could use the toilet on their floor, at which point the other interrupted him to ask what he meant by hiding place, and Korin simply repeated that it was a hiding place and that one day he found that the white packets in it had been replaced by money, and though the other tried to stop him asking what packet? which day? Korin went on saying he didn't think it had anything to do with them, that it was so far from his mind in fact that he forgot to say anything about it, because suddenly there was all this chaos, a lot of people arriving at the apartment, taking everything away then returning the next day bringing things back, and this so confused the young lady that he felt he had to look after her, and he had no idea that it was the hidden stuff that was the cause of everything, and once again began to cry in the armchair, and was quite unable to answer another question the man put to him, so that he had to do everything himself, to look through his belongings, find his passport, examine it to check that it was valid at all, then spread the clothes out in the bathroom to dry and count to see how much money there was, finally working out what to do next, then sitting down beside him again, to tell him quite quietly there was only one solution, and that was that he should get out of the country as soon as possible, but Korin did not answer and just sat beside the dummy and cried.

13.

There was just the one bed in the bedroom, a store dummy propped by the window as if looking out and in the kitchen nothing but a bare table and four chairs, one of the chairs occupied by another store dummy raising its right hand and pointing at something on the ceiling or beyond it; which left the sitting room with its TV, three armchairs, one dummy and the man, now replaced by Korin, the rest bare, practically empty, the walls alone being covered with photographs, or rather several copies of the same photograph, as was the whole apartment, one photograph in various sizes, large, middling and vast, but everywhere the same, each of them showing the same thing, a hemispherical structure clad in broken glass, and when the man, hearing a faint rustling, opened his eyes he saw Korin, fully dressed now in his overcoat, waiting, it seemed, to go, looking at the wall, examining the photographs, bowing a little to examine each of them, deeply absorbed in their contents, whereupon Korin, having noticed that the man had woken up, quickly sat down in the armchair again, next to the store dummy and fixed his eyes on the TV, not answering when the man got out of bed and asked him through the door if he wanted a cup of coffee, but kept staring at the silent TV, so the man made coffee for just one, filled himself a cup, added sugar, stirred it and sat down with it next to Korin in the vacant armchair, surprised to find that Korin was after all addressing him, asking where the woman he loved had gone, to which he replied after a long silence simply that she had gone away; and what about her? and the one in the kitchen? and the one at the bus stop? asked Korin nodding toward the various dummies, to which he answered that they all looked like her, slurped once at his coffee, stood up and took the cup out into the kitchen, and by the time he returned Korin seemed not to have noticed his absence and was absorbed in telling his story, describing the two children's faces as they peered down at him threatening to call the ambulance, and how he had managed to slip away and took shelter in the subway for a while, though every part of him was aching, he said, especially his stomach, his chest and his neck, and his whole head buzzing so that he hardly had the strength to stand, but kept going somehow and got to another subway station, then to another and another, and so forth . . . but the man stopped him at this point to say, I don't understand, what are you talking about, but rather than explain Korin stopped altogether and for a while all three of them were simply watching TV, cartoons and advertisements following close on each other's heels, rapid, jerky, silent images, as if everything was under water, until the man repeated his advice that Korin should leave immediately because it was a tough city and you couldn't hang around thinking that either someone would kill Korin or the cops would get him, which would be more or less the same thing, he said, and since he seemed to have vast amounts of money he should decide where to go and he, the man, would take care of it, but he needed to pull himself together now, he said. though he could see that Korin was still out of it and that nothing he said had got through, that he was simply frowning at the television, watching it for a long time as though it required all his concentration to keep track of the flickering images on the screen before eventually rising from the armchair, going over to the pictures on the wall, pointing to one of them and asking, and this? where is this?

14.

A temporary bed had been made up for him behind the armchairs in the living room, but though he lay down and pulled the covers over him Korin did not sleep, waiting instead for the man in the bedroom to breathe evenly and start snoring, then he got up, went to the bathroom, touched all the clothes drying there and gazed at the pictures on the wall again, leaning very close since they were just a faint glow in the murk, but by leaning so close he succeeded in examining every one, moving from one to the other, giving each one careful thought before moving on, and that is all he did that night, working his way through the apartment, moving from the bathroom through to the bedroom, then into the living room, returning frequently to the bathroom to check how dry the clothes were, touching them, adjusting them on the radiator, but then, quick as a shot out to examine the photographs again, admiring the strange, airy dome with its arches made of simple steel tubes

bent to define a large hemisphere in space, staring at the large un-
even glass panes—roughly half a meter or a meter in size—with
which the hemisphere was covered, studying the fixing of the
joints and trying to make out some text written in bright neon
tubes, pressing his head ever closer to the pictures, straining his
eyes, concentrating ever more intensely on them, until, it seemed,
he had solved something and was in any case finding it easier to
make out details that showed a completely empty space surrounded by white walls, and inside it a remarkably light-looking,
delicate contraption, a bubble of air, possibly a dwelling of some
sort, he said to himself as he moved from one image on to the
next, a version of a prehistoric structure, the man later explained to
him, yes, a dwelling, the skeleton made of aluminum tubes filled in
with broken, irregular panes of glass, something like an igloo; and
where was it? asked Korin, the man replying that it was in
Schaffhausen, and where was Schaffhausen? in Switzerland, came
the answer, near Zürich, at the point where the Rhine divides the
Jura mountains, and is that far? asked Korin, is it far, this
Schaffhausen, and if so, how far?

15.

He had called the taxi for two o'clock and the taxi arrived right on
the dot so he advised Korin to go now but first he checked the
overcoat, regretting the fact that it was still a little damp, and
looked in the pockets to see that the passport and ticket were there
before giving him some final advice on how to get around JFK,
then they were both on their way down to the ground floor, both
silent, and so they left the house, the man embracing him before
ushering him into the taxi which set off for Brooklyn and the expressway, leaving the man standing in front of the house to raise
his hand and wave uncertainly for a while, though Korin was unaware of him for he never turned his head, not even to look
through the side windows but sat quite bent over in the back seat,
his eyes staring at the road over the driver's shoulder, it being
transparently clear that he was not in the least interested in the
view but only in what lay ahead, meaning in what lay ahead over
the driver's shoulder.

VIII • THEY'VE BEEN TO AMERICA

1.

There are four of them in it, said Korin, turning to the elderly man in the rabbit-fur hat sitting next to him on the bench beside the lake at Zürich, four people most dear to his heart, and they have been traveling with him, so they've been to America but have now returned, not precisely where they had set out from, it was true, but not too far away, and now before their pursuers caught up with them, because they were being constantly pursued, he said, he was seeking a place—a *place*, he said in English—that was just right, some specific point, so that they should not have to keep running for ever and ever, because they could not accompany him where he was going since he was going on to Schaffhausen, but had to go alone, so the others had to get off, and in any case he felt it was possible for them to get off now, while he went on to Schaffhausen—at which the old gentleman's face brightened and, ah, he said, having understood barely a word of what Korin had been saying, ah, he twisted his moustache, now he understood, and using his walking stick he drew two symbols in the slushy snow at their feet and pointed to one, saying America, then, smiling broadly, began to draw a line between it and the other symbol, saying, *und Schaffhausen*, prodding the other symbol, then, signaling that all was clear at last, pointed to Korin and moved his stick between the two marks in the snow, pronouncing with great satisfaction, *Sie-Amerika-Schaffhausen, this is wonderful* and *Grüß Gott, yes*, nodded Korin, from America to Schaffhausen but what to do with the four of them, where to leave them, because this is where he should leave them, then he glanced up at the lake, and stared at it with a

sudden intensity, shouting, *ah, perhaps the Lake*, in English, delighted
to have found a solution, and was immediately on his feet, leaving
the startled old gentleman who gazed for a while uncomprehend-
ingly at the two points by his feet in the slushy snow then
scratched them away with his stick, stood up, cleared his throat and
putting a cheerful face on again strolled off between the trees toward the bridge, looking now right and now left.

2.

The town was smaller, much smaller than the one he had left, yet
it was the problem of finding his way around it that worried
him most, for despite his anxiety to prevent his pursuers catching
up with him he had got lost time and again at the airport, and
then, after some kind people had helped him onto the express for
Zürich, he had got off the train two stops too early, and so it went
on, constantly going the wrong way, getting lost, having to ask
people, and the citizens of Zürich were on the whole perfectly prepared to answer his queries, insofar as they understood what he
wanted, but even after having arrived by tram at central Bellevue
Platz he kept asking passersby where the city center was, and when
they replied, go no further, this is the city center, he clearly did not
believe them but went round and round in a high state of tension,
rubbing his neck, turning his head this way and that, unable to decide on a direction, before finally taking the plunge and choosing
one direction, constantly looking back over his shoulder to see if
there was anyone following him, then ducked into a park, confronting people and asking them, where gun? where center? most
of them not understanding the first enquiry but putting him right
as regards the second, saying, this is it, right here, in answer to
which Korin would give an irritated wave and walk on, until at the
end of the park he spotted a a few figures wearing ragged clothes
who were looking at him rather darkly, and seeing them he clearly
relaxed, thinking yes, perhaps it's them, quickly made his way over,
stopped and said in English, *I want to buy a revolver*, to which they
made no answer for a good while but examined him uncertainly,
until eventually one shrugged, saying OK, OK and gestured for him
to follow, but he was so nervous and walked so quickly that Korin

found it hard to keep up, though he kept repeating *come, come,* practically running before him, then eventually stopped at a bench among some hedges where two people were sitting, or rather sitting on its back with their feet up on the seat, one of them about twenty, the other about thirty years of age, the pair of them wearing identical leather jackets, leather trousers, boots and earrings, looking for all the earth like twins, both of them extraordinarily nervous, their feet constantly tapping on the seat of the bench and their fingers constantly drumming on their knees, the pair of them discusssing something in German of which Korin did not understand a word, until eventually the younger one turned to him and said very slowly, in English, *two hours here again,* pointing at the bench, Korin repeating in English, *two hours? here?,* and OK, he said, it's OK, *aber cash,* said the elder one leaning into his face, *dollar, OK?* and Korin took a step back while the other grinned, *three hundred dollar,* you get it, *three hundred dollar,* and Korin nodded to say that was all right, *it's all right,* in *two hours, here,* and he too pointed at the bench, then left them and set off back through the park, soon to be joined by the man who had escorted him so far, constantly whispering *pot, pot, pot, pot* into his ear and drawing some mysterious diagram on his palm with his finger until they reached the end of the park where the escort gave up and left him, Korin still repeating to himself, two hours, as he walked down to the Bellevue Platz where, with great difficulty, he persuaded a vendor to sell him a sandwich and a cola for U.S. dollars, and he ate and drank and waited for a while, watching the trams as they arrived over the bridge, turned down a narrow side street and, still clanking and ringing, disappeared; so Korin set off along the bridge to the lake, walking for ages, occasionally looking back over his shoulder, the water on one side of him with a single boat on it, a row of trees on the other and behind them the houses of Bellerivestrasse as he read on a sign, though he came across fewer and fewer people as he walked out of town, arriving eventually at a kind of carnival full of colorful booths, tents, and a Big Wheel, but the place was closed up, so he turned back and retraced his steps, the water with the single boat on it now on his other side, and then again the trees, the houses and ever more people, and ever stronger gusts of wind as he neared Bellevue Platz, and soon he was back in the park receiving the gun and some ammunition packed into a plastic bag, and was shown how to load up, to operate the safety catch and to pull the trigger, and this brief course of instruction being completed the elder man grinned at him once, put the money away and the pair of them vanished as if by magic, as if the ground had swallowed them, thought Korin as he continued to Bellevue Platz, crossed the bridge and found a sheltered place on the other side of the lake where he sat down, feeling quite drained, as he told the elderly gentleman sitting at the other end of the bench, for he had no strength left in him, but he had to be strong because the four of them were still with him, he said, and he could not go on like this, while the old gentleman nodded and hummed to himself and gazed at the solitary boat on the lake directly opposite their bench with a cheerful expression on his face.

3.

He was walking by the Limmat, then down the Mythen Quay toward the dock, for being the harbor master he was obliged to review the situation when the freezing shore presented a possible hazard, particularly to check that the service craft provided in the dock around boats anchored on the lake for the winter were doing their duty by breaking up the thin but potentially dangerous ice, in other words, he said to old cronies at the butcher's near his home, he was going along on foot, seeing it was nice weather, when in the middle of the Arboretum he suddenly notices that someone is following him, not that he bothers about this, because he thinks it's probably coincidence, or that the man has some business down there, who knows, it's perfectly possible, let him dog his steps if he wants, soon enough he'll turn off somewhere and disappear, but the man did not turn off or disappear, the harbor master raised his voice, nor did he fall behind, no, on the contrary, once they reached the steps down to the dock he comes up to him, addresses him as Mister Captain, and pointing at something on the coat of his uniform begins to gabble in a foreign language, Danish he reckoned, and when he tries to push him aside telling him to spit it out, to speak so he can understand or to leave him alone, the man, with considerable difficulty, manages to put a sentence together, a sentence he takes to mean that he wants to take a boat out, the dope, and when he answers that that is out of the question, it's winter and there is no water traffic in winter, the man simply keeps on, saying he absolutely must go out, not giving up but taking a load of dollars from his pocket, pressing him to take it, to which he can only answer that it's not a matter of money, it's winter and no amount of dollars will alter that, come back in spring, in spring it will be fine—well said, Gusti, one remarked, and how they laughed there at the butcher's—but wait, the harbor master gestured to his listeners, because by this time he had started to get a little curious himself, and asked the man what on earth he wanted with a boat on the lake, and then the guy—and here he looked around to make a proper effect and told them all to listen closely, hesitating a moment—this guy says *he wants to write something on the water*, well, he thought he had misheard or misunderstood him, but no, just imagine, it seemed the guy really did want to do all that, to take a boat out and use it to write something on the water, on the water, for godssake! he clapped his hands together as the laughter once again rose around him, well, naturally, he should have realized immediately that the man was some kind of nut, the way he was gesturing and explaining and waving his hands about, his eyes like some crazy terrorist's flashing all the time, indeed, well of course, this should have been enough to give him a clue, but, there it was, now he saw him for what he was, and for sheer entertainment, the harbor master winked at his growing audience, he decided to get to the bottom of this and to ask him what could be so very important, *very important*, he said in English, that it had to be written on water, what, he asked him, and then he started babbling again but he couldn't understand a word of it despite the fact that the man was trying everything to communicate something with him, trying to make *Herr Kapitan*, as the man insisted on calling him, understand; and then he drew a diagram in the snow with his foot, with here the boat, here how it leaves the dock, here showing it in the middle of the lake, the boat moving like pencil on paper, *like a pencil on the paper*, he had said in English, which was the way of writing on water, the message, in English again, being *way that goes out*—this at least was how he tried to get his message across at first, keeping his anxious eyes on the harbor master's face, looking for signs of understanding, and when he saw he was getting no reaction, he said, *outgoing-way*, without any more success than before, finally suggesting that they should agree on the formula, *way out*, that the boat would write these words on the water, all right? he asked hopefully, and grabbed hold of the other man's coat, but the man shook him off and set off down the steps to the dock leaving him, Korin, standing there, out of ideas and utterly helpless, finally seeing the melancholy truth of the situation, before shouting after the man, *no traffic on the lake?* on hearing which the harbor master took a few steps then stopped, turned and shouted back, as any reasonable man might, having finally understood, replying, yes, this was indeed the situation that there was, quite right, *no traffic on the lake*, repeating it, *no traffic on the lake*, and this clearly registered and continued reverberating in Korin's brain as he turned away from the lake and started walking back, his progress very slow, as if he were weighed down by a terrible burden, his back quite bent over, his head hanging as he passed along Mythen Quay, saying to himself aloud, well, all right, but now you all have to come with me, the whole lot of you, to Schaffhausen.

4.

It wasn't so difficult now to find the central railway station because he had made the journey once by tram and somehow he managed to remember it, but inside, once it was all made clear, once he had understood that he would have to pay for the tickets in francs, and once he actually had the tickets and had found the right platform, it had grown dark and there were hardly any other passengers on the car he had got onto, and those few there were did not answer Korin's requirements for it was perfectly obvious that Korin needed someone having gone up and down the train two or three times sizing up people and shaking his head because none of them seemed right to him, but then, at the very last moment before they started, that is to say just before the guard at the end of the platform sounded his whistle, a highly agitated and worried-looking woman appeared in the last car, a tall, very thin woman of about forty to forty-five, who practically exploded through the door, it being obvious from the furious expression on her face that she had undergone various trials and tribulations before getting on the train, that she had lost all hope of ever doing so but had neverthe-

less had to try, and had, by some miracle, succeeded only at the last
moment, and to make it worse her arms were laden with packages
she could hardly carry so that when the train started immediately
and the engine gave two mighty jerks she almost fell over, partly
because of the weight of the packages and partly because of the effort of rushing, and came close to striking her head on the luggage
rack, and no one came to help her, the only one in a position to do
so being a young Arab man who, judging by the angle of his body,
must have been fast asleep in the next seat, or that was how it
looked from her position, so she could do nothing but grab hold
of something to steady herself, then throw her first packages into
the nearest seat, then drop into it herself, sitting there with closed
eyes, gasping and sighing for several minutes, simply sitting, trying
to calm down as the train cut through the suburbs—which was the
point at which Korin reached the last car and glimpsed her sitting
with closed eyes among her parcels, asked in English, *can I help you*,
and hurried to lift her luggage onto the rack—suitcase, handbag,
packages and all—then dropped into the seat opposite her and
gazed deep into her eyes.

5.

*To love order is to love life: love of order is therefore love of symmetry, and love of sym-
metry is a memory of eternal truth*, he said after a long silence then seeing
how she stared at him in amazement nodded at her by way of affir-
mation, then stood up, studied the ever more distant station as
if inspecting it to see whether his pursuers were still there, then
finally sat back down again, drew his coat about him and added by
way of explanation: *An hour or two, that's all, just an hour or two now.*

6.

She didn't understand what he was saying at first, nor could she
guess what language he was speaking and it only became clearer to
her, the woman explained a couple of days later after her husband
had arrived at the vacation house they had rented in the Jura
mountains, once they had both recovered, once the man took a
piece of paper from his pocket and showed her what it said: *Mario*

Merz, Schaffhausen, and imagine that, she said, quite excitedly, it had to be Merz who was a particularly close friend of hers too, though she was absolutely baffled as to what this was all about until it slowly dawned on her that the man wasn't wanting to tell her something, wasn't spinning some story or other, but was *asking her* where in Schaffhausen he might find Merz, and even this led to a misunderstanding, she said, quite a few amusing misunderstandings in fact, for the man thought that what he was looking for was something called Merz, and she held up both her hands and laughed now as she remembered the incident, because Merz himself, the man, she told him, was not to be found in Schaffhausen, but in Toronto because that was where Merz lived, she explained, and sometimes in New York so she couldn't understand why someone had suggested Schaffhausen to him, but Korin just shook his head and insisted *no Torino, no New York, Schaffhausen, Merz in Schaffhausen*, and for a long time he couldn't think of the word he was looking for which was *sculpture, sculpture in Schaffhausen*, at which point the woman's eyes suddenly lit up and O, she cried and laughed, *What a fool!* and shook her head, because of course there was a *sculpture* by Merz in Schaffhausen, in Schaffhausen's *Hallen für die neue Kunst*, the museum, that's where it was, not just one but two, and Korin cried out in delight, that's it, the very thing, a museum, a museum and now it was all perfectly clear what he wanted, what he was looking for, where he was going and why, and he immediately told her the whole story, all in Hungarian alas, he spread his hands to apologize, since the English was beyond him and because they were on his trail and he couldn't think of the right words, or rather only one or two came so there was nothing he could do for a while but say it all in Hungarian in case the woman managed to grasp something of it, relating the story of Kasser, Bengazza, Falke and Toót, describing them in great detail, how they appeared in Crete and in Britain, what happened in Rome and Cologne, and most naturally, how they had all grown to be so much a part of him that he could no longer part with them, because, just imagine, he told his traveling companion, he had been trying to leave them for days without success, and it was only today he properly understood, at the lake in Zürich, *the Zürich Lake*, and at the familiar words *Zürich Lake* the woman's eyes lit up again, so Korin nodded, saying yes, there, there was where it became perfectly obvious that it couldn't be done, he

couldn't just drop them like that, that he knew there was no way
out, and so it was only today he realized he would have to take
them there with him, there where he himself was going, to
Schaffhausen in other words, and his face darkened and grew more
serious; you mean to the *Hallen für die neue Kunst*, said the woman
helping him out, and they both laughed.

7.

Her name was Marie, said the woman sweetly bowing her head,
she looked after him, tended him, defended and helped him, in
other words she'd give her life for him, she said; and his name,
Korin pointed to himself, was György, *Gyuri*; ah, in that case might
you be Hungarian, guessed the woman and Korin nodded, saying
yes, he *Magyarország*; and the other smiled and said she had heard
something about the country but knew so little of it, so perhaps
he might be able to tell her something about the Hungarians, because there was some time before they would reach Schaffhausen;
and Korin asked, *Magyarok?*, and the woman nodded, yes, yes, to
which he answered that Hungarians did not exist, *Hungarian no exist*,
they had all died, *they died out*, the process having begun about a
hundred or a hundred and fifty years ago, he said, and though it
might seem incredible the whole thing happened without anyone
noticing; and the woman shook her head incredulously, Hungarian? No exist? and, yes, *they died out*, Korin insisted, the process
beginning in the last century when there was a great confusion of
peoples and not one Hungarian remained, only a mixture, a few
Swabians, Gypsies, Slovaks, Austrians, Jews, Romanians, Croats and
Serbs and so on, and chiefly combinations of all these, but Hungarians disappeared, they had all gone, Korin attempted to persuade
her, only Hungary the place existed not the Hungarians, *Hungary yes,
Hungarians not*, and not one genuine memorial remained to tell the
world what an extraordinary, proud, irresistible nation they had
been, because that's what they were once, living according to laws
that were both very fierce and very pure, a people kept awake only
by the eternal necessity of performing great deeds, a barbaric people who slowly lost interest in a world that preferred lower hori-
zons, and in this way they perished, degenerated, died out and in-
terbred until nothing remained of them, only their language, their

poetry, something little, something insignificantly small; and the woman wrinkled her brow and said, what do you mean; and he didn't know, he said, but that was how it was, and the most interesting thing about it, not that it interested him at all, was that no one ever mentioned their degeneration and disappearance, nothing was said of the whole business, and that anything said now was a lie, an error, a misunderstanding or crass idiocy, but alas, the woman gestured, this was utterly confusing for her, so Korin left off and asked her instead to write down the precise name of the museum, then he fell silent, and only gazed at her, as her warm, sensitive eyes met his and she slowly started to tell him something trying to make him understand, but it was obvious that he didn't understand because Korin's mind was clearly elsewhere, that he was simply gazing at the woman's friendly attractive face, and watching the lights of little stations as they came and went, one after another.

8.

The clock at Schaffhausen station showed eleven thirty-seven and Korin stood beneath the clock, the platform quite deserted now, just a single railway man carrying a timetable, his job being to signal the train's arrival and departure, glimpsed for a second then gone so that by the time Korin had decided to address him he had disappeared together with his timetable behind the door of a room reserved for staff, and everything was silent but for the clock ticking above his head and a sudden gust of wind that swept down the platform, so Korin walked out but found no one there either and made his way down toward the town until he spotted a taxi in front of a hotel, the driver sleeping, slumped over the steering wheel, and tapped on the windshield to wake him, which he did eventually and opened the door so that Korin could give him the piece of paper with the museum's name written on it, the driver nodding morosely, telling him to get in, it was all right, he'd take him, and so it was that barely ten minutes after his arrival Korin was standing in front of a large, dark, silent building, looking for the entrance, checking that the name on the board tallied with the one on his sheet, turning first left and returning to the entrance, then right, down to the corner where the taxi had dropped him, returning again, finally circumambulating the entire building as if sizing it up, rubbing his neck the whole time and never taking his eyes off the windows, gazing and gazing at them, seeking some light, some shadow, some subtle change, some flickering, anything that might indicate a living presence, returning to the entrance, giving the door a good shake, beating and beating at it without result, and the security guard in his hut swore this all had happened precisely at midnight, his pocket radio having just bleeped twelve on the table, which seemed to be the cue for the rattling to start, not that he would claim to have known what to do right away, the noise startled him a little because no one had ever rattled the door like that at midnight or after that, not as long as he had been working nights here, so what was this about, he wondered, somebody at the door at this hour, what can it mean, and all this ran through his mind before he went to the door, opened it a crack, and what happened next, he explained the next morning on his way home from the hearing, so surprised him he really didn't know what to do, because the easiest way, he explained, would have been, as he knew full well, to chase the man off, send him on his way, just like that, but the few words he understood of what he was saying, something about sculpture and Hungarian and Mister Director and New York confused him, because it suddenly struck him what this might be about, that they might have forgotten to say something to him, that maybe he was to expect this person at such a time, and what would happen, he asked himself, slurping his milky coffee, if he chased him away, treated him like some tramp and then in the morning it turned out that he'd done something wrong, because for all he knew the man might have been a famous artist, someone they had been waiting for, who had arrived late, and suddenly there he was, without accommodation, without even a telephone number to ring, because, he might have lost it, just as he might have lost his luggage on the flight, the flight that was late, the luggage containing all his possessions, because it wouldn't have been the first time this had happened with these artists, the security guard waved at his mother in worldly wisdom, so he closed the door, he said, and thought for a moment, deciding the best thing was neither to send him away nor let him into the museum, but he couldn't ring up the director now, after midnight, so what could he do, what should he do, he pondered, and had just returned to his post, when he remembered one of the attendants, Mr. Kalotaszegi, who could possibly be called, midnight or no midnight, and he would certainly call him, he decided, and was already looking up his number in the employment book, because, in the first place, Mr. Kalotaszegi was of Hungarian extraction and would therefore understand what this person was babbling about, so if he was called out he could talk to the man and they could decide together what to do with him, and he was extremely sorry, he said on the phone, extremely sorry to disturb Mr. Kalotaszegi, but this man had turned up, probably a Hungarian artist, he said, but no one had told him anything about it, and until someone talked to him he wouldn't know what to do because he couldn't understand a word he said, only that he might be some kind of sculptor, that he might have arrived from New York and that he was probably Hungarian, and he was constantly repeating Mister Director, Mister Director, so he couldn't handle this alone, though he'd happily have sent him to hell, the attendant told the director the next morning, because he needed pills to sleep, it was the only way he could sleep, and once he does fall asleep and then someone wakes him he can't sleep a wink the rest of the night, but there's this security man ringing him at midnight, asking him to come over to the museum, and what the hell is this, was his first thought, he certainly wasn't going anywhere, because it really is scandalous that he, an acute insomniac, should be rung up after midnight, but then the security guard mentions the director's name and tells him that this weirdo keeps asking for the director, so he thought best not take a chance in case some ballyhoo ensues on account of him not helping, so he thought a bit and forgot his anger though he had every right to be angry it being past midnight, got dressed and went over to the museum, and it was good, very good indeed, in fact he didn't know how to tell the director how good it was, all that happened, because as the director knows he is not a man of many words, but what followed was one of the most extraordinary nights of his life and the events he happened to witness between half past twelve and the present time had such an effect on him that he still couldn't think of them calmly and reasonably, and because he was still recovering from the effects of these experiences, these great, quite mysterious experiences, it was perfectly possible that he might not find the right words at once, for which he asked to be excused in advance, but he really was shaken, very shaken, not quite himself, the only excuse for his condition being that he hadn't had any time, not a second, to try to get events into some kind of perspective, in fact, to be honest, even as they were sitting down here in the director's office he felt as though whatever happened wasn't entirely over and that it could start all over again from the point of his arrival a little after half past twelve when he knocked at the door and the security man came out and explained it all again to him, while the person in question, the person, as the security guard referred to him, was waiting at a point some fifteen meters from the entrance watching the upstairs windows, so he went over, introduced himself and the person was so delighted to be addressed in Hungarian that, without saying a word, he embraced him, which of course greatly surprised him, for having lived for decades in Schaffhausen, he had quite forgotten these characteristically passionate, over-excited displays of emotion, and pushed the person away, telling him his name and office, and that he'd like to help if he could, in answer to which the person introduced himself as Dr. György Korin then explained that he had arrived at the last stop in an inordinately long journey, and that he could hardly contain himself in his happiness that he could share the problems of this, for him, fateful night with a fellow Hungarian, in Hungarian, and confided to him that he was an archivist in a small Hungarian town, and that his mission, which far outweighed his position in life, had taken him to New York from where he had but recently arrived following a terrifying pursuit, because his destination was Schaffhausen, the *Hallen für die neue Kunst* to be precise, and within that building it was specifically the world-famous sculpture by Mario Merz that he desired to see, for he had been informed the work was there, said the person pointing to the building, and yes, he said, we have two works by Merz on the first floor, but by that time he could see that the person was shaking from head to foot, having presumably gotten chilled while he was waiting, so he called the security guard and suggested they continue the interview inside, for the wind was very strong, and the guard agreed, so they went inside, closed the door of the hut behind them, sat down at the table and Korin began his story, a story that started a long way back—please, the director interrupted him, do try to make your account as concise as possible—yes, the attendant nodded, he would try to make it as concise as possible but the story was so complicated, and what was more so fresh in his mind, that it was hard to tell what was important and what wasn't, and at the same time he had felt sure, said the attendant glancing up at the director, that as soon as they sat down at the table in the hut, once he had had a chance to look the person over—a tall, thin, middle-aged person with a small, bald head, feverishly burning eyes and enormous protruding ears—that he was crazy, but if he was the mystery remained of how he succeeded in winning them over in just a few minutes, because he did win them over, in fact he completely swept them off their feet, and it was plain even if he was crazy that what he was babbling was not sheer nonsense, that one had to listen to him properly, because there was a peculiar drift to his story and every word in it was of some significance, of quite dramatic significance in fact, for he felt himself to be part of the drama, an actor in it—but please, the director interrupted him again, Herr Kalotaszegi, we both have work to do, try to keep the story as short as you can—oh of course, said the attendant, nodding and conscious of his error, well, in other words he told us the story from its origins in a small Hungarian town and how one day at the office he discovered a mysterious manuscript among the archives, how he took this manuscript with him to New York, having, Herr Director, sold up and got rid of everything, left it all behind, his home, his work, his language, his house, everything, and went off to die in New York, Herr Director, all this with lots of incredible twists and turns and with one terrible unnamed incident about which he was unwilling to speak, and how he was led here by chance, he emphasized this, having heard something about some sculpture, or to be precise, a sculpture that he had seen in a photograph and decided he must see in the flesh because he had fallen in love with it, Herr Director, having fallen literally in love, said the attendant, with Mario Merz's piece and *wanted to spend an hour inside it*, at which point the director leaned incredulously forward asking, *what did he want?* and the attendant repeated *to spend an hour inside it*, a request an attendant could by no means grant of course, and he had tried to explain to him that it wasn't up to him to give such permission, in other words he rejected the request, but he did listen through his story, a story, as Herr Director could plainly see now, had quite carried him away, that overcame any resistance, even the very idea of protesting, because, he confessed, after listening to it awhile he felt his heart would break, because he felt certain that the person wasn't merely spinning stories but had genuinely come to Schaffhausen to end his life, a Hungarian like himself, a little unfortunate creature who was obsessed with the notion that the manuscript he discovered in Hungary was of such importance that he was obliged to preserve it for eternity, to transmit it, do you see Herr Director, the attendant asked him, and that was why the person went to New York, because he considered it to be the center of the world, and it was in the center of the world he wished to conclude the business, that is to say the transmitting of the manuscript as he expressed it to the attendant, to eternity, and so he got hold of a computer and typed up the entire manuscript so it should find its place on the Internet, and having done so his work was over, because the Internet, or so the person had persuaded them a few hours ago while sitting at the table in the security guard's hut, was the surest way into eternity, and he was convinced, the attendant bowed his head, that he absolutely had to die since life no longer had any meaning for him and he was most insistent on this point—the attendant raised his eyes to meet the director's—constantly emphasizing and repeating that it was for him and for him alone that life had become meaningless, and that was crystal clear to him, but as he had taken the characters in the manuscript so much to his heart, too much to heart, the person explained, the only thing not crystal clear to him was what he should do with these characters now, since they had not loosened their hold on him, and it was as if they were determined to go with him, something like that, but he couldn't be more precise, Herr Director, and the man did not explain clearly what it was he was preparing to do, except he kept asking to see the work by Herr Merz, a request he, the attendant, had to resist, constantly telling him to wait till morning, attempting to calm him down, to which Korin replied that there was no morning, and then he grasped his hand, looked into his eyes and said, Kalotaszegi úr, I have only two requests, first that I speak with the director and the director at some stage speak to Herr Merz and insist on his telling him how much his sculpture had helped him, because at the very moment the man felt he had nowhere to go to he realized he had, and he wanted to thank Herr Merz most warmly, from the bottom of his heart, for that, for he, György Korin, would forever think of him as *dear Herr Merz*, and this was his first request; the second being, the reason that he was in fact sitting here now, the attendant pointed to himself, that someone should put a plaque on his behalf, on the wall of Herr Merz's museum somewhere—and at this point he passed over a great heap of money, said the attendant, asking that it be used for that purpose—a plaque screwed to the wall, with a single sentence engraved on it telling his story, and he wrote that sentence down on a piece of paper, said the attendant, and slipped it across to him, telling him that he was doing so in order that he might remain in the vicinity of Herr Merz in spirit, Korin explained, he and the others, as close to Herr Merz as possible, that was how he explained the plaque, Herr Director, and here's the money and here's the piece of paper, and he put them both on the table, though the director was still terribly confused by what Kalotaszegi had told him, as he told his wife who had arrived in the office at the same time as the police, but at the same time he found so touching, so genuinely tragic that he had asked the attendant more questions, going over the whole story again, trying to piece together the broken pieces of Kalotaszegi's account, the last part of which was Korin saying good-bye to the attendant and going out, and he had succeeded in assembling the story after a fashion, the story being extraordinary and deeply moving, he admitted, though he swore that what finally convinced him was when he turned on the computer, checked AltaVista, a name often mentioned in the story, and saw with his own eyes that the manuscript really existed under the English title of War and War, and asked Kalotaszegi to translate the first few sentences of it for him, and even in that rough and ready translation he found the text so beautiful, so compulsive, that by the time of her arrival, he pointed to his wife, he had made his mind up, and had decided what to do, for why was he the director of this museum if he couldn't make a decision after a night like this, and that having finished his business with the police, he would see to it immediately with the help of the attendant and would choose an appropriate spot on the wall outside, for what he had decided, he declared, is that there would be a plaque on the wall, a simple plaque, to tell the visitor what happened to György Korin in his last hours and it would say precisely what it said on the piece of paper, because the man deserved to find peace in the text of such a plaque, a man, the director lowered his voice, for whom the end was to be found in Schaffhausen,

an end really to be found in Schaffhausen.

http://www.warandwar.com

This plaque marks the place where György Korin, the hero of the novel *War and War* by László Krasznahorkai, shot himself in the head. Search as he might, he could not find what he had called the Way Out.

ISAIAH HAS COME

Moon, valley, dew, death.

In the year of Our Lord—in March, to be precise, on the night of the third day of the month, between about four and quarter past four— that is to say a bare eight years before the two thousandth anniversary of what may be understood by Christian reckoning to be the new age, but far removed from the mood of rejoicing usually occasioned by such events, Dr. György Korin applied the brakes by the entrance to the NON STOP buffet at the bus station, managed to stop the car, scrambled out onto the sidewalk, then, having assured himself that after three continuous days of drunken misadventure he had arrived at a place where, with these four words ringing in his head, he would discover what he was looking for, he pushed the door open and swayed over to the one lonely-looking man at the bar, where instead of collapsing on the spot as he might have been expected to do in his condition, with a tremendous effort, very deliberately, he pronounced the words:

Dear Angel, I have been looking for you for such a long time.

The man thus addressed slowly turned to face him. It was hard to say whether he had understood any of this. His face looked tired, his eyes had no light in them and sweat was running in streams down his brow.

I have been looking for you for three days, Korin explained, *because when it comes down to it you have to know that, once again, it's over . . . That here . . . those damned bitches of a . . .* Then he fell silent a long while and the only thing that betrayed how much raw emotion he was suppressing—for his fixed expression betrayed nothing—was the way he repeated the phrase he must have practiced a thousand times: *once again, it's over.*

The man turned back to the bar, raised his cigarette slowly, deliberately, delicately to his mouth and, while the other watched him, drew deeply on it, as deeply as he could, drawing the smoke right down to the very bottom of his lungs and because it could go no deeper closed his lips and pouted slightly, keeping the smoke down for an extraordinarily long time and only began emitting it in narrow wisps once his face had turned quite red and the veins stood out on the nape of his neck. Korin watched all this without moving a muscle and it was impossible to be sure whether that was because he was waiting for some kind of response to his comments once the performance was over, or because he had suddenly turned his mind off for a while, but in any case he simply stared at the man, watching as a slowly swelling cloud of smoke enveloped him, then, without taking his eyes off him, without being able to take his eyes off him, with one blind gesture he succeeded in grabbing an empty glass and tapped it on the bar a few times as if calling a bartender. But there was no bartender to be seen, nor was there anyone else in the hangar-shaped buffet unless you counted the small booth to the left of the toilet where a pair of beggar-like figures were hunkering close, an old man of indeterminate age with a dirty unkempt beard and a good many greasy pimples on his face, and an old woman, who on closer examination turned out to be of similarly indeterminate age, thin and toothless, with cracked lips that gave her a look of idiotic cheerfulness. But you couldn't really count these two because they were sitting somehow further off, maybe just a hairsbreadth too far away, nevertheless removed in some way from the world of the buffet, further removed than might have been suggested by the positions they physically occupied within it, the boots on their feet tied round with string in one case and wire in the other, their overcoats torn, their scarves serving the office of belts, with a liter bottle of wine in front of them, the floor around them covered in a mass of commercial plastic bags stuffed to overflowing. They said nothing, simply stared ahead of them and gently held each other's hands.

All is ruined, all is brought low—Korin continued.

But he might as well have said, he added in his own clumsy almost incoherent way in an attempt to explain himself, that when you thought about it, it should be crystal clear to any notary of heaven and earth, that they have ruined everything, brought everything low, because here, he said, and this was something the man he was talking to had, whatever else he did, to understand most precisely, it wasn't a case of some mysterious divine decree driving an innocent human agency—the empty glass in his right hand was shaking at the words "divine decree"—but precisely the opposite, a disgraceful decision taken by humanity at large, a decision far exceeding normal human authority but drawing on a divine context and relying on divine assistance, which was to say that it was the crudest imaginable imposition when you got down to it, the infinitely vulgar production of an order determined by the so-called civilized world, an order that was complete and all-comprehending, and horribly successful. Horribly, in his opinion, he repeated, and, for the sake of emphasis lingered as long as he could on the word "horribly," which so slowed his speech that he almost came to a stop near the end of it, a remarkable achievement since all the way through, right from the beginning, he had been speaking as slowly and with as little passion as it was possible to speak, every syllable reduced to its mere phonemes, as if each of them were the product of a struggle against other syllables or phonemes that might have been uttered in its place, as though some kind of deep and complex war were being fought out somewhere at the bottom of his throat, in which the right syllable or phoneme had to be discovered, isolated, and torn from the clutches of superfluous ones, from the thick soup of syllable-larvae energetically thrashing about there then carried up the throat, led gently through the dome of the mouth, forced up against the row of teeth and finally spat forth into freedom, into the terminally stale air of the buffet, as the only sound apart from the sick, continuous moaning of the refrigerator, a sound heard on the edge of the bar where the man was standing immobile; hor-rib-ly, in his opinion, Korin said, slowing, after which he did not so much hesitate as come to a complete stop, and this being said it was possible to conclude without the shadow of a doubt, from the changed, clouded, ever more unfocused look in his eyes that his mind having simply and hor-rib-ly packed up at this point, he could do nothing but stand there, though the powerful gravitational force exerted on the right-hand side of his body might at any moment have caused him to tip over as he leaned heavily on the bar on his right-hand side with those ever duller eyes of his fixed immovably on the man as if he could see what he was looking at though in reality he saw nothing and was simply staring at his face for a while, without the least trace of comprehension, leaning against the bar, swaying gently and hor-rib-ly.

They have ruined the world—he said a whole minute or so later, the life returning to eyes that had regained their earlier muddy ditch color.

But it doesn't matter what he says, he said, because they've ruined everything they've managed to get their hands on, and by waging an endless, treacherous war of attrition they have managed to get their hands on everything, ruined everything—and, one should remember, they have seized everything—seized it, ruined it and carried on in this way until they had achieved complete victory, so that it was one long triumphal march of seizing and ruining, right down to the final triumph of the hordes, or more precisely, it was a long story running over hundreds of years, hundreds and hundreds of years, of seizing and, in seizing, ruining, seizing and thereby ruining, sometimes sur-reptitiously, sometimes brazenly; now subtly, now crudely, whatever way they could, that's the way they carried on, the only way they could carry on over centuries, like rats, like rats in hiding waiting to pounce; and in order to achieve this utter and complete victory they naturally needed their opponents, by which we mean anyone noble, great and transcendent, to reject, for reasons of their own, any kind of conflict, to reject in principle the idea of moving beyond bare being and engaging in some passing struggle for the notion of a slightly better balanced state of human affairs; for what was needed was for there to be no struggle at all, simply the disappearance of one of the two parties, in historical terms the lasting disappearance of the noble, the great and the transcendent, their disappearance not only from the struggle but also from the realm of mere existence, and in the worst case, for all we know, said Korin, their utter and complete annihilation, all this for some peculiar reason quite unknown to any-one but themselves, no one knowing why this should all have hap-pened the way it did, or what had happened to allow those who had been waiting to pounce and gain the victory to do so, and thereby control everything today, and there is not a nook or cranny in which you could hide anything from them, everything being theirs, said Korin at his accustomed speed, theirs is everything that may be possessed, and the decisive proportion of even those things that can't, because heaven is theirs, and every dream, every moment of silence in nature, and, to use the popular saying, immortality too is theirs— only the most common and vulgar of immortalities of course—in other words, as the embittered losers justly but mistakenly say, everything is lost and lost forever. And—his unstoppable monologue flowed on—the power in their hands is truly of no small proportions, for their position and their depraved all-pervasive strength has enabled them not merely to reduce all scale and proportion to match their own, such exercise of power being maintainable for only a short time, but their remarkable perspicuity had ensured that their own sense of scale and proportion should determine the very nature of scale and proportion, that is to say they made sure that their being should permeate any sense of scale and proportion that was inimical to them, keeping a close eye on every tiny detail so that from whatever angle you looked at them, the details would all support, strengthen, ensure and so maintain this momentous historical turn of events, this treacherous insurrection of false scales, false content, false proportions and false extents. It was a long struggle against invisible foes, or to put it more accurately, against invisible foes that might not have been there at all, but it was a victorious struggle, in the course of which they understood that the victory would be unconditional only if they annihilated or, if he might put it in such old fashioned terms, said Korin, exiled, exiled anything that might have stood against them, or rather, fully absorbed it into the repulsive vulgarity of the world they now ruled, ruled if not exactly commanded, and thereby besmirched whatever was good and transcendent, not by saying a haughty "no" to good and transcendent things, no, for they understood that the important thing was to say "yes" from the meanest of motives, to give them their outright support, to display them, to nurture them; it was this that dawned on them and showed them what to do, that their best option was not to crush their enemies, to mock them or wipe them off the face of the earth, but, on the contrary, to embrace them, to take responsibility for them and so to empty them of their content, and in this way to establish a world in which it was precisely these things that would be the most liable to spread the infection, so that the only power that had any chance of resisting them, by whose radiant light it might still have been possible to see the degree to which they had taken over people's lives

. . . how could he make himself clearer at this point, Korin hesitated . . . how to explain this more effectively, he fell to meditating, perhaps if he said it again; he ended . . . that, you know . . . that tragic lack of nobility. By embracing the good and the transcendent, he continued, his eyes not shifting a millimeter from the man, they turned them into objects that today are of all things the most repulsive, so that even pronouncing the words "good" and "transcendent" is enough to fill a man with shame; they have become so horrible, so hateful, that you only needed to say them once—the good, the transcendent—and there was nothing left to say, people's stomachs cramp up and they're ready to vomit, not because the words mean anything to them, but because it's enough simply to pronounce them, these two words, and how many more such words are there, and it's done! every time they are pronounced the victorious rulers of the world sit that much more comfortably on their thrones, are just that more firmly established there than before, and the road to the worldly throne is lined with precisely such things, for they make a nice little tapping sound, clickety-click, good and good, and there go Red Riding Hood, the hoofs of the horses, the wheels of carriages and the valves of cars as they move up and down the cylinders, good and good, clippety-clop, it's hopeless!—Korin was slowing again—but actually that was not the right word, hopeless was somehow wrong, there was no way out of this deadly loop, since it was ready and fully functioning in its own way, and calling it hopeless was not going to foul up the works, quite the contrary, in fact, it would simply oil them, bring a constant shine to them, help them to function. It was self-oiling, said Korin, raising his voice a little and looked up at the cold light shining above him, as if he thought the light was too dim, though the light in the buffet was almost intolerably intense. The whole ceiling was packed with fluorescent tubes, neon next to neon, at least a hundred tubes from right to left, from left to right, as densely and hauntingly packed as the graves in a military cemetery without an inch of bare space, the whole fluorescent, every tube burning and not one gone out, not one dark, so that the whole buffet glowed, as did the man standing at the bar with his back to it all, a cigarette in his right hand, staring fixedly at the edge of the bar and at nothing else, with Korin leaning on the bar and glowing beside him, his ditch-gray eyes fixed on the man, facing him, with these broken, painfully slow words proceeding from his mouth, and the two tramps in their booth by the toilet also glowing, squeezed in tightly next to each other like two neon tubes, the old man stroking the old woman's left hand as it lay on the table, she, by not withdrawing her hand, offering it to his to be stroked, the pair of them just sitting, their eyes gently resting on each other, the old woman occasionally adjusting a lock of her greasy matted hair with her right hand, that is to say her free hand.

I haven't gone mad—some light flashed in Korin's ditch-gray eyes—*but I see as clearly as if I were mad.*

And furthermore, he added, ever since he had started seeing clearly his brain has had to be strapped in place, figuratively speaking of course, only figuratively, but because he saw everything so clearly now he felt these straps could break at any moment, and that was why he hardly moved his head, but held it as still as he could, as long as possible without the slightest movement, and he meant this very head, this one here, for, no doubt, the other could see how stiffly he held it, not that this was of the least importance, said he, suddenly dropping the subject with a touch of annoyance in his voice, no, he couldn't see why he even brought the subject up, for it really wasn't like him to stray off the subject he had set himself and it must be that he was drunk, a fact he couldn't deny, for it must clearly have been his drunkenness that suddenly got the better of him, because the important thing was that he should be able to describe the true course of events as clearly, as unambiguously, as graphically as possible and to state as plainly as he could that, when it came to the question, the vitally important question, of why things had turned out like this, he was utterly unable to explain, because, personally, he hadn't a clue why greatness had passed from the world, how the great and noble had managed to vanish, where the exceptional, outstanding ones had gone, not the faintest idea, for how should he have a clue, the whole thing was utterly incomprehensible and that was why no one could understand it, and, as ever, when someone finds things to be incomprehensible it is usually his most acute personal sense of hurt he looks to for answers, and he had looked there himself but it hadn't got him anywhere because wherever he looked he finished up at the same place, he said, with a drab set of dull ideas and dull explanations, and though occasionally he had thought he was going the right way, along the right path, the end was still dull, infintely dull, for this disappearance or extinction, whatever he called it, was such a mysterious phenomenon that it was beyond him to understand it and, he imagined, beyond everyone else too, the only thing certain being that this was one of the greatest of human enigmas, the appearance and disappearance of greatness in history, or, more accurately, the appearance and disappearance of greatness despite history, from which one might, one just might venture to conclude that history, about which, once again, one could only speak in metaphors, and from now on in metaphors only to a certain extent, was an endless series of running battles and street fights, perhaps even one single continuous running battle or street fight, but this history, despite its extraordinary range, despite all its apparently ungovernable effects, was not entirely to be identified with all the implications of the human condition. To begin with, he said, take the example of the man in the street, that now sanguinary, now cowardly, creature adapted by nature to the street fight, who, as he crawls on through that remarkable mother of all street fights, making his way from cover to cover, possesses one, at least one, characteristic that is not in thrall to history, that being his shadow, which is not, said Korin, subject to the power of history, and so, irrespective of that which endows him with his shadow, whether it be day or night, this shadow, so to speak, escapes the infinitely complex web of the conflict, escapes, in other words, the power of history, because, just consider this—Korin waved his empty glass at the man who still gave no sign of having noticed him, or indeed of having noticed anything at all—think it over: do you think it's possible to hit this shadow with a gun? no chance, Korin answered sharply, a bullet is not going to cut down a shadow, and he was sure, he declared, that the other man would have no difficulty granting this, just as he, that is to say Korin, knew a thing or two, and had got this right in any case, the bullet wouldn't touch it and that's that! that's more than enough to show that a man's shadow was no part, no part at all, of history's surpassingly seamless and apparently all-comprehending mechanism; that, to put it in a nutshell, was the state of affairs and there was no point trying to pick holes in it, this was the way it was, end of the story, period, it was all that could be said on the subject of this shadow, and the only thing that might name or describe this shadow and in naming and describing it attempt to give it some narrative function was, naturally, said

Korin, using his empty glass once more in the hope of attracting the barman's attention, though the barman was somehow stranded there behind the counter beyond the orbit of this blindingly bright night and never looked likely to re-enter it, that thing, said Korin, was poetry. Poetry and shadows he said, his voice louder again, and by raising the issue he wished only to emphasize the fact that there existed something whose mode of being was independent of even history, something that, in its way, negated what, strictly speaking, we should regard as the present version of history, the version that has triumphed by stealth, and it was this thing alone, the existence of the noble, the great, the transcendent that mattered, because it was only the concept of what was noble, what was transcendent, what was truly great that was capable of definition, or rather could be defined as the antithesis of this version of history, for the remarkable reason that it was only the noble, the great and the transcendent whose existence could not be predicated as the product of such a historical process because that historical process, said Korin, required nothing of the sort, because the existence of such things depended entirely on the establishment of nobility as a concept, and that in turn required a better balanced kind of history to come into being, which was all the more necessary so that the historical process should not take on the absolute character it took on now, a character it took on precisely because, tragically, it lacked the concept of nobility, trapped as it was in the tangled maze of vulgar expediency, in which maze it was bound to career on unhindered, so that its triumph was perfectly obvious even to itself, as witness its own repulsive progenitors, and there it remained, in the maze, polishing and burnishing the trophies of its victory until it finally arrived at a state of unimaginable perfection. The cigarette in the man's hand had burned right down and since he had not only not taken a puff but had not moved it in the slightest the ash continued to lengthen, its own weight bending it in a gentle arc from the filter down over the waiting ashtray. In order for this state of affairs to be maintained the man naturally had very carefully to raise it millimeter by millimeter until it approached an almost horizontal position. And this was what he had been doing all the time, raising the cigarette ever nearer the horizontal, doing so moreover at precisely the rate it was burning, until it had burned right down and the ash stood in one piece suspended over the ashtray, having reached which position it had nowhere else to go, so he had to lower

it and tap it in order to avoid it falling off of its own accord, something he clearly did not wish to happen, which was why he lowered it
and flicked the ash into the ashtray, so that the ash might gather
force and be dashed and immediately disperse and only faintly suggest its earlier form, the once-straight line of the cigarette, and, later,
the arc of curving ash that had resolved itself into mere powder and
fallen to pieces. Then he threw away the remaining filter, immediately took out a fresh cigarette and lit it. Once more he drew on it
deeply, very deeply, drawing the smoke into his lungs, and kept
it there a long time. He drew just the once, very deeply and kept it
there so long he almost burst. Then he started to blow the smoke out
very slowly in one exceedingly thin wisp, exactly as he had done the
first time and while the smoke covered his face for a second or two,
obscuring it from Korin, it soon shifted again and his face was once
more exposed so he could raise his eyes and direct his gaze at the
edge of the counter as if there were something there to look at,
something drawing his eyes, something not particularly significant,
some scratch, some wound, or rather, just the usual thing, that is to
say nothing, just a faint band of light.

Mind and enlightenment, said Korin.

And what he meant by this, he continued unremittingly, was that it
was the conflict between the irresistible power of the mind and the
enlightenment that unavoidably followed from it with uncanny force;
it was the clash of this irresistibility and unavoidability, in his opinion,
that led directly to the conditions obtaining today. He couldn't know
what had actually happened of course, for how could someone like
him, a mere local historian from the back of beyond, hope to find an
answer to a question that lay so far beyond his capabilities, but it was
exhausting just to think of those good few centuries of nightmarish
triumphal march whereby the mind ruthlessly, step by step, eliminated everything that was deemed not to exist and stripped humanity
of anything it had mistakenly but understandably posited as existing,
in other words ruthlessly stripped bare the entire world until suddenly there was nothing but the naked world with the hitherto
unimaginable creations of the mind on the one side and the enlightenment with its killer's instinct for destruction on the other, for if one

agreed that the creations of the mind were unimaginably great one had all the more reason to grant that the enlightenment's capacity for destruction was laced with a killer's instinct, since the storm that broke over the mind truly swept everything away, every support on which the world had until then depended, simply wrecked the foundations of the world and in a way that proclaimed that such foundations did not exist, nor, it added, had they ever existed and there was no chance of them being resurrected from non-existence at some vainly hoped-for point in the vague and distant future. The loss, according to Korin, was immense: immense, unimaginable and impossible to recover from. Everything and everyone that was noble, great and transcendent could do nothing but stand by, if he might so put it, stand at this point where one could have no idea of the true impenetrable depth of the moment, and try to comprehend all that did not exist, that had never existed. They had to understand this and accept as a first principle that—to begin at the top—there was no god, no gods: this was what the noble, great and transcendent had to grasp and resign themselves to before anything else, said Korin, though they of course were incapable of this, simply could not understand it—believe it, yes; accept it yes; but understand it, never—and so they just stood there, uncomprehending, not accepting, long after they should have taken the next step, that being, to use an old formula, he said, to declare that if there is no god, if there are no gods, then there could be no goodness or transcendence either, but they did not take it because, or so Korin imagined it, without a god or gods they were simply incapable of moving, right up until eventually—possibly because the storm that raged around the mind drove them to it—they finally shifted and immediately did realize that without a god or gods there was nothing good or transcendent, at which point they also realized that if these really no longer existed, then neither did they themselves! His feeling, said Korin, was that this might have been the moment they disappeared from history, or rather that from the historical point of view this might have been the time from which we must acknowledge their slow passing, for that was what actually happened, they gradually passed away, he said, like a fire left to burn by itself and turn to ashes at the bottom of a garden, and the result of all this, from this image of the garden that suddenly appeared before him, was that he was now troubled by a terrible feeling that it was not so much a matter of a continuous process of appearing then gradually disappearing but of simple appearance and disappearance, but who knows what precisely happened, he asked, no one, at least not him, though he was as certain as could be about how the current holders of power had slowly and determinedly come to occupy their positions of power because that process had a kind of symmetry, a kind of infernal parasitic symmetry: for as one order slowly faded and decomposed until eventually it vanished, so the other gained strength, assumed a shape and finally gained complete control; while one retreated step by step into mystery so the other became ever more overt; as one continually lost so the other continually gained, and so it went on, defeat and triumph, defeat and triumph, and that was the way of things, said Korin, that was how one order disappeared without trace and how the repulsive other took possession of the throne, and he himself had life to realize, he said, that he had been mistaken, gravely mistaken, in believing that there hadn't been nor could there be some revolutionary moment in life, for such a revolution, he had come to see that day, had happened, had undeniably taken place. The old beggar in the nook behind him let go of the old woman's hand. But only for a moment because he immediately drew closer to her, body to body, and began passionately to kiss her cracked lips. The old woman's expression showed neither acceptance nor rejection of this advance: she put up no resistance but did not respond either. It seemed to be more that she simply had no strength left, that she was some kind of wounded bird that a shot had brought down, her head thrown back, her eyes wide open, her two arms, like wings, hanging helplessly, in other words as if she had collapsed into the other's embrace, her coat gathered round her neck to form a curious shape as the old man seized her. It was curious but all it meant was that the sudden movement had forced the coat, which was in any case too big for her, to ride up, the collar rising above her head, the effect of the embrace being to more or less wrap her head up in the cloth while the rest of her body took on the appearance of a package, a package in a coat, so from a distance it looked as if the old man were hugging a coat, for the only evidence of a body was the crown of hair rising above a thin hollow face that had quite collapsed in the blinding light, or rather its cheek as the old man's tongue flickered feverishly over it.

Moon, valley, dew, death.

Behind the counter the refrigerator shuddered and gave a loud crack as if wanting to give up the ghost but then decided against it, and started up again, rattling as it painfully resumed its business, and the two liter bottles of COCA-COLA that must have shifted in the convulsive movement now found themselves next to each other and began to tinkle and chime with the vibration.

Revolution—Korin proclaimed as the four words in his head, like four rooks circling in the darkness, were slowly absorbed into the vanishing horizon.

What is more, a revolution of world historical moment, he said, and having made this grave announcement, it was as if his strange manner of speaking were striving for some consonance, for there came a change, a change that the ravages and predictable consequences of drunkenness had made entirely predictable, a change, whereby the mind had hitherto been strapped into place, and the continuity between throat and tongue that had been maintained only with the utmost effort to prevent the words falling apart, shifted key as it was bound to do. For while the words had till now been broken up like stones into distinct syllables, there now began a complete reversal of the process so that they ran into each other, the power that had hitherto disciplined and ordered them having suddenly run out of steam, and his speech was held together only by some bitter compulsion, a compulsion that after three ill-fated days of searching for the appropriate celestial luminaries he should at all costs now finish what he had to say, what the finally and painfully located emissary of such luminaries should, in his opinion, at all costs have to hear, and his capacities being such as they were it was like watching a train crash, the engine hitting the stationary vehicle while the phonemes, like the cars piled into each other, required the notary of heaven and earth to whom the speech was addressed, to descry the word "revolution" from the ruins of "rvshon" and the sense "world-historical" from "wrldstical."

I . . . lkdnto . . . thefyoor . . . atard . . . spisl . . .
Korin declared in the appropriate new spirit.

And since this signified that he had reached a state of terminal disil-
lusion in the celestial light that had, so to say, cleared the doors of
his perception, he felt genuinely capable of having "looked into the
future at our disposal," a future—if he might condense everything
that meant anything into a single word, he raised his voice—that
frankly horrified him. It horrified him, he continued at the same volume, and it broke his heart, for so far he had only been speaking of
how the good and transcendent were defeated as the result of a
loathsome rebellion, but now that he had had a glimpse into the future he, Korin, could report that his vision of that future had clarified,
that this future that had been based on rebellion, lacked not only the
good and the transcendent, but the perspectives provided by the
good and transcendent, that is to say, he continued with increasing
tension in his voice, the way he saw it, it wasn't so much a case of the
good and transcendent of the future being usurped by the bad and
mean-spirited, but of something radically, startlingly different, a future that would lack both good and bad, that at least is what Korin
had recognized when, the doors of his perception having been
cleansed, as they say, he had a glimpse of the dark future, when he
looked forward and sought what he could not find, for the perspective was lacking, the perspective whereby the scale of the aforementioned good and transcendent might be related to the scale of the
aforementioned bad and mean-spirited; that set of perspectives required to gauge the value of actions and intentions, those shadowy
and ever more disquietingly lifeless perspectives—the empty glass
was trembling in his hand again—were broken and unusable in that
future, or, to employ a somewhat frivolous analogy, they had passed
their sell-by dates much like the goods displayed in the refrigerators
of butchers' stalls at the market, and once he had understood this,
once he had reached the bottom of that safely strapped-in mind, it
not only broke his heart, it simply and utterly crushed him because
suddenly there in front him there opened the saddest map in the
world, that of a whole disappearing continent, the true Atlantis which
was now completely and irretrievably lost. These are the words of a
broken man, quite broken, said Korin, his voice fading, and so that
there should be no doubt as to whom he meant he tried to indicate

himself with the empty glass. Since this movement meant letting go of the counter then recovering his balance, the gesture turned out to be much grander than he had intended, so grand that it seemed to include the entire buffet where nothing had changed so there was no one present who might have felt himself included in it, for the figure chiefly addressed seemed to be frozen, completely shrouded in smoke, and the pair of beggars seemed to slide ever further beyond the actual compass of the premises. Their scarves had slipped to the floor, their heavy coats were open, and they no longer sat, but in their unabated passion, seemed to have assumed a horizontal position. The old male was on top, his moustache and beard completely soaked in saliva. He was kissing the female in a frenzy, squeezing her hard, only momentarily loosening his hold on her so that he might seize her again, accommodating her to the waves of his cresting desire, seizing her with ever more convulsive vehemence. The old woman no longer simply reminded him of a dead bird, but bore it all as if the bird had collapsed in on itself, dangling in the old man's embrace as though raised in mid-swoon, spent, helpless, resigned, indifferent, surrendering like a servant to its master, obliged to let herself be used according to any command, and only once the increasingly demanding, ever more unchecked, panting and gripping kisses no longer allowed her to remain in her passive state, did she obey the imperative of response with the faintest, hardly perceptible raising of her left hand from the floor in an attempt to stroke the other's face. But since her attempt to reach the face had twice been obstructed by considerable rolls of fat, her hand grew uncertain as to how to resolve the contradiction between fat and face, and dropped back to the floor, that is to say having started to rise by reflex it hovered for a moment hopelessly then began to sink back again, past the neck, past the ribcage, past the top of the stomach, to hesitate halfway between face and floor, to intrude itself between the two tightly pressed bodies, to shift in the first place from the dome of the old man's stomach down toward her own, then, sliding further down, to locate the simple mechanism of the fly and after a certain amount of fumbling to reach the erect male member. The scarves were crushed beneath them by now, and their legs kicking and straining now this way, now that, caused considerable ruckus among the plastic bags too. None of them was completely kicked over but they were shedding items, or to be precise, items were trailing from them like the intestines of a mangy dog that had been run down by a car, the sleeve of a greasy shirt from one, the frayed electric cord of an old iron from the second, the terry cloth material of belts from old bathrobes from the third, a set of door handles tied attached to a ring from the fourth, dirty underwear from the fifth, two yellowing Advent wreaths from the sixth and so on from the seventh to the twelfth, from the pile of felt strips to the toilet paper rolls, all of which created a filthy mess between their shuffling feet, there where a thin faint light from above could expose it to view, and the mess the dirty light revealed conclusively defined the status of the owners of those legs, and equally conclusively differentiated them from the quite improbable province of the buffet, locating them in another reality, as the sickly writhing progeny of the waste dump below them, since they seemed genuinely to have grown out of the dump, and were continuing to grow minute by minute, their legs growing ever more irreversibly entangled with the waste, and their embraces, the way they were joined together on the wooden floor of the booth, added to the complexity, like a shadow that swam first one way then another caught in the thickets of a sudden, unpronounceable sentence signaling desire. They were flat out on the floor by now, the table shielding them from the eyes of anyone at the counter so that nothing could be seen of them, only an occasional elbow as it was raised to indicate in its own mysterious vague fashion what might be going on down there. The man at the counter pushed away the current cigarette and lit a new one.

Deargel!. . . . Korin leant closer to him. *Evring . . . iverd . . . zonzat . . . atliss!*

What he meant, he continued quietly, was, really and truly, that everything he ever had was on that Atlantis, everything he ever had, he repeated a few times, putting the accent now on everything and now on had, then straightened up again, regained balance by resting his right arm on the counter and was clearly struggling to gather himself so that he might continue with his account in the detached, unemotional manner in which he had begun, especially now that he had reached the point at which it seemed likely to take a particularly delicate turn. For from this point on his peculiar way of stringing words together, which seemed to be addressed exclusively to the notary of heaven and earth, was engaged in explaining how difficult it was to continue his account in such a detached yet detailed manner in the light of all that had happened, and how terrible was the taste in his mouth, a taste that extended to the tiniest detail, when he was painfully obliged to itemize all that had disappeared with the sinking of Atlantis. Let us therefore mention the mornings and the afternoons, said Korin, the evenings, the nights; all the unforgettable, enchanting hours of spring and fall, when we knew the meaning of innocence and conscience, of good will and companionship, of love and freedom, so moving in thousands of old stories; when we knew what a child was, what lovers were, when we knew what was fading away and what was coming into being, all those things that for someone waking or for someone entering a dream were so unarguably eternal; such things, he said, can no more be expressed in words than can the pain caused by the utter loss, the non-existence, of their enchantment, their heart-shaking and eternal being, for the pain ran so deep that it simply could not be circumscribed or articulated, it could only be mentioned, discussed to some extent, referred to, and so he, Korin, was now at least mentioning it, discussing it a little, no more than referring to it, to this aforementioned pain, to indicate roughly where it was and how deep it ran. For he had to confess, he confessed, that when he first decided to render this account at what, for him, was this highest and most holy of tribunals, to tell of this decisive historical turn in human affairs; when he first determined that it would be he who would finally inform the denizens of heaven that the reign of good was finally at an end, that its time, like the time remaining for him to render his account, was run; then, at that point of decision, he had hoped that he would be able to describe the fatal wounding of his spirit, the sense of being hunted and struck down by melancholy at one and the same time, to describe the punishment or price set by fate for his recognition of this state of affairs. And now he was standing here, now that he knew that this was the proper occasion, his report was concluded, and he had absolutely nothing more to add. There was nothing left that was his, he said, nothing, no possessions, no place on earth, the place where he might have deposited his personal memory was lost, that's to say he couldn't even give the things he had lost a decent burial, the place had sunk, vanished without trace, and the knowledge of a higher order of things that was once part of him had sunk with it, swallowed by the last of the waves that covered Atlantis; to put it in a nutshell, he said, this should have been the right time to tell all, but now, even though he felt its presence, knew it inside out, he was incapable of speaking. And the feeling of personal pain, the sense of being harried, of deepening melancholy, was partly borne of the bitter loss of the aforementioned mornings and evenings, the enchanting histories, the honor, the sense of eternity and heartbreaking loveliness, and partly of a recognition that defied belief, that the mornings and evenings had themselves vanished, as had the histories and codes of honor; and not only the good but the bad mornings and bad evenings, bad histories, bad faith, because, he said, it so happened that the good dragged the bad down with it, so that one day you woke or went to bed and realized that there was no longer any point in drawing distinctions between waking and sleeping, between morning and morning, between evening and evening, since the distinction had suddenly, from one day to the next, become meaningless, for at that point you understood that there was only one morning and one evening, that at least was what happened to him, said Korin, for he saw that there was just one of each thing to be shared by everyone, one morning and one evening, one history and one honor—it was only the enchantment, the heartbreaking beauty, the sense of eternity that was not shared, since they no longer existed, and furthermore, said Korin, in feeling this pain a man begins to feel that he has imagined it all, that there never had been such a state of affairs, never. That's to say, he continued unremittingly, and it was very clear from the way his voice broke from time to time, that his thoughts were leading him into such deeply emotional territory that he would be powerless to resist, that's to say, he said, that mornings and evenings no longer existed for him, he had neither history nor honor, and since it was all the same to him where he was he might as well be nowhere, that is to say, his voice broke again and again, it deeply grieved him to report that the future of mankind was standing before them in his, Korin's, person, for he was already living in the future, in a future where it had become absolutely impossible to speak of loss because the very act of speaking had become impossible, for everything you said in the language turned into a lie the instant you pronounced it, and particularly when anyone tried to speak of mornings and evenings, particularly of histories and honor, and most particularly of enchantment, of the shaken heart, of eternal truth. And this condition, said Korin, for someone like him, who saw clearly that this tragic turn of events was not the product of supernatural agency, not of divine judgment, but of the actions of a peculiarly horrible heterogeneous bunch of people, there was nothing left to do than to use the rest of his speech to lay the most terrible, most incurable curse on them, so that if reality itself were incapable of addressing them, the language of curses might at least establish such terms that the sheer weight of words would cause the ground under these unprecedentedly repulsive people to give way, or cause the sky to fall in on them, or cause all the misery wished on them to take effect. So he was cursing them, he said in a voice trembling with emotion, cursing the mean and degenerate; let the dry flesh fall from their bones and turn to dust; he cursed them once, he cursed them a thousand times; that they should prepare themselves for ruin, for the time their children, their orphans, their widows roamed the world unconsoled, as he has roamed it, starving and fearful in the impenetrable darkness, abandoned forever. He cursed them, he said, cursed those on whom curses had never nor ever would take effect; he cursed those who worked evil and destroyed trust; he cursed the cold-hearted slick ones, cursed them in victory and in defeat; he cursed the very idea of victory and defeat. And he cursed the ruthless, the envious, the aggressive, those who were so in their thoughts; he cursed the treacherous, and the way the treacherous always triumphed; he cursed the cheapskate, the confidence man, the unprincipled. Let the world be cursed, he declared, choking, a world in which there is neither Omnipotence nor Last Judgment, where curses, and any who pronounced them, were held up to ridicule, where glory could only be bought with trash. And above all, he said, curse the infernal mechanism of chance that upholds and maintains all this, and reveals it; curse even the light that by illuminating it exposes the fact that there are no worlds but this, that nothing else exists. But above even that, he said, curse humanity, curse mankind that enjoys control of the mechanism whereby it may reduce and falsify the essence of things and make that reduced and false essence the cornerstone of the deepest laws of our existence. All is false by now, he shook his head, it is all one lie after another, and these lies so permeate the most obscure recesses of our souls that they leave no room for expectations or for hope, and so, should that which will never happen actually come to pass after all and present itself anew, then he Korin had a message for this breed of humanity: that no, there would be no point in expecting mercy, that they should scurry away, for they should not trust to forgiving and forgetting, for in their case there would be no forgetting; nor should they try to mend their ways or to reform, for reform and salvation are most certainly not for them, for under no circumstances will they be forgiven, nothing awaits them but memory and punishment; for in their hands even the good has become bad; for his message to them was: perish, rot and perish, for it is enough that the mark they have left, that indelible mark, had its place in eternity. The man he was addressing neither nodded nor shook his head, in fact he did nothing whatsoever, or at least nothing to indicate that he had been listening to Korin or had understood anything. All you could say was that nothing had changed in his behavior, that he went on smoking, slowly exhaling the smoke, his gaze fixed on the same point at the edge of the counter as before, and as he blew the smoke out, blowing it before him in thin wisps, this wisp of smoke . . . precisely as before . . . rose from the side and top of the counter to more or less his own height ahead of him and seemed to stop there, forming a ball that gradually drifted back toward him, enveloping his face. It was hard to tell what was happening for a while: the ball of smoke stationary, the man perfectly still, then, very slowly, the ball drifting toward him, enveloping him, his head, as a cloud might a mountaintop, at the same time thinning, losing something of its bulk. It took a whole minute at least to make out the process, to see how the man tried to draw back into himself the whole mass of that which he had earlier expelled, trying to direct that which had formed itself into a ball back down into his lungs, and how this maneuver, he having calculated the precise volume with impressive precision, not only succeeded but succeeded gloriously, with no vestige of smoke left, how the ball of smoke did not dissipate but remained a ball, albeit of smaller mass, to disappear from the area round his head, sucked back down through his mouth into his lungs, only so that it should pretty soon reappear in the form of a thin wisp of smoke.

Imgun . . . ptfie . . . ble . . . thrme, Korin declared.

In other words he wished to announce that he would put five bullets through himself, that there would be five shots in all, that is to say he would inflict five wounds on his own body, and while he had to confess that he hadn't quite thought through where and when he should do this, he felt here and now was a perfectly acceptable place and time, for there was no particular time that seemed to him more fitting, nor a particular place, so this would do and since he had said everything he had to say, there was no point in looking further so he might as well stop right here. There'd be one in the left hand, he said, one in the left foot. There'd be one in the right foot and one, if he could manage it, in the right hand. The last, the fifth . . . he started then left off, and did not finish, but put down the glass in his right hand, reached into the outside pocket of his coat and pulled out a gun. He undid the safety catch, raised his left hand, raised it right up until it was above his head, then, from below, raised the barrel and pulled the trigger. The bullet actually penetrated the hand and lodged in the ceiling between two neon lights but Korin collapsed and lay flat out on the floor as if it had entered his head not his hand. Back in the booth it was as if the loud report had been accompanied by lightning. The two beggars leapt to their feet in terror and started touching themselves all over in case someone had taken a shot at them, then they adjusted trousers, skirts, coats and other garments, and sat down in their chairs as though obeying an order. They stared at the bar, their eyes wide-open with fright, but neither of them dared shift an inch, but sat there petrified, and it was clear that they would not move from there for quite some time, so frightened were they. The man in front of them had not moved a muscle or responded to the shot in any way, only turning his head when Korin collapsed and was stretched out, the gun having bounced three times across the floor until it stopped at the foot of the counter. He watched for a while, as one might watch the lid of a saucepan that had fallen to the tiled floor of a kitchen, then he stubbed out his cigarette, buttoned his coat, turned, and slowly walked out of the buffet. There was a long silence under the neon lights, the kind of silence you get when you suddenly find yourself under water, then a door behind the counter slowly opened a fraction, and a red-faced man with tousled hair stuck his head through the gap. He stayed there a while, only his head remaining hanging by the door, then, since the noise was not repeated, he opened the door wide and took an uncertain step toward the counter—behind which, invisible to him, lay the figure of Korin— then, anxiously glancing one way then another he started buttoning his fly with one hand. "Is there a problem?" a cracked female voice asked from behind the door. "I can't see anything . . ." "I told you, it came from the street! Get out there and take a look!" The man shrugged and was on the point of stepping out from behind the counter to the entrance to check what had actually happened out there since everything seemed to be in order inside when he froze in mid-movement as the ashtray on the edge of the counter caught his eye. The instant he did so he stopped fiddling with his fly and his hand stopped and rested on one of the shirt buttons: it was obvious that something was dawning on him, that a fury was rising in him because his red face was becoming redder and redder. "Fuck it!" He stood quite still and closed his eyes, then his fingers started to form themselves into a fist that he brought smashing down on the counter. "What's up?" the woman croaked uneasily from behind the door. "The filthy, fucking, son-of-a-bitch scum!" the man pronounced, accentuating every word with a thrust of his head. "He has fucking run off, the bastard! What's up, dear Detti, is that he's split, our stinking filthy son-of-a-bitch guest has quit, fucking run off! Our dear guest . . . the only serious thing in days . . . and . . ." "He's not in the john?" The man was almost dizzy with fury and had to hold on to the counter to steady himself. "A priest too," he growled to himself. "And not just any old priest, but one from Jerusalem! How could I be such a fool! The rat! A filthy common rat! Priest from Jerusalem! Hah! Yes, and I am Donald Duck in Disneyland!" "Béla, don't get yourself riled so! You haven't even checked in the . . ." "Listen, Detti," the man scowled over his shoulder, "stop going on about the john and all that shit, when this filthy, stinking rat has chiseled us! And left not a stinking penny behind, you understand!? He has been eating and drinking the whole day and not paid a single penny, you understand, Detti, not a penny!?" "Sure I understand, Béla sweetheart, I understand it all," the woman kept trying to calm the man, possibly from some bed, "but there's nothing to be gained, you'll not get the stinking money back by winding yourself up into a state . . . Take a look in the john, won't you?" "And all along I had this feeling," said the man, his fingers practically white on the counter, "I said to myself, listen Béla, the guy might be lying his head off? How the fuck would a priest from Je-rus-al-em get here anyway! How could I have swallowed all that shit, Detti?" "Really, Béla sweetheart, you should really . . ." The man just stood there swaying and it was a full minute or so before he could let go of the counter, straighten up, wipe his hands across his face as if wanting to erase the lines of bitterness engraved there, and was about to return to the woman, the lines of bitterness still unerased, when his eyes lit upon the petrified figures of the two beggars beside the entrance to the john. "You still here, you two shitface no-good abortions, still cooling your asses?" He bellowed at them but it was like kicking a dog, nothing came of it, nothing followed the voice, in other words rather than going over to them and chasing them out onto the street, he returned to his place behind the counter, a sad and broken figure, and quietly closed the door behind him.

The buffet was quiet again,

Korin lay by the counter, unconscious.

Moon, valley, dew, death.

Later they took him away.